Praise for *Terra*

"Prepare to be swept away by a unique and captivating fated mates romance that will enthrall you from start to finish. A fresh and imaginative take on the genre that is sure to leave you spellbound."

Judy Corry, USA Today
Bestselling Author
of Sweet Contemporary Romances

"With a Twilight feel, readers looking for a young adult urban fantasy will enjoy the hidden Elemental world of Terra. Excellent series for teen and up."

Morgan L. Busse, award-winning
author of the Ravenwood Saga,
Skyworld series, and the Nordic Wars

"Terra was a delightful surprise and kept me hungry for more. Weaving a tale of intrigue, romance, and danger, Sofia Simpson masterfully tugs on the heartstrings and crafts a tale of hope and redemption. A story to savor and an author to watch!"

Tara Johnson, Author of
To Speak His Name

Terra

Also by Sofia

Dream Weaver

An Elemental Series
Terra
Torch
Tempest

Operation Kane Novella

Terra

SOFIA SIMPSON

This is a work of fiction. All names, places, and characters are products of the author's imagination or are used fictitiously. Any resemblance to real people, places, or events is entirely coincidental.

TERRA

Copyright © 2023 Sofia Simpson

Published by Starlight Books

Second Edition Copyright © 2024

ISBN: 979-8-9874009-5-1 (paperback)

ISBN: 979-8-9874009-1-3 (ebook)

Original Cover Art Design by SelfPubBookCovers.com/S.Hardy
Updated Cover Design by: EAH Creative

Map by: Sofia Simpson

To Nicky, thank you for being the best Beta Listener a mom could ask for. I love you; you will always be my favorite baby.

CLAN TERRITORIES

FESTANS-FIRE ELEMENTALS

GYANS-EARTH ELEMENTALS

BOREANS-WIND ELEMENTALS

NERONIANS-WATER ELEMENTALS

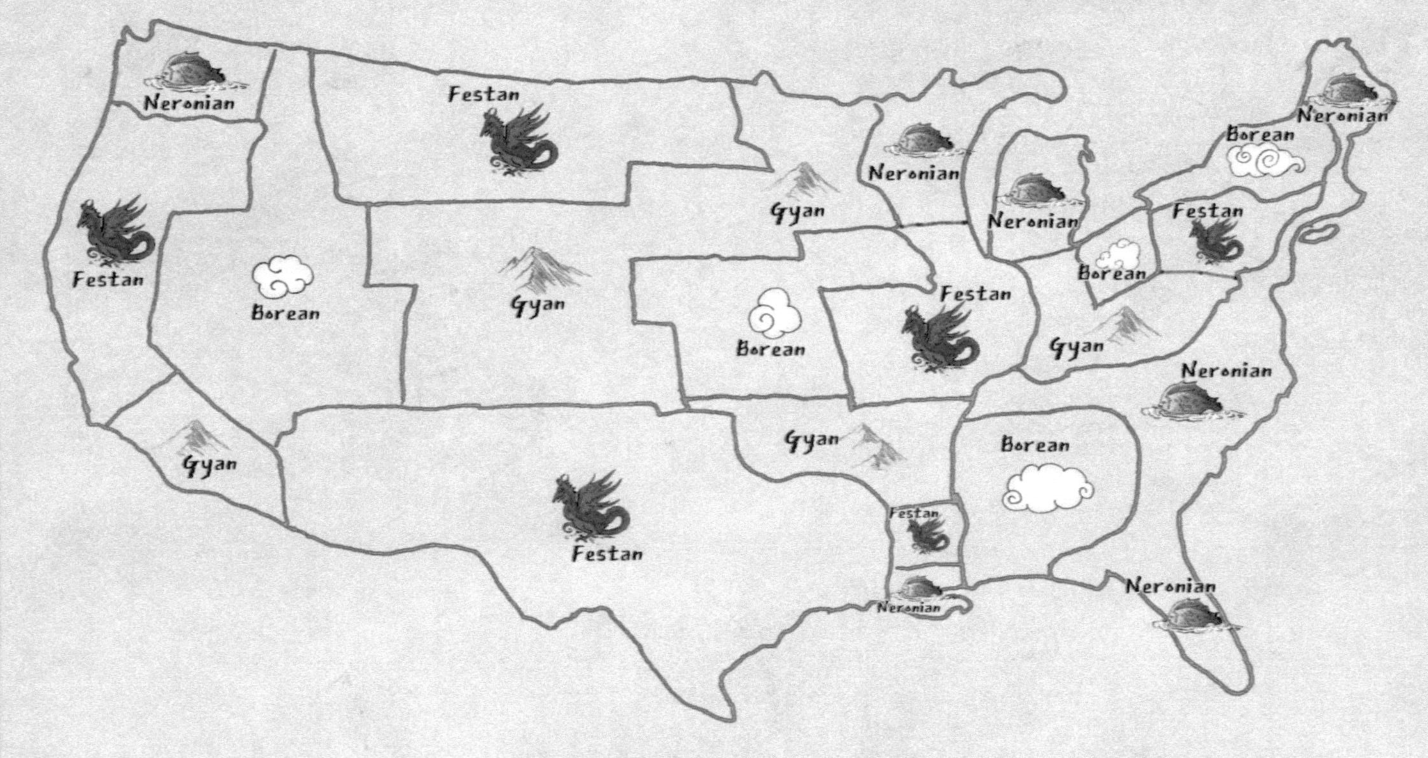

Neronian
Festan
Neronian
Borean
Neronian
Festan
Neronian
Festan
Borean
Gyan
Festan
Gyan
Borean
Borean
Festan
Gyan
Neronian
Gyan
Festan
Gyan
Borean
Festan
Neronian
Neronian

Prologue

LORD, WILL MY GIFT help us? The woman thought frantically. She put her hand on her bulging belly and looked over her shoulder, squinting through the glare of the headlights following their car. She gripped her husband's arm in an anxious question. He gunned the motor, shooting them into the night.

"We'll lose 'em," he assured her. "And I know exactly where."

She worried her lip and rubbed her belly. It was imperative they find safety.

"We need a place to stay for a few days. It's almost time," she whispered.

She breathed through the pain gripping her abdomen, inhaled, and exhaled slowly through pursed lips. She had been having contractions for a couple of hours now. Hadn't wanted to say anything about the danger. But she would have this baby in the car if they didn't find somewhere soon.

Sweat beaded the man's forehead. He gripped the steering wheel and his mouth moved silently in prayer. The headlights remained steady, shining into the car, producing worried glances between the couple.

"Get ready Baby," he said. "We're almost there."

She knew it was time and prayed she'd be able to do this. Using every mental strength she owned, her mind gripped the trees behind them on each side of the road. She commanded the trees to wrap like a net around the car that chased them, picking it up off the ground. Tires screeched on the road before being lifted, spitting gravel into the air.

The man glanced behind him, and with bright eyes, nodded and said, "Well done. Keep them there."

She didn't dare break her concentration and look at her success. Her face turned white in her strain to contain the vehicle in its tight leafy embrace. The weight of the vehicle, the energy it took to catch it and hang on was almost too much with her labor pains. She gripped her seat and groaned, bending her head. It took all her strength to keep the car in the air.

The man reached over and braced his wife with his arm. "Hold on," he said.

He spun the wheel; the tires screeching as the car fishtailed. He panicked and gripped the wheel, finishing the tight turn. He ended up at his destination, an abandoned road. Tearing down the road, spraying dirt in his tracks, the man eased his brakes just as they reached a large barn. He drove around the back of it and turned off the lights. They held their breath.

After a few moments, headlights followed around the back corner of their hiding spot. Another car must have been following the one they captured. They lost all hope. They were found. The man held his wife's stomach with his head bowed.

"I'm sorry," he said in a strangled voice. Her sobs were just as loud as his. She let go of her mental hold and a distant crash sounded. They braced themselves for the end.

Chapter One

THE AFTERNOON SUN BOASTED a day full of promise and warm rays. It wasn't such a day for Elia, Vela's best friend. Vela watched her burst through the patio door in a fit, angry as a wet cat.

Vela fought a smile. Her brother Kane had to be involved. You could cut the tension between the two with a knife, but you'll never get him to admit it. Their age difference was a problem now, but give it a year or two and she was sure that would change.

"Kane will notice you one day, bestie," Vela promised, slinging her arm over Elia's shoulder once her best friend came to stand by her. As Elia was a foot shorter than Vela, it was easy to do.

"He usually at least says hi," Elia grumbled, her head down and back slumped, her mood turning from anger to depression in the matter of seconds.

Vela glanced at the house and could see through the window her brother disappearing up the stairs. "I have an idea," Vela said, a wild thought entering her mind. "Maybe you should date a human."

A shocked look crossed over Elia's face as she peered up at Vela. "Since when do we date humans?" Her tone was low, even though they were in the privacy of Vela's fenced-in backyard. "You know a Gyan is my only future." She looked curiously at Vela, like she had sprouted two heads.

"Since the world has denied us any good options," Vela said, swinging her arm off Elia and sinking onto the ground. "Honestly, how our parents expect us to find a guy when we hardly have any to choose from is ridiculous." Sitting cross-legged, Vela called for Jack, her red rust Doberman, immediately soothed when he trotted over to her. She needed to have him in sight, or even better, by her side.

"We do have slim pickings," Elia agreed, fingering her backpack. "But once we graduate, we could visit other clans and have our pick of handsome guys. Although, I'm pretty happy with what's available right here," she said with a blush.

"Yeah well, you don't have any cute brothers for me to gush over and we're talking a year, Elia, a year!" Vela cried, suddenly frustrated. "When we graduate high school." Her spirits sunk right into the earth under her. Vela sent a tendril of her power into it, wanting to connect with her element, if only to make herself feel better. Jack yipped excitedly and began running circles around her, like he always did when she used her gift.

The earth answered and a comforting, yet thrilling rush of adrenaline filled her. She wondered how the other elements felt when practiced. She had heard, of course, but she'd never had the chance to ask another Elemental about their experience.

"You know," Vela said, musing. "I'm reading this book by Judy Corry, where a girl falls in love with her best friend, and it's so sweet and so perfect. Why couldn't that exact scenario happen to me?" Vela asked, pointing to herself. She looked out into her backyard declaring, "I'm ready, world! I'm ready to find the love of my life. If that's a human, then so be it."

Jack came, as if in response to her words, burying his wet nose in her hair, seeking affection. She gladly gave it to him, running her hands over his dark red barrel chest and sides.

"Vela! Hush your mouth! If your mother heard you, she'd kill you!" Elia whispered furiously, joining her in the soft carpet of grass. "Listen, we just have to be patient. You know we can't have a human for a boyfriend, definitely not as a husband, either. What if he found out about us?"

"So what?" Vela asked, glaring at Elia. "It's about time the world found out about us Elementals. If it wasn't for us…"

"Don't say it," Elia interrupted, looking all around Vela's back yard. She scanned the fences to make sure the human neighbors and Elemental ones weren't overhearing this treasonous conversation.

Elia talked lowly and persuasively, "Vela, you can't be desperate enough to out our entire way of life. Yes, we help take care of the earth and the other clans, all the other elements. Yes, the world would be a ruined civilization without our powers feeding the earth. But, in no way, shape or form, is the world ready to know about us? Remember history? The Salem Witch Trials? Every witch hunt ever performed has killed our ancestors!"

"It's ridiculous," Vela mumbled, frustrated at the ignorance the world had shown in the past. "Look at the Internet! That is its own kind of magic! If humans are so accepting of invisible data storage, why can't they know about us?"

"Shhhhhh!" Elia put her hand on Vela's mouth. "You said I'm the one in a grumpy mood. What's gotten into you?" Elia looked at her with concern showing in her warm brown eyes.

Vela studied her friend's pixie-like face. They had similar hair, both fell to their waist, but completely opposite color, dark brown to her blonde. Vela smiled behind Elia's hand.

She was right. Getting all worked up about nothing she could control was pointless. It was a ridiculous thought.

The world hadn't found out about Elementals yet. In what way did she think she could make a difference?

"I don't know Elia," Vela admitted. "I guess I'm just questioning things because nothing exciting ever happens around here." She fingered the grass by her legs, loving the soft feel of their blades. She sensed the water rushing through the delicate veins, feeding and nurturing the profusion of growth. As Earth Elementals, it was their gift, their duty, to nurture the land.

Vela glanced over the bounty of yellow dandelions, white daisies and red and pink miniature roses decorating the fence and the pretty white gazebo. Counting instinctively their healing properties, she smiled at them. She had planted most of these beauties.

She studied her family's vegetable garden, which was a haven in itself, too, but she couldn't claim all the rights to that space. Her entire family contributed to those delicious goodies. It was a deal in the Ashcroft home. You eat it; you help grow it. It was worth the space of half their back yard to maintain it. Vela, her two brothers, Drew and Kane, along with her parents, spent time in that prodigious area.

"Oh my gosh! I can't believe I haven't told you something immediately," Elia said, her face suddenly lighting up. "You want something exciting? Did you know a hot guy started school today?"

Vela moaned. "We just discussed how we can't date humans, Elia."

"He's not." Elia's eyes twinkled, and she waited, baiting Vela perfectly.

"Spill it, woman!" Vela demanded, grabbing Elia's perfect hand with her scarred one.

"Well, he's like six feet of pure perfection," Elia teased, suspending the moment by pausing.

Vela's heart thumped in anticipation. If a new Gyan had started school, she could only hope...

"I swear," Elia finally continued, "the air around him was as hot as he is. Which me-e-eans," she said, drawing out the word, "I think he's a Festan." Elia looked out into the yard with a contemplative glance, completely missing Vela's look of horror.

Vela's stomach dropped to the ground and a familiar anger surged through her veins at the sound of the name Festan.

"What he's doing *here* in our territory is a very good question," Elia continued in a rush of words, as if Vela's world hadn't just crashed down all around them, "but I've always loved a good mystery, so I don't mind solving this one. I've only met Gyans, like us, so it's kind of exciting to actually see or meet someone different!" She finally turned to look at Vela, who looked at her with outrage.

Vela shot up like she had fire in her veins, like a Festan, from her place in the grass. "Elia! Festans should *not* be here. They only come over here when they want to scout out new land for themselves! He's been placed here to take our property! How can you be interested in that? In *him*? You've always had too lax of an attitude toward other clans, Elia. You need to be more distrusting of them!" Jack stood too and yipped, sensing Vela's distress.

Elia waved her hand dismissively. She didn't look the least bit concerned.

Incensed, Vela continued, "Your problem is that you've never been in or seen a boundary battle. You've never had your home burn down right in front of you. You've never had to deal with *these*," Vela said as she held her arms out, showcasing the mottled brown scars that ran from her hands to her elbows. Vela threw them down, hating looking at them.

"Vela," Elia said as she looked softly at Vela, her eyes shining with sympathy, "You're right. I don't know because I've not experienced what you have. But can we look outside of the box? This guy might be here for a legitimate reason."

Vela looked hard at her friend. Phantom pains in her arms made her run her hands over them. Her whole body stilled, and she breathed through the sudden pain she felt from the edge of the wall pressing on her mind. A flicker of fire appeared in her thoughts, teasing her sanity. She ruthlessly squashed it down. She had erected the wall to keep certain memories out, but sometimes a slip of control happened. Jack whined again.

Vela shook her head of any memories. "You don't know that. We need to *suspect* him, not try to solve a good mystery!" Vela rubbed Jack's smooth head when he nudged her and let him know she was okay. Sort of.

"Can't we at least find out why he's here? That's what a good mystery is all about! Solving your suspicions!" Elia begged, her big eyes sparkling with hope.

"Well, your suspicions are way different than mine," Vela sighed, giving up on getting through to her optimistic friend. "I won't trust him as far as I can throw him," she vowed. "I suggest you do the same."

"I'm not saying I trust him, Vels, he's a Festan, but I don't think one teen guy is going to do all that much damage to our clan. Why would they send a teenager to scout our territory?"

"All the more reason not to trust his intentions, Leelee. They're trying to get us to let down our defenses and trust someone young. For all we know, they've trained him for years on what to look for and report all he sees back to the mother ship, wherever that is," Vela said and grimaced. "Take your pick. He could be from the south, north or west of us!" She crossed her arms and huffed. All her good mood vanished, like the wind.

"I swear," Elia mused, seeming to ignore Vela's dark mood, "I don't know how humans don't notice his heat signature. That he's not human."

"Well, anyway, I want to know more about him," Elia said. "I mean swoon! Aren't you the least bit curious?" she giggled, enjoying the topic a little too much, in Vela's opinion. Elia sighed dramatically.

Vela answered with a curt, "No. I have no desire to meet any Festan and never will."

Elia's eyebrows raised, and her eyes sparkled with mischief.

"I'll tell you what is disturbing to me, Elia *darling*, is your tendency to downplay your schemes."

"Schemes? Like when I had the brilliant idea to sneak back into track practice last year? Climbing that fence saved us two extra miles of sprints!"

"Climbing that fence nearly got me killed; it's twenty feet high off the ground! You're lucky tearing my shirt was the only thing that tore that day, because I nearly tore the limbs off your..."

"Girls, girls!!" Vela's mother admonished. Sticking her head around the gazebo, she yelled for Vela to come and help her with dinner.

"Can Elia stay for dinner, Mom?" Vela called out. When she heard an affirmative, she glanced at Elia. "You're staying, right?"

Elia jumped up off the ground and stood next to Vela, wrapping her arm around her shoulders. "Yes, of course. And I'm telling you, Vela, I have a very good feeling about this new guy. I just know he's going to change everything around here."

"Change our state to a Festan one, you mean," Vela grumbled. "Do you really think he is a Festan?" she asked, her nose wrinkled with distaste, stiff as Elia side hugged her.

"I don't know, but I'm going to find out," Elia promised again, dropping her arm as they walked into the house.

Vela called Jack to follow, his presence calming her worries, like they always did. "You worry me, girl. One of these days, you're going to kill me. I can't keep up with you half the time."

"Oh Vela, you don't need to keep up with me. Just jump on my train and enjoy the ride," Elia said, giggling.

"Yep, like I said, your schemes are going to be the death of me." Vela wished that would be that last she heard of the new Festan, but sickeningly in her gut, she knew it wouldn't.

Chapter Two

VELA WALKED INTO THE dining room with Jack and stopped to appreciate the scene. The room sparkled with light from the crystal chandelier hanging over the table. A hundred little crystals hung prettily, watching the lively dialogue that happened below.

At a large mahogany table, with intricately carved edges of fleur de lis and leaves, stemmed water glasses and white shiny plates sat in front of each of her two brothers, who were next to each other in sturdy chairs that matched the table with their backrests carved as beautifully as the table edges. Her parents sat at each end of the table, both engaged in conversations with who sat closest to them.

A cream rug with bright orange and green swirled patterns rested under the old table. It brought color into the dark room. The walls were cherry wood panels holding wall sconces that provided more of an ambiance to the room than light.

Her father had captured images of their garden in a warm sunsets and bright sunrises that decorated the walls.

Vela took her seat between her mom and Elia with Jack, who sat beside her chair, licking his chops in anticipation of what he could beg for. She looked around the room and smiled. Dinner in the Ashcroft home was always noisy. Everyone tried to get their two cents in for every topic that came up. Today was no different. Currently, a heated discussion had sprung up on the teenager with the Festan element.

Vela's two brawny older brothers, Drew, with his wavy dark hair and serious grey eyes and Kane, whose hair was on the lighter end, but still brown, both lounged in the beautiful wooden dining chairs. The large dining room table and two corner hutches sat with an old but elegant China cabinet that completed the ensemble of furniture.

Her dad manned the helm at the end of the table. He looked especially handsome tonight. Pride swelled in Vela's chest as she looked at his grey cardigan and dark slicked back hair. Pictures showed him as a knockout when he was young, but his features were still striking. She glanced over at her mom, who graced the other end of the table and who must agree with Vela. Love shone from her eyes as she mooned over her dad. Her mother, too, looked stunning with her blonde hair and curls that framed her oval face perfectly. She carried a soft look with big brown eyes that sparkled often. Barely there lines caressed the edges of her eyes and forehead, but Vela loved them. They showed she laughed more than she frowned.

Vela surveyed the feast and noted the table might be beautiful, but the large layout of food was even more so. A wealth of vegetables, which would always be the main course at her mother's table, made her mouth water just looking at it all. Platters and bowls full of colorful yumminess assaulted her senses.

Cold garlic and butter broccoli, steamy green beans and pine nuts, buttered corn on the cob, smashed turnips, a leafy salad stocked with cucumbers and tomatoes and spices, twice-baked potatoes full of cheese and bacon were just some vegetables she could see on her end of the table. Add to them the slow cooked roast and steaming rolls and Vela's stomach grumbled.

Jack, of course, sat as close to the tantalizing smell of food as he could get, right next to Vela's chair. He stayed because she would sneak him treats throughout the meal. Healthy ones, of course. She knew she was a bad pet owner for feeding him under the table, but she really didn't care. He was such a good dog; she wanted to spoil him.

She got away with it, too. Her mom and dad and brothers knew about her slipping him food, just pretended not to see her do it.

Elia, Vela and her parents were barely getting servings in between her brothers' many grabs for the delicious home cooked meal.

"He should not be here!" Drew demanded, his dark eyebrows scowling. "Why is he here? I don't know of any Festan in the area." He clenched his hand on his fifth roll of the night. Vela couldn't help counting as she chuckled to herself at his enormous appetite, but completely agreed with him.

"I say," Elia interjected, "let him come; it's a free country. Elementals shouldn't have to stay in their own territories. He brings with him something new; it's a mystery I wouldn't mind solving." Her finger traced the printed design on the cloth napkin at her side.

"And why is that?" Kane asked with a cool look in his eye, one that Vela noticed immediately. "Because he's hot?"

"I have my reasons," Elia answered, her lips twitching at the corners, but Vela could tell she was trying not to smile. Looking directly at Kane, she said, "And of course he's hot. He's a Festan, Kane."

"That's not what I meant," Kane grumbled, glaring at Elia. "He can't be your Intended, so why bother?"

"Kane, it *is* possible for a Festan to be my Intended," Elia fired back. "We just don't ever find them because we never mix with other clans, which is a shame, in my opinion. It's so rare to find your Intended, that it wouldn't surprise me if I did find my soul mate in a Borean, Neronian or Festan. God intended us to live together, remember, not apart. Territories happened because we chose to live apart and we're suffering for it. I know you all might feel different, and I understand that, because of all the bad history between our clans, but it's affecting our Intended bondings.

"The way we keep our clans separate; I literally have a one in a million chance of even finding my Intended. Wouldn't it make sense for us to unite so we can meet our one and only? Think about how finding our Intended enhances our abilities. It would strengthen us as a race!"

Vela glanced at her parents and knew that their connection was a miracle. And she knew her mother was an even more talented landscape designer because of her and her father's bond. And he, too, benefitted. But it was almost impossible to find your Intended. She knew that her parents only found each other because her dad had been on a sabbatical, traveling through various Gyan territories when he chanced on her mom.

"There's nothing wrong with marrying someone who isn't your Intended," Kane said, shredding a roll apart. "It's been done a million times and will continue. Our clans aren't going to merge anytime soon."

Vela glanced at his frown and wondered if he was upset at not finding his bondmate or the fact that Elia wanted to find hers.

Drew pounded the table. "The girls only care about how *hot* this new Elemental is! They're in high school. It's the only reason they're interested in him."

"Wait a minute! I couldn't care less!" Vela disagreed loudly. "He could be a Greek god and I wouldn't notice one way or another. Don't lump me in with this conversation! He's a Festan, and I don't want him here." She moved her green beans around her plate. "They're all alike, throwing their fire around like they own any place they set their sights on," Vela said. "They're nothing but land pirates."

"Now, Vela," her mother, Whitney, admonished in a soft, but firm voice. "It was years ago; we need to come to peace with what happened."

"I agree with Vela," Drew said, slapping the table again, his sixth roll bouncing to the ground. "They're land pirates, huh? I like that Vels, excellent description."

"Mom, I've had four years to think about what they did. And don't get me started on Cooper!" Vela argued. Her blood raged through her and a wide leafed plant that sat in the corner combusted in growth. Vela cringed. This was why she couldn't be close to humans. This happened sometimes when she got upset or emotional.

The table went silent. As it usually did when Cooper was mentioned, but especially at her slip of control.

"Sorry," she said, breathing deeply. "But we're constantly at war with that clan. They won't go easy on us. We shouldn't go easy on them, either!"

Whitney glanced at the plant before she said in her soft voice, "As much as I agree with you that Festans are dangerous and volatile, but they had an accident that night, too." She looked at David meaningfully and said to him, "It's time, honey. They should know the truth."

"What truth? That their fire had gotten out of control?" Vela's laugh barked. "I don't believe that for a second. Their element is fire; *of course* they have complete control of their gift. That's like saying I could be buried alive. It's impossible!"

"We launched a full investigation, Vela," her father, David, said firmly. "They lost a family member to that fire."

Shocked expressions reflected around the table. The only one not surprised was her mom.

Vela was the first to react. "How did I not know about this, Dad? And how could a Festan die by fire? Isn't that impossible?"

"It wasn't something they wanted to get out, and it still isn't. You've never been old enough to have this conversation. I guess now seems like as good a time as any. But this conversation does not leave this table. Is that understood?" David questioned. He cast a stern eye about the room, capturing everyone's attention.

Affirmative answers sounded around the table. Drew's expression was grim, his mouth a tight line. Kane's angry gaze stayed focused on his plate, and Elia's eyes were wide with disbelief.

"How did the family member die, Dad?" Vela asked again, curiosity burning through her. She was completely shocked; her stomach had dropped at the news.

"Just like everyone on this Earth, we need clean air to breathe," David answered. "We had in a shed between our properties old paint that apparently is toxic to breathe when it catches fire. The Festan died because of the fumes from the fire." David shook his head. "A senseless death is always sad."

A heavy silence filled the room. Vela sat, stunned. She slowly processed what she just heard. She agreed. It was sad. And a heat filled her with the injustice of what happened and someone losing their life in the process, too.

"Why did God allow that all to happen, anyway?" Vela said, voicing the questions in her mind. "He could have prevented it."

"Why do bad things happen to good people?" David asked, a thoughtful expression crossing his face. "That is a question that's been asked across the ages. And to answer that, you need to remember one thing." His deep voice caressed the room. Everyone hung on his next sentence. Vela's own breath caught as she listened intently. "Free will."

"You mean, like we have the choice to do right or wrong?" Drew asked, his serious expression matching the conversation being said.

"Yes," David said succinctly. "A fire broke out, one that a Festan started, probably to frighten us out of our home. That was their choice, one God freely gave them."

"The result wasn't worth it," Vela said quietly, her gaze locked on her plate. She fisted Jack's collar tightly.

"No," David agreed. "But free will is like that. Consequences will always follow every decision you make. All of you, please be sure you remember that as you go on in life. Whether they are good or bad, depending on your choices, results lead from your decisions. It's pretty simple."

"I say it had something to do with the Elemental Extremists," Kane said, throwing his napkin down. "They're always involved when it comes to suspicious activity."

"What's their deal?" Vela asked. "Why haven't they been stopped?"

"Because they're very good at remaining a secret," David answered. "They set their sights on preventing the old prophecy of a Chosen Child uniting our clans from coming true. But their actions have been tied to other questionable activities, as well."

"Like..." Vela said, motioning with her hand for him to continue.

David glanced at her mom before answering. He shifted in his seat and finally said, "There's been talk that you can hire the E.E. for services only Elementals can provide."

"What?" Kane and Drew barked at the same time.

"Are you saying that the E.E. markets themselves for things like healings and fires?" Vela asked.

"And get a pretty penny for them too," he answered solemnly.

"Why would people..." Vela started, at a loss for words.

"Desperate people will do desperate things to save a loved one or a crop from failing," Whitney said softly.

"It's actually pretty smart," Drew said thoughtfully. "If you overlook the prejudices our clans have and help one another, it would be one step closer to uniting the clans."

"*That* is not their intention," her dad said in a gruff voice. "That's actually the opposite, to cause division. The E.E. want nothing more than to keep their lucrative profits coming in. They've started many boundary battles to keep things the way they are just so uniting, like you say, Drew, never happens. Chaos and prejudices need to remain the same, according to this group. It keeps us apart and hating each other."

"Not enough to stop the E.E. from finding customers," Vela retorted.

"That's true," David said in a deep voice.

"It just seems wrong to me," Vela began, "to sell our services to the highest bidder. Our gifts are just what they're called, God-given gifts. To sell them when they're meant to be used to further our world and... our people? It makes me uncomfortable to think of selling my gift."

"I don't know how they're convincing their members to do these services," Whitney interjected, "but one thing I do know, is if the Chosen Child comes along, or someone comes along to unite us, their methods will no longer be needed."

"This is that prophecy where the Chosen Child will get rid of our territories?" Elia asked, a hopeful look taking over her face, probably related to the Intended conversation.

"That would actually be pretty great," Vela said thoughtfully. "It would stop the boundary battles."

"Well, right now, we Elementals all have our own spaces," David stated, folding his hands together, his elbows on either side of his plate. "The Neronians have most of the coastal areas, as you know, Florida and the Eastern seaboard. The Boreans have most of the Midwest states. And how can we forget that the Festans control most of Texas and California, with some Northern states and the ones around us?"

"And us lowly Gyans have the states no one else wants," Vela grumbled.

"No," David said, drawing out the word. "We have the states that we have fought well and hard to get and keep."

"It's ridiculous that we haven't gotten control of California yet," Kane grumbled.

David responded, "Gyans and Festans have been battling over that state for a hundred years. The Gyans with the earthquakes and fires for the Festans. It's been bombarded with territory disputes for too long. It's done too much damage to the state and the residents there, humans and Elementals. That's why we moved here to a less combative place. We're in a safe place, thank God. We're not in a border town where we could see territory disputes."

"We moved here," Vela said in a hard voice, "because our house, which sat on a territory border between us and the Festans, was lost to that stupid dispute. Our home became a casualty of war. And we almost were too. Do I have to remind any of you of all of our losses?" Tears pricked her eyes, but she forced them back.

"Be careful of your anger, daughter," Whitney warned. "It'll be a vice against you that you sorely don't need in this world. There's enough out there battling for you to lose faith in humanity and God. Don't allow its poison to enter your heart and your mind. Forgiveness helps you let go of your anger." She had spoken with a warning censure in her voice but ended with a gentle and caring tone. Vela's raised blood pressure cooled, and she sat grateful for the reminder.

Vela nodded. Jack nudged her knee with his nose, sensing her emotions, as always. She rubbed his head, assuring him and herself she was alright. Then she snuck him some roast beef. It was as much therapy for her as a snack for him.

"Why do we have to wait for a Chosen Child to unite us, anyway?" Vela asked. "If it's for the better of our race, we should unite now."

"Boundary battles are the reason we couldn't unite now. There are too many hard feelings between the clans to do something so extreme," David answered.

Territory battles were a constant threat and shifting boundary lines didn't make living as an Elemental easy. You were always on the news watching what natural disaster hit what area to see which Elemental was taking over what area. She knew it must not be an easy job to be an Elder, managing their defenses. She didn't envy her parents' roles as Elders, at all.

During the rest of dinner, their conversation ran through Vela's mind, possessing it completely. She hardly noticed when dinner was over. One thing was for sure, she couldn't wait for their soon-to-be vacation on Labor Day to start. After this conversation and its revelations, she desperately needed it. Two weeks seemed too long for Labor Day to arrive.

Chapter Three

AFTER HELPING HER MOTHER clean up after dinner, Vela took a step outside on their wraparound porch. She called Jack to her side as she closed the door. It was completely dark; the moon covered with a cloud. Filling her lungs with the night air, she squinted her eyes to see into the darkness. Her vision limited; she opened her ears to the musical evening.

Cicadas droned on loudly, their loud song one only they could appreciate. She wished an owl would make its melody; she loved their hooting in the night. Keeping Jack close to her, she didn't want to lose sight of him. He liked to explore.

Taking a deep breath, Vela relaxed slightly. The dinner left her feeling out of sorts. She thought about the elementals selling their gifts to other clans. She understood if they needed a healer's touch to contact a Gyan. But to sneak around and contact the E.E. for it? That didn't sit well with her. She was lucky enough to be in a Gyan territory, so she could receive healing anytime she needed. As long as it wasn't a terminal sickness, Gyans could heal most anything.

Jack, sensing her mood, bumped her legs with his side. She rubbed her hand down his smooth coat and took another deep breath of the fresh night air, chasing the peace it brought.

Vela looked around. Her father and two older brothers had laid each board of this beautiful porch. The corners of the patio boasted sturdy wooden posts that held up the roof that her brothers and dad also built, shingles and all. Their hard work was always something she would admire, considering her brothers were teenagers when they helped build it. They'd always been mature beyond their years.

Looking around, she sank into one of the rockers and ran her finger lovingly down a wooden vase inscribed with a floral design seated on the small table beside her. With one command from her, Jack made himself comfortable next to her chair as he scanned the yard.

Vela ran her fingertips over Jack's smooth coat as she watched fireflies dot the garden and the pergola in the back. She loved seeing their little lights dance the night away and considered herself a free spirit like them. If she could choose to be anything other than an Elemental, it would be a firefly. But then she wouldn't have a home to live in.

Examining her thoughts, she wondered what was it about a home that made her feel so safe and secure? She thought back to the childhood home she had lost and loved. She recalled a host of memories just thinking about her old stomping grounds. A lot had been forgotten over the years, but she remembered details that still meant the world to her.

Resting her head back, she slowly rocked the chair and remembered. She had had a tire swing, and it was one of her favorite pastimes when she was a child. At six years old, she had spent hours swinging her childhood away in it. The kittens born under her porch were a delight only puppies and kittens could provide. She would sneak under the porch that was a tight crawl space and play with them every chance she got.

She smiled, remembering. Her mother hadn't wanted her under the porch. Vela had eventually gotten stuck under there one day and it took some careful engineering from her father and both her brothers to get her out. Vela shuddered at the memory. She still didn't like small places to this day.

Other details of her home filtered through, cycling through her mind. She had read to her heart's content in the nook window in her bedroom. As a child, she would always hide in the closet under the stairs when she played hide and seek with her brothers.

She wondered at her feelings. Nostalgia crawled through her, but mainly she was angry, furious even. Still. Because they had barely escaped the fire unscathed. And she had failed her best friend.

With that thought, she was back in the flames.

Squeezing her eyes shut, her heart rate climbed, and she shook her head, forcing the images to recede farther back where they belonged. She would not go through those memories again. She wouldn't.

Imagining calm rivers with light sparkling on the surface, and warm, sunny days she could get lost in, she soon relaxed when the memories finally receded.

Sighing heavily, Vela had known from the moment she had moved, she would never forget what the Festans had taken from her. And she would forever carry scars that would remind her of her failure and what the Festans took from her. God taught her to forgive, but she wasn't sure she had managed to do that yet. And now, she was to face a Festan for the first time since the fire. She knew this boy was not the one who had set flames to her home, but she wouldn't trust him within an inch of her and those she loved.

The disturbance of someone with that Element was just what she did not need at that school. She sighed heavily, rocking her chair. Why couldn't a gorgeous Gyan Elemental start classes? Why was it her luck that a Festan may have now added to the chaos of her high school? She thumped her head against the chair and repeated the motion until her head complained from the bumps she gave it.

"No sense in starting a headache now. There's an even bigger one waiting for me on Monday," she whispered. Abandoning her peaceful rest on the porch, she walked back to the French doors that opened into the back of the house. Jack whined and followed. He could sense right now she was still on edge. Vela rubbed his head, assuring him, loving his concern for her.

She spied her mom making tea in the cheerful kitchen they all shared. Its yellow paint reminded Vela of sunshine, which was her mom's personality, too. Chocolate brown cabinets with glass allowed her to see the pretty colorful plates nestled inside. It was a modest space for a modest home.

Her mom stood leaning against the Formica counter that looked like marble but was just as good. Already dressed in her pajamas, it didn't surprise Vela to see her mom like that, even though it was only eight o'clock. Her mom looked up at her and Vela could see her eyes were already drooping. She went to work before the birds woke the day, which required an early bedtime, so Vela knew she had little time to talk to her.

Her mom co-owned a landscape company, designing the perfect gardens for her customers. The other owner was her mom's best friend wo Vela called Aunt Lila. Her real aunts lived all over the country. So, she loved Aunt Lila for being close and loving Vela as much as she did. Vela hoped she would be just as lucky as her mom one day to do what she loved with people she cared about. Her father did something very different, managing people's investments. He worked better with numbers.

Holding her cup to her chin and blowing softly on it, Whitney raised her eyebrows, indicating Vela could talk.

Vela asked, "Are we still going on vacation? Please say yes."

Whitney nodded. "I guess it's a vacation for you. Your father and I have business to take care of in the town close to where we're going. But your dad and I'll get some time to play. Labor Day can't come quickly enough."

"And it's in Utah?"

She nodded, saying, "It's a little place called Vernal. There's a campsite north of there we'll be staying at. Steinacker State Park. The locals pronounce it 'Stanacker' though, kind of funny."

"Huh. Sounds great," Vela said, exhaling. "I love camping. There's something about a campfire every night and sleeping under the stars. That's such therapy for me." Vela had a thought that worried her, and she decided to ask it, "Is that on the border, Mom? And is it Gyan territory?"

"Of course, it's our territory, sweetie. And, as a matter of fact, it is on the border. That's partly why we have to go. There's been some issues their Elders need our conference on. But don't worry, there's been no sign of the Borean Elementals that border the land in quite some time. Your dad and I have already researched it and confirmed it should be safe."

Vela nodded. She never wanted to get in the middle of a border battle. They were serious and sometimes deadly. Lightening the mood she had created with her question, she asked, "What's there to do around there?"

Her mom's stiff form visibly relaxed, and she answered cheerfully, "Well, there's swimming, fishing, hiking. There's actually a really cool rock formation area I want us to hike to that's close. Moonshine Arch. I think you'll love it. The lady who works at the campsite says Labor Day is a great time to camp there. It's the perfect temperature for swimming."

"You sound like a brochure for the place," Vela teased. "I can't wait." She sighed and fingered the fringe of her shorts. Suddenly Elia's words at dinner got her thinking. She wanted to know more about her parent's Intended bond. Her whole life she had watched their bond at work, but she couldn't help the questions that popped up.

"What is it that's bothering you? Talk to me," her mom urged.

Puffing out a breath she didn't realize she was holding, Vela blurted, "Dinner just had me thinking."

"What could be rolling around that crazy head of yours?" Whitney smiled gently at her.

"Well, when you met Dad, was it, as they say, a fireworks-like feeling of sensations and amazing scent?"

"You're worried about finding your Intended, is that it?"

Vela wrapped her arms around her middle and said, "I was just thinking about what Elia said about the probability of finding my Intended and how it's highly unlikely I'll find him. Elia's right, the chances are so small. But in case I do, what can I expect? Am I going to be forever pulled toward that person for the rest of my life? Will I have a life of my own at all after that moment? You and Dad make it look so easy."

A faraway look crept into her mom's eyes and she said softly, "Your Intended will have the beat of your heart going so strong, you'll crave being around him as much as breathing."

"Breathing, Mom? How can I crave the act of breathing? That just doesn't make any sense," Vela said, her nose scrunching.

"No," her mom said, smiling, "it makes little sense. That's the beauty, the magic of it. You'll be completely drawn to him and he to you. Like two magnets, you won't be able to resist him."

"So, you fall in love instantly?"

"No, I wouldn't say that. It still takes time to fall in love with him. Get to know who he is and what he loves and vice versa. He'll need to get to know who you are, too. But you'll find each other to be a perfect match in every way. It'll be easy to fall for him. It was for me, anyway."

"Sounds intense," Vela said, frowning.

"What scares you about that?" Whitney asked, laughing.

"I just want to have choices in my life," Vela said, pacing. Jack whined again, and she petted his head absentmindedly. "It sounds like some of your choices get taken away if I meet my Intended. Like the life that I planned and worked hard for completely alters to meet a brand new path. I don't know, Mom, I'm not sure I like that. I've got dreams, you know?"

"Vela, one thing I can tell you, everything falls into place if you ever meet him. A lot easier than you think. And if you give God control of your life completely, He'll work out those details to fit *His* plan. He has a wonderful plan for you and whomever you're tied to. He promises in Jeremiah 29:11, For I know the plans I have for you," she quoted, her eyes shining. "Plans to prosper you and not to harm you. Plans to give you a hope and a future."

Vela's heart swelled. She knew talking to her mom would help settle her anxiety, but nothing was like hearing promises from her Creator like that. She reached for her mom and drew her into a tight hug.

"Thank you, Mom," she whispered into her hair, inhaling the scent she always associated with her, a unique blend of vanilla and traces of lavender. "You always help me see the big picture. I love you."

Whitney squeezed her back and said, "Anytime, baby. It's all going to work out."

Vela let her go to bed and wondered where her brothers had disappeared to after dinner. With those two, you never know what mischief they were involved in.

Scanning the house, she looked for one of them. Still restless, she wanted to know their opinions. The new information about the childhood fire they had been told had to have affected them, too. Vela was relieved to see Kane bounding down the stairs.

"Kane! Can I talk to you?" she asked, intercepting his path.

"Sure sis, what's up?" Kane walked over to a stuffed chair in the living room and plopped down. He called Jack over to him and frowned when Jack ignored him and remained by her.

"Why'd he become your dog anyway? He was supposed to be a family dog."

Sitting across from him, she smiled down at her loyal companion and said, "He fell in love with me, and I with him. It was destiny." Studying her brother and his handsome looks, she could see what Elia saw in her stubborn brother. She really did hope things would work out between those two. Changing subjects, she asked, "What did you think of what Dad said about our old home and the fire?"

Taking a deep breath, he answered, "I think it's really sad. It makes you re-think the whole thing, doesn't it?"

"Yes! I've always blamed the Festans for taking our home and land. And now knowing it really did get out of control makes me feel..."

"Sympathetic?" he finished for her.

"Yes! But it still makes me so mad! I..." Vela folded her arms across her chest. How could she explain the terrible pain that still wrapped around her heart when she thought of her lost friend?

With a short bark of laughter, he asked, "Are you wanting to stay angry, Vels? Would that make you feel better?"

"I don't know Kane, I thought I forgave them and moved on with my life, but..."

"If it makes you feel any better, I doubt they wanted the fire to get that bad where it burned our house to the ground and you know..."

Nodding curtly, Vela chewed her lip and whispered, "I can't stop hearing his crying. I wake up sometimes in a cold sweat just remembering."

He looked at her with sad eyes and said, "I wish I could give you good advice. It feels nearly impossible to let go of such a terrible hurt, but from what I hear from Mom and Dad, it is possible to let it go. I'm not in the same boat as you, but I am in the same ocean. I loved Cooper too. Let's just try to do as our parents asked, now that we know the truth. It's easier to forgive someone when they aren't completely in the wrong."

"Yes," Vela agreed. "I'll try to let it all go..." Then, to lighten the mood, she asked, "Like you letting go of that comment Elia made about the hot Festan tonight?"

A shocked look came over Kane's face. "No, I was just..." his hands fisted on his knees and he stared off to the side, looking a little lost for words.

"Mad?" Vela made a valiant effort not to smile. She failed.

"Mad? Me? No! I don't care who she thinks is hot. It's none of my business," he said, straightening in his seat.

"Would you like it to be your business, Kane?" Vela couldn't help it. She laughed at his expression. It was part outrage and part curiosity.

He turned and glared at Vela. "Look, this conversation is over. And don't push it okay? Elia is young and not—"

"Kane," Vela interrupted, "I can be sympathetic too. This conversation never happened. I got it."

"Let's keep it that way," Kane grumbled. "I've got something to do."

Smiling, Vela let him leave with her promise in mind. As much as she wanted to share with Elia this very interesting conversation, she had to stay out of it. But she had a feeling Elia was going to be her sister one day, both in name and in her heart.

Chapter Four

"Vela," her mother said with a sigh, studying her daughter's face. "Don't look so depressed. It's not like you have to fight in a battle or suffer some major illness. You're going to school. Really," she sighed heavily. "It's like you're on your deathbed. Now turn around so I can work on this braid."

Vela dutifully turned around and fumed. Normally she could braid her own hair, but there was something immeasurably soothing about hands combing through her hair. And her mom's touch felt even more magical in how relaxing it was. She suspected her mom to be infusing her with calming, healing energy.

It was a few days after having Elia over for dinner, *and* it was a Wednesday. Vela groaned. Two days into a week at school with two days to go, three if you included today. Her parents forced her to attend school, but she wished they still homeschooled her, where she could attend her Gyan classes outside, breathing in the rich, clean air.

Instead, she had to suck in the air-conditioned environment, and it took its toll on her gift. The fake air that blew through the classrooms and flowed unnaturally through the halls stunted her abilities, making them less, making her less. She longed to rebel against attending the toxic place. At least she was a Senior.

Vela shook off her anxiety and had to admit, she was more nervous about running into the Festan. She hadn't come across him yet, and she was stressed about her reaction when she did. So, she had asked her mom to come in and give her a hand with her braid. Even Jack's presence had failed to calm her spirits.

She glanced in the mirror at her outfit and frowned at the bright colors in her dress. Why did she have to like yellow so much? It did not in any way reflect her mood today, so she didn't know why she had picked it out. It was too late to change now, so she shrugged and turned away from the mirror.

"Mom, that school is so full of germs and bacteria. It creeps into everything I own. It wouldn't surprise me if I dropped into a coma one of these days." She dropped her head, only to have it gently yanked back up for her mom to finish her braid. "Why can't you homeschool me in high school? Why is it so necessary to go to that decrepit place?"

"You know very well why. You're experiencing society in a local environment," her mom said patiently, tugging on her hair as she braided. "By going, you're learning to cohabitate with the human population. And understanding about their history will help you in the future."

"How? How will learning their history help me?" She knew full well she sounded like a whining brat, but she didn't care.

"By learning from their mistakes, dear," her mom said as she wrapped an elastic on the end of her long golden braid. "Now go, or you'll be late."

Vela thought the only mistake she was learning about was her attending school. But she wisely kept those thoughts to herself. Saying a mournful goodbye to Jack, her heart clenched at, literally, his lost puppy expression. "I'll be back by 2:30, baby, don't worry. You know I won't stay there a minute longer than necessary." Smoothing her hand down his head, she kissed his wet nose.

Straightening, she met her mom's gaze in the mirror. "Don't worry, I'll watch over him, like I always do. He's perfectly safe with me, honey," Whitney promised.

As satisfied as she could be with that promise, Vela went outside and waited at the end of her street for the school bus to pick her up. Waiting for a bus was annoying. She really should buy a car. She had her driver's license. It was time. She made a mental note to look at cars online after school.

Breathing deeply, she was glad it was just starting the fall season. The delightfully clean, crisp air was refreshing. As much as she hated the air conditioning blasting through school, she was more than happy at her house with all their windows open, catching the cool breeze.

She lived in a small skiing town called Breckenridge. It was popular for tourists in the winter months to come and enjoy their winding trails.

Her family was lucky enough to be in a neighborhood that didn't butt up against one another. They had a beautiful white two-storied home that looked colonial. In fact, they had found a home with a reserve that stretched behind their home for miles. *No, not lucky,* Vela corrected herself, *blessed.* Her mom always reminded her luck has nothing to do with things, they're blessings.

Each home boasted a nice yard, which, in their family's case, was necessary. They not only needed space to grow a garden, complete with their own vegetables and herbs, but it was far from prying eyes. With the inclusion of a high privacy fence, they could perform their gifts without the eyes of human neighbors watching them. They didn't have to necessarily worry about anyone seeing behind them, because of the reserve, but their neighbors could get an eyeful without the fence there to protect their secrets.

Human neighbors were a fact Elementals had to accustom themselves to, as they couldn't afford to claim whole neighborhoods for only Elementals to live in. That didn't mean, however, Elementals got close to their human neighbors.

They actually had an Elemental family on one side of them, which was usually great, besides when Vela spouted off treasonous words like she did with Elia a few days earlier. But other than that family, the rest of the street were humans. She used to wish she could befriend the other human children, but Vela had always gravitated toward other Elementals as friends. In fact, her parents encouraged that. But she had some human friends. To say they were friends was stretching the term, though, mainly acquaintances. She couldn't risk it.

Looking over her shoulder, she wondered where Elia was, nodding her head at a few humans who had joined her at the bus stop. Then she saw her best friend strolling down the street. She had her headphones on and sang along to an upbeat song. Vela leaned in to hear which one and smiled when she heard it was Taylor Swift's *Love Story*, then promptly frowned when she remembered the Festan at her school she had yet to run into.

When Elia reached her, she took her headphones off and Vela asked, "Well, aren't you a chipper thing this morning?"

"Yes! And aren't you a grouch?"

"What? No! Hey, did you hear about the breach in security the other day?"

Elia shoved her headphones off her head and demanded, "Spill. What and who?"

"What happened and who let their element show, you mean?" Vela said, talking in a hushed voice so the humans couldn't hear.

"Yes! What happened, Vels?"

"Well, apparently, Maria was showing off or mad at someone and bent a sapling in half, unknowingly in front of a human."

"So, the Elders are taking care of it?"

Vela nodded and said, "My mom was getting the poppy seed formula ready for them to use on the human this morning."

"That Maria, she's such a blonde, and she's a redhead! She needs to be more careful. Thank God for that formula. What would we do without it?"

"We wouldn't be able to alter the memories of humans without it," Vela said, shrugging.

Elia studied Vela's face and took her by the shoulders. "What else is wrong?"

"Besides the fact that I now need to share my breathing air with a Festan? Nothing."

"Oh, come *on*, he's not going to be that bad. And you haven't even met him yet since you don't have any classes with him! It shakes things up a bit around here! We could use a little spice in our lives, especially of the hot variety!"

"How do you even know he's a Festan, anyway? How can you be so sure?"

"You can feel the heat signature just radiating off him. He's definitely a Festan, Vels."

"Whoopee, that's just great," Vela muttered.

"Honestly, you're making too much of this. It's going to be fine! I'm sure of it!"

Vela could only hope that was true. But she couldn't help the bad feeling that snaked throughout her.

Chapter Five

VELA WALKED INTO HER first class and stopped dead in her tracks. A tall dark-haired guy stood at the front desk having a conversation with her first period teacher. He was new to her class, and it looked like he was accepting a textbook from the teacher.

Her gut clenched, and she hoped he wasn't the Festan Elia talked about. This guy wore his dark jeans and black shirt well. From the side, it looked like he was attractive to the nth degree and she hoped he was like her, a Gyan. *He can't be the Festan*, she thought, her heart pounding. *That guy started over a week ago. This must be someone new.*

Vela would have to pass him to get to her seat, so she'd find out sooner rather than later if he was an Elemental. Vela knew if she passed close enough to him, she'd sense him. If he was Festan, heat would radiate off his skin. A rush of energy will rush through her veins if he was Gyan. If he was human, there will be nothing.

Vela studied his stance. He stood tall, lean, but confident. That much she could easily see. He was strong, too. She could see the ropes of muscles in his arms as he stood talking to the teacher. She slowly started walking towards him.

When she finally passed by him, a fragrance hit her, so mouthwatering, she stopped dead in her tracks. It smelled like the tantalizing aroma of a hundred pine trees and an even sweeter, smokier fragrance of... marshmallows melted by an outdoor fire. The smell of fire and smoke usually terrified her, but for some reason, heat bloomed under her skin. Never had anything smelled so good to her. She leaned toward him unconsciously, not able to help her reaction. *This can't be happening.* Panic crept into her body.

Her fingers tingled like she was using her gift and she looked at her hands like they were strangers to her. Her gift fired up her arms, and she looked with horror at them. But it wasn't her scars that terrified her, it was her reaction to... him.

She needed to move and just get to her seat. But she stood frozen in place. Feeling the heat radiating off him, he was definitely a Festan. There was no mistaking that. As for his scent and her body's reaction, her panic escalated with this very unwelcome development. Only her Intended would make her gift come alive and only *he* would smell this good. Her gut dropped, and she held her breath to avoid scenting him again.

She squeezed her fingers, attempting to get rid of the tingling. Sliding her hand up her shirtsleeve, she fingered the rough skin of her scars, which grounded her, bringing her back from wherever she had disappeared to. If there had been plants in the room, they would have combusted in a profusion of growth.

He finished his conversation with the teacher. But because Vela had stopped right behind him, when he turned, he slammed into her. She fell, but his quick hands grabbed her, preventing her from falling to the ground.

"I'm sorry." His deep voice said. He held her to him, pausing, she guessed, to be sure she could stand and her face and hands were pressed against his chest. "I didn't see you standing there. I was just transferred into this class and needed my...book." the voice faltered, and he finished his comment like a question.

Her pulse pounded, and she was sure he could hear both it and her rapid breathing. Vela was mortified. Her face flamed with a blush that rivaled any she had had before. And their proximity flooded her senses with his amazing, woodsy scent he carried. *It can't be! Please, Lord, tell me no!*

She didn't want to look up, but when she finally did, it was to view wavy hair that fell to his shoulders, a confused look in his midnight blue eyes, a straight nose and a strong chin, with a dimple in it of all things. It was a classically handsome face. She really hated that she liked that dimple.

"I didn't realize it was a welcoming ritual in this school to..." He stopped talking just as his nostrils flared. He took a deep breath, just as she had, and looked at her with bright astonishment in his eyes. He must have noticed her shock, too, and he straightened his arms, holding her away from him, looking her over from head to toe. Her surprised gaze took in that his dark shirt had a band name on it. He tightened his grip on her arms, not letting her escape, which she wanted to, badly. The heat from his hands flared, getting hotter, and she winced at the sensation that it felt... nice. He looked like Vela could push him over with a feather, if she wanted.

Stunned, she knew then that what her senses were telling her was true. She shook off his hands and ran.

Vela nearly bowled over two students in her mad dash to leave the room. Tearing open the door to the classroom, she ran to the nearest bathroom. She needed some time alone. Locking herself in the bathroom stall, Vela plopped herself down on the toilet seat and put her head down between her legs. She began taking huge gulps of breaths, trying not to hyperventilate.

"He cannot be my Intended, there is absolutely no way," she whispered fiercely as tears leaked from her eyes.

Every Elemental had an Intended, the one person they connected to perfectly and would usually, one day, marry. But Vela would literally give up her kidneys for that person to be anyone but a Festan. Her reactions to this guy told her he was her bondmate. The scent, the wild energy rush ratcheting up her heart rate and her gift flaring up spelled out this new disaster.

What will she say to him? What will she do? How was all this possible? She raised her head and breathed deeply, hating the chemical smell of the bathroom and hating her new position.

Her thoughts churned. *Let me think about this logically,* she started thinking. *Just because he smells good—really good—cannot mean he is my Intended. Maybe he just went camping and hadn't showered or changed his clothes. Yeah, that has to be it.*

Blowing out a breath, she knew she had to face some reality, however. If, and this was a huge *if*, this guy does smell as good as she remembered, and it wasn't because he had just gone camping, then this was going to be a secret, she decided. The kind of secret where even if he dares to bring it up to her, she will completely deny such a connection exists. How could she deny the other signs, though? She moaned into her hand.

Having an Intended was entirely a choice. Intendeds don't always get together if they choose not to. And that was her choice. She just needed to keep this Festan away from her. She would avoid him like the plague. And telling Elia she was going to do this would not go over well. But she had handled worse.

Like losing her home to Festan Elementals.

Chapter Six

Sitting at lunch with Elia later that day, Vela slammed down her drink. "Elia, you said this day was going to be fine. Remember when you said that this morning? You said everything was going to work out. Is this what you call working out?"

Vela and her Gyan friends all sat at a round table in a crowded lunchroom that smelled of subpar food and fake air with a noise level that rivaled a football game. Everyone was trying to be heard, and it was making Vela's already bad headache worse.

Lillith, a blonde curly haired friend, asked, "What's going to be fine?" She chewed a french fry and eyed Vela curiously.

Vela knew she looked wild with worry. Schooling her expression as best as she could, she said tersely, "It's nothing big."

"Yeah, it is," Elia said cheerfully. "She has a problem with the new Festan."

Vela glared at Elia, who caught the hint and snorted, but went quiet.

"Well, you're the first," Lillith remarked with a huff. "The humans love that guy. He's fast becoming the most popular guy in the school. Why, that is, I couldn't guess," she said with a sneer. "He's got charisma, I'll give him that. But he's a *Festan*. He shouldn't be here."

"Good for him, and I completely agree that he shouldn't be here, not that he's got charisma. He must have everyone fooled," Vela said dryly.

"If he thinks he can waltz in here with his beautiful face and charm everyone he meets, he's got another thing coming," Lillith fumed. "We Gyans stick together. They have plagued our borders for far too long for us to ever trust them."

Evan, another Gyan, spoke up. "I'd like to show him a thing or two of what it means to cross a Gyan. Like bury him in dirt. See what his fire can do about that," he muttered darkly.

A pretty Gyan Vela never cared for, Maria, searched through the lunchroom for wherever the Festan had found a seat. "I don't know. He's confident. To walk into a school full of Gyans? That's power, if you ask me." She twirled her long red hair with one manicured finger.

Vela snorted. She wasn't the least bit surprised Maria set her eyes on this new guy. There was no limit to her flirtatious nature. Humans or Elemental, she went after them all. Vela would never date a human. She wanted to be herself around someone she cared about, not hide the deepest and most personal side of her, her powers. Maria must not feel the same way, because she did not discriminate. She dated everyone.

"What?" Maria asked, her shoulders stiffening. "I have every right to like who I want to like. I'm not as prejudiced as you all."

"That you would say that to those of us who have been affected by the acts Festans are capable of says a lot about your character, Maria," Vela bit out.

Maria's wide blue eyes grew even wider. "Who says I haven't been affected? I just happen to have a forgiving nature. Besides, there's only one of him and hundreds of us. What could he possibly do to us?"

"Plenty," Vela said curtly. "Believe me, it would take him all of thirty seconds to set this entire high school on fire."

"I doubt that's his intention," Maria disagreed.

"No," Elia chirped, "He has other *intended* targets." She smiled smugly at Vela, who narrowed her eyes at her in a warning to keep quiet.

"Well, I aim to find out what those are," Maria promised, her eyes narrowed at Vela.

Vela's stomach sunk. Thankfully, the conversation changed to the upcoming football game.

Once Elia was sure none of their tablemates could hear her, she zeroed her attention on Vela and whispered, "So, spill. Tell me every single minute detail." Telling Elia had been the next worse thing to have happened to Vela that day. Elia had jumped in the hallway and squealed as loud as she could. It had taken everything in Vela to calm her down and then fess up to what she was going to do about it, which was nothing.

"I told you everything," Vela whispered back. "I smelled him. He smelled me. I ran away. And that's that. I plan on ignoring him for the unforeseen future. He can't be my Intended, there's no way."

"Ignore him? That's your plan?" Elia hissed at Vela. "What if this guy *is* your bondmate? You think he would let this kind of thing go? You're crazy to think he's going to do nothing but follow you to the ends of the earth. Did you even go back to first period?"

When Vela shook her head, Elia laughed. "This is the highlight of my year. I cannot wait to see what happens."

Despite Vela's protests, Elia wouldn't stop talking about it. "Oh my gosh, who would have thought that would have happened? I still can't believe it!" Elia squealed and her face lit up with excitement. "So, you didn't talk to him at all?"

Vela turned to Elia slowly and continued to whisper. "What on Earth would possess me to talk to him? I have serious issues with anyone with a fire element. I'm trying not to hate them, but you can't expect miracles from me right now. And it would be one huge miracle for me to just accept a lifetime tie with someone who's a Festan. You think I would welcome this into my life?" With Elia's expectant look, Vela answered with a big sigh, "No, I did not talk to him. Happy?"

"Hmm, would I call myself happy right now?" Elia asked quietly with big smile still trying to keep their conversation private. "I think not. I think my emotion is pure excitement and anticipation. Yes! Anticipation is the perfect word. This is going to rock your world, my dear friend," she said, resting her chin in her hand as she looked out over the cafeteria. Sitting up slowly, Elia's grin somehow got bigger, and she announced, "And I think Round Two is just about to start, folks. Your love is looking right at you, Vels, and yep! He's on his way over now. Get ready bestie!"

Vela looked up and, sure enough, the Festan walked in a determined stride toward her from across the cafeteria. Their gazes locked. She watched as his dark form easily glided around people standing in his way, never once breaking eye contact with her. It was like she could feel his heat from across the room. Everything in her couldn't wait until he reached her. But her emotions and head collided in a battle of wills. Run or see what he wanted? Mostly, she wanted to hide. Crawl into the smallest hole imaginable. Even Alice in the Wonderland's rabbit hole would be preferable at this moment. She'd gladly brave a big-headed queen and a talking rabbit over this.

But she knew she had only one option. The closer he got to the table, the more her mind rejoiced that he was coming. Her pulse skyrocketed, and she had trouble catching her breath. Her fingertips went crazy with her element again and Vela, annoyed, shook them out. That could not be a good sign. It was also yet another serious sign that he was her Intended.

Time to put her plan in action. It was time to run away.

"Sorry to do this to you, Els, but it's time I got lost," Vela said, hurrying to grab her backpack. "You deal with Fire Boy, I've gotta go." Ignoring the sensation to stay, she turned and practically ran to the lunchroom doors. She was going to find that small hole she wanted earlier and hide.

Chapter Seven

HIDING DURING LUNCH HAD proved pretty easy. She had found a cozy nook in the library in between two enormous bookcases that kept out of sight, but she could watch the front doors to the library in case she needed a quick getaway.

She was home now and waiting for Elia to call or come over, or knowing her best friend, both. Just then, her phone rang and after looking at the caller ID, she could see her wait was over.

"Vela! Where did you go during lunch?" Elia screeched into the phone. "I can't believe you ran away like that! Are you crazy? You just dug yourself into a deep, deep hole! You will not believe his reaction to you leaving!"

"Elia, breathe, breathe, relax," Vela cautioned. "It's going to be alright."

"Yea, you say that when you hear what he said to me, Vels" Elia said in a sing-song voice.

Dread pooled in Vela's stomach, but she had to ask, "What did he say?"

"Your Fire Boy just got more interesting," Elia said with a big smile in her voice.

"What. Did. He. Say, Elia?"

"Okay, picture this. He saunters up to our table, watching you leave like a hawk watching his poor defenseless prey."

Yes, Vela could picture that easily.

"Then he says in this beautiful voice, 'If she keeps running away, doesn't she know it's the chase that makes the capture that much sweeter?' Never once taking his eyes off you or the doors you disappeared into. Then, just like that, he walks away."

Vela's head felt like it exploded in outrage. "He said, WHAT?"

She couldn't believe this. Her mind spun, her breathing erratic and quick. She never would have imagined that she would dodge her Intended, the person she should want to spend the rest of her life with. But that was the situation. And the crazy thing was, it seemed he liked the chase.

"The capture that much sweeter?" Vela repeated. "Does he think I'm going to just fall in his arms with that kind of comment?"

"I think he likes that he has to chase you, Vels. So, keep it up. You're doing a great job, bestie."

"A great job with what?" Vela growled.

"With that fishing line you just threw out there. All you have to do is reel him in!" Elia laughed.

It was possible he felt the draw to be around her every bit as much as she around him. And she wanted to be around him. She felt like her emotions betrayed her in their pull to be near him. But so far, she had ignored every inclination. And it also looked like he was every bit a predator she wanted to avoid.

Who enjoyed being prey? Not her.

"Why can't my Intended be my element?" Vela asked, moaning into the phone.

"It's definitely unusual. I mean, when are we ever around any Elemental who isn't in our clan?"

"Well, lucky for me," Vela said dryly. Putting her head in her hand, she asked, "Why would this happen to me, Elia? I get this incredible chance at happiness, and it happens with a Festan. Just my luck. I'm trying to be understanding of them and what happened when I was a kid, then this gets thrown in my face!"

"Vela, give him a chance," Elia begged. "He's probably a great guy! He must be if you're connected to him. Please don't run away from him! I want to see you happy! He's your destiny!"

"And you think that being connected to a Festan is going to make me happy? He's lucky I didn't break his neck! He's the last kind of person for me, Elia! I cannot believe this. I'm only seventeen, I'm not ready to be tied down. Do you know what it was like recovering from third-degree burns, even with my mom's healing touch? Why would I want my Intended to be a walking fireplace? And Cooper? What about him?"

"Vela, honestly," Elia said in a somber voice, "What happened to Cooper and you is tragic. It's the stuff you can only read about in books. But you're asking me why being tied down to someone who's your perfect companion is bad? Who's incomparable to any other? Who's the perfect yin to your yang? Yea, that sounds terrible, Vels."

"You just sound jealous."

"Because I *am*! I would love to find my Intended. Now, put your big girl pants on, find out what and why he's here in our territory, get your answers, then live your happily ever after!"

"But a Festan, Elia? I could never trust one of them! Oh my gosh, what am I going to do? Sorry, I've gotta go. I need to think about this for a while."

"Okay, but do me a favor? Talk to your mom about this. Your parents need to know what's going on."

"Not yet, Elia. There's still a chance this can end," Vela answered quickly.

"How?" Elia's exasperation was plain.

"He might decide he doesn't like me," Vela said hopefully.

Elia laughed outright. "Who? You? Of course, he's going to love you. Seriously, think about telling your parents," Elia said, finishing the conversation.

If there was one thing she would not do, it was tell her parents right now. She wondered how they would react to this news. Would they hate that he's a Festan or would they just hear that he's her Intended and be ecstatic with this news? Would they try to push her toward him or away?

It was a hard guess and one she couldn't make.

"Not making any promises, Elia, just don't tell anyone, please?"

"I won't, but what's stopping him from not talking?"

"Let's hope he doesn't."

This was turning into a veritable nightmare. But, with a heap of avoidance and a touch of rudeness, she just might wake up from this much happier than she is now.

If she was lucky.

Chapter Eight

Choosing to run away from Fire Boy was easy. But Vela found it easier said than done. It was close to the end of the week, a Thursday, but it had been murder constantly being on her guard.

Everywhere she went, she saw his tall form either coming her way or turning the corner toward her. If she could melt into the shadows by wearing dark colors, she would. The school, however, boasted brightly lit hallways, terrible at slinking around in. So, she continued wearing her normal bright colors. She'd at least find happiness in what she wore.

And first period was a complete nightmare. She had to make sure she was the last person to arrive and the first person to leave, sitting right next to the door for a quick getaway. She could feel his stare at her back during the entire class, but she resolutely kept her gaze at the front of the class and took meticulous notes to keep herself busy from turning to meet his penetrating gaze. It tempted her. She unconsciously gravitated toward him, but she forced herself not to. Lunches were now spent in the library nook she had found.

The teacher had called out his name, and she had learned it was Lincoln, which he had then corrected and shortened to Linc. And from what she saw in her glances at him, her friends were right about his popularity. Humans constantly surrounded him. She wondered how he could blend so easily into the human world. It was hard for most Elementals to mesh with humans, but he seemed to have no trouble.

Glancing at the cliques standing around the busy hallway, she wondered how humans made sense of Elementals sticking together away from humans. There was no rhyme or reason to their groups in a human's mind. Human jocks and cheerleaders usually gravitated toward their own groups and the artsy students with one another, too. Then, there were the rednecks and the western set as well as the emos with their black hair, eyeliners and black painted nails, even on the guys. But the Elementals mixed despite preferences like that. Not only that, but as she watched, she could see Elementals physically shying away from humans, remaining in their groups. What did the humans make of it, she wondered? And how did Linc navigate both worlds so well?

Speaking of, Cassie, one of her human acquaintances stopped her in the hallway. Vela was so lost in her thoughts she hadn't noticed her friend.

"Whatcha' up to stranger?" Cassie asked sweetly. Two deep dimples showed up with her smile and her eyes studied Vela. "I feel like I haven't seen you in a week! You look cute in your little white dress. Where've you been? Usually, we walk to second and sixth together, but I haven't seen you. I didn't do something wrong, did I?"

"No! Of course not!" Vela's mind spun with all the questions and comments fired at her. "I've just been spending all of my free time..." she paused, thinking, *Hiding from a certain Festan Intended*, but said instead, "getting a head start on a couple projects."

"Oh okay," Cassie said happily. "Going to class?"

Vela looked around. Today was no exception to her pattern of hiding from Linc. She and Cassie had just turned the corner when she saw him coming down the hall. He walked awfully close to Maria, her fellow Gyan. Maria laughed at something he said and tucked her arm in his. An irrational jealousy rose through Vela, which she ruthlessly squashed down. He could walk with anyone he chose and make them laugh.

Just then, Linc looked directly at her. Unable to give Cassie any explanation, she shrieked and waved her goodbye. Ducking through a door and into a stairwell, she molded her body to the wall next to the door. She hoped Cassie would forgive her, but she'd have to worry about her later. She'd wait a few minutes to leave her hiding spot, which was going to make her late to her next class.

It was well worth it.

Vela could tell when Linc was close because her traitorous body lit up like a beach bonfire. Her heart raced, astonished at its rate when she wasn't even close to him. Probably because he was getting closer. She turned her head toward the wall. In case he looked in the stairwell, he wouldn't see her face.

Just when Vela realized he probably sensed her as much as she could sense him, the door to the stairwell opened. Her heart froze, and she hoped it wasn't Linc who opened the door. She kept her head turned toward the wall and her eyes squeezed shut, but an overwhelming pleasure filled her senses. A delicious, sweet scent washed over her.

Vela jumped when a warm, deep voice spoke into her ear, "Caught ya'. My ghost has nowhere to fly now."

She jumped and turned toward him, opening her eyes, and found herself trapped in a dark blue gaze. Vela stepped back and continued to do so until she found herself tucked into a corner. Then yelped when he shut the heavy door with a loud thud. Leaning against it casually, he looked completely at ease when he crossed his arms and legs. She looked down at herself. She looked like a ghost compared to him with her white dress and his dark colors he favored.

A ghost to his dark shadow. There couldn't be more of a contrast between them.

"Ghost?" she asked. He put her under a spell, and she didn't know the incantation to diffuse it.

"Yes, ghost, spirit, apparition," he said, inhaling deeply. "You're definitely her; the one who's been haunting me all week. You're even wearing white, like a ghost. The question is, what do I do with you now? And why do you keep running away from me?"

"Stop blocking my way, Linc," Vela ordered, ignoring his question. Frustrated he caught her so easily, and equally frustrated that she enjoyed having him close. She never should have hidden in this stupid stairwell. Vela hid her damaged arms behind her back. She didn't want him to see her scars; she didn't want to share her memories of that night with a *Festan*.

He moved smoothly, opening the door. "You're free to go. Don't let me stop you." His eyes challenged her.

She couldn't move, found she didn't want to, and fury raced through her veins at her body's betrayal. She was *curious,* but didn't want to be.

"You found out my name." He smiled, looking entirely too pleased.

Vela's eyes narrowed. She could race up the stairs so she wouldn't have to pass him on the way out. He still held open the door for her to leave, if she wanted. *Why didn't I want to?*

"You know, usually Elementals would be ecstatic to find their Intended," he said good-naturedly as he let go of the door and stepped toward her. "But mine, for some reason, wants nothing to do with me. Why is that, I wonder? Do I smell?" The door slammed shut.

"No, definitely not," she said, before snorting. Vela instantly hated her quick reaction, basically admitting that he smelled wonderful. And her heart sunk with the casual way he mentioned an Intended bond. Why wasn't it the end of the world for him like it was for her? How could he be so easily accepting of a bonding with a Gyan?

She racked her brain for explanations.

"Ah, I see I have just as much of an effect on you as you do on me. Good. And since you don't want to offer your name, I'll say it for you. You're Vela. Vela Ashcroft."

Vela decided to feign ignorance; she had to try something. "I actually don't know what you're talking about." All she could picture suddenly was her old home in flames. She blinked, forcing away the image, convincing herself that memory wasn't his fault.

"You don't know what I'm talking about?" he repeated, oblivious to her torment. "You mean that you're Vela Ashcroft, or that you smell like flowers and honey... like, like... the sweetest blend of roses, gardenias, and honey butter rolls? It's intoxicating. And I think you know exactly what that means."

Looking into his eyes that had become rather hypnotic, she repeated, willing him to believe her, "I don't know what you're talking about, please excuse me." Before she could leave her corner, he moved a half step closer.

"You don't know what I'm talking about?" he said with his hands raised, asking her to wait. "You know what we have," he said firmly, "and we have to talk."

"Talk to a guy who has a lot to gain by being my Intended?" she spat.

He cocked his head. "Explain."

She scoffed. "As if we don't both know what will happen if we *are* each other's Intended." She cocked her head, too, and narrowed her eyes. "I'm sure the fact that you'll enhance your already deadly gifts isn't what motivates you at all to accept me as your bondmate."

"The same could be said for you," he said smoothly, his eyes boring into hers.

"I never said I wanted this. For the record, I don't. You're the last person I'd want to have a lifetime bond with," she fired at him, hoping her words hurt.

"You don't even know me," he said, his eyes troubled as he studied her.

"I don't have to. You're all the same."

"Who's all the same?" he said, crossing his arms. "Don't tell me you're one of those who hates men because of one person's mistake."

"Try an entire clan. You Festans have done nothing but bring pain and loss to my life. Why would I want to tie myself to one of you?"

He paused, studying her, leaning back in his stance. Running a hand over his jaw, he commented, "We've really done a number on you, haven't we?"

Angry he had brought forth the memories she tried so hard to leave behind, she stamped down the horror, the devastation, the loss. Flames showed up in the corner of her eye, and she could smell the smoke again. She whimpered and hugged her middle to keep herself together.

His eyes widened when he looked down at her arms that were practically on full display. Horror crossed his expression. "What hap... never mind," he said, seeming to remember they were strangers.

"That is nothing I want to talk about." She shook from the memories leaking from the vault she kept them in. Leaning as far away as she could manage, she would not reveal more to him in this moment. And not care that he seemed to care about her, very much.

They had just met. He couldn't. There was no way.

"You can't deny you're not the least bit curious."

"About?" she croaked, her mind swimming from her distress.

"What an Intended bond is and how it can benefit your life."

"From what I know about Intended bonds, the Maker wanted to have a way of keeping our clans from disbanding. He wanted to unite us. Look how well that turned out."

"I think," Linc said in a soft voice, "it's an excellent plan. It could unite us again, eventually, one day. If enough people find their other half in other clans, those bonds could lead the way to a united land again. Who would fight their own families?"

"Who are you?" Vela asked, her eyes tracing his features again. "You talk like an Elder."

"I'm young for an Elder in training, but I am one, you're right. My mother is the Grand Elder of the Festans."

Vela's eyes widened. She was talking to practically royalty. There were only four Grand Elders in the world. And Linc was the son of one of them.

"Does your mother hold the same lofty ideas as you?" she squeaked.

A sad smile snuck over his face at the mention of his mother. "Yes, in fact, she does. But don't go telling everyone that. Those are her personal ideas, not office goals."

"Have you ever thought that maybe I don't want this? I don't want *you*?" Her breath constricted in her chest. Choosing to let her Intended go in her mind was much easier than saying it out loud. It felt completely wrong to throw him away. Her rejection started a physical chain reaction, paralyzing her. It started with her heart; it felt like she had just fed it to a meat grinder.

Vela winced at the pain and tried to ignore her body's reaction.

His eyes narrowed, and he moved a fraction closer. Too close. "So, you *are* admitting to our connection. That's much better. But to say you don't want me isn't going to work. Not for me, anyway." He looked over her facial features.

She finally braved a long look at him. Vela cursed inwardly at how handsome he was. He had a strong jaw below cheekbones bronzed from the sun. Lush eyelashes framed each eye to perfection. His lips were currently holding a smirk in place, which she found annoying considering his response to her throwing away their bond. His bottom lip was much fuller than the top. *Why did I just notice that?*

"Why wouldn't that work for you? As if you have a choice in my decision," she said, glaring at the look he gave her. She fought her intense feelings toward him, longing to give in to it. Her every breath was torture, breathing in his unique sweet, smoky scent, and she wanted more than anything to touch his skin to see if it was as smooth as it looked.

"I very much have a choice," he disagreed. "I choose to follow through and try to get to know you. The question is why would you reject me, reject being *my Intended* without even knowing me?"

"That's something you'll never understand," she said bitterly and turned her face away from his handsome features.

"Oh, but I can, if you gave me half a chance to," he said. He seemed to defy all stereotypes when a stranger first meets someone. Boundaries obliterated between them when he walked a couple steps toward her, put his finger under her chin and gently turned her face to him. His warm finger ran up her cheek, setting it ablaze with a blush and zinging sensations. "You'll come to find out I can be single-mindedly devoted to unearthing mysteries, and you're one mystery I won't let go of easily." His eyes drilled into hers.

At his touch, her mind went on lockdown. Vela couldn't imagine a more infuriating position to be in. Just his one finger had pleasantly electrocuted her. Trying to find her voice, she gritted out, "Well, consider this mystery unsolved. Because I will never want you."

"We'll see," he responded, dropping his hand and backing away from her. He walked over to the door, gave her a smile and said, "Based on what I've just seen, you want this very much. See you around, little ghost. Vela."

And with that promise, he left. Her face still tingled from where he had touched her. She put her hands over her face and tried to forget his piercing gaze and disturbing words. How was she going to forget what his presence did to her?

How was she going to resist him if he wouldn't let her go?

Vela needed to get rid of these feelings around him. To do that, she needed to know how to abandon her Intended, she needed to know what to do to make her choice. But the real question was, after talking to him, did she really want to? And it didn't look like Linc would make it easy on her to accomplish a true break.

Vela groaned loudly and put herself into motion to go to her next class. By now, she was ridiculously late. She hurried out of the corridor and walked briskly, resolve planting itself firmly in her mind with each step.

She would not fall for a Festan Elemental.

Chapter Nine

VELA WRESTLED WITH HER tangled hair Saturday morning. She suffered a couple of sleepless nights after her meeting—or was it her confrontation with Linc? Sighing, she slammed down her brush.

She looked down at Jack and complained, "You don't have this problem, do you, boy? You don't have a silly Intended bond to worry about with a dog you don't want. And your hair is as short as it comes. Not fair."

Having gotten a late start, she cringed looking at the clock. Wrestling open the mascara, she dashed it quickly across her lashes. Studying her eyes, she jumped in place when she fixed her smears. After cleaning up the extra mascara with a cotton swab, she stuffed her favorite strawberry flavored lip gloss into her pocket. She smoothed down her jean shorts and shirt that showcased a bouquet that read, 'Flowers are my Friends'. Satisfied with her choice of outfit, she put on her sneakers, then squatted down to Jack's level and crooned, "Ready to go, boy? This is one class you can go to!"

He didn't need a leash. He followed her like true puppy dog fashion, but she fastened one on him, anyway. Her neighborhood required all dogs to be on a leash or behind a fence. She hated that it looked like she dragged him around everywhere. He was so well trained; she wanted to show off his loyalties when he stayed by her no matter what. But such is life. You don't always get what you want.

Sometimes you needed to conform to rules.

Vela had a full day ahead of her. She was teaching a seven-year-old class of Elementals and after that, was taking an advanced class for herself. Her parents had asked Vela to help fill in for the seven-year-olds today and she was happy to say yes. She, in turn, had asked to Elia to help assist. And Jack was the perfect partner in these situations. Even though he had a tough Doberman look, he was as gentle as a puppy. The kids ate him up and instantly relaxed with his easygoing ways.

This was the perfect opportunity to forget about Linc, too. To immerse herself in her gift surrounded by other Gyans.

Running through the house, she grabbed a quick breakfast and dashed out the door with Jack on her heels. Elia, who had her hand raised to knock on the door, was nearly bowled over with Vela's rushing.

"Whoa!" Elia yelled, grabbing Vela's shoulders as she tried to steady herself. "You nearly killed me!"

"Sorry," Vela said, rebalancing herself after running into Elia. She quickly grabbed Elia's hand with her free one to pull her down the steps, her other hand gripping Jack's leash. "We gotta go, Elia! We're going to be late to our teaching class! Why weren't you here earlier?"

"Were *you* ready earlier?" Elia asked as Vela dragged her away from the house.

"No," Vela admitted, "But I could have been ready earlier if you were here to remind me to leave!"

They hurried down the sidewalk and Elia mumbled, "I was late because I was primping and hoping to see..."

"How are you supposed to see my brother if you're running late?"

"I didn't realize I was late. I was busy with my hair and... stop pulling me, Vela!" Elia yanked her hand out of Vela's and started walking slower. "We have twenty minutes till class starts! Don't worry so much. The Elders Center is a fifteen-minute walk. We'll get there on time, barely, but on time."

"If I had a car, we'd get there a lot sooner. We're so lucky the Elder's Center is so close to our neighborhood. I just wanted to be there early, and I woke up later than I wanted. I've been so stressed with this whole Linc thing, I barely got any sleep last night." She sighed. "Elia, come on!" Hurrying down the sidewalk, Vela looked behind her and nearly tripped. Elia was going to get her wish to see her brother.

Kane jogged toward them. Vela was jealous when he reached them, barely out of breath. He kept himself in great shape where she did not.

"Kane!" Elia's eyes were wide with surprise. "What are you doing here?"

"I'm to teach the seven-year-old class, so I thought I'd walk with you two."

"Oh. Mom didn't tell me you were teaching," Vela said with a confused frown. "She just mentioned Elia could help me. She must have changed her mind. I guess that's okay."

"Glad to know I have your approval, Vels," he said, ruffling her hair. She ducked away, annoyed he was messing her hair up. She didn't have a brush with her to fix what he rumpled.

Giving Kane a big smile, Elia's dimples made an appearance and Vela hoped her bestie would charm Kane this morning. "*I* don't mind, Kane. That sounds great! Just great!" Elia gushed. "We'll have a great class now!"

"*Great*, huh?" Kane baited, looking down at her best friend, his eyes twinkling.

"Well, you're perfect to teach the younger kids," Elia explained, blushing. "Between you and Vela, I'll have nothing to do. This is actually perfect."

"Trying to get out of work, Elia?" Kane asked, gently poking her with his elbow.

"Yes," Elia said quickly, "I'll be happy watching you teach… er, and Vela too, of course," she said. Her face became a bright shade of red.

Kane nodded; his look pleased as they all walked down the sidewalk.

"Vela, how are things going at school?" Kane asked.

Frowning, she thought a moment before she answered, "Things are a little complicated."

"Because of the Festan?" he guessed, giving her a sympathetic look.

"How'd you know?"

Shrugging, he answered, "I just figured. That's the only change there's been. You've seemed a little… different lately. I thought it was you not having a date to Homecoming yet, but I think a Festan at the school is much more upsetting."

Vela elbowed him. Of course, she didn't have a date to Homecoming. All she'd been able to think about for the past week and a half was Linc.

Elia giggled.

Kane's head whipped toward her. "What? Am I right? Is he giving Vela trouble?"

Elia giggled again and answered slyly, "Yep and plenty of it."

"What's going on? How's he bothering her?" Kane stopped and grabbed his sister's hand. "Vela, what's he doing to you?"

"He's not doing anything! He just exists, okay?" Vela shrugged off Kane's grip and stormed down the sidewalk away from this conversation. She couldn't escape Linc no matter what she did.

As frustrated as she was that Kane would bring up her new torment, it thrilled Vela that Elia got to spend time with her older brother.

Leaving them alone was her motivation in walking away from the conversation, she tried to convince herself as she sped up her and Jack's pace toward the center.

Elders across the world, as far as Vela knew, held classes in privately owned businesses humans and Elementals both could access. Here in her town, it was called; The Breckenridge Learning Center, but Elementals knew it as the Elder Center. It sat on the edge of the commercial side of the city, close to her neighborhood. It made for an easy walk.

Vela always admired the red brick two-story building surrounded by a tall privacy fence, noting it could pass for a house, and at one time maybe it did. Pillars held up a small patio on the second floor and welcomed clients into the large front porch. Vela knew in the back they kept a large yard and garden where Elementals could practice their element.

So lost in her thoughts, Vela didn't notice when she and Jack approached the Center. Her fingers had tingled a block back, and she shook them out, ignoring their flare up. Confused why her gift would act up, she jumped when Jack began barking and pulling on his leash. Hushing him, she looked up the steps to see what had him so excited.

Her lips parted with surprise when she saw Linc standing by one of the pillars. He wore his usual style, dark colors complimenting his dark hair. He had a band shirt on, a band she didn't recognize, Sonic Youth. Come to think of it, she had never seen him wear anything bright, even down to his black Vans. He looked like a sentinel standing there, doing a good job of scaring her off.

Bracing herself, the closer she walked to the Center, the more flustered she got. Her heart raced, blood flew through her veins, and she clenched her hands, trying to soothe their tickle.

He greeted her with an observation, glancing first at her scars then her shirt. At first his gaze looked troubled, looking at her arms, then a lighter look came over him. "Flowers are your friends?" His lips turned up in a smile.

She looked at him, confused, until he pointed at her shirt.

Blushing, she said, "Don't judge." Then asked, "What are you doing here?"

"I can say the same for you."

"This is *my* Center, a Gyan Center for *Gyans*. Why wouldn't I be here?"

"No need to get testy," he said, pushing off the pillar stepping down the steps toward her. "I'm just teasing you."

Frowning, she watched him approach with a mixture of pleasure and dread. She didn't want to see him, but her body had other ideas. She forced herself to stop leaning toward him.

"I would like to get a tour of your center. But the door's locked. They must not have gotten my uncle's message that I was coming," he said. She noticed he clenched his hands open and shut before stuffing them in his pockets.

Jack strained at the leash, wanting to sniff Linc, and she finally allowed it. Linc held out his hands, which Jack investigated before thoroughly exploring everywhere he could reach, mainly his pants and shirt.

Linc laughed and looked at Vela, cocking his head in question. "Can I?" he asked, still holding his hands out.

Surprised Linc didn't seem intimidated by Jack, Vela hesitated. She didn't want to share her Jack with Linc, but Jack, it seemed, really wanted to be friendly. Jack's interest in him was strange. He sat next to Linc licking his hands and rubbed himself on his legs. Jack rarely responded so well to strange men.

Vela finally agreed and squatted next to Jack, nodding at Linc. She held onto Jack's collar as Linc squatted too, rubbing Jack's head and back, who ate up the attention.

Linc laughed when Jack jumped up, placing his huge front paws on his shoulders. Jack began washing Linc's face with his long tongue, and Vela felt slightly betrayed. It was almost as if Jack could sense who Linc was to Vela and immediately broadcasted his approval of their connection.

But she wasn't sure she wanted this connection, so she needed Jack to be on her side, not his.

"Jack! Stop that." Vela ordered.

"No, It's okay, I don't mind," Linc said, still chuckling as he rubbed Jack's sides. "He's a great dog. How old is he?"

"Four," she said curtly before standing up and pulling Jack's leash to keep him away from Linc. This was one time she was glad to have the leash on Jack.

Linc's eyes carried a hurt glance that she had taken Jack away, but resignation took its place and he straightened, too.

"So, can you and Jack give a guy a tour of your center? Like I said, it's locked."

"There's actually a brilliant reason it's locked," Vela said proudly.

"Oh, yeah?"

"It's how we keep the Elemental classes a secret from humans. It's all in the scheduling."

"Mmm, hmmm."

"When Elementals have classes, humans aren't scheduled to come in for tutoring."

"And when humans need tutoring, Elementals won't be there," he said, nodding his head at the building. "I see."

Vela knew from her parents that they conducted other business in this building. Again, they usually scheduled these meetings at night when classes weren't being held. When they called an emergency meeting, they would cancel all appointments for the day.

"Don't they do that where you come from?" she asked, curiosity forcing her to ask.

"Actually, we have a private location way outside of town. Only for Elementals. To have free rein of our fire power."

"Makes sense." How else could you hide their kind of gifts except keep them out of sight?

"Well, we're about to have a class," she said, fishing her phone out of her pocket to text one of the Elders to let them in. She wanted to teach her class and try to forget about this Elemental who kept her from sleep and peace in general. But it looked like he would dog her waking hours and her sleeping ones. "So, I can't give you a tour today." Once the door opened, she took off Jack's leash, as relieved as he to have the contraption off.

The tall, thin middle-aged Elder who opened the door, Pierre Eldin, sported a friendly smile that faltered when he saw Jack, then Linc who stood behind her.

"Hi, Vela, uhh, who's this? I thought you were alone," Pierre said, viewing Jack nervously and blocking the doorway with his lanky frame.

Flustered, Vela said, "I am alone. This is Linc. He's a Festan who now attends our school. When I came to the Center, he was already waiting. He'd like a tour, but..."

"Ah! Yes, you're here with your uncle, right?" Pierre said, his eyes lighting up in recognition.

"Your uncle?" Vela cast a curious look at Linc.

He glanced at her briefly before stepping forward to offer his hand to Pierre. "Yes, sir. My uncle is grateful for the Gyan Elders' support."

Vela gaped. The Elders *knew* the Festans were here? And they *supported* them?

"It's a pleasure," Pierre clapped his hands around Linc's. "Your uncle's research could be a turning point in the war between our clans."

Linc held a patient smile, like he had heard these praises before. Maybe he had. Vela's mind spun. This is why he's here, really? And why did he live with his uncle and not his parents? Questions fired through Vela's mind. Maybe she should spend some time with him, just to answer these interminable questions. *Did they actually believe this garbage, a researcher, really?*

And then as Linc and Vela walked inside, she hissed suspiciously, "What kind of *research* would bring Festans into Gyan territory?"

"My uncle is writing a history of the Elemental clans." He leaned closer, his lips pressed into a crooked smile and whispered, "It's helpful to actually talk with a Gyan or two if you're going to write about them. So... a tour? My uncle sent me here to get a bird's eye view of this place," Linc looked to Vela to see if she would agree now.

"Oh, she couldn't possibly do a tour right now, so sorry," Pierre said, his hands waving around looking visibly flustered. "Her class is starting too soon for her to do the honor."

Vela glanced at them both and said, "Well, then, I'll just get to it then." She started for the hallway with Jack.

Before she could leave, Linc's voice stopped her. "I can wait."

Pierre's shocked gaze matched Vela's. "She teaches a class and then takes a class of her own. It'll be some time before she's done."

"If it's alright, I'd like to observe both classes. Then Vela can show me around when she's finished. It's actually a perfect scenario. To observe classes while I'm here and get a tour."

Vela's mouth dropped open and she stuttered, "You can't... wait around for me to finish!"

"Sure, I can," he said, his eyes twinkling. "I'd love to watch your classes. That is if you don't mind."

Vela fumed. Of course, she minded. But, to voice that in front of Pierre's enthusiastic nodding made her look like a child, so she bit back her retort and gritted out, "Not at all. Let's go then."

Linc's victorious grin followed her inside the center.

Chapter Ten

VELA STOOD IN ONE of the classrooms, a white room decorated with beautiful prints of nature all around her. The floor stood empty of chairs as her students would sit on the floor. Her nerves caused her to jiggle her leg. Linc stood caddy corner to her giving him a perfect view of her, but she couldn't do anything about it. He was there to watch her whether she liked it or not. She couldn't believe he charmed his way into this class. And her next one, too!

Looking over the children all mingling before their class started, she couldn't help but smile, relaxing a bit. The kids were a cute mixture. These seven-year-olds were growing more quickly than others, but they all still held onto the baby fat in their little faces. It always made her happy to teach the younger Elementals.

Jack nosed his way through the group making friends. Children weren't as afraid of him as adults for some reason. She stilled though when she observed one student, a cute African American girl whose hair was in twin poofy piggytails. The little girl backed away from Jack and even Vela could see the little one was terrified of him. Jack paused watching her retreat, then he sat and whined pitifully, his cue for the little girl to pet him.

Another student approached him but he turned his head to the cocoa skinned girl and Vela guessed he was encouraging her to pet him. Jack waited patiently and after a moment the little girl paused to watch the other boy petting Jack enthusiastically. She cautiously approached them. Vela had been about to intervene and spring to the little girl's side, but it looked like the situation worked itself out. The little girl reached out to pet Jack's head, and he licked her hand causing her to squeal in laughter.

Huh, she thought, *maybe he should be a service dog.*

Turning her attention back to the class, she called out for the kids to sit in their respective places. They were a perfect age to teach, in her opinion. The kids weren't too young or too cocky with their gifts, not yet anyway. Give them a couple of years and they would change. They all did. It came with a mastery of their gift.

Linc appeared next to her, and she jumped not noticing him leave his space in the corner.

"Are your children homeschooled, too?" he asked, looking over the group.

"Yes." Suspicious of his real purpose of being here, she vowed not to give him too much information. He, of course surprised her when he started talking.

"Festan children are homeschooled until their teen years, learning to control their gifts from Elders. Once we reach high school age, our educations are split between human schools and Elemental classes. It looks like our system is the same as yours."

She paused, before saying, "Yes, it seems like we have that in common."

"We might have a lot in common. Tell me anything about yourself and I'll see how we compare." He leaned back in his stance with his hands behind his back.

"Okay," she said surprising herself, "I've noticed you seem very comfortable around humans. Care to share how you accomplish that?"

"That's something about me. That's not what I asked."

"How about you first?"

"I've been raised to lead my clan. My mother being the Grand Elder and my father, an Elder, are both anxious for me to fall in their footsteps. They've made sure I'm very comfortable around humans, since I'll be required to be among them quite a bit, when it's my time to lead. I'll work among the humans, most likely, when I'm grown."

"Now, you," he said. "Feed my dying curiosity. Tell me something about yourself. I'll take anything."

She conceded. "I'm not that great around humans. I mean, I have some human friends, but I keep them as acquaintances."

"Really? They aren't that different from us. You should give them a chance."

"I don't want to be responsible for them having to take the poppyseed drug to alter their memories if I ever accidentally showed my gifts to them." Vela shook her head. "I'd feel too bad. It's not a fun concoction to take, from what I hear."

"At least we have it, just in case. It keeps our secrets secret."

Changing the subject, she asked, "Where are you from?"

"Dallas."

"Huh, a solid Festan state."

"As is yours, a Gyan state, I mean." He eyed her.

"That's if our southern borders aren't taken over by your Festan brothers and sisters." She watched his reaction carefully.

"And vice versa," he said. His face was smooth of any reaction at all.

Good poker face.

Crossing her arms, she decided to announce, "I don't buy it."

His eyebrow raised and he asked, "Buy what?"

"Your story. You're no more of a researcher than I'm a Borean."

"I'm not a researcher. You're right. I'm just an observer, who gives my eye-witness accounts to a researcher, my uncle." He cocked his head and waited for her response, as if he knew she would have one.

She did.

"Why can't he do that alone? Why does he need you?"

Linc chuffed a laugh. "He doesn't need me. My parents don't either. They all think I need to learn to deal with other clans, so they shipped me off to every clan known to existence to learn firsthand."

Surprised he revealed so much about himself, she said, "Sounds to me you don't agree with them." She couldn't imagine not being raised by her parents.

"What can I say?" he said shrugging. A hard look crossed his eyes, and she wondered if he hid a lot behind that look. "I'd rather have the white picket fence. A house that I grew up in, parents to call home. I guess, you can say that I don't agree. It's not how I'd raise my kid."

"Do you have brothers and sisters?" she asked, suddenly curious about him.

"Had," he said, his voice a hushed murmur. She barely heard him say, "One sister."

Sympathy rushed her to say, "I'm sorry. What's her name?"

"Olympia," he said in a tone that didn't sound open for conversation.

Before Vela could say anything more, Kane approached them then and stuck his hand out to Linc. "I'm Kane. Who might you be?"

Linc blinked and looked at Kane's hand like he was just remembering where he was. He took Kane's hand in what looked like a firm grip and shook it answering, "The name's Linc. I'm a Festan visiting the area."

Kane's eyebrows shot up and he said snatching his hand back, "You're the Festan going to my sister's school?"

"If Vela's your sister, then, yes, that's me." He had a sad smile, but to Vela, he looked haunted. She knew the feeling. Linc schooled his face into a neutral expression. "I'm here to observe your class. I hope you don't mind."

"We'll have to continue this later," Kane said, glaring at Linc then glancing at the now noisy class.

The class congregated on the floor were antsy. The volume of the room became too high for conversation. Kane looked over at the kids, frustration furrowing his brow.

Knowing Kane, Vela could tell he had questions for Linc, but it looked like those would have to wait.

Finally greeting the settled group, Kane introduced himself, Elia and Vela. He announced Linc's presence as a guest and Linc resumed his spot in the corner.

"Now, as Earth's Guardians, God has entrusted us with many gifts," Kane began. "But I want to talk about our main responsibilities. Let me see what you all know. Can anyone tell me what Gyans' gift mainly contributes to Earth?"

One of the students' hands, a red headed boy, shot his hand up, "Food to eat?"

Kane responded, "That is one thing, but not what I'm looking for. Think about what we in our valley help with."

"Helping with the sick?" another student, a tow headed boy asked.

"We do have the ability to heal and identify and treat different poisons and illnesses in our bodies, but no, that's not what I'm looking for either. Anyone else?"

No one raised their hand and Vela asked, "Maybe I can help?"

Kane moved over and gave Vela the floor gesturing for her to take his place.

"Breathe deeply," she instructed. They all did, then she asked, "Now, why can you do that so easily?"

"Because the Borean Elementals are in charge of the wind and keep the air clean?" asked a dark-haired boy.

"They do keep the air clean from pollutants, but there's another reason," Vela looked around for another raised hand.

A little blonde girl with worried eyes put her shaking hand up, and when Vela chose her to answer, she answered tentatively, "Keeping the plants healthy helps the air?"

Vela clapped her hands. "Yes! By maintaining the trees and the plants, we provide oxygen to keep Earth healthy."

When all the little faces smiled and nodded, Kane asked the group, "What about Neronian Elementals? What is their main contribution?"

"Keeping the water healthy?" asked a boy in a football jersey.

Kane shook his head and chose another student.

"Rain? They can do that!" A light had dawned in that girl's eyes.

"Yes!" Kane exclaimed. "Rain waters the earth which keeps our plants healthy, and water sources full. How about the Festans?" With a glance at Linc, Kane focused his attention to the class and asked, "Who can tell me what they contribute to the health of the Earth?"

"My mom says they're only good at taking land from other Elementals. That they're bullies," a lanky boy with a gravelly voice answered. His honesty surprised Vela, and she snorted, unable to stop herself. She watched Linc's face for his reaction, but it just held a smooth, calm demeanor. He must be used to this kind of reaction to his clan. There were a lot of prejudices with her clan and Festan Elementals.

She was one of them, after all. But after his surprising revelation of his sister, she felt a little guilty for it.

"Well, we're not talking about land boundaries right now, Evan," Kane said, "So anyone else have an answer?" Vela smirked at how easily he changed the topic.

"Fires burn through fields pretty often where I come from," an older girl with long orange braids said. "Does that help the fields somehow? I always wondered. No one seemed mad that they were doing it."

"Yes! That's right," Kane told her, "While we often fight with other clans over boundaries, sometimes we do help each other. Fires are really helpful in fertilizing soil. That's how we grow our world's vegetables and fruits. It puts much needed nutrients into the soil helping vegetables grow best."

Vela chanced a look at Linc and noted he looked pleased with that answer.

The little blonde girl timidly raised her hand again. At Kane's nod, she asked, "What *good* are forest fires though? There seems to be a lot of those."

"Well, that's a good question," Kane answered. "The ashes from a forest fire saturate the floor of the forest with many good nutrients providing a way for healthy new growth.

"Now," Kane said, clapping his hands together, "We've talked about how Gyans take care of nature helping with the oxygen levels of the Earth. Neronians provide much needed rainwater," Kane recapped. "And we've just talked about

Festans and what they do. How about Boreans? Who can tell me their main function in being Earth's Guardians?"

Vela spoke up, "Well, one student already mentioned their main use in one of your other answers. Who can remember what they said?"

A host of hands shot up, and Vela chose the most enthusiastic waving.

"They keep the air free from yucky pollutants," the red-haired girl answered proudly.

"Good! You've been paying attention!" she cheered.

"What about those funny wind thingies that help with electricity?" a large-boned boy with freckles asked.

"Windmills?" Vela guessed. "There are windfarms that some territories use to help aid with electricity but it's not their main function as Guardians."

Kane came to her side and said to the class, "Now how about we go outside to demonstrate some of our abilities? And you can work on what you've been learning all week."

All the students cheered excitedly at the prospect of using their gift. The tall and lanky boy groused, "We have to do mostly silly math and history all week. The weekends are the best classes where we can work on really cool stuff."

Vela enjoyed their precocious natures. She fondly remembered feeling much the same way. Jack jumped up with the kids and yelped excited to go outside, too. He knew the word 'outside' very well so when he heard it, he had jumped up and began spinning in circles. Knowing he wouldn't stop until she let him out, she laughed and led him to the door.

All the students already stood in a line to go outside.

Elia sidled up to Vela and whispered, "I wonder if Linc's going to come outside too." She had looked wide-eyed at Linc when she first stepped into the room but had adjusted easily to his presence. Typical Elia, Vela thought.

"I don't know," Vela answered wondering the same thing herself.

Chapter Eleven

Linc followed them as Kane, Elia, Vela, and Jack led the group through the center and its library, which served as the sitting room. Books lined the walls above and around a cozy fireplace. It seemed kind of dangerous to Vela for books to be near fire, but that was just her protective instincts for her beloved tomes.

She walked through the French doors that led to the outside training area and she promised herself she would be back to see if there were any new books on the well-oiled wooden bookshelves. She knew they were well oiled because she took it upon herself to make sure the home for her books were looked after.

Once outside, Vela looked around. Linc had placed himself next to the warm brown fence in the back that protected the class from view. He had his arms crossed and folded together and he glanced around the area, taking in the rosebushes that lined the fence and a tall tree that gave plenty of shade. The sun shone down, warming the area nicely.

She tried to study him unobtrusively. His comment about his parents and lost sister struck something in her. It made him more real, more likable; his heartbreak broke through her defenses. If he wasn't a Festan, if he wasn't her Intended, would she look at him twice? She studied her shoes after noting his handsome features. He would definitely have gotten an easy second glance, and after their conversation, he would have turned her head. But can he now?

Jack barked happily and ran around the group of kids. Once at the head of the class again, Kane began the outdoor class with a demonstration. Vela gave her brother her full attention.

With his arms raised, the ground rumbled. The students cheered, delighted with his show of a small earthquake. Vela scowled at Kane when Jack slumped to the ground and whimpered. Usually, he loved a display of their gifts, but obviously did not like tremors. Vela went to him and rubbed his ears, assuring him it was alright.

She brought him over to her side furious Kane didn't warn her what he was going to do. Kane looked at her apologetically as she continued soothing Jack. The fur on his back stood up, but he had stopped whimpering, at least.

The kids, on the other hand, loved Kane's display of power. It took a moment for him to calm them down. He said, "I talked to your usual instructor for this class, and he gave me permission to show you that. Can anyone tell me what we use earthquakes for?"

"Doesn't it stop the Festans, Neronians and Boreans from hurting us?" a freckle-faced boy asked.

"Yes, it's a defense and attack maneuver. One thing about us Elementals is that we like our borders. And we defend ourselves with earthquakes to keep the other clans from our lands. Proof of our battles is all over the news. So, you may have heard of these fights happening."

An older girl with braids spoke up, "Is it true we're going to win against the Festans at the bottom of our state?"

"If I knew the answer to that question, I'd be a rich man," Kane said with a laugh, "land boundaries are hotly contested here in Colorado. Our northern and southern borders are right next to Festan territory. But remember, sometimes forest fires are accidents and not done by Festans. Just like some earthquakes are natural and not done by Gyans."

"Now I know you would love to do what I demonstrated," Kane said solemnly. "But because of everything I just mentioned, I hope you see that it is too dangerous to teach you. You all are too young and too inexperienced to do this. Earthquakes are an advanced level ability."

A chorus of groans filled the air.

"But there are other defenses I can teach you. You may need to know how to defend yourself one day if another clan tries to take over your home." That quieted the kids down and he had their full attention. "For instance, there are hundreds of roots under your feet, you'll be able to sense them. Let's work on tripping each other by bringing the roots up. The trick, however, is doing two things at one time, holding the root then wrapping it around your opponent's ankles.

"Now Vela, how about I show this technique on you?"

Vela hesitated before walking over. She motioned for Jack to stay by Elia. "Umm, Kane, you might want to do this with Elia. Jack's not going to like this," she warned, looking at her faithful sidekick.

"He won't attack me. I've known him since he was a puppy," Kane said, standing with his hands on his hips looking completely confident.

Vela shrugged and said, "Don't say I didn't warn you."

Kane ignored her warning and continued with his instruction. "OK, so if you have this attack in mind, you need to sense what you're working with before you attack. Reach your mind down into the dirt. Feel with your senses for where the roots are underneath your victim. You'll feel the water rushing through the roots. You'll sense how thick and long they are. Go to the end of the root. That's the part you need to do this lesson.

"Then, grab the end of the roots you find and pull hard, because you not only need to bring the root up, but you're going to quickly wrap the root around the ankles of your target."

Vela had been standing easily until Kane demonstrated his ability. The ground broke open, dirt bursting underneath her and roots quickly cinched her ankles together. She toppled over with the two long roots Kane had called up. When she fell, however, Jack had jumped up and Elia had barely grabbed his collar to prevent him from disrupting the demonstration. He was too strong, however, for her to control and he ripped free from Elia's grip and raced straight toward Kane, snarling and jaws snapping.

How he knew it was Kane's fault that she had fallen. Vela would never know, but she screamed out to him, "Jack! Stop!"

It was almost comical how her words worked.

He had jumped toward her brother, but turned his body midair to avoid his attack, obeying Vela. He landed away from her brother, but growled and bared his teeth at him until Vela called him to her.

Everyone held a collective sigh of relief until Jack obeyed and walked over to sit next to her, who was still on the ground with the roots wrapped around her ankles. He sniffed her and checked her over, and Vela looked up at Kane, smirking. "And you were saying?"

Kane's arms were still in front of him, and he stood frozen in a crouch, his eyes wide and face white.

Vela couldn't help but notice Linc, too, had reacted when she had fallen. When she caught his eye, he nodded at her proudly. It looked like he approved of her control over Jack. Or was it Jack's protectiveness of her he approved?

Turning back to her brother, she asked, "Kane, do you mind?" She jerked her chin at her ankles.

Shaking his head, Kane collected himself and said, "And that's another part of this lesson. The caster can only release the roots. The Gyan could get out of it, but they'll need to overpower the efforts of the caster to get free."

Vela tried mentally wrenching the roots from her brother's control, but he had too firm a grip. He must be trying to make a point with the class. She growled and released Kane's roots, deciding another tactic was in order. Sending her senses under the earth, she zeroed in on the roots she found there. Roots differed from the rocks and the clumps of dirt she came across. She could feel the water rushing through them. Clamping her control over them, she mimicked her brother's move and soon roots burst free from the earth in a spray of dirt and grass, wrapping his ankles like hers.

Kane toppled over.

"Or, if you happen upon a Gyan with similar strengths as yours," Kane grunted from the ground, "you can always manage an offensive move like Vela here has done. As you can see, I lost the connection to the roots I had her tangled up in when she went on the attack. And she's now free."

Linc smirked and nodded at Vela as she kicked off the now loose roots, then clapped at her show of offense. The class soon followed him, and the sound of applause filled the air.

Vela didn't think she needed Linc's approval, but it felt good, nonetheless. She smiled to herself and stood up, brushing her legs off. She decided to be nicer than Kane and released the roots around his ankles.

Kane got to his feet, shaking himself from the now loose roots, and instructed, "Pair up everyone. You'll each get a turn, so don't worry. And try to wrestle control of the roots if you do get tripped."

Vela walked around and watched the students as she practically hurtled over Jack. He seemed uneasy after Kane's attack. He kept looking at everyone around her like they'd be the next one to attack Vela. She smoothed his fur down on his head. He'd ease up in a minute.

Unfortunately, Jack's aggressiveness had now made the students uncomfortable around him. They shied away from him when he came near. He wasn't helping things either by studying the students around Vela. She motioned for Jack to follow her, and she had him lie down in an area away from the students.

Confident he would stay put, she resumed walking around. The kids stared at the ground in intense concentration before roots started sprouting from the ground. The range of control over the roots varied. Some roots shot up in a small explosion of dirt, while others crept through the topsoil of the yard more slowly. A few students couldn't do it at all.

Jack couldn't resist the amount of raw energy in the air. Vela laughed when he yipped, jumped up, and began running circles around the group. The kids were too focused on the exercise to give him any notice, so she allowed him to run.

She, Elia, and Kane continued to encourage the students and helped those who needed some constructive criticism. She could see, too, that some students wrestled control over their attackers and some could not.

Vela stopped by the African-American girl Jack had befriended earlier. The little girl had brought up the roots under her target but couldn't seem to get them to wrap around the other's ankles.

"It's hard," the girl complained, her little face scrunched in frustration.

Vela smiled understanding completely and squatted next to her, so they were at eye level. "Well, you're doing two different things with this root. You gave the first command perfectly. You brought it up from its normal resting place. Now, you need to, while holding onto the first command, give it a second one to wrap around your opponent's ankles."

"I can't," the girl said, her voice breaking. "It's too hard!" Her roots fell limp to the ground.

Vela jumped when Linc squatted next to them. He looked at Vela and asked, "May I help?"

"With a *Gyan* ability? How are you going to manage that?"

"She's trying to do two things at once, right?"

Vela and the girl nodded.

"Well, that's something we do, too. Can I give her some advice?" Vela could only nod again as surprise robbed her of speech.

He turned his gaze to the little girl who had started sniffling and stood wiping her tears away. With a low and soothing voice, he said, "There's a trick to doing two things at one time. I had to do this as a child, too. Maybe it will help you, like it helped me."

The young girl's eyes went round with hope. "Really?" she squeaked.

"Yes. It's quite simple, really. Now, be patient with me. But I want you to do a silly exercise. If you can do this, you can do two commands at one time."

"Okay," Linc's new pupil said uncertainly.

"What's your name?"

"Carla," the girl said shyly.

"Carla, can you pat your head for me?" Linc asked.

Carla looked at Vela with round eyes. Vela shrugged at her. She had no idea where Linc was going with this.

Carla reached up and began patting her head with both hands.

Linc reached up and took one hand down, saying, "One hand only. Now, with this hand, rub your stomach in circles. And then do both things at the same time."

Vela had to cover her mouth with a laugh. It was ingenious, really. She saw where he was going with this now.

After several attempts, Carla got the exercise right. Laughing, she squealed, "I'm doing it!"

"Good!" Linc praised, smiling widely at the girl. "What you need to get the root exercise right is basically the same principle. You're using one of you brain muscles to control patting your head. And then another muscle will rub your stomach. It's the same way with the roots. One muscle will give one command, holding onto the root..." he paused, glancing at Vela with uncertainty, looking for help.

Vela did laugh then. "Let me take over."

She looked at Carla and instructed, "While you hold on to the root in your mind, and like he said, you're going to use another part of your mind to tell it to wrap around your opponent's ankles."

"Like the exercise I taught you. You're just doing two things at one time. You can do it!" Linc encouraged.

Carla patted her head and rubbed her stomach in circles. Nodding briskly, she announced, "I'm ready." Her opponent had waited patiently and now stood with his arms crossed and foot tapping. Carla concentrated hard on the ground, commanding control of the root that had fallen to the ground earlier. Then, after a pause, Vela held her breath while Carla continued to stare at the root. Suddenly, the root shot over to the boys' ankles, cinching them together tight. He fell over, crying out in surprise.

Vela and Linc both cheered, clapping loudly.

"You did it!" Linc praised, raising his hand for a high five to Carla, who stood over her opponent with her fists clenched. She blinked at his raised hand and unclenching her little fists, shook herself off and jumped high fiving Linc as hard as she could. She cheered and wiggled happily in place.

Vela straightened and turned toward Linc, who had stood and turned toward her as well.

"I'll have to remember that little trick," Vela said, smiling up at him, happy for the young girl.

"You can have that one for free," Linc said, returning her smile.

"Free?"

"I normally charge for my brilliant tutoring services," he said, as he seemed to try and fail to stop smiling.

"Oh," Vela said, huffing a laugh. "You do? I'll have to remember that next time I go trying to steal your pricey ideas."

"You do that."

"Thank you," she said. "Really." It surprised her that she meant it.

"You're welcome. It was fun. There seems to be a good range of abilities here," he said, looking around as the class continued practicing their lesson.

"Yes, I should get back to helping them." Vela suddenly felt uncomfortable with how easy it felt to laugh with her Intended, whom she didn't want, she reminded herself firmly.

Linc nodded and turned to walk back to his spot against the fence. She watched him go, not surprised that he was good with kids. Like everyone else, he could befriend anyone.

After instructing the kids to switch partners, Kane walked around with Vela and Elia, helping struggling students. Soon, with their help, there weren't many. Most were laughing and seemed to be having fun tripping each other.

Kane clapped his hands and announced, "Now, that's all for today's class. We have to clean up this mess before the next one. Hopefully, we'll get the chance to fill in for your regular teacher another time."

Kane talked to some students as the rest left the yard. Vela was anxious to start her own more advanced class, where she could further her own training. She had bottled-up energy that needed to find its release. Spending so much time in classes at the toxic high school was the culprit, she knew. Her uncertainty with Linc, another.

Elia walked up to her and asked in a low voice, "So Kane was spectacular, don't you think? He's so good with the kids. He's going to make the best dad one day," she said as she looked over at him wistfully.

"He will. Why don't you go tell him that, Elia?" nudging her friend with her shoulder toward her brother.

"What? No!" Elia whispered furiously, her face blushing as she pulled away. She threw a dirty look over her shoulder and left, just as Kane walked over and joined his sister.

"What'd you do to Elia?" Kane asked.

She smiled. "Oh, I just got under her skin."

He raised his eyebrow, but then changed the subject, "Do you want me to say something to the Festan for you? Tell him to leave you alone?"

Vela sighed, scuffing her foot in the dirt. "It's not that easy, Kane." She didn't want to tell him about her bond with Linc, not yet.

"It'll be a pleasure to say something to him, believe me. It's not right that he's here. He should be back in his own territory," Kane said, leveling a hard look at Linc, who stood off the side waiting for what Vela couldn't tell.

"No. I've got it covered. But thanks."

"If I didn't have somewhere to be right now, I'd be having a talk with him, but I can't," Kane said as he cracked his knuckles. His face strained like it physically pained him that he couldn't get his questions answered.

"Just go. I'll be fine. Elia's with me, anyway."

"Like she's a big help with her five-foot self," Kane said, smirking. A fondness came in his eyes as he looked over at Elia.

"I heard that!" Elia called out. "That's five foot two, to you, mister!"

His eyes lit up, and he coughed a laugh. Vela smiled and then remembered, "Oh! Can you take Jack home?"

"Sure," he said, turning his gaze away from Elia. "Why? Don't you normally keep him during your classes?"

"Well, I'm not sure what we'll be doing today, but he really didn't like the tremor you did earlier. Just in case we do something like that, I think it'd be better if he went home."

He nodded and called Jack to him. After she retrieved the leash where she had left it, handed it over to her brother, who attached it to Jack's collar and left the yard. Vela's heart clenched. She did *not* like to leave Jack. It was hard enough to go to school without him. She couldn't help it. She was as protective of Jack as he was with her.

With a heavy heart, Vela joined Elia as they got busy cleaning up the ripped-up yard. They grew grass over the dirt patches they created after ordering the roots back into the ground. Between the two of them using their gifts, they made quick work of cleaning up the place. Vela glanced around, looking for Linc. She didn't see him.

Maybe she'd gotten lucky for once and he left early. She could only hope. He was starting to humanize himself. He wasn't just an unwelcome Festan. He now had a story, a past that saddened him, a future he wished he had. And it was scaring her as she began to care.

Chapter Twelve

"Stop fidgeting!" Elia scolded. She and Vela stood in the backyard of the Center, waiting for their advanced class to begin. Students her age were trickling in, but only a handful were there, so far. They were early, after all.

Linc hadn't appeared, so Vela assumed he left earlier, and she had gotten out of giving him the tour he wanted. She wasn't sure though, so she worried he would show up again.

Deciding to blame her nerves on something else, she said, "I can't help it. I'm full of pent-up energy." Vela shook her hands, trying to loosen up a little. A certain Fire Boy had completely gotten under her skin.

"Maybe you just need some time with me," a lanky, cute blonde-haired boy drawled, swinging his arm over Vela's shoulder.

"Evan, please," Vela groaned and ducked under his arm.

"Hey, I'm just sayin', I'm not anything if not helpful," he said cheerfully.

Vela took in Evan's appearance and shook her head. His tall form wasn't unpleasant to look at. He had a surfer boy physique and charm, but he just didn't do it for her. His bright green eyes looked at her expectantly, but he couldn't be serious. She would never fall for those lines in a million years.

"I'm pretty sure this was mine and Elia's conversation and not yours. And besides, I've told you before. You're not my type. But again, thanks for the compliment." She turned around and hoped her back would signal that this conversation was over.

"Vela. When are you gonna give me a chance?"

Vela looked over her shoulder. "And why would I do that?"

Grinning, his green eyes sparkled and commented, "Because you don't know what's good for you." He sauntered away, thankfully.

Vela turned back, shaking her head, refusing to add to that train of thought.

"Vela," one of the other students whispered in Vela's direction. Maria looked at her expectantly.

Seeing her reminded Vela of Maria's lack of control earlier that week. Before Maria could say anything, Vela asked, "Hey I heard you did something that caused a human to have their memories erased?"

"Oh, really? You too? *Everyone* is asking me about that." Maria flipped her bright hair over her shoulder. "How did you hear about that?"

"My parents had to make the poppyseed formula." Vela folded her arms across her chest.

"Oh. Well, it was stupid. Mark and I were talking, and he took something from my hand and threw it up a tree. I couldn't reach it, so I did what I had to do to get it down." Maria turned away like that was the end of the conversation.

"You bent a sapling in half, Maria. How did you not think that wouldn't attract a human's attention?"

"You and everyone else have such little minds. I just thought they would think I reached up and bent it with my own little fingers." She waved said fingers in front of Vela's face. "Besides, I didn't hurt anyone. Our formula took care of my mistake, so no harm done."

Waving Maria's hand away, Vela's voice climbed, "Maria, that formula is terrible to take! Don't you know that?" That was one scenario she did not want to have happened because of her actions.

"Who told you that?"

"Uh, my parents? It's not a fun experience. It's very uncomfortable from what they've said."

"Oh, always so dramatic." Maria waved her hand.

She was about to turn away when Elia backed Vela up. "It's true, Maria. That formula is an absolute last resort. Can you imagine what it's like to have your memories erased?"

"I'd imagine I wouldn't remember," Maria answered with a half-lidded look and smile. A couple of her friends snickered with her. They were two girls Vela never cared much for. They only parroted anything Maria said or did and on her best day, Vela didn't have the patience with any of them.

"Nice, Maria. It's disorientating and scary. They usually need to be monitored afterward to be sure there aren't any bad repercussions."

"My bad," Maria said, rolling her eyes. "Anyway, I was trying to tell you that Evan's a catch. You should be happy he's paying attention to you." Her eyes held a knowing look that Vela wanted to confront, but decided to play nice and ignore.

"Evan's always playing the field," Vela retorted. "I'm not interested in being one of his many players. I'm not that desperate."

"He just needs to be tamed, Vela. You might be that girl, that's all I'm saying."

Vela wasn't sure why Maria was pushing Evan on her. She looked over and him who stood a distance away now, but still watched her.

"If he's so easily tamed, Maria," Vela said, "why don't you do it?"

Lillith, who had just walked up, laughed. She must have overheard the last part of their conversation. She said, "Evan's too easy a conquest for our Maria. She needs someone a little harder to get."

"It's because," Maria said with a hard look in her eyes, "I know a crush when I see one, Vela. You would see it, too, if you didn't have such big blinders on. Or maybe you've set your blinders on someone else?"

Vela shook her head, hard. "No, I don't. And I don't think Evan genuinely likes me. He's just fishing to see if he can catch something. He's not being serious. I've known Evan for years now and he's always been like this."

"Suit yourself," Maria said airily. "But you're crazy. He would be fun to be around."

Vela wasn't so sure. She wanted to be with someone she could take seriously, and Evan just wasn't that person.

"Maria has her sights set high, anyway," Lillith teased. "I hear she's looking to tame a guy of her own. Like that new Festan."

Maria grinned unabashedly and looked directly at Vela. "Some of us, unlike others, aren't afraid of a little heat. What can I say?" She stood with one hand on her hip. She had a look in her eye that Vela didn't trust, never had.

There was no way Maria could know about her bond with Linc, but it sure seemed like she did or suspected. Then she realized Maria must have overheard Linc's comment to Elia after Vela had run away in the cafeteria. That was the only reason Vela could come up with. She must want Vela to chase after Evan now so she can make a play for Linc.

Shaking her head, Vela realized she really wasn't that surprised. This was Maria she was thinking about. Who did anything she could to get the guy she wanted. And she didn't trust Maria even more, knowing she trusted the Festans. Where were her loyalties?

"Well, what can I say? It seems like Linc and I have more in common than you might think," Maria announced, folding her arms over her chest.

"What could that possibly be?" Lillith asked, with heavy sarcasm.

"We both want to be Elders, for one," she said with a proud tilt to her head, daring anyone to contradict her.

"You? Want to be an Elder?" Elia asked, laughing outright. Vela couldn't agree more. Maria would be the last person she wanted to see with some control over the clan. She was way too self-absorbed and vain for that role.

"Of course I do," Maria said, sniffing.

"How are you going to manage being an Elder for us and him an Elder for the Festans? How exactly would that work?" Elia snorted.

"Look, I'm not saying I'm going to marry the guy. We just have similar goals. It gives us lots to talk about," she boasted. "Did you guys know his mother is the *Grand Elder*?" Her eyes gleamed.

Shocked gasps went around the group.

"Are you serious?" Lillith asked.

"Why would I joke about that? He's practically a prince."

Whispers broke out among her friends. This was why she had only told Elia about Linc being a Grand Elder's son. It seemed she wanted to protect him from insatiable curiosities and fake interest. Why she was doing this for a Festan, Vela couldn't figure out. But she did.

This will spread like wildfire, and she knew everyone in her clan will want to have a piece in the tasty pie that was now Linc Stevenson. He used to be a curiosity visiting her clan. Now he was a meal ticket. Even if they were enemies with his clan, it wouldn't hurt to get in his good graces.

Vela viewed Maria with contempt. Not only was she wanting a part in leading her clan, but she was announcing her interest in Vela's Intended. Not that it mattered that no one knew of this development, but still. Vela couldn't help but be jealous. And Maria seemed much more interested in Linc's mother's title than what Linc himself had to offer.

Then Vela groaned inwardly. She couldn't escape Linc, even when he wasn't here.

Their instructor, an Elder who was a balding, middle-aged man with a potbelly, saved her from any more conversations. He stepped up to the front of the now full class and began speaking in an agitated voice. "A Nor'easter just ravaged the coast of Maine. Can someone tell me why this was a bad idea for an Elemental to formulate a storm like this now?"

Vela's foot started thumping on the ground. She did not want to have a lecture right now. This was terrible timing. She had to get started using her gift or she would combust.

But he continued when no one answered. "This storm is going to draw unwanted attention of the human population. Can anyone explain why?"

He encountered a group of blank faces. "I'll answer this question for you all, since we don't have these types of storms here. Only coastal towns in the Atlantic will experience them, and *usually* during certain months of the year. Between the months of November and March, Nor'easters develop, but it's August!"

His outraged expression amused Vela. Other Elementals were going to have a heyday, trying to explain why Elementals were causing this kind of storm now.

There were Elementals in weather stations across the world who would downplay phenomena that defied science. But that didn't seem to pacify this instructor.

"The Elementals who caused this storm should be hanged! Never," he warned, shaking his finger at the group, "Cause large scale travesties without having the proper science to back up its existence. Now, the tornadoes that the Boreans in Mississippi caused last week were pure genius! They only lasted a few moments and did not cause any damage."

Vela couldn't understand his glee that the Boreans had channeled the wind to create tornadoes that could have potentially hurt someone or property, even. They might have once she thought about it.

"The point of our gift is to enhance the Earth, not harm it," he stated firmly. "But, to keep our boundaries protected, demonstrations of large storms—or, in our case—earthquakes are sometimes necessary."

That explained his attitude then, Vela thought. They were defending their borders, which clans did, at the risk of harming people or places. Territories were fiercely guarded which shifted often because of these boundary wars.

Planting his feet, he raised his arms. "Now, how about we work on one of our defenses, earthquakes? Earlier this morning, a younger instructor demonstrated a small tremor. That will help explain our earthquakes, as well. Now," he said with his arms still raised, "We will keep our quakes small and insubstantial. As soon as you feel you've caused a little shake, stop."

Vela grinned at the words, 'little shake.' She was also thrilled. This would be the perfect venue to vent her frustrations. This was a major feat to master. It was their top defense, after all. She would love trying to conquer this tough skill. She had been jealous of Kane earlier when he had effortlessly produced a small tremor.

Vela stood and, like the instructor, planted her feet and raised her hands till they were perpendicular to the ground.

"Now," he said in a commanding voice, "cast your senses miles down into the ground."

"How far down do we go?" Vela asked, excitement making her voice high.

"There are plates about sixty miles down into the earth that you want to reach. They're on the Earth's crust and are actually called tectonic plates. They fit together like a jigsaw puzzle, but it's the cracks in these plates you want to focus on."

Sweat formed on Vela's brow as she held her arms over the soil and cast her senses deep. She had never reached for this depth before.

She would do this, promising herself. And would succeed.

Her arms trembled as she focused. She pushed all her energy into her subterranean search. Down, down she reached. Digging deep into her recesses of energy, she fueled her efforts and kept going.

"You should be getting close to reaching one of the plates," her teacher said. "When you reach them, feel along it. They are enormous slabs of rock, and you need to find a crack. Those are called fault lines. When you do, rest. You'll need to re-energize."

Vela was deeper into the Earth than she had ever been. Her emotions flew. She had never pushed herself this far and relished expending herself this way.

When she touched on a plate, she knew she had reached it because the teacher had described it perfectly. Sending her senses out, she could feel that it was a monstrous, irregular shape of rock. She crept along one until she found a crack in its surface. Stopping there, she held her place and tried to relax the rest of her muscles. Complete exhaustion seeped into her body. Sweat ran down her face. She had wanted to use up her energy, with this exercise and she succeeded.

Vela glanced over at Elia and wondered if she had reached the plate yet. An intense look was on Elia's face, so Vela was sure she was still searching. Evan, who stood next to Elia, looked at her and winked, which she ignored. He must have found the plate, too. Maria and Lillith were concentrating, like Elia.

In the corner of her eye, she noticed a familiar form slipping to the back of their group. Linc had just returned. Vela's attention wavered, and it took everything in her to concentrate on keeping her position underground.

Turning her gaze back to the ground, she realized she needed to address her dwindling energy supply. Breathing deeply, she allowed the rose bushes that surrounded the group to re-fuel her depleted resources. She hated taking from their life source, but she was dangerously low. This was the only time she would take from their energy instead of replenishing it for them.

Vela drew from the bushes' sweet power and felt a boost of energy, breathing a sigh of relief. Checking to be sure she hadn't taken too much; she saw the leaves were a little wilted but no lasting damage. Perfect.

Vela investigated the area below, feeling the rough texture of the rock and crack she needed to focus on. It was a hive of energy; she could feel the heat of the earth underneath it and could only guess at how hot it was. Elders had taught her the core of the earth was 10,000 degrees. Thankful she didn't have to manipulate anything hot; the teacher then commanded her attention.

"Ok, nod when you are ready to continue," the Elder said.

Vela nodded, holding her position.

After a few moments, he got everyone's nod and said, "It seems like everyone's where they're supposed to be. Now the cracks in the tectonic plate you found are where I want you to focus your attention."

Vela obeyed, eager to continue.

"I want you to barely push the crack together. I don't want you doing a big 'quake, so only move it a little. And feel what happens."

Vela felt where the two places the crack in the rock met and, with all of her mental energy, slightly pushed the two together. Immediately, the ground shook under her feet, almost making her fall. Rebalancing herself, pure adrenaline raced through her. Her head swam with the knowledge she had done that.

Vela laughed. She had made an earthquake.

It was a slight tremor, but she knew she could have strengthened it if she had pushed the crack together more. The ground continued to rumble as more students got the hang of the exercise. Vela planted her feet to keep from stumbling again. Exhaustion creeped up on her.

"Ok, stop," the teacher commanded the class. "That's enough seismic movement for today. What you did was shift the plate around. If you had manipulated the cracks more, a stronger earthquake would have ensued. Good job class."

Vela let go of her connection deep under the ground. Instantly, her muscles felt languid and tired and her legs felt like limp noodles. So much so, her knees buckled. She felt herself falling, but never reached the ground.

Two muscular arms encircled her waist and prevented her from crashing. A swirl of heat and energy rushed through her at Linc's nearness, because she knew it was him. No one else made her feel this way. Only her Intended. Vela leaned back into him, relishing the feeling of adrenaline rushing through her, restoring her. Not knowing if he did it intentionally but was happy he revitalized her.

Giving herself a moment, she enjoyed the sensation of energy spiking in her tired muscles and breathing in his unique sweet, smoky scent. She closed her eyes, wishing more than anything he was a Gyan, like her. Why must things be so difficult? Why did he have to be a mysterious Festan in Gyan territory?

When she felt like she could stand, she forced herself to breathe through her mouth to avoid the mouthwatering scent Linc had and pulled away from him. Vela stood with her back to him, getting command of her senses. Every nerve ending flared to life, and she felt like she could jump a ravine with her renewed energy.

"Are you okay?" Linc asked, concern in his voice.

Nodding, she finally turned to look at him. Vela tried to control the blush that raged across her cheeks. He laid her completely bare, revealing a side of her she had never witnessed in herself. There was attraction. Then there was this thing she and Linc had. No one had ever made her feel so alive and safe the way he did. But she didn't want that, right?

She felt eyes boring into her and she remembered they had company. Maria and her cronies, Alice and Jen, bunched together in solidarity and all glared at her. Maria flicked her eyes between her and Linc, then stalked off. Her friends followed.

Elia and Lillith walked over, both looking worse for wear. "Ugh," Elia complained. "I feel like I got hit by a Mack truck." Lillith nodded like she could relate.

"Didn't you guys replenish your energy from the garden?" Vela asked, then glanced at Linc. Did their bond help her get her strength back?

"Yes, but I didn't want to take too much," Elia said.

"Me either," Lillith said, holding her back like an old woman would.

"You guys really should go home and get some rest," Vela suggested.

They both nodded, then limped away.

Vela turned toward Linc, who had waited for her to talk to her friends. "Thanks. I guess I needed your help. Did you do something to give me energy?"

"I felt some of my strength leave when I held you," he said, his eyebrows scrunched together. "I guess our bond knew you needed it more." He then smiled and stuffed his hands in his pockets.

"Well, thank you, I guess, even if you weren't willing," Vela said, embarrassed.

"Who said I wasn't willing? I'm happy to help you, Vela."

"I thought you'd left for the day." Vela suddenly found the ground very interesting as she scuffed her foot in the grass.

"You noticed?"

"I notice all kinds of things now." Vela's blush burned at the admission. Linc's unabashed grin set her on fire, and she shot at him, "Don't be so proud of yourself. It's this thing we have, not you, personally."

He chuckled, making his smile wider. Vela fumed.

"How about that tour you promised? You seem better after that little earthquake lesson to give me one."

Affronted, she said, putting her hands on hips, "What? You mean the earthquake that could have swallowed you completely up if I wanted?"

"The one that shivered the ground. Should I be *shaking* in my boots now?" He laughed outright.

Vela bit out a response. "You know that shiver was just an example of what we can do. It could've been much stronger."

He infuriated her as much as he affected her every nerve. She fought the pleasure racing through her veins. She should not enjoy his presence. Especially when he made fun of her hard-won victories, like the new skill, she just mastered. She contemplated doing a tremor right under his feet, just to really shake him.

Before she could, he said, "I'm just teasing you, Vela. It was actually very impressive that you picked that up so quickly. It doesn't surprise me. You, however, do."

"What do you mean?" Vela asked, thrown off a little.

He explained, "I pick things up quickly, too, so it's no surprise to see we're matched in our abilities."

"But what did you mean by being surprised by me?"

"Oh, just that I'm enjoying learning things about you. I'd like to know more. But what I do know, like you're the cutest ghost I've ever seen, or your determination to master a new skill is precious. It's fun just watching you."

His words appeased her. A little bit. She turned her head to hide her blush that wouldn't stop burning her. "I guess now's a good time for a look around."

"I'm pretty happy at what I'm looking at right now."

Vela could feel his gaze trained on her, and her blood sang at his attention. She squashed the feeling and shook her head as she walked away, knowing he'd follow. She didn't want that fact to please her, but it did just the same.

Stupid bond, she thought angrily as she stomped across the yard toward the Center.

Chapter Thirteen

Linc did follow Vela. In fact, he almost bumped into her when she stopped to open the door to the Center. Was he as distracted as she was by the bond?

Clearing her throat, she awkwardly stood when she went in, then went to close the door. They both walked into the sitting room and walked over to the small library of books surrounding the red brick fireplace. Linc was about to get the shortest tour he had ever gotten. She didn't trust how she'd act around him. She promised herself, in that moment, to try to be nice.

Gesturing toward her favorite area, she said, "So, as you can see, here's our library." She eyed the fireplace, as it currently hosted a small fire and really hoped a spark wouldn't burn her favorite cache of books. She had lined them up as far from the fireplace as she could get them, but if any of the books caught on fire, they would all burn. She knew she wasn't an employee of the Center, but the Elders allowed her to manage their little library on a volunteer basis.

"Why are you frowning at the fireplace?" Linc asked with a frown of his own. "Is it because of me?" His troubled eyes sought hers out.

"What? No! Why?"

"Because it reminds you of my fire ability." He looked down at his shoes, then back at her.

She shrugged, trying not to like his vulnerability. "No. I just think it's a terrible place to put the books. Right next to a fire, you know?"

"But isn't that the best place to read a book?" He wore a confused smile. "By a roaring fire? With a cup of hot chocolate?"

Her lips parted with surprise. He just spelled out her favorite scene in the world. "Yes. That's actually pretty perfect."

"So, why can't books be by a fireplace?"

"Books," she stated, running her hands lovingly over the spines closest to her, "can be brought by a fire and enjoyed, but not stored near one. What would happen when a spark got too close to one unlucky page? It'd be a massacre!"

"Yes, let's describe books like people. Massacring them by fire. I love it," he said, laughing.

"It's true! They have their own personalities and evoke more emotions than some people I know."

"True, true. So," he said, turning toward the books, scanning each section, "let me guess which book is your favorite."

Rubbing his hands together, he walked over to *her* section, spotting a book right away. "I'm going to guess your favorite books will be over here, since these're the farthest ones away from the big, bad fireplace."

She grinned, despite herself.

He stretched up and reached for a black book. It, in fact, was her favorite book in her stash.

Turning, he brought the book to her, and she looked at the cover that bore two hands holding an apple. "My guess is that *Twilight* is your all-time favorite book." His eyes twinkled, and she fought back her grin.

"So?" was her only response, folding her arms across her chest.

"So? That's all you have to say about this amazing example of literature?" He sounded serious, but his sparkling eyes gave it away that he was teasing her.

"It *is* amazing!" she blurted, not able to help herself, holding her hips. "Stephenie Meyer is a brilliant example of one unique story paving the way for an entirely new section at every Barnes and Noble and Books A Million in the country — the world even!"

"A new section, huh?"

"Yes! The only popular books for teens before *Twilight* were the Harry Potter books. So, between J.K. Rowling and Stephenie Meyer, hundreds, no, thousands of books had the chance to be published."

"*So* passionate about books." He smirked, putting her book back on the shelf. "Yet another quality of you I'm finding fascinating."

"Happy to amuse you."

So much for a quick tour. They had only been in one place, and it felt like they'd spent an hour together already.

Time should fly by when you're not having fun, she reasoned. That would only be fair. But, in all honesty, she didn't hate being around Linc, which annoyed her. She should hate it, but he had a way of making her feel comfortable. It must be what attracted the humans to him, too. He was magnetic. She would not be another magnet, she promised herself.

Walking away from the books, she turned toward the kitchen that boasted a counter facing the library. Walking a couple steps into the small space, she motioned toward the pots and pans hanging above a stove island, saying simply, "Kitchen."

He followed and said, arching his eyebrow, "What, I don't get to find your favorite pot, like I found your favorite book?"

Ignoring him, she walked out of the kitchen, and into the hallway leading to the study rooms. After naming them, she showed him one and then closed the door.

Then they walked into the conservatory, housing all their delicate plants. She started breathing in their scents, immediately happy. Linc's aroma still called to her, but she welcomed the myriad of flavors she now inhaled.

"I like to call these plants the babies," she said, strolling down the path. She affectionately grazed the flowers she passed with her fingers, feeding them a bit of her now replenished energy.

"Why? Besides, they're new plants?" Linc followed a step behind her.

Vela smiled softly as she stopped and studied an orchid, making sure it rested healthily in its pot. Satisfied it did, she looked over her shoulder and said, "They require the most care and attention, like a baby."

"You really care about each plant, don't you?" He stepped up to her side, looking down at the delicate blue and white flower.

"I do. They have a life and energy that's unique to each one. I admire their loves."

"Their *loves*? I didn't realize plants had the capability to love." He turned to study her expression, which she ignored, as she tried to form the right answer.

"They don't love in our sense, but theirs. They absorb the light and heat of the environment around them, and in turn, they give the best thank you they can, their beauty. They live to love. Their entire being expresses their love for God, who created them, and they reward us with their simple act of living, of loving." She blushed when she looked up from the orchid she fingered to find Linc staring at her.

"It's breathtaking," he breathed.

"It is."

"No." He shook his head. "*You* are breathtaking. That was probably the most beautiful and caring way of describing a flower's purpose in life."

Blushing furiously, Vela turned to walk away. Linc gently grabbed her elbow, stopping her.

When she wouldn't turn, Linc asked, "Vela, look at me?"

Despite willing herself not to, she turned slowly. Her breath caught at his expression. He pleaded for her with his eyes to listen to what he had to say. She found she very much wanted to.

"You know the story of Romeo and Juliet?"

She nodded.

"I was forced to read it during my homeschool years, when I was young. But I'm glad I did because you remind me of that story. What I didn't understand then, I can now, very much."

"In what sense?" she found herself asking.

His eyes burned into hers and she felt his gift flare in his fingertips that still held her elbow. Goosebumps erupted at the warmth he emanated. She stood still, confused at herself for wanting to hear what he had to say.

"There's a scene that has always stayed with me. Romeo watched Juliet when she stood a distance away, on her balcony. Romeo described being jealous of the glove on Juliet's hand. He wanted to be the glove, just so he could feel her cheek. I never understood that when I read it. But I do now."

When Vela looked at him curiously, he explained. "Seeing you touch the plants, care for them in such a loving way, makes me jealous. That I can't be on the receiving end of your care, like they are. I would give anything for you to even look at me like you do one of your flowers." He looked down, a soft blush coming over his cheeks, and Vela very much knew how he felt. She had blushed earlier, too, and had tried to hide it.

She found she wanted to see it, though, see this side of him she was sure not many ever saw. She *was* a magnet; she realized. Finding herself leaning toward him, she reached out to tip his chin up, like he had done to hers in the stairwell the day before.

Shame leaked out from his expression before he cleared it and smoothed his face of any emotion. She couldn't make sense of what she just saw and what he wore now on his handsome face.

"Linc?" she asked, wondering where the enigmatic guy who said such beautiful things went.

"Never mind," he said, shaking his head. He turned and walked out of the conservatory, leaving her to follow him for once. Puzzled, she walked after him until he reached the front door of the center.

"Thank you," he said with his back to her. "I appreciate the tour. I have to go."

And with that, he left taking with him his delicious aroma, charismatic personality and everything Linc.

"Bye," she whispered, very much wondering who exactly God bonded her to.

Chapter Fourteen

For the next week, Vela didn't see Linc. She wondered if he was avoiding her as much as she avoided him.

It was Wednesday; she had almost made it to her family's vacation weekend. She had spent her evenings either on the phone with Elia arguing about her complete avoidance of Linc or cloistered in her room. Elia thought Vela needed to pursue and try to spend more time with Linc, which Vela wholeheartedly disagreed with.

She needed space.

After the tour she had with Linc, she didn't know what to make of her feelings toward him. She knew the bond would make it hard for them to be apart, but she didn't predict that she suddenly wanted to get to know him.

And that frightened her more than anything.

He had displayed such gentleness and genuine feelings that day that it tore through her defenses like paper. In fact, he, like his element, set her on fire so easily, so effortlessly that she didn't know anything about herself when she had contact with him. She was afraid that she'd, like paper, go up in smoke with his presence. That she would disappear into whatever their bond was losing herself completely.

If she acted on what their bond wanted and had a relationship with Linc, what would happen to her dreams, her reality? He was on track to be an Elder, and she wanted a little life as a flower shop owner. Would she have to give up her dream to meet his? If so, that was a hard pill to swallow. How would she fit into a Festan community? What would she do with herself? Many married couples, like her parents, were Elders. She could never earn that distinction in a Festan world. She ran her hands over her scars, studying them. Could she be honest with herself and live among the people who were responsible for her scars, her nightmares?

So, this week, she avoided him. She needed to think things through, not be barraged by her feelings and the sensations evoked while around him.

Trying to avoid Elia's non-stop questions, however, was her new catastrophe.

Vela sat in her room with Jack for company on her bed, staring at a blank page as she attempted to get a paper started on the Iliad and the Odyssey. Why her teacher would assign a paper on Labor Day weekend was an anomaly she could not figure out. A knock on the door interrupted her thoughts, and she looked up just as Elia quietly slipped in.

"When is this going to stop, Vels?" Elia sighed, sitting next to her on the bed, getting right to the point.

"I don't know what you're talking about." Vela studied her notes.

"You know exactly what I'm talking about. I hardly see you anymore. You keep to yourself all the time. At school you're a ghost, never staying in one place and constantly looking over your shoulder."

At Elia's description, Vela's heart lurched. That's how *he* described her too, a ghost.

"I'm just staying out of the way of the Festan. I don't want to talk to him," Vela said, tired of the situation.

"He has a name, Vela, it's Lincoln. Stop de-humanizing him. He has feelings just like anyone else. I get you're staying off his radar, but I have a news flash, sister, you will have to face him. You can't keep hiding."

"It's all I can do right now, Elia. I just can't. He makes me feel too much. It's like I don't know what *I* want when I'm around him."

"Won't, you mean. You won't face him. What if he's a great guy, Vela? Why won't you even give him a chance? And since when are you afraid of feelings? And of course you're not going to disappear, Vela. He would hate that. He just wants you."

Vela threw her notebook down and yelled, "Because *I* want to be in control of my own feelings! Not be led around the nose by them. I'm not the girl that will just fall at the feet of my Intended, because I'm supposed to. And the sooner you realize that about me, the better. Honestly, I'd thought you'd understand me. I'm kind of hurt that you don't."

Elia's eyes flashed with pain. "If you're going to be this stubborn, maybe I should leave. The best friend I know, and love, would never back down from a problem this easily. So, whoever this is that just lashed out at me can take a hike. I'll see you later."

With that, Elia left the room as quietly as when she entered.

Vela put her head down in her hands. She couldn't explain her determined feelings. She didn't want Linc. She didn't. He was the last person she should want to be her Intended. He was a Festan, her enemy.

But what was this nagging feeling she had to let him talk to her again? After their last conversation, though, it scared her how effortlessly he had pulled her into a wonderful talk about all her favorite things.

She finally admitted to herself, he scared her witless.

Was he really that bad? And what was he doing at their school? If she gave him a chance, she could find out what his real purpose was in being in their area. She did not believe the researcher reason. And he might answer some questions she had about why Festan Elementals were taking over so much territory with their fires. Everything felt confusing and to top it off, she had just hurt her best friend's feelings. When were things going to start being right?

Her phone lit up with a notification. Hoping to see Elia's face with a message, she flipped her phone up to see it.

It was a DM, a private message on Instagram from a Linc Stevenson. Her heart beat faster, taking her breath away when she read the message.

Since you are the queen of avoidance and bent on ignoring me, I have no choice but to find you on Instagram. I'd make a good friend if you gave me a chance. I thought I proved that on Saturday. Friend me.

Throwing her phone down, she jumped up from the bed. Jack barked, thinking she wanted to play.

"No, Jack, lay down."

Thinking it through, she decided this might be better than being around him. At least this way, he couldn't wreak havoc on her emotions, like when they were face to face. It would make a good buffer zone. Her decision made, it didn't mean she would make it easy for him, though.

Are you stalking me on social media now? How does that make a good friend?

Instantly, she got a message back.

I wouldn't have to if you were man or, sorry, woman enough to actually face me.

She laughed out loud, more exasperated than anything else.

I have my reasons.
What could possibly induce you to completely turn down a perfectly good opportunity at a really good friendship?
Are you saying you're perfection?

All their answers had been fired back and forth pretty quickly, but this time, she had to wait for an answer.

I'm not saying I'm perfect. I'm far from it. But I'm also not a coward. That I can say. You're afraid of something only we can have and not even giving it a chance. I'll leave this with you. What could be so bad about me you will throw away a God-given gift? Is it because I'm not a Gyan, like you? I don't hold to the same prejudices everyone else does. Unlike you, I choose to get to know someone before I cut them out. But it seems like you will cut me out before giving me a chance. I hope whatever it is, it's for a really good reason. See you around.

With that last message, her breathing hitched, and she knew she was being hard on someone she didn't even know. Because he was right. This was a God-given gift she was throwing away. Why she would meet her Intended now, she did not know. But she at least needed to let him try to have something with her.

And with that decision in place, she opened up her Instagram, found Linc, and clicked a button to follow him. She made her move; the ball was now in his court.

Chapter Fifteen

VELA MOVED HER FRIES around the styrofoam plate. The school cooks did a miserable job on the fryer today. Her fries resembled cooked carrots more than the fried goodness they should be. She wanted to distract herself with food today; the alternative was facing the quietness permeating her table.

With her and Elia not talking, she just wanted to sit alone. She didn't want to face meaningless conversations in her normal group. They all eyed her from another table curiously, but she ignored them.

She and Elia didn't fight, like ever. This was new, and she looked around the crowded cafeteria for a glimpse of her best friend. She didn't see her.

A familiar euphoria filled her veins and her breath caught. She should be used to Linc approaching her by now.

After last night's Instagram conversation, she decided to stop running. He so easily called to the deepest parts of her, things she barely recognized in herself. He made her face her fears of the Festans, even when he didn't know the full truth of them or the knowledge of her terrible memories.

The feeling intensified until a tray appeared on her right and Linc dropped into the chair with a groan. His shirt was a light gray, she noted, the lightest she had ever seen him wear, but still a subdued color. There was yet again another band name on it.

Vela looked at him, waiting for an explanation for the groan, but it didn't come. So, she asked, "Are you an old man now? Bones, not what they used to be?"

He huffed a laugh and shook his head. "Just a late night with my parents."

"I thought they were in Dallas?"

"It was a phone conversation. A long one."

"You mean, after you Insta'd me, you talked to your parents for a while?"

"Yep." He dug into his food. He didn't seem to mind the soggy fries. She eyed his plate. Maybe his fries were better than hers. Were they in a good enough place where she could dig into his fries?

Deciding against it, she wondered, *Should she bring up their conversation last night?* His body language screamed pure exhaustion. He sat with his shoulders slumped, his posture terrible. *No, not now.*

"Must have been a long talk," she said instead.

He sighed heavily. "It was. They want to know every little detail of my life. It's exhausting."

"*Every* detail?" Vela asked, curious if he told them about her. "Like...me?"

"I might have mentioned it," Linc said with a smile, popping a fry into his mouth.

Vela's jaw dropped.

"Why're you surprised? Didn't you talk to your parents, too?"

"No!" Vela dropped her voice and whispered, "I actually don't want anyone to know."

"You're keeping our bond from your parents?" When he saw her glance at her Gyan friends, he said, nodding, "And from your Gyan friends, too." He looked troubled. "Why keep me a secret, Vela?"

Vela cringed, wondering what her Gyan friends and family would think about her Intended being a Festan. It wouldn't be an easy sell, if she accepted him.

"In case, you know... if this doesn't work out," she stumbled through her words.

His eyes wide, he leaned toward her. "Why wouldn't this work out? Are you already brushing me off? Just like that?"

"No!" she sighed and said, "I guess I just keep waiting for the ball to drop."

He huffed. "The only ball that's going to drop is the one that's completely in your court. I have no problem with you. It's you that has these insurmountable walls up."

Linc now sat, his shoulders tense and fists clenched. Vela couldn't stand his frustrated expression. He couldn't help who he was. She knew that. "I just have some major trust issues with..."

"Me. A Festan," he gritted out.

"Yeah." She ran her hands over her scars to remind herself that she had good reason not to trust him.

"Look," he said with a sigh, eyeing her, fingering the scars. "Maybe one day you'll trust me enough to tell me what happened to you." He ran his hand through his hair and suggested, "Until then, how about we just pretend there's no bond at all and just get to know each other, like we're just one guy and one girl? Simplify things."

Vela paused before she nodded and said, "OK." Looking at his shirt, she remarked, "You're into music, aren't you?"

"What makes you ask that?"

"Every time I see you, you're wearing a different band shirt. Ones I don't recognize."

"How do you not recognize The Smiths?" he asked, leaning back to look down at the graphic on the front of his shirt.

"I'm kind of the average teenager. I listen to the newer pop songs and the Beatles, of course."

"Ah, classic, The Beatles. Even though they performed in the 1960's, they're iconic. Though, so are The Smiths. Would you like me to introduce you to them?" His eyes gleamed, and he looked at her with a hopeful expression.

"Maybe," she said, relieved their conversation turned into a lighter one. "Do you go to their concerts?"

"No, sadly they broke up. I keep hoping they'll reunite at some point, but it's not looking promising."

"So, on to a harder question." When he turned toward her, she plowed on with it. "Why aren't you the least bit weird around Gyans or humans for that matter? You're comfortable with everyone I see, especially me. Aren't you... you know... the least bit bothered by us?"

"You're special, first of all," he said, ticking off a finger, "Of course, I would treat my Intended, you, on a more personal level. The rest of you though," he mused, scanning the Gyan groups sitting around at their different tables, "are like the humans, in my mind. I keep them at arm's length but am friendly enough to chat or socialize. I don't hold it against your friends because they're Gyans. Like I don't hold it against humans that they're human. I wouldn't have a human as my best friend if I have a choice in it. You can't really choose your friends, though. Sometimes people just worm their way into your life unexpectedly."

He eyed her thoughtfully, then continued. "I'd like to be my complete self around those I'm close to. I couldn't do that around a human, since they can't know about us. So, I'm careful when I choose my close friends. But I don't mind talking to different crowds. In fact, it's kind of a challenge to me."

Almost as if on cue, a human girl stumbled toward their table as she tripped on her wedges. She avoided a face plant by holding out her hand and catching the lip of the table. She picked up her bright red face and smiled awkwardly at Linc behind a curtain of long, dark hair.

He smiled gently at her, probably to make her feel better about her clumsy entrance.

"Hi, Linc," she greeted in a breathy voice, "sorry I almost fell into your lap, which would have been disastrous." She looked away and drew in a deep breath and continued, "Anyway, I was wondering, well, my friends and I," she pointed behind her at a crowded, giggling table of girls, "if you were going to go the party tomorrow night? Since there's no school on Monday, it gives us extra time to unwind."

"Oh," Linc said and paused, looking at Vela. "Can anyone come?" he asked as he gave his attention back to the blushing girl.

"Oh!" she mirrored, "Who? Her?" eyeing Vela. The girl tried to hide her disappointment that he would want to bring a date.

"Yes," Linc said firmly, so there were no allusions to what he meant.

"Umm, yeah... I guess," the girl stammered.

"I'll have to see," Linc said. "Not sure of our plans yet."

Vela's eyebrows raised at his use of his word, "our".

"OK, great!" the girl gushed, completely ignoring Vela and granting Linc a white winning smile.

When he didn't say anything, clearly finished with their conversation, the girl giggled and turned away to join her friends.

"Our plans?" Vela asked, folding her arms on the table. "That was presumptuous of you."

Linc had the decency to look chagrined. "I was going to ask you what your plans were this weekend, anyway. Wanna' go to a party with me?"

"A party with humans? No. Definitely not. And anyway, I'm going out of town this weekend."

"Really? With who? Your friend? Where is she today anyway?" he asked, looking around.

"No, not with Elia," Vela said, not wanting to get into the reason Elia didn't sit with her today. Annoyed he was the reason for their argument, she said curtly, "With my family. We're going camping."

He thought over that for a moment, then said, "Be careful, please?"

"What do you think I'm going to do, fall out of my sleeping bag?"

"All kinds of things can happen. Where is your family camping?"

"Utah."

"That's Borean territory!" He looked alarmed.

"We'll be on the border of our land and theirs, I guess."

"Just another reason to be very careful." He looked down. He did *not* look happy with her news.

"I won't go looking for trouble, if that's what you're saying."

"Good." He toyed with the food on his plate.

Someone else walked up to their table. This time, Vela cringed. Maria sauntered to their table with a predatory smile on her face.

"Hi, Linc," she said, all her attention on Linc, ignoring Vela completely.

"Hi, Maria," Vela announced, outright ignoring Maria ignoring her.

Maria's eyes flicked to Vela, then away just as quickly. "I was wondering," she said, her attention refocused on Linc, "if you wanted to come to a little get together I'm having at my house this weekend."

Linc answered easily. "Sorry, Maria. I have plans."

"Plans that couldn't be broken?" Maria asked in a flirty tone, her finger tracing the table's edge.

"Maria. He has plans, okay? He just said he did. Get the hint," Vela said in a tight voice. Vela burned with indignation. If Maria came on any hotter, she'd be burning up. This was getting ridiculous.

Maria's eyes narrowed, and she looked between Linc and Vela suspiciously. She was glad she hadn't told anyone in her group about her and Linc's bond. Who knew what measures Maria would take to steal him away from her? Wait, she couldn't steal what Vela didn't own. Yet. She shook her head in frustration.

Maria, judging by Linc's silence, got the hint he wouldn't change his mind and finally left in a huff.

"Sorry about that," Linc said, running his hand through his dark hair.

"What are *you* sorry about?" Vela asked with a laugh. "I'm pretty sure Maria is the one who needs to lay off a little bit."

"You know? She might actually be doing me a favor," he said, leaning back in his chair studying Vela with a grin.

"What favor?" Vela's indignation rose fiercely.

"Getting you to admit you like me more than you think. Like me enough to care if someone else flirts with me...or asks me out," he said with a triumphant smile.

Vela spluttered. "I'll admit nothing," she finally managed to say. "Maria's just..."

"She's not your enemy, Vela," he said, his tone suddenly soft. "And, just for the record, you have nothing to worry about." He covered her hand that rested on the table with his.

"She," Vela spat, unable to calm herself down, pulling her hand away, "is a piece of work. Who will stop at nothing to get what she wants. And you're right. A fellow Gyan isn't my enemy. You keep making me forget that the Festans are." She regretted her harsh words as soon as she said them.

He reared back like she hit him. "Look," he said in a deep voice, "I keep trying to show you, to tell you, that I can't fix what's been wrong with our clans for three hundred years. Since the Salem Witch Trials, our clans have done everything they could to claim their own lands so they can manage their gifts their way. Hide them away and not get persecuted for them. I can't fix history. But what I can fix right here and right now is us. Or the chance of us, anyway. Vela," he asked, grabbing both her hands this time, "what can I do to show you I'm a good and decent person? Worthy of having a bond with?"

Vela looked down at their hands, wincing at the electrical pulses and warmth his touch generated.

"I don't know," she answered honestly. Then she looked up. "Give me time, maybe? To think about this?" Confusion made her head swim.

Just then, she spotted Elia walking into the cafeteria.

"I have to go," she said, pulling her hands away and snatching up her bookbag and tray of food. Regret tore through her as she left Linc's tortured expression behind as she said goodbye and rushed to her best friend.

Reaching Elia, she stopped and leaned on one foot, then another, unsure of what to say. Elia looked at her with troubled eyes, her knuckles white as she grasped her backpack.

"Were you sitting with *Linc*? I thought you hated him," Elia finally said.

"Yeah, I was. I do… I mean," Vela sighed heavily and shook her head fiercely. "I mean I don't know how I feel about that guy."

"Don't let me stop you," Elia said, her eyes wide. "In fact, I encourage you to go back over there."

"Elia, I'm trying," she said, sighing again heavily. "I can only take so much of the feelings he makes me feel. I can hardly think. And our argument is killing me. Please, can we talk somewhere?"

Elia's lip trembled, and a tear filled her eye. She whispered, "I'm not going to say it's okay that you went off on me like you did. But I understand the stress you're under. And I really want to know what seems to have progressed with Linc. So, let's go. I was in the library. There's no one there. We have about ten minutes left before class."

Vela breathed out a sigh of relief, stuffing her confusion and fears away deep inside, then dumped her tray of food in the trash before she left with Elia.

Vela couldn't see ahead on where she stood with her Intended, but she was willing to think about it. And she needed to make things right with her best friend. That was one relationship she did not want to mess up.

Chapter Sixteen

VELA THREW HER SUITCASE on the bed. Saturday had finally graced her with its presence. It was a relief to go on a trip she had looked forward to forever now. And to get away from a very confusing, very frustrating individual who had crashed into her life like a Mack truck.

Life just felt better after she apologized to Elia, too. Vela got to work throwing her bathing suit and plenty of exercise clothes into her bag. She planned on swimming until she turned into a raisin and doing a lot of hiking and exploring once they reached Utah. She couldn't wait to get away. Getting out of her head for a while and a change of scenery was just the ticket.

She leaned over her bag, remembering how Linc had gotten her attention the day before, and smiled despite herself.

Vela walked with Cassie chatting with her about school when she noticed Linc ahead of her in the hallway. Vela stopped when he did, and he cocked his head. She knew he felt her presence and waited for her to catch up with him. Cassie looked curiously at Vela, then said something about needing to get to class and left her in the hallway.

Vela was wary of another encounter with Linc where he made her feel conflicted and confused, so she waited for him to move along. He waited for a second, then looked over his shoulder, giving her a resigned smile. She remembered wondering what the smile was for. Like he knew, she was hesitant to move forward with a relationship she wasn't sure she wanted.

He was being exhaustingly patient with her, and she couldn't decide if she was pleased with that or infuriated. She waited for him to continue walking, which he did, but instead of walking forward, he stepped backwards.

And he didn't stop until he was right next to her. Vela didn't know what made her wait for him to reach her, instead of using the opportunity to race by him, but she waited. It must be her infernal curiosity. She clenched her hands, upset with herself.

"Hey new buddy," Linc said.

"I'm not..."

"Your buddy? You're right, you're much more than that," he said, his eyes warm.

Resistance seemed futile when it came to Linc. Sighing, she said, "Yes?"

"Yes, you are more than a friend?" he asked with a smile.

"Time, Linc, remember?" she asked, shifting her backpack nervously, suddenly nervous he could see right through her crumbling defenses.

"Can't I say hello to my new friend? Is that a crime around here?" He looked around them, stuffed his hands in his dark jean pockets and said, "Nope, it seems like something everyone does when they see their friend in the hallway." He leaned toward her, and she leaned back. "I'm just being friendly. Can you do that?"

He straightened, which she did also, frowning because she had gotten a nose full of fire and candy. "Yes, I can be friendly, Linc." She didn't like being rude and that's all he seemed to bring out in her. Now she just felt guilty.

"Well, it occurred to me I know next to nothing about you. Tell me about yourself. What are your dreams and aspirations?"

Vela looked around her, just noticing people were having to walk around them to get to their next class. She pulled his arm toward the side of the hallway, where they could get out of the flow of traffic.

"We have seven minutes between classes, most of which were already spent. So, in the next," she checked her watch, "three minutes you want to know what my *dreams* are?" She shook her head, bewildered.

"No, you have three minutes to start telling me your dreams, and we have the rest of our lives to finish the conversation." He smiled wickedly at her.

Her eyebrows pulled high and her mouth open, she spluttered, "How are you so accepting of our bond?"

Winking, he said, "Ah, ah, ah, those are all secrets you are just going to have to peel off me in our next lifetime together. I can't give away all of them at once. Or in two minutes now."

Flustered, she adjusted her backpack to give her hands something busy to do because she wanted to smack the silly smile off his face.

"Come on, tell me one thing about yourself," he begged. He looked at her uncertainly and it surprised her to see this side of him. Not so confident.

Biting her lip, she made a decision, hoping it was the right one. In a flurry of words, she said, "I want to own my own flower shop one day. I know it seems like an obvious job to have knowing what I am, but I really want one, a good one." She braced herself, waiting for him to say something about a Gyan wanting to abuse their powers to make a profit.

"I like it," he said instead, surprising her. "You'd be beautiful surrounded by nothing but flowers. Now, come on or we really are going to be late for our next class."

She walked in a daze as he took her elbow gently and steered her down the hallway. Every Gyan she had told about her dream had sneered and criticized her for wanting to use her gift for a job. He didn't know how her heart warmed through her chest with his words and what they meant to her. Her insecurities of owning a flower shop as a Gyan melted away, and his simple answer obliterated every argument she had against the idea.

On top of that, the whole way down the hall, her gift flared, sending sparks through her with his touch. He deposited her to her next class. She wondered when he noticed she had this class. Dipping her head to hide her blush, she half waved at him and walked into her class, floating on a cloud.

Coming back to the present, she sat on the edge of her bed and tried to recall her distaste for him or her distrust. He had obliterated what her preconceptions of what a Festan would act like and she wasn't sure how she felt about that. She still distrusted the idea of him here. *Why* was he so accepting of her? Didn't Festans dislike other clans as much as Gyans disliked them? *What* was his deal? Fisting her hands, she decided there was nothing she could do about it now. Those questions would have to wait. She had a glorious weekend to prepare for, all without him.

She was determined to enjoy it.

Vela walked into her bathroom tossing her favorite shampoo, conditioner, body wash and lotion into a bag.

Within thirty minutes, she had packed her bags downstairs, and they were ready to go in the car. Kane and Drew soon joined her. She gave them both a wide smile and asked, "Ready to go on vacay boys?"

Jack whined at the door. He always knew when it was time for a trip. The minute he saw the suitcases, he got antsy, whined and paced the floor. Sometimes they had to leave him, but this vacation they could bring him since they were camping.

"More than ready." Drew groused. "Now where's Mom and Dad? Even Jack's ready before them. We've got a four-and-a-half-hour car ride ahead of us."

"We're coming, we're coming! Sorry boys, I should have packed last night. I'm sorry," Whitney rushed down the stairs, David on her heels dragging two suitcases behind him.

They were on the road as soon as Drew packed the new additions in the family SUV.

Drew was up in the passenger seat as their dad drove. She had her mom in the back seat with her and Kane was in the back row with Jack, who had finally settled down. Jack wasn't crazy about car rides and cried unless someone was in the back seat with him, which Kane was. So, he contentedly rode with half his body draped over Kane's lap and nose to the window. He would have been even happier with his nose out the window, but the back windows didn't go down, so he'd have to do without.

Vela was glad she had her mom completely to herself. Drew and her dad were in an in-depth conversation in the front, and she checked over her shoulder, noticing Kane had earbuds in. It was time to tell her about her and Linc's bond. "Mom?"

Whitney propped her elbow on the headrest of the seat next to them, adjusted her body to where she was facing her and said tiredly, "Yes?"

Vela took a deep breath and measured her words. "How likely is it to get the wrong bondmate?"

Concern flashed across Whitney's face for a moment, but then was gone just as quickly. Confusion took its place, and she asked, "Are we talking from personal experience, Vela?"

"Maybe."

"Why don't you tell me what is going on? You're young to be talking about an Intended."

"You and dad didn't meet till you were in your twenties, right? I realize that I'm young, but this question is important. Can someone you think is your Intended not be him?" Vela asked, wringing her hands.

"Honey, as far as I know, if you experience the signs, the aphrodisiac-like scent, the awareness when they are around, the longing to be together, it means they are your Intended. Even though it's a permanent bond, it is one you can reject if you so choose. But you need to be absolutely sure that's what you want to do. You don't reject it lightly."

"Yeah, I know, I can understand that. It's just that, well, I'm as surprised as you are about this conversation, but there's something I've been kind of dealing with. I've tried to deal with it on my own, but I'm not doing such a great job of it. And I need your advice."

"Honey, you will always have me to come to for anything. Did you find your Intended? At school?"

"Yes. As much as I wished I hadn't. Oh, Mom!" She promptly burst into tears. She was a mess inside. All her uncertainty and frustration rushed to the surface, and it actually felt good to release it.

Vela felt her mother's arms come around her and a soothing caress on her back as she cried. After a few minutes, Whitney leaned back and pushed Vela's hair away from her face and asked, "Now how about you tell me what happened?"

"Mom, my Intended is the new Festan Elemental in school." More tears leaked. "Of all the Elementals across this whole world, why him? Why him?" she repeated.

"A *Festan Elemental* Vela? Are you sure, honey?" She held Vela's face in her hands and searched her eyes. Fear flashed across her mom's face.

"I'm sure Mom. I told him I wanted to reject the bond, and he's asking me to reconsider. But I'm sure it's him. His scent is incredible, like the most beautiful aroma. And when he's around me, my skin jumps just being near him, and I never want him to leave. I can sense his presence when he's near, too." More tears welled in her eyes, and she asked, "I'm sure he's my Intended. But why a Festan? I thought Elementals would always be drawn to their own kind."

"No, not always. It's rare to find your Intended because they could be any Elemental and we don't see any but Gyans. But the fact that you're both different elements reminds me of a prophecy I heard. But it can't be you, at least I hope..."

Before her mother could finish, Vela asked, "Prophecy? The prophecy someone mentioned at dinner the other night?"

"It's not important, baby. If you're sure you don't want this boy as your Intended, maybe it's best you reject his bond."

Suspicious that her mom came to that conclusion so quickly, Vela asked, "Because of this prophecy? Mom, what does it say? How could it be about me?"

Whitney quickly said, "It couldn't be. Forget I said it." She turned toward the window, a worried line between her eyes appearing.

"No. Mom, please talk to me. What should I be worried about?" She refused to allow her mom to get out of this conversation so easily. Not when it came to such a big moment in her life.

Whitney turned back toward her, her face pinched, and said, "There have been several prophets, not just one, who have all foretold of someone who will bring all the clans together."

"Right. What does this have to do with me and Linc?"

"Linc? That's his name?"

Vela nodded.

"One prophet mentioned something different about this person, a child actually, and one thing they say is that the parents of this Chosen Child, they call him or her, will be different elements. So, basically any Intendeds who do not have the same element are under a lot of scrutiny."

"I can guess why," Vela breathed. "Wow, so Linc and I could be parents of this child?"

"The Chosen Child. And, technically, yes, but I don't like that you are even put in that position. It's a lot of pressure. I don't want that for you, baby." She turned away to look out the window and Vela thought her mom hid her expression.

And she was being cryptically vague. Vela didn't like it. But she figured that was all she was going to get out of her at the moment. Well, they had plenty of time this weekend to talk about it. She would get more out of her mom then. Her chest squeezed with worry. Yes, this prophecy is life changing, but there was more her mom wasn't saying.

"Mom? What aren't you telling me?" Vela pushed one more time.

"Nothing, honey," her mom answered firmly. "That's all I want to get into right now. Now, let's just relax."

Settling into her seat, Vela looked over and saw her mom had laid her head down and chewed on her fingernail in a nervous habit she had.

Snuggling into her seat, dragging a blanket to cover her body, she tucked it under her chin. First, she had to stop worrying. Second, she needed to pray.

Vela needed God's peace right now.

Usually when this upset, she tried to handle it on her own, but maybe she'd calm down by reading her Bible. Sitting up, she dug it out of her big purse. Opening it up to where she had read last, she found she was in Isaiah. One of God's prophets. Interesting. It was like she was meant to read this exact passage. *Okay*, she prayed, *Please God, calm my heart.*

She read from Chapter 43:

> *But now, this is what the Lord says-he who created you Jacob, he who formed you Israel. "Do not fear, for I have redeemed you; I have summoned you by name; you are mine.*

Her heart settled a bit in her chest and felt less restrictive. Warmed by the thought of belonging to God and reading this exact Scripture just when she desperately needed it, she continued reading.

> *When you pass through the waters, I will be with you, and when you pass through the rivers, they will not sweep over you.*

Her chest felt lighter. She praised God and kept reading.

When you walk through the fire, you will not be burned, the flames will not set you ablaze. For I am the Lord your God, the Holy One of Israel, your Savior....

She stopped reading just then and closed her eyes. Thankful beyond words, tears leaked through her closed eyes and dripped off her face one by one. She was so humbled that God would give her this passage to read. The fire reminded her of Linc and his gift. And now she had read it in the Word that she wouldn't be burned by the fire. As she panicked about her future and whether she should choose Linc, she knew she was led to these Scriptures as a sign that she shouldn't worry about accepting the bond. They reminded her she was in capable hands, God's hands. So, no matter what came her way, God would give her the courage, the strength, and the endurance to get through it.

Now, she just needed to believe this with all her heart so she could face her future again. And whether that would include a certain Festan Elemental, only time would tell. First, she needed to get to know him. After this weekend, maybe they could try this friendship thing.

With someone she never thought she'd even be friends with.

Chapter Seventeen

AFTER A COUPLE OF breaks letting Jack out to do his business, they finally made it to Vernal, Utah. It was late when they got in. They set their tents set up in the dark and after pumping their air mattresses, they all crashed to sleep.

In the early hours of the morning, Vela stepped out of the tent and stretched. It hadn't been a bad drive last night, but she was still a little stiff. She reached up to the colorful sky for several minutes till she heard her shoulder joints popping, then twisted her torso in a satisfying stretch. The sky was a kaleidoscope of colors: soft pinks, bright oranges and iridescent yellows, all blending together in a spectacular sunrise. *God's perfect beauty.* She delighted in the terrain's view, too.

Sage bushes scattered all around her, and she stepped onto the packed red, orange and brown dirt. Immediately, she connected to the surrounding nature, allowing it to rejuvenate her. She noticed every shrub and tree; their presences soothing her. She had needed this and badly.

Vela called Jack over to her, who had explored the area behind the tent, and he bumped into her side. Leaning down, she kissed his head and took a few licks to the face before she sent him to explore some more. She knew he wouldn't go too far, but monitored him just in case.

The sunshine came down on her bare shoulders. Her bright pink tank top was the perfect shirt for this kind of weather. Soft golden goodness surrounded her, and she noticed the lake they were camping by. It shimmered in the morning sun, and she planned on getting personally acquainted with that bit of water soon. Her brothers would start fishing at the first available minute. They had heard that there was rainbow trout, bluegill, sunfish and largemouth bass to catch, and their mouths were salivating to have a fish fry. She wouldn't see much of them, but that was fine. She was good at hanging by herself. That was one thing about herself she liked. She wasn't dependent on other people to have fun.

The campground itself was the perfect size to Vela, only like thirty or so campsites. Since it was Labor Day weekend, the sites were completely full. Vela started a walk to the bathroom, leaving Jack with her parents, who were just stirring awake. There was an assortment of RV's and tents. Her stomach rumbled, ready for breakfast, but coffee was her most immediate need. She had heard that it was in college when students became addicted to that beautiful little bean, but she was a full-on addict as a teenager.

During her walk, she took notice if there were any Elementals camping. They were still in Gyan territory, so she expected to see other Elementals like her. But, on a vacation spot, this was the only time she would see other elements. They never socialized with them. Her parents had taught her to keep to her own element. She wondered what it would be like to know other Elementals, however. If this Chosen Child she had heard about could combine their separate ways and integrate them, would their deep-ingrained prejudices be demolished, too?

Her dad had said God intended for them to live together. It was the Elementals who allowed prejudice and hatred to divide themselves. With her distrust of Elementals, especially Festans, she was now one of them.

Would that ever change?

For now, other Elementals were a danger to her. Not necessarily here, at vacation spots, it was a peace treaty of sorts to set aside their differences for a small amount of time.

Vela just hoped that this Chosen Child would come soon, because she was tired of distrusting other Elementals. It didn't seem natural.

During her walk, she had noticed a few other Elementals, and they had noticed her as they had nodded at her when she walked by. There was a mixture of Boreans and Gyans. She hadn't noticed any Neronians or Festans. The rest were human, which was fine.

After she reached the bathrooms, she noticed a sign posted advertising an outside night class about the stars, called a Star Party. It looked like there was one tonight and she mentally cataloged the time. As she thought about dragging Drew and Kane to this, she grinned. It was she who loved the stars and the stories about all the constellations, not them. She loved stories in general, so centuries-old ones about her starry guides in the sky was definitely something she didn't want to miss.

Vela decided to explore a little bit before she made it back to the campsite. Finding a perfect rock to perch by the lake, she looked out over the water. Light glimmered off the expansive space, and she delighted in watching the smaller fish jump out of the water to catch bugs for their morning meal.

Not seeing flowering trees around them, she glanced around and saw there were only the sage bushes she noticed earlier, and it looked like Juniper trees and scrub oaks. Soon, the latter would turn into an array of fall colors as they transitioned to winter. Vela was sorry she would miss it. It wasn't late enough to see their autumnal beauty, but maybe one day she would be here to see it in all its fall glory.

Sometime later, she made it back to their campsite and appreciated the homey touches her mom and dad had made to the place. A sign hung at the entrance that read Happy Campers, with their family name printed on the bottom. Her busy parents had hung up tarps around their campsite, so they could have a little privacy from their neighbors. There was even a potted flower by their tent. Vela smiled and shook her head. Her mom couldn't stand not having something flowering near her. It was a weakness of hers and her strength, Vela supposed. Where did she even get the little plant? Did they pack it? Currently, her parents were pulling off light strands off tree branches.

"Why are you guys taking down perfectly good lights?" Vela asked.

"Oh, we didn't know the park was an International Dark Sky Park," her dad answered.

"A what?"

"Someone from the park came to tell us they are part of an international program where they are one in 105 parks in the world that celebrates their starry nights. There's a list of qualifications they have to meet to become one of these parks."

"And that means you can't have lights in the campground?"

"No. It's not a specification of the park, but we don't want to contribute to what they call light pollution. It's fascinating. We want to enjoy the full experience of the park and if that means taking down our lights to do this, we will," her mom said resolutely, wrapping a string of lights around her arm.

"Light pollution, huh," Vela said. "That makes sense. They're having a Star Party later too. You guys would love it." She explained what the sign down at the bathroom had said about it and they made plans to attend.

"We saved you a plate of breakfast... and coffee," her mother sang.

Vela groaned happily. "You guys are the best parents in the entire world!"

Whitney softly laughed and looked over at David. "You see honey, for one cup of coffee, we have the best title a parent could ask for."

"Glad it doesn't take much," David quipped.

"If you only knew what this drink does for me, you wouldn't be saying that." Vela happily sipped her warm beverage.

She enjoyed her breakfast. Since she already had her bathing suit on under her clothes, she grabbed her sunscreen, towel, phone and a Bluetooth speaker and called for Jack and headed down to the lake.

Vela was determined to have a full day of suntanning and swimming ahead of her. She couldn't wait. Neither could Jack. His red coat gleamed in the sun, and he ran circles around her as she walked. She laughed and tried to catch him when he got close. She'd have to find some sticks to throw out to him. Dobermans weren't natural swimmers, so it always took some encouragement to get him to swim with her. But she'd do it. He would love it.

Jack had gotten ahead of her, so she ran ahead to catch up to him. On the trail, Vela scooted around a couple of teenagers, human by the looks of them, a guy and a girl. She breathlessly said her excuses as she ran after Jack. He reached the water before she did, and she laughed as he jumped out of the lake as soon as his paws touched it.

"You wimp, Jack! It can't be that bad. Is it cold, boy?"

Vela slipped her flip-flops off and touched her toes to the water's edge and saw it was a perfect temperature. Not too cold or hot and so she dropped her bundle, shed her clothes, and ran in.

Splashing Jack as she passed him, he backed up even more. Laughing, she turned and dove into the water, submerging herself completely. She emerged to Jack barking, running the length of the lake of where she swam. The teenagers she had passed on the trail eyed Jack warily as they skirted around him, walking to a section of the beach close to where she had dropped her towel and things.

Vela called out to them, "Don't worry about him, he just doesn't like when I'm somewhere he can't get to. He won't hurt you. I promise!"

The teen boy, a medium-sized guy with long blonde hair, waved at her and smiled. The girl, blonde like the boy, still eyed Jack and Vela knew they would just have to prove to her that Jack wasn't dangerous.

Walking toward her skittish dog, Vela was waist deep in the water when she called for him to come to her and he whined at the water's edge. "You big puppy! Get in here." She splashed him. He didn't like that, and he ran even further from the lake. He stayed a distance away watching her, with his tongue lolled out of his mouth and panting. He seemed to understand she was in no danger but wanted to be near her regardless and so he whined.

Vela looked around for a stick she could toss into the water to get him to start swimming. As she walked toward him, she wrung her hair out and pushed it behind her.

Spying a stick over by the two teenagers, she ran over to them, adjusting her bikini. She had picked the yellow and black polka dot one and had to make sure it didn't move on her. The bottoms tied on the sides and even though she double knotted it, she obsessively checked the knots to make sure they didn't come free. Patting her knots, she approached the girl and boy. Not wanting them to be afraid of Jack when he reached her, she patted his head, saying, "He really is a gentle giant. Please don't be afraid of him. But he can be a little distrustful of men, at first."

The guy acknowledged her warning with a nod. "I think I heard you say his name is Jack?" He must spend a lot of time in the sun, she thought. His skin was sun-kissed, more so than the girl.

As though he knew he was the subject of the conversation, Jack yipped, startling both the guy and the girl. Vela commanded Jack to sit, which he promptly did.

"Sorry. He's a good boy, just doesn't like me in the water. But he'll warm up to it soon enough."

"May I?" the guy asked, braving a touch by holding out his hands to pet Jack, but he waited for her permission.

"Sure. Let him smell you first. Just go slow."

Jack smelled the guy's offered hands for a full minute, then stepped back toward Vela sitting next to her, in protective mode. He kept his gaze trained on the stranger.

"Sorry, it's going to take some time for him to warm up to you. He doesn't like strange men. Not that you're strange! You're just someone new he doesn't know, so you're strange to him." She blushed at her rambling.

He looked at her with bright blue eyes and said, "It's no problem. I'm pretty likeable, though, he'll soon see." He gestured toward the girl, "My sister and I wanted to get some sun and swim for a while before we go hiking over to Moonshine Arch."

"Oh! I heard about that place; it sounds amazing! I saw some pictures of it. It looks absolutely beautiful. I'm going to get over there before we leave for the weekend, too."

"We always go see it when we come. It's kind of a tradition. It's very close to get to, you can hike there from here. It's only three miles."

By that time, the girl had slowly approached them, and Vela encouraged her to pet Jack, too. When she allowed Jack to lick her fingers, the girl put her hands behind her back. Vela guessed to prevent her overenthusiastic dog from licking her again. Vela hid her smile.

"You guys come here often, then?" Vela asked, rubbing Jack's head, complimenting him for his good manners.

"Every year," the guy answered. He seemed much friendlier than his sister. "If this is Jack, what's your name?" he asked.

"Vela." Unfortunately, it was time for this conversation to end. She didn't mind being friendly, but she couldn't be friends, not with these two. They were human. She could tell because they were blank slates, nothing emitted from them. She couldn't risk them ever seeing her perform her gifts. It was for their own protection.

"My name is Ellory, like Mallory, but without the "M" and with an "E" in front," the girl said shyly. She blushed as she looked at Vela and quickly looked away. Vela knew that probably took a lot for her to say. She seemed very shy.

"Hi Ellory, it's nice to meet you. And your name?" she asked the brother who squatted down to better to reach Jack. She asked, only to be polite.

"Vance," he answered with a friendly smile.

She looked around to see if her family could see her talking with these two.

Vela took a good look at Vance; she was curious about them. Even though he was of medium height, he had some muscle definition. He was wearing a sleeveless shirt, and she could easily see he was building the physique he had. Looking away quickly, she hoped he hadn't seen her noticing his muscles.

"Is it okay if we sit over here?" Ellory asked in a small voice. Blushing, she rushed to say, "I only said that because I saw that your stuff was right here, too. So, if you want this place to yourself, I, I mean, we totally understand your need for space."

Vance put his hand on his sister's shoulder and said gently, "I'm sure Vela doesn't mind that we set up camp right next to her. Right?" he asked Vela. That's when she noticed that his eyes were almost the exact color of Linc's eyes. They were a sapphire blue, and she almost forgot to answer his question.

"Oh! Ummm, yeah, I mean, no! I don't mind at all," she spluttered. She blamed her quick answer on her ridiculous feelings toward Linc, despite her resolve to distance herself from these two. She didn't want to be reminded of him here, of all places. With their things right next to hers, she guessed she'd see more of them than she'd like.

Ellory seemed very sweet though, so Vela looked up, smiled at her and asked, "Do you mind if I put some music on? I brought my Bluetooth speaker, but I won't play it if it would bother you guys."

Ellory shook her head, her face burning red, and got to work laying down her and Vance's towels. Vela did the same with hers. Picking up her phone, she scrolled through her music, trying to pick something they wouldn't mind listening to. She tended to listen to pop and old songs from the fifties and sixties. She absolutely loved the Beatles, who played then. She chose one of her favorite playlists of great Beatles songs.

Once the music started, Ellory's head popped up from bending over her towel and she gushed, "The Beatles! I love them! They're the best band of all time! I mean, sorry," she said, realizing she had blurted that out. "I just love that band, too. It's nice to know a fan, like me." Her face was now a deep red and Vela's heart went out to her.

It had surprised Vela at Ellory's outburst, but wanting her to feel comfortable, she said, "I completely agree! They contributed so much to the music industry. I wish I had been born when they were performing concerts. I would have been one of their wild, screaming fans, for sure!"

Ellory looked like she had a lot to say, but she was holding her words in.

"You just made a best friend in my sister," Vance said, with a huge smile. "She has Beatles posters all over her walls in her room and owns more Beatles shirts than I own in my entire wardrobe." Laughing, he urged his sister, "Go on, be honest. People like honesty more than anything. You don't have to be ashamed of your crush on eighty-year-old men."

Ellory giggled, and Vela joined her. It felt good to laugh. She had been so stressed lately; she forgot how to let loose. And she was doing it with not one human, but two! Who would have thought?

"Do you guys want to help me get Jack to swim? If we throw this stick enough times, he'll eventually go after it," Vela asked, and picked up the stick by her foot. Surprised at herself for her offer, she fidgeted with the branch she had grabbed.

"Absolutely!" Vance said, tugging it from her hand. "Are you sure he'll let me? You said he was uneasy around manly men."

Vela laughed but in the corner of her eye, she saw Jack dash off into the brush. Her heart froze, and she whipped her head around to pinpoint what he was chasing.

"Jack!" she called, with no success at bringing him back. She watched as an orange fox darted through the brush, escaping for dear life with Jack hot on its trail.

Vela broke out in a cold sweat. Fear lodged in her chest. Jack was always with her, always. *I can't lose him!*

"Jack! Come back!" she called, and her heart sunk even further when he ignored her shout for the call of the wild.

Vela ran after him, crashing into the small brush that framed the trail, ignoring the stabs of pain in her legs and arms as she fought to chase after her disappearing dog.

"No, no, no," she breathed, looking around wildly for the last place she saw him, barely registering Vance and Ellory right behind her, catching up to her when she paused.

"Does he do this often?" Vance asked, looking around for a sign of Jack's rust colored coat.

"Never," Vela said, her voice breaking.

"We'll find him," Ellory promised, her voice sure for the first time Vela heard, and for that she was glad. Vela needed promises right now.

Vela heard, rather than saw, rumbling in the bushes ahead, then a growl sounded in the air, then a fierce barking.

"Jack! Stop! Come here!" Never had her heartbeat so wildly and froze at the same time as she waited to see if Jack would listen to her command. Terrified the fox would hurt Jack in defending itself, she strained her ears listening to any more sounds.

Protectprotectprotectcannotlosecannotlose.

Her mind spun with all the frightening possibilities of why he wouldn't respond to her calls. "Jack!" she called again. Vance and Ellory called for him, too.

Vela led the way to where she last heard him, but he had gone silent. Surely, she would have heard a fight between the two animals. She had only heard Jack barking. *Please God, let him be okay!*

"Jack, please come back," Vela whispered as she edged around a tree, searching the bushes and brush that made up the area. Vance and Ellory spread out, looking in other directions. Vela wanted to be in all places at once, but she couldn't, and that frustration gnawed at her fiercely.

"Do you guys see anything?" Vance asked, moving brush aside to investigate the smaller spaces.

Vela shook her head and despair rushed over her. She had always known where Jack was, to the point where her life was completely entwined with her beloved dog. He was more than a furry companion; he was her best friend. She felt lost without him.

Her heart lifted when she had a thought. She only knew of one thing Jack loved more than anything: when she used her gift. But to use it in front of humans was a serious infraction in her world, so she would need to be smart.

Sinking to the ground, she bowed her head and pretended to sob softly. This gave her access to the ground, and she sank her fingertips into the earth.

Spearing her gift into the hard red dirt, she sent a shock wave of power out as far as she could. The humans had no way of knowing it wasn't the wind perking up the surrounding plants, but her infusion of power they responded to.

"Come on Jack, you know you love this," she breathed under her breath. She sent another shock wave out, praying he would respond like he always did.

A happy barking filled her ears, and Vela's head whipped up to watch her beloved dog crashing through brush and bushes, bounding up to her and licking her face with an exuberance she matched.

"Jack! Jack, you came back!" Vela cried, burying her face into Jack's wiggling neck. Her heart soared, and a giant wave of relief crashed through her. He hopped up and placed his two giant paws on her shoulders to give him better access to her cheeks and nose.

She turned her head, saying, "Jack, I need to breathe, please, relax for a second." When really, she didn't for one moment want him to calm down. She wrapped her arms around his body and squeezed before he wiggled free.

He ran circles around her, and it thrilled Vela that she thought to use her gift to call Jack back.

Vela looked up to a stunned look on Vance and Ellory's faces. "Did you have a treat in your pocket or something?" Vance asked. "How did you get him back?"

"He must have lost sight of the fox," Vela said smoothly, rubbing circles on Jack's head. There was no way they would know the truth. Her face was a picture of relief, so they couldn't know she was lying through her teeth. It was the one time she felt no guilt at lying. It was for their protection.

"Come on guys, let's get out of here," Vela announced, getting up from her spot on the ground. She almost wished for Jack's leash in her hand, but he had never needed it before today.

"I'm so glad you found your dog," Ellory gushed as she fell into step at Vela's other side. Her right side currently keeping one dog very close to her. She did grip his collar, just in case.

"Thank you for helping me look," Vela said sincerely, meaning it, holding first Ellory's then Vance's gaze. "He... means a lot to me."

"I can tell," Vance said with a smile. "If this was my dog back home, I would have needed fifty treats to get him away from chasing anything. Brave dog, Jack is to chase down a fox, by the way."

"Yeah," Vela grinned. "He's not afraid of anything." As they walked back to the trail and the lake area, Vela almost didn't notice a change in the weather. Until an unusual burst of air threw her hair around, she thought the day had just turned windy. Holding her hair down, she studied the wind pattern more closely. Wind burst through the tops of the Cottonwoods that stood close to the water they had now reached.

Why would the wind be just at the tops of the trees and not through them entirely? And why was she feeling strange drops in the air pressure? Her ears were popping, and she continued to scan the area. The water was choppy in some places and not in others. That's when her eyes widened at her realization.

This was no windy day. She'd bet her life on it.

She didn't see any Boreans but knew some must be close. This was too much wind for one Elemental to be doing it all on their own, too. There must be several around. And that could only mean... her heart froze, and she tried to school her features so as not to alert her new human friends to her fears.

They were close to Vernal, a city that had a Borean border. Vela had never dreamed she would see it for herself. But, as the wind picked up, she knew she was right.

Vela was about to experience her very first boundary battle.

Chapter Eighteen

Vela called for Jack and was never happier to see he had returned to being an obedient dog. He came right to her. Vela rushed Vance and Ellory to their stuff and begged them to pack up quickly.

Vance stopped her frantic movements by holding onto her arms. He looked in her eyes with her fright reflected in them and asked, "It's just a little wind, Vela, don't worry, we'll be fine. What's the matter?"

"I just have a feeling it's going to be a bad storm. You guys need to go. Go back to your campsite and buckle down. I have a pretty good premonition about the weather. Please go inside somewhere." Vela pushed his hands off her arms and attempted to act normal. Collecting her things with shaking hands, she cringed when the wind bracketed up. It was getting worse.

Making sure Jack was right by her, she didn't know what she was going to do with him. They had a tent! Where was she going to hide him?

Vela pushed her new friends down the dirt lane that led back to the campsites and prayed for their safety. By helping her find Jack, they had ingratiated themselves to her, and she was thankful to have met them. But she needed to get to her family. The wind continued to howl, and she picked up her pace, rushing the three of them and Jack, ignoring their protests. But they soon quieted when the wind picked up even further.

Vela made it to her campsite first, and she watched as Vance and Ellory held onto each other as they walked back to their campsite as the wind threatened to push them off the path.

Whitney grabbed her attention when she called out, running toward her, "Vela! We need to get over to Moonshine Arch! That's the best cover we're going to get." Grabbing Vela's arms, she yelled, "Dad and I have already called the local Elders! They'll meet us there!"

"So, this is a boundary battle, then?" Her mom nodded and then Vela grabbed and pulled her back to her, crying in a frantic voice, "Where's Drew and Kane?"

"Your father is getting them. Come on! We need to get in the car and wait for them."

Vela dropped her bundle on the ground, wondering if they would survive this unscathed. She prayed as she ran to the car and, after getting Jack in, quickly buckled in with trembling fingers.

"And are you sure this place is the best place to go right now?" Vela asked.

Whitney started the car, looking out the windshield and windows for the rest of their family to make it in. "Yes. Those rock formations will protect us from the wind the best. Those Boreans will try to do a lot of damage with flying debris and even uprooting trees and bushes. We can deflect the ground cover, but it's in our best interest to be somewhere we can hide. Those huge rocks aren't going anywhere. "There they are!" she said with relief when she spotted her sons and husband running toward the car in the rearview mirror.

"What about the humans, Mom? How will they be safe?" Her breathing hitched, thinking about her new friends terrified they would get hurt in the crossfire.

"If they stay here, they should be safe. The Boreans will go after where we are, and we'll be at that Moonshine place. So, they should be fine. We'll make sure to evacuate that place of humans first, though. If the humans are smart, they'll leave on their own."

Vela's brothers and father jumped in. Her mom impressed her when she peeled out, backing out of their space in her rush to leave.

With her dad giving instructions to her mom on how to get to Moonshine Arch, Vela knew it would be a quick drive. If it was only a three-mile hike from the park, it would be even quicker in the car. Along the way, her parents made her promise to stay under the protection of the rock formations. They were very firm in saying that Vela was too young to fight back. They wanted her hidden.

Vela rebelled at the thought.

They would need her, and she intended on helping. A sudden hot anger filled her. This was too much, too dangerous. People could get hurt. People she cared about. She fisted her hands as they parked and practically fell out of the car in her haste to leave.

"Dad! Should I leave Jack in the car? What do I do with him?" Vela cried, trying to bring her voice above the noise of the wind howling.

"No," he yelled. "The car could flip in the wind. He's safer with you under the rock formations!"

They rushed toward the huge rocks and, at first, Vela's eyes went wide at the number of people who were there. But they weren't humans, she realized. They were Elementals. When she got closer, she understood. Gyans were gathering to counteract what the Boreans were doing. They must have come from the neighboring town.

Her vacation had just turned into a nightmare.

Vela had Jack close to her, and they followed her parents and brothers to the biggest orange rock formation she could see. Her mom tucked her and Jack into a niche in the rock wall. "Stay here, Vela. You cannot participate. You are not old enough. Do you understand?"

Vela hated lying to her, but she nodded, quickly agreeing. But as her mom ran off, Vela saw other Gyans were bringing other young Elementals to where she and Jack sat.

Looking around at the number of children being brought over, she knew she had an important job to do. To help protect these little girls and boys, most of whom were crying. With determination, she studied each one's terrified face and vowed to keep them all safe. She counted twelve kids.

Vela watched as her family and the other Gyans fanned out and waited for the Boreans to reveal themselves. They might not, preferring to hide so they couldn't be attacked. But the Gyans would flesh them out. The Boreans couldn't hide in nature for long. She grabbed the two kids closest to her and hugged them to her with Jack whining and laying in front of her. It was like he couldn't get close enough.

Vela could see several small swirls of air in different places from her vantage point. She knew from her classes that a Borean would create a vortex of air, but had to be relatively near it for it to sustain itself. By the looks of it, she and the other Gyans could now pinpoint where the Boreans were hiding. They needed to go after them! Vela approved when she noticed several Gyans run in the direction of the wind formations.

The vortices strengthened in size and power and Vela hoped her fellow Gyans made it to them quickly before they combined forces and created a monster sized tornado. Elementals were stronger when they put their powers together.

Vela bit her lip. She felt powerless sitting there and not doing anything. Huge rocks stood in her line of sight. She then saw that some vortexes she had seen in the sky were gone. Good, those Boreans must have been found and stopped.

Her peripheral vision had her whipping her head to the east. Several more vortexes climbed into the air. Her heart rate jumped. The wind gusts around her rose and she turned her head, only to see the same thing to the west was happening. They were surrounded and running out of time.

The Borean Elementals threatened the Gyans right now. They knew if the Gyans were scared enough of a devastating storm, they would give up. The Boreans could win this just by a demonstration. They could create a huge tornado capable of wiping out everything in its path.

Vela didn't know what she wanted. This wasn't her home, so she wasn't attached to it, like the Gyans who lived here. This was only supposed to be a vacation, but she wanted to support her fellow Gyans at the same time. Her heart tore. She didn't want to die or see her family hurt in this potential giant storm. Thinking of her new human friends, she also wanted to protect them, too. They were defenseless in this. She cried out to God for protection and instruction.

Almost as if in answer to her prayer, some of the wind swirls to the east popped out of existence. Hugging the kids to her side, she breathed in relief. Good, that meant they had to find the Boreans to the west. She sucked in a gasp when a figure popped up in front of her. Jack instantly jumped up and barked wildly at him. She didn't know the Gyans in the area, so she wasn't sure if she was looking at a Gyan or a Borean. She sensed something in him, but he wasn't close enough for her to sense what he was.

He stood tall and lean with a shock of blonde hair blowing in the wind. And by the wild and angry look Vela could see, she guessed he was a Borean. He held his arms out, and the wind picked up. That was her answer.

Chapter Nineteen

"YOU WOULD ATTACK KIDS, really?" Vela yelled, outrage coursing through her.

"You're all filthy Gyans. The guy was right. It's time you left. He said you all were going to attack us. But not if we attack you first. This place is ours," he growled.

Vela slowly stood, sliding up the rock face. She racked her brain about what guy he was talking about. Who would incite these Boreans? She had a bad suspicion. This had the E.E. written all over it.

Unsure if she should go on the attack or stay on the defensive, she stood tense and undecided. Jack did not have her indecisiveness. He jumped toward the Borean, teeth bared, his full body stretched out in a reach that would kill. With one sweep of his arm, the attacker threw a wind gust that shoved Jack away and her beloved dog yelped when he hit a rock face hard, his body sliding down, not moving.

"No!" Vela yelled. Her vision tunneled to meet the eyes of this Tasmanian Devil who would dare hurt her dog and threaten these innocent kids. She stepped forward and gestured for the kids to move behind her, and then stepped to the right to keep them out of this fight. Every atom in her body was primed and ready to do damage. She couldn't sense any roots underneath them—the immediate area was bare of any greenery — but she had other weapons in her arsenal.

The rocks around her answered her call. They would make fantastic weapons.

The Elemental threw currents of air at her with quick snaps of his hands; she dodged. Bending over, she winced and glanced at her arm where one current caught the side of it, slicing into her. Snapping her body in an upright position, she whipped her head at him and growled. Those were wind knives. Vicious and deadly. *He was going to pay for that;* her face twisted and fierce. With all her might, she threw every rock she could mentally grab at him.

Like her, he ducked, then covered himself with his arms, trying to fend off the storm of stones hitting his body. She was brutal in her assault, not allowing him to get up and counter what she was doing. While he cowered, she walked toward him, nailing him viciously.

Dropping her hold on the stones, Vela reached for him. She threw her knee up into his face, hearing a satisfying crunch. He looked up, blood spurting from his broken nose.

"I'm going to kill you for that," he snarled, his words garbled with blood that slid down his throat.

"You can try." Vela watched as he straightened. Fear uncurled through her. She knew a little hand-to-hand combat from the Elder classes but was no black belt. Making a quick decision, she'd use the little she knew and surprise him.

Before Vela could, however, he threw a punch. Her body instinctively swung to the right, avoiding his reach. Recovering quickly, she feinted with her left. When he flinched, he turned his head, leaving a perfect opening. She punched his trachea with her right fist, putting all her anger and strength into it. He dropped, choking, holding his neck and trying to breathe. She needed to get around some trees or bushes for offense and defense.

Vela ran back to the kids, herded them, did a quick count, and made sure she had all of them. Forcing them around the towering rock where they had been hiding, they went around to the back of it. She stopped for a minute, unsure where to take the children, and suddenly thought of Jack.

Hearing a branch snap, Vela turned to look behind her, when a violent wind picked her body up.

She spun wildly in twisting currents of air, wrenched from one direction to the other. The Borean pulled and jerked her like a rag doll. A burst of pain in her shoulder and then her knee had her crying out. *He was going to tear her apart!* The wind ripped around and through her and she couldn't gather her thoughts and will to defend herself. Just as Vela thought, all hope was lost. The winds disappeared. She dropped to the ground in a limp tangle of limbs. Somehow, her arms cushioned her head from hitting the ground. Moaning, she looked up.

Jack made her fiercely proud. He stood on top of the fallen and screaming Borean, who lay on his stomach with his face in the dirt. Jack ripped into the man's back and shoulder with a vicious bite. Jack had a good grip, and the Borean couldn't get up with Jack's ninety-seven pounds on him. The dog growled as his weight and bite held the man down. Vela couldn't be more proud and thankful that her protective dog was alright. He must have woken up and attacked him from behind. Now she could focus on the kids. This Wind Devil wasn't going anywhere with Jack there.

Vela tried getting up on her hands and knees and cried out, falling onto her left hip. Her right knee screamed in pain, and she bit down, clenching her teeth, trying to hold in her cries. Her right shoulder hung limply, and she couldn't move it. It had popped out. Her whole body felt sore, but other than her right knee and shoulder, everything else checked out.

She wished she could heal herself, but Gyans could only heal others, never themselves. No use wishing for something that couldn't happen.

Even though Jack had disabled the Borean, there were others out there. She looked around, assessing. Vela had to get the kids to a safer point. Squinting through the pain in her shoulder and knee, she looked around at all the huge rock faces. She quickly picked another rock face that had three faces and only one opening. She could defend that place; they would be safer there. A red-haired kid, who looked to be about ten, came up to her.

"Do you need help walking?" he asked in a raspy voice.

Grateful, she replied, "Yes, my knee and shoulder are shot. Thanks."

He nodded, then he motioned for a smaller boy with red hair, his brother by the looks of him, on her other side. Careful of her hurt shoulder, the brother tucked into her left side and wrapped his small arm around her waist. Being as gentle as they both could, they painstakingly helped her walk. The pain in her knee tore through her and she held back her cries as she told them which direction she wanted to go. The boys, sensitive to her breathless instructions, called out to the others to follow them.

They slowly made their way over to the huge rock face she had picked out that had a thin shelf of rock hanging over them. It looked like a squared upside down "U". She instructed the kids to hide behind one of the walls of rock. A menagerie of tall behemoth-sized red rocks stood around them, and small oak trees and bushes dotted the landscape. She nodded to herself; those roots will do. They could defend themselves from here. The kids can help. She would just tell them what to do.

Shouts sounded, alerting her again to the fight raging around her. Scanning the skies, she grew alarmed at the number of vortices dotting the view. They had grown in number and strength.

"What's happening, miss?" asked a gap-toothed young boy. His face scrunched with worry. He and the others all looked to her for good news. She had none to give.

Trying to breathe through the waves of pain radiating from mostly her knee, she said, "We need to take cover, boys and girls. You're all going to be fine," she assured them. Vela didn't know how to tell them that the Boreans were about to make a power move that could kill them all. An idea sprang, one she couldn't ignore. Shutting her eyes, she shook her head, but it took root, forcefully and aggressively. No one had ever done this before, as far as she knew.

Vela opened her eyes and projected more confidence in her voice. More than she had. She ordered, "Let's sit in a circle. Sit as close as you can. We're going to do something together." She looked them all over, determining how old they were and trying to remember her skill level at their ages. "No matter what, listen closely to me. Do exactly what I say, okay? Or do the best you can, at least."

The way the skies were combining forces into one giant storm, this wild and crazy plan was the only one she could come up with. It would destroy the plant life in the area, a casualty she regretted. Hopefully, her parents and the other Gyans would recognize her plan and hide behind the many rock faces and combine forces with her small unit of tiny fighters. Like the Wind Devils, which she had taken to calling the Borean Elemental, Gyans could bring their powers together to do major damage.

As her plan cemented in her mind, she saw that the children had listened well. They sat in a tight circle and even joined hands. They were all looking up at her, waiting for her next command. A mixture of emotions—fear, worry and uncertainty crossed their faces, but the dominant one she wore too: pure determination.

The red-haired boys helped Vela hop with her one good leg over to the tight circle and balanced her until she awkwardly bent, somehow sitting with her bad leg stretched out in front of her. She took a minute, breathing through her nose, trying to manage the pain her knee caused her. The brothers sat on either side of her. With her good hand, she grasped one brother's hand, then nodded toward her limp hand, directing the other brother to grab it, trying not to wince as he carefully took hold. Once he did, she spoke slowly, choosing her words to make the most impact on these young minds.

"These storms you see everywhere are going to do something bad. It will become one enormous storm. But we are going to turn their attack into our weapon." Searching their eyes, she willed bravery and confidence into them. "This won't be easy. But we can do this. You're all powerful Gyans, remember that. We will not allow our parents to be hurt without our help. I believe in each of you. You need to dig deep and give this all your energy, all your fight! We won't let those Borean Devils hurt those we love!"

A wild light entered the children's eyes as her words registered. Fierce pride and a will to protect what was theirs took over each face, even the youngest, who looked to be about six years old. Fear left their faces to be released into the very winds blowing all around them.

Vela explained as best she could about her plan and watched carefully to be sure the kids all understood her. Satisfied she had done the best she could, she studied the storm.

Looking up, her stomach dropped as she watched the tornado the Wind Devils had threatened them with all along finally form. Smaller vortices fed into a giant destructive tornado, and its enormous form made Vela's determination falter. Doubt coursed through her, and she wasn't sure if her plan would work.

This was a Hail Mary and she knew it.

Vela focused on her small band of warriors. They were wide-eyed watching the tornado take shape, but at her nod, they closed their eyes and intense concentration filled their expressions. She, too, dug deep within her and grabbed onto the well of power she had within her. With their hands held, they shared energy, and she focused on filling herself with the boost in power. Every ounce of strength she owned went into this attack, and she noted when each child nodded until they were ready.

"Now!" she yelled as loudly as she could, turning it into a war cry.

Big and small trees and bushes ripped from their roots and, with a sweep of her one good hand, she and the kids slung them into the deadly storm.

"Keep going!" Vela screamed. "Get the rocks, get every single thing you can grab!"

Vela watched with hope in her eyes and willed her plan to act in the way she had imagined.

Strain etched into the faces of her young charges, but soon, Vela could see that more vegetation than her little group could manage flew into the storm. Fellow Gyans flung trees and bushes from a field. The others were joining forces with them! Others could see what she was doing.

Vela's breath caught in her throat when she saw the storm move. The Devils were counterattacking by moving the storm toward their little group. She watched as Gyans searched for Boreans responsible for this cyclone. One, no two found Boreans hiding, and they fought using a mixture of hand-to-hand fighting and their elements. One Borean blew a Gyan back, and she watched with horror as he landed hard on his back and did not get back up. The Borean then returned his focus to the storm, fueling it with his power, too.

With her teeth gritted, she threw as much power as she could into ripping up every tree and bush and throwing it into the storm. She had to help her fellow Gyans! With her group combining powers, she felt a rush fill her close to bursting of combined energy. These kids might be small, but they packed a punch. Pulling energy from the vegetation she was killing anyway, she put all her focus, all her strength into this fight for their lives.

With the trees disappearing, Vela could see more of the figures controlling the storm. Men and women dotted the landscape in front of her. A group of about twenty stood with their hands raised, their stances confident and strong.

Until the winds started turning in the Gyan's favor.

The storm started spitting out debris, flying around the storm faster than bullets. And faster than the Devils could block, much to Vela's immense satisfaction. Cries sounded from the exposed Boreans as they were being knocked down left and right with projectile missiles from their own tornado.

The Gyans were manipulating the projectiles easily, slinging them away from themselves, but the Boreans weren't as lucky. They couldn't feed the storm and block at the same time. In fact, she could see that most of the Boreans had abandoned the tornado and were fending off the branches and bushes firing at them.

Her plan was working!

Where Vela and the kids hid behind the rock wall, it shielded them from the debris. The Boreans started getting the same idea and fled to the other rock faces around Vela. She prepared herself if any got the idea of coming to her hiding spot. The storm began losing strength. She pumped her good arm and felt like jumping with exhilaration, but sadly, her leg would never allow it in its condition.

"Keep it up, kids! It's helping! We're almost done! You're doing great!"

She gripped her good hand tighter, the stress of the moment causing sweat to make it slip a little. They just needed a few more moments, and this whole thing would be over.

"I can't go much longer, miss," one of the brothers yelled, his hand slipping from hers. Even connected, their limit was fast approaching. The energy that had coursed through her waned. She could feel her little group struggling.

"Almost there." Between the tearing pain in her knee and her limp shoulder and her energy lagging, she almost dropped in exhaustion. A child slumped over, breathing in and out harshly.

The tornado had shrunk in size and had stopped moving along the ground. Her hair, instead of lifting and blowing around her face, had died down a little.

The children hunched their shoulders, eyes shut tight, and exhaustion lined their small faces. She admired her little warriors, who were going strong and waiting for her to tell them to stop. It was time. Vela couldn't tax them too much.

"Stop!" Instantly, their shared connection fell away. Vela let go of the hands she held, but she continued finding plants and throwing them into the storm, using the last of her strength.

She bent her head and trained her eyes on the ground to concentrate as much as she could. She was rewarded.

Within a few minutes, the winds died down dramatically. Vela looked up. The storm dissipated. Everything whirling around within it crashed to the ground in a heap of tangled branches, roots, and leaves.

A cry went up, Gyans cheering and grabbing each other as they hugged and cried. Many were walking toward and guarding the fallen Borean Devils and the ones hiding behind the many rock faces. There would never be another name for them, in her mind. They were Tasmanian Devils, in the flesh forever.

A tear slipped from Vela's eye, and she sank into the dirt, as much relief filling every part of her as the pain of her injuries. Her adrenaline faded, and she slipped into a kind of daze.

"Vela!" her mom cried, dropping to the ground with her. She ran her hands over Vela to determine where she was injured.

"I need Drew," her mom said under her breath as she studied Vela's knee. She ran her hands over Vela's shoulder, but she barely felt it when her mom popped it back into place. She knew her mother would have dulled the pain, but she should have felt *something* when it happened. Shock had settled into her bones like a weight, dragging her into a coma-like state. The enormity of what she and the children had instigated threw her mind into a buzzing hive of wasps, stinging her with surprise over and over again.

"Where's Drew?" her mom asked, looking over her shoulder. "He's the best at healing, and I don't think I would do the right kind of healing for this knee. Vela, *what* made you think of the crazy idea of flooding the tornado with trees?" Her eyes looked wide with disbelief.

Vela shook her head slowly. She focused her bleary gaze on her mom. "I don't even know. I just thought that the storm would kill us all and those kids were so helpless until they weren't. Did you see what they did? Where are they, by the way?"

"their parents are collecting them. I saw from a distance what you and the kids started, and it was brilliant! I am so proud of you, Vela."

As Vela looked around, she saw Drew and Kane come around the corner of the large rock wall. "Mom?" Drew asked, eyeing Vela. "Need some help?"

"Yes," her mom said briskly. "Drew, come here and see what you can do with this knee. It's torn in every direction I can see. I've dulled the pain, but the rest I need you to look at."

He settled by Vela's leg and ran his hands over the damaged tissues, examining them carefully.

"Will it heal alright?" Vela asked anxiously.

"Give me a minute, Vels. I need to really concentrate. What happened to you? Why is your knee like this?"

"A Borean got me in a wind funnel, and it pulled me in ways I shouldn't move. You should see the other guy, though."

"Where is this guy?" Kane growled.

"Jack has his teeth in him currently. Back there," Vela motioned with her chin behind her.

Kane promptly left.

Drew grunted in acknowledgement, then went to work. She could feel his efforts, a tug in her kneecap, a pressure first on one side of her knee than another. Thankfully, because of her mom managing the pain, she didn't feel a thing. Before she knew it, he had finished, breathing hard from the effort it took to heal her.

"All done?" her mom asked, standing at Drew's side.

"Yes," he said tiredly and picked himself up off the ground. "I think it healed nicely. She should be fine."

"Drew, you're a miracle worker!" Vela exclaimed, bending her knee and unbending it. "I'm so glad you're going into the field. You'll make a wonderful doctor."

"I wish I could help humans like I'll help Elementals," he commented, frowning.

"You'll be the best doctor they've ever seen, regardless of healing them in our way," her mom said, putting her hand on Drew's shoulder.

Vela rolled the shoulder her mom re-set. She was a little sore but in much better condition than before. "Thank you, Mom, thank you, Drew," she said in a heartfelt tone. "Thank God we're Gyans and have this ability. I almost feel bad for the other clans. They don't have our ability to heal."

"The other clans get by just fine," her mom commented. "They take a little longer to heal, but they have gifts we don't, and we get by without those, too."

Vela nodded. If this Chosen Child she had heard about came, their world would be so different. Helping each other would be commonplace.

Exuberant licking all over face helped Vela come back to her senses.

"Jack!" she croaked. Her chest swelled with love for her big, beautiful animal. "You're the best dog!" She dug her face into Jack's neck and hugged his wiggling form. "You saved my life, you big oaf! I love you!" Tears leaked onto Jack's fur, and he finally sat, sneaking licks onto her wet face now and then.

Her mom pointed around her at the families collecting their young ones, now milling around where she lay in the dirt. "I think they want to talk to you, sweetie."

"Talk to me? Why?"

"We want to thank you," a tall burly man said, with a shock of red hair.

"You must be the twins' father," she said with a smile.

He nodded. "We just wanted someone to keep an eye on our boys. We never thought you would mastermind a genius plan and put them to work at it," the man boomed in a deep voice. He was the equivalent of what a lumberjack looked and sounded like in Vela's mind, his look complete with red flannel and jeans. Both boys moved close to his side, and he held them in a protective gesture. His face beamed and Vela smiled back.

Her mom helped her stand up. In her peripheral vision, she could see the other parents coming closer.

One woman hugging a young girl close to her said with a grateful look in her eyes, "I never thought my Betsy would help fight. I just wanted her somewhere safe. And look what they did. What you had them do. It's amazing what happened it is. Thank you, miss."

Others murmured their agreements, all wearing thankful expressions.

"We're indebted to you," the lumberjack father said, talking for all of them. "You and our kids saved the day today. We won't be forgetting that."

"Everyone helped," Vela insisted. "We couldn't have done it without all of you aiding us."

"We never would have won this, if it wasn't for your idea. This is your victory, young lady, and that's a fact we all know and agree with," the lumberjack said firmly.

Whitney's face beamed with pride and Vela ducked her head, embarrassed by all the attention.

"Just say thank you, darling, because he's right," her mom said, squeezing Vela's hand.

Obediently, Vela said, "Thank you, but everyone did help. And I couldn't be prouder of your kids. They won the day. I couldn't have done this without them."

Clapping suddenly started, and a blush crawled over Vela's face, burning into her skin. She walked over to a brown-haired girl, who looked eight or nine. Vela held up her hand in a high five, but the girl took one look at her hand and lurched toward Vela, knocking her back and squeezing her stomach tight.

Vela laughed. She squeezed the girl back, but another child surprised her by latching onto her back, wrapping their arms around her. Another one hugged her from the side and yet another on her only free side. More and more joined in this impromptu group hug. A mixture of giggles and laughter rose from the crowd of children, and Vela's heart felt like it would burst.

This result had been an answer to a prayer, and she thankfully bowed her head and whispered another prayer of thanks.

Somehow, amid all the commotion, she heard her brothers and dad's voices asking what was going on.

Thinking of how brave the children had been, she raised her voice to be heard over the fuss they were making. "You guys are my heroes. You were fearless, and you will always, in my mind, be my little band of warriors. I'd be honored to go into battle with you anytime."

At that, a cheer went up and the kids all started jumping. As they held her, she had to jump or they would jostle her into another injury.

Happily, she complied.

Her brothers joined her warrior's group and jumped and laughed along with her.

Jack added to the celebration, barking and running circles around their group. *This experience couldn't be more perfect.*

With that thought, Vela just enjoyed the moment.

✦

Chapter Twenty

Exhausted, Vela's family limped home, or to their temporary home, anyway. The campsite looked relatively unscathed by the horror of the storm they'd all faced in Moonstone Arch. Three miles must have been enough of a distance to prevent any major damage to the small campground, and for that, Vela was thankful.

Sunset crawled across the sky, giving a filtered light to some of the mess the distant tornado did cause. Tree limbs littered the ground, some in the campsites and some on the gravel road that stretched through the campground.

"Vela!" Turning toward the direction of her name, Vela saw that Ellory and Vance ran over to where she stood. Relieved they were alright, she waved at them. They wore twin expressions of disbelief and, as they reached her, they enveloped her into yet another group hug. *They must have felt bonded with me over finding Jack, too,* Vela thought happily as she accepted their hugs.

"Are you guys alright?" Vance exclaimed as he held her at arm's length. "There was a tornado just west of us! I don't know how it missed us, but thank God it did!"

Ellory looked around and asked, "Where's Jack? Is he okay?"

"He's just fine don't worry about him. He saved my life," Vela blurted.

Releasing her, Vance looked her over and asked, "How?"

"Well…" Vela faltered. She had said too much. Her body froze. How could she explain that away easily? "Ummm."

"Vela," her dad appeared from around their car, saving her from answering. "Who are your friends?"

"Uh, Dad," Vela said, swinging her arms. She had never been so glad to see him. "Meet Ellory and Vance. They're a brother and sister I met earlier this afternoon."

Vance glanced at her family's car and asked, "Where are you guys coming back from? You didn't stay at the campsite during the storm?"

Unsure how to answer, Vela's dad saved her.

"We were in the area," he said vaguely, "but went over to Moonshine Arch after the storm because we heard some people needed help being evacuated." Putting his arm across Vela's shoulder, said, "So, we helped in any way we could."

And by help, Vela recalled what they had to do to make the area look like a tornado had blown through. The uprooted bushes and trees dumped in one place after the storm dissolved were a dead giveaway something unnatural happened. To avoid attention, they scattered the vegetation around like the cyclone had passed through.

Nodding, Vela asked, "Did your camp have any damage? Are you guys in tents or an RV?"

"Tents," Ellory quickly answered. "Shockingly enough, we didn't have any damage to our car. Our tents, of course, blew apart, but we holed up in the bathrooms during the storm."

"Good," Vela said, crossing her arms. Her body protested her standing up. She needed to lie down, pronto.

"You look dead on your feet," Ellory said. "We'll see you tomorrow. Come on Vance." She grabbed her brother's arm and began pulling him away.

"Are you guys leaving tomorrow?" Vance asked, pulling his arm away from his sister.

Vela looked at her dad for an answer. He shook his head. "We're actually leaving today."

Vance's face fell. "Oh okay. Well, do you have Insta? We can keep in touch that way," he said to Vela hopefully. "And you can tell me how Jack saved your life." He laughed like she had been kidding about Jack saving her. She hoped he thought that.

She nodded, told him her Instagram name, then watched as he allowed himself to be led away by his sister. After watching them leave, she uncrossed her arms and wearily turned toward her tent.

"Vela," her dad's deep voice stopped her from moving. It held censure, and Vela didn't know if she had the energy to follow the coming conversation. She knew what was coming.

"They're *humans*."

"I know." Vela hung her head.

"You know you can't continue this friendship. It's too dangerous." She looked back up and his gaze held an unrelenting sternness she knew he wouldn't back away from.

"I *know.*"

"And what was he talking about, Jack saving you? How did he know that?"

Her shoulders slumped. "It slipped out." She rubbed her face. "I didn't know how to take it back."

"He seemed to think you were kidding."

"Yeah, I got pretty lucky, I think. I hope so anyway."

Putting his hand on her shoulder, he nodded, understanding her position. "Let's hope he thinks it was a joke then."

Vela watched him walk away. She wondered if this kind of close call had happened to him, too, that he must have befriended humans in the past. And had to give them up. To protect them.

It was the only way. But she wondered with social media if things could be different for her and her new friends.

Weary beyond measure, she went to her tent repairing where the stakes had pulled free, even if they were just going to break it down soon. She needed a nap. Vela found her phone in the car, where she had left it before the storm, relieved to see it had some power still in it. Crawling into her tent, she flopped on to the sleeping bag. Too tired to even turn over to her back, her preferred sleeping position, she just lay there and willed her mind to sleep.

The problem was, she couldn't turn her thoughts off. They revolved around all that had happened and her subsequent break up with two perfectly good friends she had made that day.

Vela forgot she still held onto her phone when it buzzed in her hand. She looked down and saw that Linc messaged her.

> **Linc:** Hey Flower Girl, hope you are having a great weekend in Utah. I'm going to ask you to go somewhere with me, but don't shoot me down immediately. I have to tell you it's the best flower shop in town. I thought you'd have fun dreaming.

Vela smiled, her depressed feelings over losing her human friends lifting a little bit.

> **Vela:** Wow. You really go for the big guns.
> **Linc:** I'm nothing if not a go big or go home kind of guy. ;)

Vela: I never pictured you as a winking guy.
Linc: There's a LOT you don't know about me, Flower Girl! So, are you distracting me on purpose?
Vela: Not really. I would love to check out that shop. Maybe?
Linc: :(
Vela: Believe me, I'd much rather be home doing that. I've had just about the worst weekend ever.
Linc: Talk to me, Flower Girl.

Vela smiled again and quickly typed out a condensed version of what had happened.

Linc: Are you seriously telling me you fought in a boundary battle? Are you okay? Injured at all?
Vela: I'm a Gyan, remember? Awesome healing abilities.
Linc: Right. But were you injured?
Vela: Yes. My mom and brother took care of it. A Borean got me in a wind funnel. Almost tore me apart.
Linc: What? I wish I was there. That wouldn't have happened.
Vela: I can take care of myself, Linc.
Linc: Obviously not.

Vela's mouth hung open in shock. She may have gotten hurt, but she held her own against that Borean before he snuck up behind her and trapped her in wind. And thankfully she had a kick-butt dog who had her back. She did *not* need a knight in shining armor. Especially one with an attitude. She powered down her phone, not wanting to see any more messages from him.

"Vela!" her dad called. "Get that tent broken down. We're going home."

Slumping into her sleeping bag, she groaned. Looked like she'd have to get a nap on the drive home.

Chapter Twenty-One

"Go team go! Go-oooo Hawkeyes!" the cheerleaders chanted, and Vela winced. Not a fan of pep rallies, she tolerated them, usually only for Elia, who loved to cheer their high school team on.

A week had passed by since the Linc text-incident, she was calling it, and Vela was still as mad about Linc's insensitive comment as when he had first made it. She had finally gotten some of her Gyan friends' attention off her, too. When they had found out about the boundary battle, there were endless questions and they exhausted her with wanting to know every detail. She didn't mind reliving it once or twice, but the cajillion times it took to satisfy their curiosity seemed excessive.

Vela looked around after she had skirted the cheerleading team on the sidelines in the gym. Avoiding the Gyans, she looked around for her trusty best friend to sit with, hoping she sat alone.

When her school had pep rallies on Fridays, normally she would half-heartedly cheer along with Elia just to make her happy. The crush of people and the hot, stifled air made her feel sick, but she weathered it. And she didn't want to see Linc now any more than she did Monday when she had returned from the disastrous weekend in Utah.

His statement that she couldn't properly defend herself still made her blood boil. He had really hurt her with that small but powerful comment, and she played the avoidance dance with him. Again.

They were spending more time apart than together.

She just couldn't face him until she could have a productive conversation with him. So far, Vela had been successful in keeping her distance. She thought he wouldn't give her space, but he wasn't pushing himself on her, which surprised her. Not to look a gift horse in the mouth, she looked back on the week, not able to decide if she really wanted Linc to be distant or if she wanted an apology. Was he avoiding giving her one? Until she knew, having an audience right now would be a good thing, and she wouldn't have to be alone with him just yet.

Before the comment, Vela had wanted to get to know her Intended. She would have looked around the gym for his tall, dark form to catch his eye. She shook her head, because that was neither here nor there right now. And almost forgot that she would sense when he was nearby and so didn't need to worry about running into him. But would that be such a bad thing? She thought about it again.

Why shouldn't I demand an apology? Why wait for it? Maybe I should have it out with him with tons of witnesses around.

It would force him to be civil and give her a chance to speak her mind. She would not put up with a cocky, rude attitude from anyone.

With that thought, Vela looked around the gym again. Not feeling his presence, she realized there must be a limit to how far she could sense him. Spotting his dark head with dark shirt and pants across the gym, she could see he was there, almost directly opposite her.

Walking as fast as she could, she walked over to the other side of the gym and toward the set of bleachers that contained Linc. She wished Elia was with her to bolster her confidence and wondered where she was in the large gym. Vela had filed in with her calculus class and had not seen her best friend, yet.

The closer she walked toward Linc, however, the more aware she was of his presence. She relied purely on her instinct at that point, and her senses began screaming at her, telling her when he was close. Analyzing these feelings coursing through her, she didn't know if she could get used to them. She heard from her parents as time went by, Intendeds got used to the feeling and the exhilaration never dampened, more like mellowed.

"Vela!" Elia jumped up and down in the aisle above her. Vela climbed the steps near where Linc sat.

Reaching her, she was relieved to have inadvertently found her friend, then looked over her shoulder at Linc.

"Vela, I saw you heading this way and figured you had seen me! I'm so glad you did!"

People surrounded Linc. *Wait*, she thought darkly, *Is that Maria standing next to him?* She growled under her breath.

"Vela, did you even hear me?"

Vela turned back to Elia. "Sorry, what did you say?"

Scanning where Vela had been looking, understanding settled in Elia's eyes. "Ah, I see. You were distracted."

"Yes, sorry."

Vela's gaze turned toward a sight that tore at her heart. A girl struggled to walk up the stairs and Vela put her hand up to stop Elia's questions. She wanted to help this girl. It looked like she had a disability that made walking difficult and climbing near impossible. When she twisted her body to yank her legs up the steps and pulled herself up a stair, Vela's heart went out to her.

"Hold on Elia." Vela jumped up and ran down to where the girl struggled at the bottom of the steps.

Vela reached her and a rush of anger went through her at the number of people who shoved their way around the struggling girl, bumping into her as they rushed past. Not wanting to offend the girl who had finally noticed Vela standing a couple steps above her, Vela asked, "Would it be easier if you leaned on me, and I helped you?" Vela asked with a soft smile on her face, hoping it came across as helpful and not pitying.

The girl's eyes furrowed, and she looked down, hiding her face.

"Please don't take this the wrong way," Vela begged. "I just want to help."

"No," the girl finally said. Her breathing was rough, as if the few steps she had managed took a lot out of her. "It would help. I just wish I didn't need it," she said as yet another person pushed their way around her and now Vela.

"We all need help sometimes," Vela said gently, glaring at the rude student over her shoulder. She returned her attention to the girl. "Some just need it more than others. May I?" When the girl nodded reluctantly, Vela leaned over to wrap her arm around her, then asked, "What's your name?"

"Julia, but my friends call me Jewels."

Vela smiled and said, "Jewels, then. Let's get a seat, shall we?" All the seats close to the ground were taken and so, up they had to go. Vela had been looking down at her new acquaintance, so when Jewels startled at someone new leaning into the two of them, Vela looked up.

And came within an inch of Linc smiling at them both. Shocked, she jumped too, but with her hold on Jewels, she couldn't back up. "Linc! What are you doing?" His proximity made her blood sing, and she quickly became short of breath.

"The same thing as you, obviously" His eyes twinkled, and he stepped down to wrap his arm around Jewels' other side. "Hi Jewels," he said casually, like they were good friends. Maybe they were.

"Hey Linc," Jewels said, rolling her eyes.

"We go way back," Linc said to Vela with a smile.

"All of two weeks," Jewels returned, smirking.

"I told her I have never met such a needy damsel in distress."

"And *I* told *him*, I am never needy, just a little helpless is all," Jewels stated firmly.

Vela's eyes went wide with how comfortable they seemed around each other.

"And I said, even her name sounds like a damsel to me." Linc's comment only made Jewels laugh.

It shouldn't surprise Vela that Linc had made a friend in Jewels, but she couldn't help it. She *was* surprised. It warmed her, and she smiled gratefully at Linc. She had noticed Jewels around school but had never helped or talked to her before. Jewels was also human, so there was that. Linc, again, obliterated all notions of not befriending humans.

"On the count of three," Linc said, bringing Vela's attention to him, as he nodded at her over Jewels' head. "We'll both help her walk up the stairs."

Vela's right arm held on tight and with her other hand feeling useless, she took hold of Jewels' arm with her left hand. Once Linc counted down, Vela laughed when Linc then said, "And away we go!"

It was slow going, but with her and Linc's help, they soon reached where Linc had been sitting with his friends.

He looked down at Jewels, who looked around uncertainly and asked gently, "Want to sit with me?"

Maria glared at Vela from her spot in the row like it was Vela's fault Linc left to help Jewels. Vela glared back at her until Maria looked away. Vela looked over the rest of his friends and noticed some of them were the ones who had pushed and shoved their way past Jewels to get to their seats.

Jewels must have noticed the same thing, because she shook her head firmly. Linc frowned at his friends, then looked over at Vela and asked with his eyes if Vela would offer to have her sit with her.

Of course she would.

"Jewels," Vela said brightly. "There's a friend of mine I'd like you to meet. We'd love it if you sat with us. It's just a couple more steps up."

Linc's eyes looked warmly at her, and she forgot why she had been mad at him. Nodding again at her, they both helped, nearly lifting Jewels completely off her feet up a couple more steps. Linc's strength alone could have done the job easily, but she was glad to have helped.

Elia's eyes, once they reached her, were wide but welcoming. She nodded at Jewels and Vela said, "Elia, meet my new friend, Jewels."

Elia scooted over the bench to make room, smiling brightly at the new girl. Vela was glad Elia didn't have a sympathetic look to her. In the short time Vela had met her, Jewels seemed pretty independent, which Vela respected enormously.

Once Jewels settled onto her seat, Linc said to Elia, "She's the neediest damsel in distress I ever saw."

Vela and Jewels both said, "Not needy, just a little helpless." And they both looked at each other and laughed.

"Well, I'll leave you girls to chat," Linc said, chuckling. "I know that's what you like to do."

"So, first I'm needy, now I'm a mindless chatterbox?" Jewels asked, crossing her arms over her chest. But her eyes sparkled, so Vela knew she was kidding.

"I have never met a mouthier chick in all my life, either," Linc said with a straight face, but he fought a grin.

Vela, Elia, and Jewels all cried out together and shooed him away from their seat. He laughed as he left.

"He was talking about me, right?" Jewels asked, still grinning. "Or was he talking about you?"

Vela looked at her with mock horror. "Me mouthy? Never!"

"Okay," Jewels said, squirming to get comfortable in her seat. "He *must* have been talking about you, then."

Laughing, Elia nodded and said, "Probably."

Vela watched Linc as he bled seamlessly back into his crowd of friends. Being a part of Linc's selfless act warmed Vela's heart more than words could say. Talking months with a guy could not show Vela more about Linc's character than what she witnessed him doing and had been doing. He had left his seat to help someone who needed a little kindness. She could see herself friends with this kind of Linc.

Even if he was a misogynistic pig at other times.

She could work with this. A little disappointed he didn't blow off his rude friends to sit with them, she shrugged to herself. Maybe he knew Jewels would like a little girl time. She then glared at the back of Maria's head, wishing she'd leave her Intended alone.

He must have felt her eyes on him because he looked over his shoulder. He smiled, nodding warmly at her. Smiling back at him, her eyes full of gratitude, she nodded back.

"So, Jewels," Vela heard Elia ask, "what grade are you in?"

Vela looked over at them when Jewels sighed heavily and answered, "A senior. Finally. The end of the year can't come fast enough."

They both laughed, commiserating with her. "We are, too," Vela said. "How come I haven't seen you until recently? Are you new?"

"Yes," she answered with a frown. "As if it's not hard enough to have this," she gestured to her legs and back. "I transferred here this year."

Vela's heart went out to her again. "That is hard. I can't believe you had to change schools your senior year. Where are you from?"

"Denver, I transferred here from South High."

"Wow," Elia breathed, "Close enough to stay in touch with good friends, but…"

"Far enough to lose touch, too," Jewels finished, her eyes sad.

Vela looked at Jewels. She was small, a little taller than Elia, maybe five foot five. She had a pixie look about her, with a cute face, brown curly hair that came to her shoulders. She held herself well, looking around at where they sat with an intelligent gaze and a curious one, even with melancholy in her eyes. As Vela watched, Jewels' sadness melted away and a conscious decision seemed to have her sitting up straighter, determined to enjoy the moment. With her sitting, Vela would never guess she had a condition that made it difficult to walk. She wondered what it was.

"Where do you sit at lunch?" Vela asked. With Jewels' head turned, she couldn't see Elia's wide eyes, but Vela sure did. What could she do? Not befriend someone who obviously needed a friend or two? She also couldn't help but wonder if, as a Gyan, she could heal this girl of her malady. She, again, wanted to know what it was. Maybe Drew could help. Before she could think more about it, Jewels' answer surprised her, and made her more resolved to befriend this girl. And then, shook off her notion to try to heal this girl. That was a big no-no.

"I eat in the library." Jewels shrugged. "It's easier than walking all the way to the cafeteria, only to not know..."

"Where to sit?" Elia finished gently. She looked at Vela with understanding in her eyes, but also a little warning.

That was right. Vela had seen Jewels in the library during lunch now that she thought about it.

Vela thought about the friends she had resumed sitting with at lunch. How could Vela bring Jewels over to a table full of Gyans? They might not be as accepting as she and Elia of Jewels, and then there's the issue of their conversations. They would all have to be careful what they said around her.

She and Elia could get around that. "Well, you can sit with Elia and I."

It was like what Linc had said about not choosing friends. Sometimes they chose you. And this felt like that. Making a decision for Elia without discussing it with her probably wasn't wise, but she couldn't sit by after today and know this charming girl sat alone in the library eating lunch. "That's if you want to make the trip to the lunchroom."

Jewels smiled prettily, "That sounds great! I guess I could make the trip."

Eating lunch with a human wasn't the same as inviting her into their lives. Vela looked at Elia intently, telling her with her eyes, they would figure it out. In Vela's mind she could see her sharing a different table with just Elia and Jewels and might she venture to say, Linc?

She would see what happens with this infuriating boy. But, looking at her new friend, her old friend, then at her

Intended below her, she thought she could get on board with that scenario.

This small act today seemed insignificant by itself, but to her she knew it was a good place to be in this strange dynamic she and Linc were in. To start a friendship or more, she couldn't say. The rest of the pep rally continued on in a blur, as Vela planned the next steps she would take to forging a friendship with her Intended.

Chapter Twenty-Two

VELA WALKED TO HER first period class the next Tuesday, dodging rushing students as they all tried to make the bell. She was late for the second time this week. Vela blamed it on her conflicting feelings about Linc making her lose sleep, and when she had finally gotten some rest, had ignored her alarm.

She had spent the weekend with Elia, who had successfully distracted her from thinking about her Intended, but Vela still had reservations about facing him today. She had even texted with Jewels a few times, who, it turned out, had a great sense of humor and had her cracking up all weekend. Linc had texted her too, but she either ignored him or gave him short answers.

Over the past several days, she struggled with her feelings. To invite Linc into her life was welcoming him... with his fire. Fire was her worst fear. She was trying to come to terms with the fact that fire was what Linc embodied, carried around inside himself. With the thought that he was flame, her heart instantly pounded, and her temples would sweat.

She looked at her hand, with its mangled scars, as it twitched against her leg and terrible memories crept into her mind. Before she could stop them, a sudden onslaught of sensory feelings ambushed her. She stopped and shut her eyes, her body stiff with tension. The scent of smoke, flames licking up a wall, and the sounds of whimpers assaulted her.

Lord, help! She fisted her hands, willing her mind to shut down, to forget. She needed to hide behind her wall again; it was the only chance of staying sane. Vela pictured it going as high as it could in her mind. Every fear, every thought, she pushed behind it.

People brushed by her as she fought for control. She didn't care. She would not move until she was victorious once more.

Her body began to slowly relax. Her method was working. Shoving and forcing every memory she didn't want behind the wall, she recovered her peace. When it was safe to do so, she opened her eyes and took a calm breath, thankful it was easy and not shaky.

Gripping her bag slung over her shoulder, she marched into her class, well after the late ball rang. Her teacher gave her the stink eye, but thankfully, didn't bark at her for being late. With every step to her desk, Vela thanked God for helping her calm down. Repressing her trauma might not be the healthiest way of dealing with her past, but for now, it was all she was capable of. Vela also ignored the fact that Linc's gaze burned into her back when she sat in the only available seat in front of the classroom.

After a ten-minute intro worksheet, her teacher assigned an essay you had to do with a partner. Vela picked up her backpack and determinedly walked over to Cassie's desk, when an arm was thrown over her shoulder and she was pulled into the side of a tall body. It was not Linc.

"What's up, good lookin'?" the voice drawled in her ear.

"Evan," she groaned. "Not today." She swatted his arm away and glared up at him. She did not need this right now.

He threw his arm back over her shoulder and said, "What? You're not taken. Who's stopping me?"

"Um, me." She firmly moved his arm away from her again and moved a couple of steps away.

"Come on, Vela, do this assignment with me. Be my partner," Evan begged.

Vela didn't want Linc to see Evan close to or draped over her. She knew how she felt when Maria flirted relentlessly with Linc, and he might feel the same. In fact, she was sure he did.

Her hesitation to answer Evan cost her.

"Yes! I knew you would," Evan crowed and started pulling her over to his desk, taking her silence as acceptance of his offer.

She looked over at Linc. He sat with a dark look, glowering at Evan.

Vela kept Linc in the corner of her eye as she sighed. "Evan, leave me alone today. I'm really not in the mood."

"Really?" he asked, looking stumped that she would turn him down.

"Yes," she said firmly and started walking back over to Cassie's desk, hoping she didn't claim a partner yet.

Vela glanced around the classroom and in the back of her eye, she could see Maria slinking over to Linc's desk. Of course, Maria would want to be his partner, and Vela burned at the thought. Suddenly determined to head Maria off, she approached the desk next to Linc, since she was closer.

Standing before it, she debated. Taking a chance, she set her bookbag down on the desk and sat, quelling her jumping nerves. She looked up at Linc.

He was grinning at her.

Maria, on the other hand, glared at her and flounced into an open seat a couple of rows away, completely ignoring her new partner. If looks could kill, Vela would be dead.

"You actually want to be my partner?" Linc asked. She wasn't sure if he was aware of Vela and Maria's eye showdown, so she put Maria in the back of her mind and looked over at him. He wore a smile that was so wide, it set off the dimple in his right cheek perfectly, and his eyes sparkled at her indecisive seat-sitting. He must be over his annoyance at Evan, which was good.

Taking a deep breath, she said, "I need to talk to you. About that text you sent me? I was wondering if I should give you the benefit of the doubt."

Linc took out his notebook to prepare for their assignment and said, "The benefit of the doubt that I'm a decent guy and I am not actually out to ruin your life?" He leaned forward in his seat so he could whisper loudly. "That benefit of the doubt?"

The corner of his mouth tugged up in a small smile, and Vela couldn't help responding. If he really wanted to get to know her, he would find out sooner rather than later she could give as much as she got.

She had two older brothers, after all. She'd had plenty of practice to defend herself.

"That I very well can defend myself when I'm in the fight of my life *if* you would have given me a chance to explain myself. I also don't need your attitude. And you are most definitely out to ruin the plans I have for my life, so pick another benefit of the doubt." Running out of air with her impromptu speech, she sucked in a breath, then pushed her hair back from her face to see his reaction better. She had shaken her head in her vehemence, and it was all over the place.

"So, my little ghost doesn't just have an invisibility factor going for her, but a bite as well. That's good to know," he said, looking down at his notebook and writing down both of their names.

"Are you going to acknowledge what I just said to you?" Vela asked, glaring at him.

He looked up and apologized in an earnest tone. "I'm sorry. I shouldn't have undermined you when I said you couldn't defend yourself. But I can't help but be a little protective of you, Vela. You're my Intended," he added in a dropped whisper.

"I am perfectly capable of handling myself, Linc!" she whispered harshly, leaning toward him as well. "Which I proved, by the way." She valiantly tried to ignore his glorious scent and concentrate.

"Touche. I'd actually really like to hear how you got away from that Borean and his wind funnel." He leaned back and resumed lounging, tapping his pen against the desk.

They were already behind on their assignment at this point, but she didn't care. She blinked at his change of pace and said, "I'm surprised you haven't already heard from the gossip mill what happened."

"Oh, I heard a few things. But I want to hear it from your lips."

"Well," she began, blushing as his gaze went to the subject of his last request. "I got away because I had help."

At his raised eyebrow, she began explaining the entire story, thankful the teacher hadn't noticed that they had not started the essay yet.

After she was done, she sat back.

"Huh."

She expected more of a reaction than that. "Awesome, right? I had the best help in the world!"

"That's all I meant, you know," he said, leaning forward again, his eyes drilling into hers.

"What?"

"That you needed help in your fight against the Boreans. You had your dog with that lone Borean, then the children, to help you later. You couldn't do it alone. I just wanted to have been able to help you, too."

She spluttered, at a loss for words, but he continued in a heated voice. "If you had given me the chance to explain myself this week instead of shutting off your phone and running away from me *again*, I would have told you I *hated* hearing about you getting hurt. It took everything, and I mean, everything, in me not to drive to Utah and make sure you weren't playing down your injuries. If I hadn't seen for myself that you were fine that Monday, I would have tracked that Borean down and..." he stopped himself from finishing and inhaled through his nose. "You told me you were almost *torn apart* in a wind funnel. Am I supposed to be happy about that? I could have helped you defend yourself. That's all I meant when I said it wouldn't have happened if I was there."

He sat back, crossed his arms and continued, "Now, as far as me being out to," using his hands to motion air quotes, 'ruin your life' that is not my intention. An Intended bond only enhances a couple, making them stronger, closer. *That* is the benefit of the doubt I'm looking for."

His comment made her stop and think. She had been turning him away left and right, constantly ignoring him, threatening to ignore their bond. She did not like the version of herself she could now see Linc had been seeing. She was better than that, she chided herself. She needed to give him a chance. More than the half-hearted attempts she had made. At that thought, a thrill of satisfaction ran through her.

Relieved, too, that his explanation meant he wasn't as much of a jerk as she first thought, then a little scared that she was starting to really like this most recent version of Linc. Between his actions at the tour, pep rally, and his explanation, he was making a pretty strong case for himself.

Also, he had called her *his* little ghost, which made her stupidly happy. Deciding to lighten the conversation and not address the heavier thread of their conversation, she said, "I don't know if I should feel complimented right now or horrified that you think I'm a scary specter, which is it, I wonder?"

"Specter?" Linc coughed a laugh. He didn't seem to mind the lighter conversation and went along with it. "Where are we? In Transylvania? I'm pretty sure I said ghost and not specter. And you're about as scary as a little kitten, so how's that for a compliment? Kittens are cute and cuddly, to be specific, so I'm definitely attempting to compliment you."

The teacher called the class to order. Vela bit back a retort. She would *not* be compared to a kitten. They also now had nothing to turn in.

She tried to ignore the wide smile he gave her so she could focus on the very boring lecture her teacher was currently giving. She was attempting to be friendly, but he was making it hard for her when he teased so much.

The class continued with her sneaking peeks at Linc every now and then.

He continued to lounge in his seat and his answers to the teacher's questions only added to the fact that he seemed to own this class. His responses to the questions were polite, however, and respectful. Linc also was discreetly writing in the notebook they were supposed to have written their combined essay.

Waiting through the rest of the class was a chore, but Vela bore it as best as she could. To her surprise, Linc turned in a page he ripped out to the teacher at the end of the lecture.

"Can't have you getting an F on my account, can we?" he asked with a wink.

After he sauntered back to his desk, she couldn't help but thank him. "You didn't have to do that."

He put his books in his bookbag and said, "My kitten needs to have good grades. I'm only being a responsible pet owner."

"Owner? Kitten?" She glared at him. "And since when are kittens cuddly? All they want to do is to bite, scratch and be left alone."

"Uh, have you ever even had a kitten before? Pretty sure you're wrong. And are you saying you want to be left alone? Are we back to that?" He tossed his bookbag on his shoulder and looked at her expectantly.

"No, that's not what I meant at all!" Frustrated, she continued, "I am not going to be owned to make that clear, and so we are on the same page," she mimicked his words, "I am *trying* to be friends. Isn't that what you wanted? Well, I want that, too, now. It can't hurt to get to know each other." Her heart fluttered at her declaration. She couldn't take her words back, now that she had said them.

"Well, as long as we're being dead honest, I'm going to tell you right now, if we stay in this class much longer, we're going to have to hear another boring English lecture. This class is over."

Vela looked around and gasped. The room was empty. Their teacher looked at them curiously. Linc grasped her elbow to steer her out the door. "Come on, let's continue our *getting to know you chat* in the hallway."

A spark lit her veins again when he touched her elbow. Embarrassed at her reaction, yet again, to his touch, she let him lead her away.

Vela stopped him in the hallway and asked, "Don't you think we're young to find out about our bond? Why'd we find out so soon?"

Towering over her, he ducked his head as he gave her a warm look. "You don't think other Elementals have found their Intendeds in high school?"

"I guess so. I've just never heard of it."

She thought about the Chosen Child her mom had mentioned on the way to Utah. And how his or her parents would be different Elementals. Could that be them? Her heart sped up at the thought. Maybe they had a destiny together that was long foretold, and that's why their bond flared to life so soon. It was a stretch, she knew, but she wanted his opinion. She had so many more questions, so she blurted, "Have you ever heard, too, of different Elementals becoming a match?"

Leading her down the hallway, he seemed to pause before he answered, "I have heard of it, yes."

"And what have you heard?"

"Look, let's talk about this after school, okay? How about I call you later and we can go over our theories?"

Disappointed they hadn't gotten anywhere, she agreed, but looking him in the eye, asked firmly, "We *will* talk. You'll call me?"

"Wouldn't dream of missing out on a conversation with my *specter*," he said with a straight face.

"I'm going to have to get used to your dry humor."

"Dead right." He said and turned into his next class. She couldn't see his expression, but she was sure he had a smile on his face.

Hurrying to her class, she wondered what she had signed up for in being Linc's friend. No wonder he found himself in the popular crowd. He was entertaining, to say the least.

But he was still a piece of work, and it might be a long time before she understood him.

She smiled to herself. Now it didn't seem like such a chore to get to know him better. In fact, she was looking forward to it.

Chapter Twenty-Three

VELA BLEW A HAIR out of her face. She frowned at her homework, not able to concentrate on the math equations she tried to solve.

If only it was so easy to solve the tricky equation that was Linc Stevenson.

It was early evening, so Vela knew Linc would probably call later. She wasn't sure why she thought that. It was probably because he would hold her in suspense, waiting for his call as long as possible.

That sounded just like him. In the past hour, she had obsessively checked her phone a hundred times. When no calls had come in, she had become anxious in both a good and bad way.

Good, because maybe she might get some answers to all her questions. Bad, because he was starting to make her feel things, she might not be ready to feel right now. She was stubbornly trying to hold on to her independence. To be a strong girl who would stand on her own two feet, not just depend on someone else for whatever she wanted out of life. But that was good, right?

Not when she started playing games with her head, waiting for his call. This wasn't just a high school romance she was considering, but her Intended. Someone she might be with for the rest of her life.

Sighing, she turned her head toward a potted marigold she had on the windowsill by her bed. It looked a little lifeless, so she ran her fingers over the waxy leaves and soft orange flowers. Imbuing some of her powers into the plant, she leaned back and enjoyed the rush of energy. She had been meaning to replant the flower in her parents' garden since it had outgrown her pot, but she hadn't had the chance. It only had this one season to grow so she should plant it outside where it will thrive best in its short life.

Deciding she would love to get her hands in the dirt outside, Vela gave up on her math homework, sat up, and called for Jack to come with her. She grabbed the plant and headed for the garden. Not seeing anyone in the house wasn't unusual, but she could hear her parents in the kitchen talking in low voices while they prepared dinner.

Once she stepped off the back porch, Vela let Jack explore the rose garden off to the side. When she reached the multi-colored zinnias, red geraniums, and white potato vines, she looked around for a good home for her little marigold. Finding one, she kneeled in the dirt, thanked God for such a pretty day, as well as her lovely flower that she blessedly hadn't killed yet, and got to work.

Sinking her hands into the dirt, she remembered her mom telling her to be thankful for even the little things.

So, she would try to remember that. Even when dealing with infuriating boys who liked to get under her skin. She shook her head and concentrated instead on what she was doing. Vela ran her hands over the flower's petals and leaves, sensing its roots crowding the pot.

Vela, like the plant, would breathe much better once she reassigned its home. She wished she could untangle her mess of a life as easily as this plant.

The flower was in good health, aside from the overcrowding issue. She tugged it free from the pot. Without touching the plant, she drew the mass of roots down, gently untangling them one root at a time.

She waved her hand over the ground. It wasn't necessary to use her hands to make her element come alive, but she liked to sometimes. It was a dance with the give and take of using her element, and she relaxed as she spun a hole in the ground. She watched as the dirt made room for her marigold about a foot and a half deep. She carefully cradled the plant and placed the roots in its new home. With another sweep of her hand, she moved the earth over the now transplanted flower. Jack ran over sniffing her work, happy she used her gift. Vela laughed and nudged him back.

Focused on her work and Jack, she slowly became aware of a slight bump against her hair. Figuring it was a bee, she swatted the little nuisance away. She focused on her flower and, with a rush of energy, rooted it deeper into the dirt.

Another gentle bump had her swatting above her head to get rid of the pest bothering her. Several more taps followed, and she finally looked up to investigate.

If it was wasps or bees, she would have to get moving; she did not want to get stung.

When she looked up, however, her mouth dropped open. Hovering over her head was a cloud of fireflies gently bouncing in the air. They surrounded her. She just hadn't noticed them. They twinkled in a little cloud she saw clearly in the dusky light. She held her breath at the wonder of it.

The sky transitioned to pink and orange streaks, and it only added to the moment. With the fireflies orbiting around her and against the stunning sunset, she couldn't believe the magic she was witnessing. Jack, it seemed, couldn't either. He began jumping in circles and trying to catch one in his mouth.

Their little lights blinked on and off, like tiny lightbulbs dancing in the air.

Laughing, she lifted her hands and carefully tried catching one, too. She would never hurt it, she just wanted to study it while she had enough light to see its little body. She stood up carefully so as not to disturb the hive of activity around her. Twirling in place, she giggled as she attempted to catch one. They bounced around, always a grasp away. How an insect could glow amazed her. Jack turned and, she thought, barked at another firefly and bounded after it.

A deep voice spoke a little distance away. "I think it's easier to catch one when you're standing in one place, not twirling around."

Vela shrieked and spun. Linc stood with one hand hovering toward the fireflies and the other rubbing Jack's ears, who investigated Linc's pant leg. He wore another band shirt and dark gray jeans. His dark clothes stood out in the garden's color and the sunset.

Eyeing his stretched-out arm, Vela blurted, "What are you doing?"

"Controlling my surprise for you."

"My surprise? The fireflies?" Glancing at Jack, it shocked her again that he warmed up so easily to Linc.

"On my way over here, I began collecting these little lightning bugs as I went. I didn't figure you'd be outside. I thought I'd have to get you out here somehow. I got lucky you were already out."

Vela's brows knotted in confusion.

"I have a way with anything with a heat source."

"You can *control* insects?"

"Not control, but influence. Because I'm a Festan, I'm attracted to anything with a heat signature. I can sense animals or insects and they, in turn, are drawn to my heat. The only way I can describe it is that I mesmerize them, and after that happens, I can convince them, or influence them, to do what I want."

"Wait, are you influencing my dog right now?" That would explain his exuberance toward him.

He shook his head, affectionately petting Jack's head. "No, he naturally loves me."

She eyed her dog, who licked Linc's hand and frowned. "He loves magic. He must sense our bond and treats it like he would our gift. That's the only explanation I have."

"Why can't he just like me?"

"He's never liked a strange guy before. He's naturally distrustful of them. He only really likes women for some reason."

"Well, I'll consider myself lucky then."

"You should."

"So, do you like my surprise?"

Vela looked around at the little light show of fireflies and breathed, "This truly is amazing." She marveled at what Linc brought her. She'd never heard that Festans could do this before today. Alarm washed over her. "Hey, can you convince humans to do things, too?"

"If I could, don't you think I would have convinced you by now to give me a chance?" he asked with a crooked smile.

At her shocked look, he said, "No, complex minds like humans aren't easily manipulated like animals and little creatures like these lightning bugs."

"And these little *fireflies* have enough heat to attract your gift?"

"Anything with life has a heat source, so yes, they do. Did you like them?" He grinned, seemingly amused by her reaction.

"I *love* them! I've always loved them." Vela smiled up at the tumbling little gems. "They're like tiny Tinkerbells flying around."

"Well, then instead of bringing you flowers, which you seem to be in abundance of," he gestured at the lush garden, "I'll bring you lightning bugs. Or butterflies or rabbits, whatever you like. But not kittens, since you don't think those are very cuddly. What else do you like? I seemed to have lucked out with the *lightning bugs*."

Ignoring his question, she asked, "Why do you keep calling them that? They aren't lightning bugs! They're called fireflies!"

"Where I come from, they're called lightning bugs. Do you mind if I let them go now? I'd like to have use of my arm again." He held still and waited.

"Yes, of course," she said reluctantly. The little lights dispersed as he dropped his arm and let them go. She watched them filter into her garden. It was a lovely sight. They caught the night breeze and floated away into the multicolored sunset.

This night had just gotten very interesting. Vela was never sure what to expect with Linc. He was always surprising her. She'd just have to wait and see what he would do next.

Chapter Twenty-Four

"I HAVE TO ASK you something that's been on my mind for a while," Vela said to Linc.

They meandered over to the rose garden, with Jack in between them. They stepped on a flagstone path that led to the rose, vegetable, and herb gardens. The aromatic scent of rosemary added to the sweet, smoky scent Linc always brought with him.

"This area has been Gyan territory for a long time now. Are you scouting for potential new land for Festans to take over? *Why* are you here?" Suspicion clouded the tone of her voice.

Confusion crossed his face, and he shook his head. "No, I told you. I'm staying here with my uncle. He's conducting research on Gyans and I'm just tagging along. I'm not scouting anything out." This time, his eyes held hurt.

"What kind of research? How to exploit our weaknesses? What our territory looks like, so you can have it?" They passed the full red, pink, and yellow roses.

"No," he answered to each of the questions she fired off. "My uncle is conducting research on all the clans, which he'll give to them when he's finished. It's purely for historical purposes. So, there can be a clear picture of each clan's accomplishments, for history's sake."

That made sense. Guilt coursed through Vela and an apology rose in her throat. "I'm sorry. I shouldn't have said that. It's just... never mind."

"What?" Linc walked to her side, concern etched in his furrowed brow.

She waved her hand as she continued walking. She stopped at the vegetable garden. "It's nothing. Ancient history."

"You can confide in me. We're friends, right?" Linc cocked his head. Then he said in a soft voice, "Sometimes talking things through is the best medicine."

Wrinkling her nose, she skirted a tomato plant that edged the vegetables. "I don't know if you're guilting me into this conversation. It definitely feels like it. But, okay."

It took a few minutes for Vela to walk around the lettuce heads and cornstalks to the back of the yard, where a white gazebo stood. It sat prettily between the vegetable and herb garden and shaded four black wrought iron benches placed in a circle.

She chose a bench, and he joined her, their knees touching. She scooted closer to the edge. Linc, coming into her space, felt personal, and she fought the wild feelings he caused. Her heart felt like it would race out of her chest, her blood jumped around in her veins, and she suddenly forgot what she had been talking about.

Linc seemed to understand, because he said gently, "It's a lot, isn't it?"

She stammered, "This... this bond takes a lot to get used to. I'm never sure where I am when you're..." Not finishing, she simply looked at him, willing him to understand.

"Near me?" he finished.

Vela nodded.

"But I seem to take it a lot better than you are. Why is that?"

His comment instantly reminded her of what she had spaced out on, her childhood trauma.

"Well, that's what I was going to talk to you about."

"Ah, I see. Do Festans have anything to do with this?"

"How'd you know?"

"Let's just say I recognize the signs. This isn't the first Gyan settlement I've lived in."

"Really? So, you've experienced some problems before me?" Vela flushed at her admittance of being prejudiced.

"So, I'm right? It was a Festan that hurt you?" Anger came over his features and she relaxed, appreciating his concern.

Jack had settled next to Linc, and she called him to her. Rubbing his sleek side soothed her. Taking a deep breath, she began, "Festans started a fire near my childhood home. They wanted to scare us out of it, but it burned my house down instead. And with it, my..." her breath caught, and she could feel the familiar pain swamping her. "I'm sorry. I can't talk about it anymore. It's too painful," she whispered.

Linc laid a hand on her arm. She flinched and tried to escape the memories leaking through her wall.

"I'm sorry for what my people did to you, Vela. This is the reason, isn't it? Why you don't want to accept our bond?"

Her eyes burned at the pain she felt remembering that awful night. She shook her head. "It's more than that."

"What is it? What can I do?" Linc asked, desperation making his voice hoarse.

She looked into his eyes and felt surprised at how far they had come that she could suddenly want to be this honest with him.

"I want to be my own person," she declared. "I've watched my parents my whole life commit to each other wholeheartedly, without a thought of doing otherwise. I'm not sure I'm ready for that, Linc. You're a catch. I know that, trust me, I see it every time I look at you! But to give myself, my life over to someone else when I'm still discovering who I am, seems impossible right now."

Linc sat and digested her burst of words, looking out into the distance. Then he tilted his head, giving her a crooked grin. "So, you think I'm hot?"

Vela stared at him, her mouth open in shock. "That's all you have to say? That I think you're hot?"

"So, you do."

"Yes! But that's not the point!"

"Ah." Linc laughed. "But it's a start."

"A start to what?"

"To a relationship. It always starts with attraction. So, despite your hang-ups, we've already begun our whirlwind romance."

"I will not have a *whirlwind* romance with you!"

"Okay, maybe it'll take longer than a whirlwind romance to claim your heart, but I'm willing to wait it out. To wait your fears out."

"How? How... can you be so certain of me?"

"Vela," Linc said, his eyes suddenly serious as he grabbed her hands. "I've never been more certain of anything in my sad little life."

"Sad life?" she asked, confusion and bewilderment settling in. He was the prince of the Festans. How was his life in any way sad?

"Oh, you know, the boy whose parents cast him off like he's a problem they don't have time to deal with. All because of one terrible mistake. To live with someone who has more time for pen, paper and his endless research to pay attention to the boy he's been told to raise." He let go of her hand to run his fingers through his hair. His pained expression tore at Vela's heart. Her mind spun with all that he shared.

"To think that I've found the one person designed just for me to love makes this trip invaluable to me. I couldn't be happier, Vela. I just need to convince you what I already know."

"And what's that?" Vela asked, her heart in her throat completely caught up in his words.

"That we're meant for each other." He reclaimed her hand and rubbed circles onto her now overheated skin with his thumbs. Their bond flared to life once again, sending a rush of adrenaline racing through her veins.

The pain she felt remembering her tragedy went forgotten as his proximity ran her emotions through havoc. Every sensory motor in her body was alive and buzzing.

"Would it help you if I sit over there?" Linc asked and gestured to the bench across from them.

Vela appreciated his thoughtfulness. She didn't know how these feelings could lessen over time. He zapped her every time he barely touched her.

She breathed, "Thank you."

After he moved, he said, "No problem. So, you know, I feel it too." Warmth emanated from his gaze.

"And it doesn't bother you?"

"No, it definitely doesn't bother me."

"You're saying that you don't mind feeling like you're being shocked every time we're near each other?"

"I'm a Festan, remember?" he said with a laugh. "I like heat and any sensation that resembles it. So, no, I don't mind the electrical storm you seem to generate."

"*I* generate? It's *you* that's doing all of that! I mean, isn't it? With your heat powers and everything?"

He laughed and shook his head. "No. There's a lot you don't know about Festans. This thing we have between us is just with us. *We* are creating these sensations. You are a gift personally crafted just for me. Just like I'm made just for you."

Vela looked everywhere but at him. She didn't know what to say.

"Remember, too," Linc added, "I can't influence humans with my gift. Just creatures."

"Oh yeah, you said that earlier. Sorry, I didn't mean to accuse you." She studied him as she said, "You don't seem to mind this connection we have. Like it fits perfectly into your plans. I'm jealous."

He seemed to mull over her statement. "I'm not saying it fits perfectly in my plans. Accepting a Gyan as my Intended is no problem for me. I always expected to be surprised when I found you, but I definitely didn't expect to have to chase you down."

"Chase me down?" She thought for a minute and shrugged. "Well, maybe you did."

"That's why I'm here, by the way."

"You mean this unexpected visit?"

"Yes. I wanted to talk to you."

A funny feeling entered her chest. "You could have talked to me over the phone."

"But I can't bring you lightning bugs through the phone." His lips smirked, and she found herself grinning at him.

"Fireflies," she corrected. "How did you know where I live?"

"If you had to do what I've had to do for the past couple of weeks, you'd be able to track me down, too."

"What've you had to do?"

"I've had to tune in to my senses on where to find you." He stretched out his legs and crossed them.

"You mean, all those times I hid from you? You knew where I was?" she whispered. Embarrassment took over.

"Let's just say it has been excellent training for me to pinpoint exactly where you are." A lazy smile drifted over his face. All the times she hid from him was just an elaborate game of hide and seek. She would never to be able to hide from him again, she realized.

Vela didn't know how she felt about that.

"So, that time in the stairwell?" she asked in a small voice. "You were toying with me?"

"No, I just decided it was time I found you." There was a softness to his tone as he regarded her with amusement. "You had gone so out of your way to be nowhere near me, I thought it was time we met. I had been able to clue in to where you hid for a while before that."

"Linc," she began uncertainly, "I don't know how to say this. But please just give me time. That would help me process all of this. And maybe, one day, accept us as easily as you have."

Vela played with her fingers in her lap and couldn't meet his gaze. She didn't know what she would see. Braving a look, she raised her head.

His expression surprised her. Instead of frustration, it was acceptance. "Would it help to tell you I'm grateful for your honesty?" he said. "I'm sorry about what happened to you and your family. I can't imagine the pain you've experienced. Maybe it was God's intention to bring us together to help you realize Festans are as complicated and trustworthy as you Gyans. We have the same desires, needs, and wants as anyone and make just as many mistakes."

"The fire, it turned out, was a mistake," she admitted. "A Festan Elemental actually died in that fire, breathing toxic fumes from some chemical near our land. Their fire went out of control, taking over the land near us and our home, too."

"Wow, a Festan dying because of a fire. That's unheard of." He ran his hands through his hair and winced. "I wonder who it was? Where did this happen?"

"California, El Dorado, actually. It's between Lake Tahoe and Sacramento. Have you heard of it?"

"Hmm, no, I haven't heard of that town."

"We have great history there. It's where the California Gold Rush originated. It's a beautiful land. There are mountains with these amazing trails all throughout the area."

Linc studied her. "You seem like you miss it."

"I do. It was a wonderful place to grow up. Plenty of room to explore and be a kid. But here's nice, too."

He looked around their garden and nodded. "It *is* peaceful. Colorado is a lot different from California, though."

"Yeah, but the mountains are similar. I'll always need to be around them. There's nothing like a profusion of trees and wildlife to nurture my gift, which will *always* be needed, in any part of the world."

"My fire element is needed everywhere, too. Since we are the most lethal clan, we're the best protectors."

"Destroyers, you mean. Your gift doesn't create, it eliminates."

"That's not true," he said with a frown. "Vela, we're more than a weapon. Our gifts enhance the earth just as much as water, earth and wind. I believe God gave us our gifts to better the world. We've just done a terrible job of abusing our power. Somewhere in our history, because of greed, prejudices, and bigotry, we've divided ourselves. But that isn't what God designed us for. Yes, Festans are superior in our fighting skills, because of how dangerous our gift is but just because there aren't many who can beat us in hand-to-hand combat or a bigger battle, doesn't mean we should take advantage of that."

"Gyans' gifts are pretty lethal, too," she said in a hard tone.

Ignoring her subtle warning, he asked, "In what way? You heal and nurture the land. That's what you do best."

"You don't think we can defend ourselves?" Vela asked, her voice ending in a shrill pitch. He acted just like he had after the boundary battle. That she couldn't defend herself properly. This attitude Linc owned probably reflected all the clans' attitude toward Gyans. She agreed that fire could devastate. It was a lethal gift, but she wanted to prove a point. Her gift could be just as lethal. Maybe she should show him. That would help convince him. She sensed the plant life around her and saw the possibilities of offense and defense.

Tilting his head back, he ran his hands through his hair and moaned, "Why must things be so difficult with you? Why are we even arguing?" he asked.

"*Me* being difficult? How about *you*?" she squinted her eyes at him. "Look, I, like all Gyans, can take care of myself. We defended ourselves pretty well against the Boreans in that boundary battle, which we won, by the way." She waited for him to acknowledge that feat. When he nodded, she announced, "You know, I could fight better than you any day."

"Would you like to make a wager on that?" A glint came in his eyes, and he half smiled as he waited for her answer.

"What kind of wager?" she asked warily.

"A duel between you and me. A date with me, if you lose. Freedom from me, if I lose."

Vela watched his eyes. They were very expressive and usually announced his intent. Right now, they reflected excitement and anticipation. Like he wanted this. She couldn't believe he offered her a way out of their relationship this easily. Just if she won. She didn't believe him.

"You will give me up if you lose?"

"Believe me, it'll never come to that," he said firmly.

"You're that confident?"

"Very."

Regardless of whether he would give her up or not, the thought making her uncomfortable, Vela itched to challenge him. She couldn't resist going up against a Festan.

"Agreed," she announced.

Chapter Twenty-Five

"Come, Jack! I don't want you near fire." Vela opened the back porch door and Jack whined and resisted, but she firmly nudged him inside with her knee. No way could she handle her dog getting hurt over a silly duel.

After closing the patio door and ignoring Jack's puppy dog look, she walked down the stairs and scouted a suitable area to have whatever this was, a showdown, she guessed.

Vela walked over to a spot a couple of yards away from the gazebo in a grassy part of their lawn. She needed a good area to pull from the resources at her disposal and a place that would be free from permanent fire damage. She glanced over at the gazebo, suddenly worried a spark would light it on fire. Linc walked over and stood about twenty feet from her, away from the pretty wooden structure. When she arched her eyebrow at the gazebo, he seemed to read her question right and nodded his head, confirming he wouldn't do any damage to the building.

"Are you sure you're ready for this?" Linc asked, challenging her with his gaze.

"I'm ready to show you what my gifts can really do."

Vela shook her hands and eyed her opponent, wondering what his first move would be. She gathered control of the nearby vines trailing up the gazebo's canopy, thinking about her attack sequence. Her hands tingled in anticipation, and she clenched them at her sides.

He didn't seem to notice the slight movement the vines made when she got control of them. He stared straight at her, and he looked like he was deciding on what offense to start with, too.

She didn't plan on letting him see his strategy through.

"When do we start?" she asked.

"On the count of three." Slowly, he counted backwards.

At the sound of one, Vela threw up a cloud of dirt. Knowing dirt can put out the hottest of fires, she tossed up as much as she could. It worked. He had lobbed several fireballs, but the dirt snuffed them out immediately. Fear clenched her chest at fighting fire for the first time. She ruthlessly quenched the feeling even though a cold sweat trickled down her back.

With her senses, she grabbed hold of the long vines that hung over the garden benches and ripped them free from the gazebo's poles. Wielding them like rope, she wrapped Linc's chest, pinning his arms to his sides.

Surprise came over his features before the leafy plants covered his face. He went still with shock before he started struggling.

Vela walked toward the house with a jaunty step. A rush of wind and heat flamed at her back. *Oh, no.* Linc was free from the vines.

Vela turned to see flames engulf the vines, incinerating Linc's temporary prison. Linc emerged from behind a curtain of smoke, his silhouette stark against the smoldering remains of her vines.

The smell of the smoke reached her nose, and the fear rose again. An image of her house in flames popped into her mind.

She shook her head to clear it.

Linc's mouth was in a tight line, his eyes scorching hot as he strode towards her. His fingers flexed against his sides. She dug her feet into the earth, widening her stance. Steeling herself, she waited for his next move.

Expecting another fireball assault, she prepared to fling up more dirt if she needed to. He shocked her when he completely engulfed himself in fire, every inch covered in flames. He slowly walked toward her like an avenging angel.

She darted backwards into the garden, not taking her eyes off his fiery frame.

He moved around bushes and plants, avoiding setting those ablaze.

Suddenly, old memories rose in Vela's mind. She couldn't stop them. Her body froze, absolutely unable to move.

Her old terror engulfed her. This time, the old vision consumed her. With Linc on fire in front of her, behind her eyelids, her old house burned, Cooper cried, smoke rose.

Linc had just become her worst nightmare. He advanced closer.

All of her senses screamed at her to run, and in the back of her mind, she knew she needed to react to chase away this horrible memory. Between Linc's fire and the vision of her past, she was trapped in a trauma of such proportions; she didn't know if she would recover.

Finally, before he could reach her, she turned and ran, terror blinding her.

Before she made it ten steps, however, a monstrous fire wall flared up in front of her. She stopped just in time. Scorching heat baked the front of her body and her face. Her heart stalled in her chest. She backed up quickly.

Vela spun around. Her body felt like a statue, this time unable to make herself move or act. Another wave of memories assaulted her. The blaze triggered everything she had forced into hiding to come out.

She wasn't ready.

Vela faced Linc, who stood oblivious to her turmoil and terror. She succumbed to the onslaught she remembered and crumpled to the ground.

Putting her arms out, she whispered, "Stop."

Looking at his advancing body of flames approach her, terror climbed in her throat, and she screamed, "Stop! Please. Stop."

Linc must have realized he had gone too far, and something more was wrong with her.

Dousing himself in one fluid motion with his arms, he stood looking at her with concern while smoke billowed around him in a dark cloud.

Unable to look at him, Vela dug her head into her arms and tried to stop her body's shaking.

"Vela," Linc whispered, now crouching next to her. "You're shaking." His hands ghosted over her arms, like he didn't know if touching her would make her break.

It probably would.

"I just need a minute," Vela said in a choking voice. Her chest was so tight, she could barely squeeze in breaths. She felt like she would hyperventilate.

In her little cocoon of darkness, she imagined her beautiful wall as high as she could make it. The memories of fire and smoke and sounds of crying, she relentlessly pushed behind it. The terror and sorrow she felt, she did the same to those feelings. Put them where they needed to be. Away. Then she pictured a thick door that she slammed shut, closing in those memories so she could continue as she had.

"Vela?" Linc asked in a tentative voice. "Are you okay?"

Her mental strategy to forget worked. She breathed a little easier, relishing the lack of pain and terror engulfing her.

Her nose dripped and tears stuck hot on her face as she looked up and asked in a strained voice, "You really were going to *burn* me?"

"No!" Linc cried. "I would never hurt you, Vela. I couldn't." He reached out to her, but when she flinched, he pulled his hands back.

"You were on fire in front of me and the blaze behind me. How did you expect me to escape that?" she asked in a hard voice.

He smiled softly and said, "Vela, I literally can't hurt you. You're my Intended. Our gifts would never harm each other."

Vela inhaled sharply. It was true. She remembered now. Her parent's powers were harmless against one another. The shock of seeing him on fire and the fire wall surrounding her had clouded her mind with terror, making her forget.

"Can I show you?" he asked gently.

"I'm not sure I can handle that," Vela answered honestly, pushing herself up off the ground.

"You need to believe me, Vela. The best way is to show you what I mean."

Vela examined the wall she had built in her mind. Now that she could prepare for the shock of being so close to fire, she thought maybe she could handle it.

Reluctantly nodding, she held out her hand. Time to make giant steps toward her fear of flames.

Linc sat back and again, a rush of orange encased his body.

Prepared for the sight, she sucked in a breath as she watched his lips formed of fire smile. Where she thought she would see a formless globe of flames on his head, instead now she saw she could easily discern eyes, nose, mouth and chin.

It surprised Vela she could also see emotion in the fiery depths of his eyes.

"I only wanted to get your attention." His lips turned up in a grin, his eyes burning into hers.

"You certainly did that," she said, in awe of the details she could now see.

"Being my Intended grants you immunity from burns, from me, anyway. I don't know if that's true of all Festan Elementals, though."

"That's right. I forgot somehow."

"Now it's time to test this out. Please trust me." He reached for her hand, which was tempered down to a low flame.

Watching his hand reach for hers, her eyes widened when he gently picked up her frozen fingers from her lap and held it against his chest.

She took stock of what she felt. Warmth encased her hand and part of her arm. It was pleasant and not the least bit hot. It thawed out the stiffness from the terror she had just experienced.

"How on earth?" She was in awe. Full of wonder, she looked up at him. "You're right. It's barely hot. It just feels warm."

He extinguished the fire all over them in one practiced move. Smoke billowed on the ground.

"That's what I feel, too," he said. Happy to see the fire gone and his face in view again, Vela shuddered. The flames he wore had scared her, but after he asked her to trust him, she could see the beauty of it, too. "I register the increase in temperature, but it doesn't hurt me, just like it won't hurt you."

"You know what else I was right about?" he asked with a smile. "My gift *is* stronger. You owe me a date."

Vela shook her head fiercely. "You are not getting a date today. You cheated! And offensively, you may be stronger, but I could have opened a hole in the ground and buried you."

"And I would have thrown more fire at you, distracting you until I escaped the hole," he countered.

"Well, you don't win this duel. You played dirty. So, about this fire wall behind me. Care to douse it? I think my dog is about to have a coronary in there." She gestured toward the sliding glass door. Sure enough, Jack was barking his head off. She started panicking over what her parents would think of this situation.

"That all depends," Linc responded.

"On what?"

"On whether you'll cooperate." One side of his mouth lifted in a half smile. He leaned toward her.

Before she could figure out what he was doing, she heard a loud, "What in Sam Hill is going on here? What is all of this? Drew, get the hose!"

Vela could hear Jack now barking outside.

Her eyes widened. It was her father. And he didn't sound happy. She had a lot of explaining to do.

Chapter Twenty-Six

"Vela! Vela, where are you?" her brothers called out frantically. She heard the hose start up and water beat at the flames at her back.

Leaning in to Linc's face that held more than a hint of annoyance, she whispered, "I told you."

"What?" he growled.

"That you weren't going to get that date today." It felt good to tease him, like she could finally get back at him.

The water soon beat out the firewall. Scorch marks stained the ground where the fire had stood. Vela could see other spots in the yard where other fireballs had landed. As soon as the fire disappeared, Jack lunged toward Linc, who shot up his arm, using his powers to gain control over her furious animal.

"Jack, stop!" she cried. Her command was unnecessary, however. Linc had Jack completely under his spell. Jack stood a few feet from Linc, his back quivering and legs shaking. Linc had his mind, but it looked like Jack fought for his body back. She grabbed a hold of Jack's collar. Tilting her head, she gave Linc an exasperated look.

He gave up control of Jack, who, at her command, sat next to her. Jack hadn't forgiven Linc, yet. He trained his canine eyes on Linc relentlessly.

Lowering his arm, his attention went to the tense silence from her family members, who stood around in a semicircle around them. He asked warily, "So this is your family?"

"Vela? Would you mind explaining *what* is going on here?" her father roared and, without letting her answer, turned his furious gaze to Linc. "Who are you? And what did you do to our dog?"

Her dad apparently did not know about the Festan ability to control animals, either.

"Dad, it's part of his gift. He can mind control animals. All Festans...." Vela glanced at Linc before she let go of Jack, tilting her head in question. He nodded at her. "Have this ability."

"Influence," Linc corrected.

She straightened her back at the pregnant pause while everyone studied each other. To break the awkward silence, she blurted, "Mom, Dad, Drew and Kane? Meet Lincoln, he goes by Linc."

"That's all we get, his name is Linc?" If her father could spontaneously burst in flames, like Linc, he would have, as mad as he looked right now. "We rush outside when we see a wall of fire in our backyard, thinking you're in terrible danger and all you have to say for an explanation is, 'Meet *Linc*'?"

"Sorry Dad, but I kind of spoke about him to Mom already. I thought you would know by now. He and I have discovered a connection between us. He's kind of my Intended," she said, awkwardly twisting her hands. She did not expect to have this conversation at seventeen.

His fury morphed into disbelief, but just for a moment. Concern took over his face. "Your Intended? Him?"

Vela looked over at her bondmate, who seemed to take offense at that question. His body stiffened and his fists clenched.

"It surprised us, too, Dad."

Linc nodded in agreement.

David's eyes ping ponged between the two of them and seemed to measure his words, "I see. And he decided a wall of fire would convince you of his intentions?"

Embarrassed to be caught dueling, she answered, "You can call it that."

"What do you have to say for yourself, *Linc?*" her father asked in a hard voice. "Is this how you woo my daughter? With dangerous antics?"

"Not to mention nearly burning a second house to the ground!" Drew spat. He was leaning aggressively toward Linc. But Linc just stood and seemed to wait for an opportunity to speak.

Vela didn't like the aggression directed toward Linc. A protectiveness surged through her, and she moved in front of him, trying to block him from their view. The moment charged and surprised her.

"Leave him alone!" she cried. "He's not responsible for this! I am."

She glanced back at Linc, trying to reassure him with her eyes she would defend him. Linc's face went from calm acceptance to surprise. He looked at her with a question in his eyes.

Vela realized in that moment she cared more for Linc than she thought possible. All the moments of him waiting patiently for her, *wooing* her like her dad said, rushed through her mind. It sunk in how deeply he committed himself to her. She suddenly wanted to explore what could be between them. He's made such an effort; it was time for her to do the same. She would tell him of these new feelings, and soon. But she still needed to be wary. There were still too many unknowns about Linc she needed answers to.

"Well, it was kind of both of us," she finally said and turned around and rushed to explain. "I wrapped him in vines, and he had to burn his way out and we were just..."

"You had to *wrap* him in vines?" her father interrupted in a quiet voice that could have just as easily been a shout. "Please explain why you felt you were in some kind of danger *to warrant wrapping him in vines*." He trained his eyes hard on Linc; her brothers, too, glared at him.

Vela reached her hands out, trying to diffuse the situation. Looking at her mom, she asked, "Mom? Can you help me?"

"Answer the question, Vela," her mother said.

Vela watched her family warily and searched for an explanation. Especially one that wouldn't result in Linc buried in rock.

Moving her gently to the side, Linc stepped around her. "Maybe I should explain," he said.

"Maybe you should," Kane agreed in a hard voice.

"We were talking when we came to a disagreement," Linc began.

"A disagreement?" Her mother's eyes sparked with indignation. "That would result in a firewall?"

"We disagreed on who was the stronger Elemental, Festans or Gyans," Linc explained calmly. "We dueled to prove who would win. I tried to stop her attack with the vines, knowing my fire wouldn't harm her. But maybe my actions were too drastic—I tried to warn her I am the stronger Elemental."

"Hmm, that remains to be seen. But you're right," David said, nodding his head. "If you are her Intended, your fires won't hurt her."

"Can someone explain to us," Kane said, motioning between him and Drew angrily, "what you guys are talking about?"

"It's a bond thing, Kane," Vela explained. "Apparently Linc knew my gift wouldn't hurt him and vice versa. His fire won't hurt me." Vela completely understood Kane's remark. She had forgotten, too. And her brothers were protective at the best and obsessively obtuse about her safety at their worst.

"I'm sure there was more to this duel than a way to see who's strongest," Drew said with a sneer.

"No. That's really what..." Vela said before Linc interrupted her.

"I was going to kiss her," Linc admitted with a sheepish grin. "But things got out of hand."

Vela whipped her head in Linc's direction. Her lips parted. She couldn't hide her shock. It was more than shock, though. Merely a pleasant surprise. She wondered if she would have welcomed a kiss. She was a little embarrassed, though, to have this conversation in front of her entire family.

Kane snorted, thoroughly amused.

"You think this is *funny*?" Vela asked her brother.

"Vela, anyone who tries to kiss you and gets wrapped in vines needs to have some kind of defense. A Festan just conquered you, little sister."

"He did not. And he didn't try to kiss me." She eyed Linc, who looked as embarrassed as she did.

"What? You didn't know he was going to kiss you?" Kane asked, incredulous. "Wow, you guys are off to a great start."

"Kane," her father barked. "Keep your enlightenments to yourself. This is not the time."

"Sorry Dad."

"No, *I'm* sorry," Linc apologized. "Your daughter has a way about her that took over my good sense. I apologize for any fear you felt for her."

Her father looked at Linc with a grudging respect, which relieved Vela. "I accept your apology. But does Vela?"

Linc looked over at her. "Vela, do you accept my apology? I hope I didn't scare you."

"It's okay. You're fire body is a bit intense, I'll admit. I thought I was in some kind of nightmare for a minute."

"The element of surprise for that particular skill of mine is now gone, so you won't see that side of me coming for you ever again," Linc promised.

Nodding, she was still shocked Linc had wanted to kiss her. She had no clue he'd had those intentions. When would he stop surprising her?

Never, was probably the only answer she would get.

Chapter Twenty-Seven

"Linc, Vela, come into the house," Whitney said with a tired voice.

Vela knew her mother had cause to sound exhausted. She exhausted herself on her best day, especially when it came to Linc.

Her mom went on to claim they had some important things to discuss with them both. Jack molded to her leg as she walked inside. She almost tripped twice over him. She supposed it was alright after not being able to get to her during the duel. He wouldn't let her out of his sight now.

Her brothers followed close behind and she wasn't positive this wasn't an ambush.

Her protective feelings resurfaced, but she pushed them back down. Whatever the conversation her parents wanted to have with them, she would face with Linc beside her. Her heart warmed again at the revelation of her feelings. She wanted to tell him what she was now feeling. That would happen later, she vowed.

She sat down in a creamy loveseat with bright flowers, her back straight and her leg jiggling. Jack jumped up on the loveseat and draped himself over Vela's lap. She smiled. He always sat like this and it instantly calmed her. Linc sat on what was left of the loveseat, squeezing himself next to her oaf of a dog. Linc sat stiffly and released a short sigh as he tried to get comfortable.

"Want me to get him down for you?" Linc offered, gesturing toward Jack.

"No," Vela said, smiling, "Your moojoo powers aren't needed. I like him like this."

He seemed amused, nodded and gave his attention to her parents.

The family settled in the living room. Her brothers took the two stuffed chairs that framed the red couch her parents sat on.

Her father began, "Now, let's get right to the point. You're both young for Intendeds, but that's not the worries your mother and I have." His eyes held a deep concern that worried Vela. Her father was nothing but calm, and she had never known him to overreact.

"Vela, you know that as Elders we have the privilege of learning things about our clan and the others, as well, that you don't have access to. Your and Linc's bond are a great concern for your mother and I."

Vela searched her mom's eyes and saw the same anxiety she saw in her dad's. Worry settled in her stomach.

He continued after a pause, "You, as a Gyan, and you, Linc, as a Festan, are an anomaly to connect the way you have. It does happen but rarely. Our concern, however, is that the times it has happened before have not gone well for the couple."

"Why Dad? They aren't compatible?" Unease crawled through her. She felt like spiders cavorted under her skin. Worry mixed in with the euphoria she experienced being around Linc. *What an odd feeling*, she thought. She rubbed her arms as she waited for her father to continue. She looked at Linc and he looked back at her, his face unreadable. She felt like a unit in that moment, solid and unbreakable.

David paused, seeming to choose his words carefully. "The Elemental couples that were from different clans have all mysteriously disappeared. As soon as word gets out about their bond, these couples drop off the face of the Earth."

A pregnant silence followed his revelation, and Vela's heart lurched. She looked over at Linc with horror and saw resolve, rather than fear, take over his features. He clenched his hands on his knees. His knuckles were white with tension. His face looked like it was chiseled with stone, which happened, she noticed, when he tried to hide his reaction from her. What did he know that he wasn't saying?

Drew was the first to break the silence. He fired off questions. "Does anyone know what happens to these lost couples, Dad? And why are they being taken? Who's taking them?"

Whitney spoke up, her words clipped, "Everyone knows of the old prophecy, The Prophecy of Connection, about the Chosen Child, right?"

Vela looked at Linc with a questioning glance. She knew the prophecy, but did he? His answer didn't surprise her as much as his tone when he spoke.

"Yes, I've grown up knowing about this prophecy," he stated. His voice carried a heaviness, like it stressed him to even talk about it. And he looked like he took it very seriously.

A blush stole over her at the thought. If she and Linc would marry, this Chosen Child could be theirs. It seemed a bit presumptive to think about children when they hadn't even shared a kiss.

"Um, Dad," Vela began, a million questions racing through her mind. Not sure which one to start with, she asked, "Are you worried that Linc and I will disappear, too? All because we might have a child together?" Her face continued to blush furiously. "And this child might unite the clans? Am I getting this right?"

Drew, with a dark scowl, said, "Wait, this is where one child will bring peace to our clans and stop the territory disputes, right?"

David answered with a brisk nod. "And there are people, Elementals, who are very determined that this child never exists."

"What do you mean, Dad?" Kane asked. "That they'll kill the child?"

"Not only would they kill the child," David answered in a solemn voice, "But they're obliterating any couple that could even have this prophesied child."

"Where do these people come from? Who are they?" Drew asked, fear taking over his tone.

"I'm sure you've heard of them. They're a secret group, The Elemental Extremists, or known as the E.E. They're linked with almost every disappearance. They take this prophecy seriously. They don't want any changes made to our way of doing things, or any potential for change."

"You've talked about this group before," Kane said. "The ones who are hiring Elementals to sell their gifts to the highest bidders. By changes, Dad, do you mean the way we defend our borders?"

"Yes. A child who can bring the clans together, unite us, is an attack on our world as we know it. Who would rule the clans? What kind of hierarchy are we looking at? It would be a monumental change."

"They don't want this child to ever exist," Vela said in a daze. To comfort herself, she patted Jack's head, running her hand over his sleek head. "And the couples that could have this child together vanish."

"Who are these crazy people, anyway?" Kane asked. "Do they belong to a certain clan or what?"

"Our suspicion is that they're recruiting and getting followers from all the clans."

"Wouldn't that be ironic?" Drew snorted.

"What would?" Vela asked.

"If they're from different clans working together to kill a child, who would unite the clans? They would be doing exactly what they are trying to kill. Uniting."

Drew's words rang in Vela's ears. It was true. This group's motivation was to prevent the clans from coming together in peace. If they were willingly working together to annihilate the prospect of peace, they were doing exactly that, working together. With horrifying results.

"I want to know," Drew continued, "why no one has caught this group. How are they staying secret when couples are disappearing? How is this not a priority to find these people?"

"It *is* a priority," David said. "This group must have a lot of money and connections along with a top rate computer system to track Elementals' social media accounts. That's where we think they're finding these couples. They get wind of their relationships and track them down. It's disturbing that they know the clans operate independently from each other and are making it hard to combine our efforts to find them. The E.E. is definitely using that to their tactical advantage to remain hidden.

"So," her father said solemnly. "It's critical that no one knows about your bond. You must not announce it in any circle, on any social media account, anywhere. Vela, Linc," he reiterated in a firm voice, "No one can know about you two. Who knows?"

Vela thought hard. "No one besides Elia and you guys."

"Okay, the first thing you do after this conversation is to talk to Elia and tell her how important it is that she does not speak about you and Linc to anyone. Got it?"

When Vela nodded eagerly, David turned to her Intended.

"Linc?" David questioned. "Who have you told?"

"My parents," he answered. A touch of worry crossed his face, but he quickly masked it.

"Not your uncle?" Vela asked, her voice tinged with disbelief.

"No."

"Is there a reason you wouldn't tell your uncle, Linc?" Kane asked with a suspicious glare.

"It was personal, and I don't share much of anything personal with my uncle. I wanted to keep it to myself, besides my parents, of course. But they wouldn't say anything, believe me."

"Linc," her dad started, seeming to think through what he was going to say, "It's unusual for you two to meet, because our clans don't usually converge into each other's territories. Why don't you tell us more about your uncle's research?"

"My uncle," Linc said slowly, "is a national researcher. He's traveling the United States, eventually Europe too, learning about other clans' cultures, since it is unknown among Festans how other clans operate. He's interested in learning about Gyans, Boreans, and Neronians and wants to put his research into a book, or a series of them. He plans to make it available to all Elementals."

"He's *studying* us?" Drew asked, distaste turning his mouth down.

"He's not being obvious about it. He's just trying to study as much as he can without being intrusive," Linc said with a shrug.

Vela's parents exchanged a look. "And your parents? Tell us about them."

"Vela hasn't told you?" he asked, surprise crossing his face.

"Not yet. I can hardly believe it myself," Vela confessed.

"My mother is the Grand Elder of the Festans. And my father is an Elder as well. They stay very busy running the clan, so they felt it best they send me with my uncle to study how other clans operate."

"Your *mother* is the *Grand Elder?*" her mother asked in shock. "How did we not make that connection, David?"

"So, your last name is Stevenson?" her dad asked with a shocked look, as well.

"Yes," Linc answered, chagrin taking over his expression. "It's a lot to take in."

"You're like a prince among the Festans," Drew scoffed, looking away.

"It's something I'd like to keep between us, if you don't mind," Linc requested.

"Of course," David replied, looking around at their small group. "Do you have siblings?" her father asked.

Vela had noticed he hadn't mentioned his sister he had lost. She wondered again what had happened to her.

Linc's stoic look fell, and he looked down, collecting his thoughts. "I had one sister," he finally said, holding his knees, his knuckles white with strain. "She passed away a couple years ago."

"I'm sorry to hear that," her mother said softly.

"And when did you start traveling with your uncle?" her father asked in a kinder tone.

"A couple years ago," Linc said, flexing his hands and a ghost of an anguished look crossed his face. He eventually looked up, composed again, and closed his face off.

From the few things he had told Vela, she knew he didn't want to be traveling the country with his uncle. He'd rather be home. What happened a couple years ago that resulted in his sister's death and him being shipped off to his uncle? Questions tore through her mind. They would have to be answered later. He didn't seem to want to talk about these subjects with her family he just met.

"I'd like to meet your uncle," Vela said, trying to keep sympathy off her face. He probably didn't want her broadcasting his problems with his family.

"You will. I'll bring him by," he told her with a strained smile.

"You two are in danger from this E.E. group," Drew interrupted, "And all you two think to talk about is meeting family? I think you should both reject this bond, and the sooner, the better."

Linc's eyes flashed with anger, and he said quickly, "That's asking for a lot."

"Yeah well, in case you didn't hear my dad, couples like you two are disappearing, doesn't that concern you?" Drew asked, his face in a deep scowl.

"Yes, of course it does," Linc answered in a hard voice. "But it's not easy to disconnect from an Intended. It could cause major pain in Vela and myself. Ignoring our bond and distancing ourselves from each other would cause excruciating pain, leaving Vela writhing around for weeks and that's not even mentioning the emotional pain our separation would cause. That would last months, years even. I'm not going to just do that. And she is my *Intended*. I'm not letting go of her easily. If we keep quiet, we can avoid danger from the E.E."

"Yes." David interrupted their heated exchange. "You can keep it quiet, which it seems you've done, besides your parents, us, and Elia knowing, but your actions will tell more than words."

"You mean if we act like a couple, people will know?" Vela assumed with a sinking feeling in her stomach. She had just decided she wanted something more. Now they had to stay secret?

"Yes," David answered. "No one can know there's a connection between you two."

"How do we hide something like this?" Vela's voice was bleak. "I mean, what kind of future is this?" She slumped back against the couch cushions, suddenly feeling hopeless. She moved Jack off her, needing space. She felt like she had just lost something she only had for a moment. Jack whimpered, nosing her hand.

She looked over at Linc, tears swimming in her eyes. "What do we do?" He looked lost for a moment, like he didn't know how to help her, sympathy finally taking over his face. He reached and took her hand in his.

Whitney jumped up and rushed to Vela's side. She stood by her, holding and supporting her sagging weight. "Vela, no one said this will be easy. But we can't risk anyone finding out about you two. It's too dangerous."

"Which is why it may be easier to just break the bond," Drew repeated. He leaned forward, resting his arms on his knees. "Vela, it's no life to live. Pretending to not be together is too hard."

Vela leaned against her mother, feeling weak. She didn't know what decision to make.

"We are talking about *our* lives here, not *yours*," Linc snapped. "You're asking us to break something God intended. Who do you think you are to play God by tearing something apart He designed to be together?"

"Explain that to the missing couples," Drew spat. "That their God-given relationship killed them."

Linc shot up from his seat. "Vela and I will decide once we've talked about this. There have to be other couples like us, in hiding, somewhere. I will not give up easily on something so important to me! And I think to her, too." He looked down at her, raising his eyebrows.

She nodded. Vela's aching heart warmed. She didn't know what the future held—who did, for that matter? But it made her feel good knowing someone was willing to fight for her, for them.

For a reason she couldn't explain, she just knew that she couldn't let go of Linc yet. Not with her newfound feelings and even knowing there was a danger for the both of them. No one knew about them yet, so they were safe.

Standing next to Linc, she put a hand on his arm and announced, "A secret relationship wouldn't be impossible. Difficult, yes, but not impossible. And we're still getting to know each other right now. It's not like we're getting married soon or anything. We can take this slow," she added, looking up into Linc's darkening eyes. He didn't seem to completely agree with her, on prospective wedding bells or their secret relationship, she wasn't sure, but he stayed silent.

"Very slow," David emphasized to Linc. "Vela's mother and I will support both of your decisions, but only if you're both very careful. You're taking our daughter's life in your hands, young man, and we don't give our trust easily. You'll have to earn it. We've only just met you. And as much as we respect the Intended bonding, Vela's life is too important to put her in danger needlessly."

"Needlessly?" Linc asked, his voice flat. He huffed, shaking his head. His voice grew stronger as he asked, "And what of a potential child? We could have what the prophecy predicted. Isn't that important to any of you?"

"It's such a slight chance that that will happen, son, that I'm not even the least bit concerned about that. It could be anyone, anywhere, who will fulfill that prophecy. We'll cross that bridge if we ever get there," David said firmly, his eyes hard as steel. "There's no reason to talk about a child just yet."

Vela sat down before her knees gave out, suddenly exhausted. The day had caught up with her. First the garden duel, and now this conversation shredded her emotions trying to keep up with this conversation. Glad her father put a stop to talking about a child between her and Linc, she relaxed into the couch.

"I'd better go," Linc announced, turning toward Vela. "My uncle will wonder where I am."

"Okay," Vela said softly. Was she ready to talk to him? She bit her lip as she thought about it.

"It seems I've picked a good time. You're tired," Linc said, smiling at Vela.

"Am I that obvious?"

Linc gave her a tender look. "Only to me."

"Thanks," she said, her cheeks warm. This would take some getting used to. She decided impulsively she did want to talk to him.

"Linc? Can I have a minute before you go?"

"Sure," he offered her his hand to stand. She appreciated his thoughtfulness and willed energy she didn't have into her body. When she touched his hand, however, a now familiar energy filled her chest and limbs, inherently fueling her. He was her personal battery charger. She loved it.

Her mom gave her a knowing look when Vela pulled Linc away from their group. Vela hid a smile. She led him by the hand into the mudroom, away from any prying ears.

Standing before him, she blushed and looked down, getting her thoughts together. Linc unlinked their fingers and tipped her head up gently.

"What is this adorable blush? For me? I'm honored."

Breathing out a soft laugh, her face turned even warmer, and she said suddenly shy, "I have to let you know something."

"I'm all ears."

She finally looked up at him, into his warm eyes and smile, and she wondered if he knew what she was going to say. She didn't care if he did.

Not wasting another minute, she stumbled through her words, "I want to try... with us. In secret, but still. I'm not saying I want a lifetime commitment here yet, but I'm willing... now... to try. To start this thing we have."

Grabbing her hands, he brought them to his chest and put his forehead on hers. His grip got warmer, but it wasn't too hot, and wouldn't be. But he seemed to struggle for words and Vela waited, holding her breath.

He had made it clear he wanted a relationship, but she still felt like she was throwing herself on the line for him to reject. *What if he did?* She suddenly wasn't sure, and her chest grew tight with tension.

"Vela, I can't tell you what this means. What you mean to me. I'll take this... thing you called it... and be happy with it. You're my world now and where you'll be, I'll be there too, to protect and cherish."

At his words, she gave him a wide smile. It was the perfect kind of moment she wanted to remember forever. She basked in it for a second, then couldn't help herself. She leaned in where he stood, oh so close, and brought her lips to his in a soft kiss.

Their lips fit together perfectly, and he cupped her face and angled her head for an even better kiss. She thought of their bonded energy like adrenaline, and it sped through her making her dizzy. She held onto his arms because her knees suddenly turned to jelly. She did *not* want this moment to end because of her stupid body's inability to handle the best kiss of her life, so she hung on and matched his kiss.

He pulled away, bringing them back to their first position, foreheads touching.

"Vela," he moaned again. "You're going to kill me. I never thought a kiss would feel like that. I could burn a house to the ground right now."

At that, she took two steps away, ice filling her veins, and looked at him with horror.

"What did you just say?"

Looking at her, confused, he said, "I never thought a kiss would feel like that."

"No. After that," she said in a hoarse voice, her heart beating wildly.

"What? That I could burn..." Realization dawned in his eyes, and he rushed to say, "Vela, I'm sorry. I didn't mean to say it like that. It's an expression where I come from!"

"But *why* would you say that? Burn a house down? Would you, could you, do that?"

Her old fears rose to the surface faster than a striking snake, and she choked on the smoke she could somehow smell from her childhood memories. All of it, Cooper, the lost pictures, the lost mementos, their old life, crashed through her memories.

"Vela," he breathed, reaching for her arms. "No. I would never. I could, I mean, I guess, if I wanted to, but no! I'd never burn a house down. It's a stupid expression we Festans say." Eyeing her distressed look, he said, "Obviously, I said the absolute worst thing I could. I'm sorry, Vela, I would never harm you."

Shaking her head, she held her hands out and said, "I resisted you this whole time because I've always feared the Festans. First you guys burned down my house, which gave me these scars, then we moved to an area where you terrorize our northern and southern borders. Do you know how hard it's been to trust you enough to believe you wouldn't do just what your expression," she quoted with her hands, "said? I'm putting aside years, a lifetime of fears, trusting you, Linc."

Throwing out her arms in a wide arc, she continued, "You have this mysterious background with parents who just let you roam the country with your researcher uncle that you just expect everyone to believe. Well," she said with a hard laugh, "I'm sorry. But it still raises questions in my mind. I almost forgot what you're capable of. What your kind can do and has done in my life." She forced tears back, refusing to let them fall. "I'm trying to put aside my prejudice for this... this... connection we have. Do you realize how hard it is for me?"

As if approaching a scared animal, he made a small step toward her and held out his arms to her, reaching for her hands.

Warily, she watched him approach her and swallowed thickly, fighting panic as it clawed her throat. She allowed him to softly touch her hands.

"What we have," he said in a fervent voice, "is priceless. It's not common, I know, for our two clans to trust each other. But I'm not trying to change our world's view, just our two hearts. Let our hearts decide if this is safe. Trust them to guide our unusual connection and go from there. Let's just take it a day, no, a moment at a time, learning to trust each other, because your people are just as terrifying as mine. Until it's as easy as breathing to trust... and love each other."

She had been staring down at his hands, barely holding hers, and she stilled. Her mom had said that about an Intended bond. That she would crave being around him as much as breathing. She sucked in a deep breath and warred with trusting her mom's and Linc's advice.

"Okay," she finally said and looked up at him. She gave him, not his people, a chance to prove to her he would be trustworthy.

Squeezing her fingers, his face lit up, and he beamed a smile, stretching the dimple on his chin wider. "Really?" he asked in a hopeful voice. "I'm sorry," he said as if he begged her. "I would never want to scare you with my gift, and I'll be more sensitive to what I say from now on. And for the record," he said, bending his knees to look her fully in the eyes, "I would never burn down a house. Ever."

She couldn't help her smile and she said, "That's good to know."

He looked away from her and said with regret in his tone, "I really have to go. But thank you, Vela. For trusting me. And even if you only trust me with a sliver of your heart right now, I'll take that for the gift it is. Until the day you give me your whole heart, I'll collect the pieces you offer and keep them until they're complete."

"Like a puzzle," she said, smiling.

"You are a puzzle I'll have the joy of putting together one day, Vela." Cupping her face almost reverently, he asked, "Can I have one last kiss? To chase away the terror of scaring you like that?"

In answer, she leaned in and softly kissed him. It was gentle. It was sweet. And just what she needed. She smiled against his lips and breathed out, "Thank you."

"I should be the one thanking you," he said. He looked reluctant to pull away.

"I'll see you tomorrow?"

"I'll count every minute till I do," he promised.

She blushed and nodded.

He turned, like he would leave, but then whipped around, held her face in his hands and pressed his warm lips to hers, more firmly than her kiss had been and deeper. He expertly moved his lips communicating to her the depth of his feelings. Okay, she was wrong. This kiss was what she had needed.

Vela gasped for air.

He leaned his forehead against hers. "I had to kiss you one more time. For memory's sake," he whispered against her lips.

"Memory's sake?"

"My memory of your lips against mine."

"Didn't we just kiss?" She giggled.

"Not the way I wanted to," he answered and claimed her lips again.

Vela lost herself in Linc's arms and his kiss drove away all thoughts of their argument and who his clan was, the gift he harbored, their future. All was lost in the tangle of their mouths. She kissed him back as equally as he kissed her, and her heart soared.

He broke away from her panting. "I need to stop."

"Okay," she said, just as breathless.

He leaned in, pressed one more hard kiss to her mouth and stepped two steps back, his fists clenching and his chest heaving in breaths.

"You are going to kill me," he breathed.

"Vice Versa! You know, I could get used to this," she added with a smile, equally out of breath. He had literally taken her breath away.

"Plan on it," he said with a wicked grin and walked to the door.

With that, Linc slipped out of the mudroom door, and Vela drifted to her room. She was sure of three things. As she ran her hand over her swollen lips, she counted them. One, she no longer hated Linc. Two, she had feelings for him that were unparalleled. And three, she'd have to fight her fears. She knew they wouldn't go away in a day.

But she left them in God's hands. If He thought she could handle this, she would. Vela just had to believe that.

Chapter Twenty-Eight

AS TIRED AS VELA was, she could not hold off on calling Elia. She needed to be sure Elia hadn't talked with anyone else about her bonding with Linc. It was impossible to know with her. When she got excited about something, she usually couldn't hold it in. But she was sure that her best friend had respected Vela's private nature and not blabbed about it.

What she and Linc had just discussed, she would keep to herself, however. She wanted to hold it close to her right now. It was too new to expose to anyone else's scrutiny. Even though she was sure Elia would be ecstatic over their new understanding. For now, she just needed to find out what her best friend may have said and to whom.

There was only one way to know.

Picking up her phone, Vela dialed and when Elia picked up, Vela sighed with relief.

"What's up, Vels?" Elia asked in a chipper voice.

"Elia, my mom and dad are really worried about something. It has to do with Linc and I being different Elementals. Have you told anyone about us? About our bond? Any other Elemental?"

"I don't think so." Elia's voice sobered quickly. "Hold on a minute, let me think. I told my mom, and she probably mentioned it to my dad. Why Vela? Why would your parents be worried?"

"No one else knows Elia? No other Elemental?" Vela asked again, holding her breath.

"No. Unless someone can suddenly read minds, no one else knows. Maria has been glaring at you lately and with her little crush on Linc, I wondered if she suspects. I would never have told her, though! Vela, what's wrong?"

Vela sat back on her bed with a huge sigh of relief. Maria was a cause for concern, however. She'd have to be extra careful around her. "Oh, thank God. Okay, we'll need to talk to your parents right away. I'll have my parents call yours."

"Vela, explain to me right now what is going on."

"Elia, you know about the Prophecy of Connection? That there's a child who will unite the clans? And that this child will have two different Elementals as parents?"

"Yes," Elia answered slowly. "I have heard about it. *What about it?*"

Vela filled Elia in on what she had discussed with her family and Linc that afternoon.

"They would target you and Linc?" Elia asked after listening quietly, her tone grim. "What do you mean, target?"

"I mean, no one ever sees these couples again. Elia, never. No one can know about Linc and I. We could disappear if the wrong people find out about us. We could disappear forever."

Elia was quiet for a minute, then yelled away from her phone. "Mom, Dad! Call the Ashcroft's! Call them now!" She got back on the phone. "This is crappy news. The worst. What's the plan?"

"Staying alive and secret. Absolutely no one can find out about this. Apparently, once word reaches this group, that's it for the couple."

"I'm going to research this group," Elia announced.

"I don't know if that's a good idea." Vela thought through what her parents went over this afternoon. "They could track Internet searches for their name. They're too dangerous, LeeLee."

"They are stealthy, too, from what it sounds like. To get away with this, I mean. How would one go about joining a group like this? If they are so secret, how can they be found?"

"What are you getting at, Elia?" Vela didn't like this question one bit.

"Well, what if we took the bull by the horns and contacted the E.E. like we wanted to be members? That way, we could find out so much…"

Horrified, Vela yelled, "No! That's out of the question! I cannot believe you would even go there, Elia. No. Absolutely not. Don't scare me with your insane ideas!"

"It was just a thought," Elia mumbled. She gained momentum when she continued in the same breath, "But think about it, Vela. It's the perfect way to know if you and Linc are safe. By being in the lion's den. Spying on them."

"How on Earth would we do that, Elia? They're secret. No one knows how to find them." Vela couldn't believe she was even listening to this.

"I'll bet they have an online presence," Elia mused. "They must stay connected that way. I'm sure I could find them."

"No! Elia, no," Vela groaned. "This is madness to get in touch with a secret group of goons and gorillas who murder people! This is your craziest idea yet. You are *not* going to try to find them. Promise me, Elia."

Vela's heart raced at the thought of her dearest friend going into danger because of her. She had to put a stop to her friend's scheme. There was a measure of truth to it. She'd give her that. But it was still too dangerous.

"Look Vela. I would do anything to keep you safe. And if that means joining some online group to keep an ear out on these people, then so be it. Who knows, maybe I can help some other poor couple out there who need to know they're in danger!"

Vela swiftly countered, "I will not put you in danger just to save someone else, Elia! What you're doing is what the Elders should do. They're adults, Elia. We're just kids."

"Exactly, who would suspect me of being anything other than who I say I am? I'll be a twenty-something Neronian. Who would guess?"

"Someone could. And that's a chance I'm not willing to take."

Silence came over their conversation. Vela could hear Elia furiously typing in the background.

"What. Are. You. Doing?"

"Just looking around," Elia answered evasively.

"Well, stop that! I know you're looking!"

"And why not Vela? Do you want to be a sitting duck? Just waiting for the worst to happen? Or," Elia said with determination in her words, "do you want to take control of your own life?"

Elia waited while Vela thought. She in no way wanted her best friend to put herself in harm's way. But, if she was just reaching out to an online community, she could keep her identity a secret and stay safe. All while she gathered information. What if she helped her and they could stay anonymous? It was the only way to rein Elia in. For Vela to get involved.

"Elia, listen to me. If you're determined to do this, I'm going to help you. But we need to keep our identities secret. We can't tell anyone our real names or anything about us. This is crazy," Vela breathed.

"Vels, it's just a harmless search."

"Until you contact someone! Elia, please be careful. What're you finding? Tell me the website." Vela sighed, resigned to a night of researching.

She opened up her laptop and got comfortable on her bed, stacking pillows behind her, laying her computer on her lap.

"I don't have a website yet. I'm just searching right now," Elia said, sounding distracted.

Vela pulled up her favorite search engine and typed in *Elemental groups.* She grew curious when she saw one result that said, *Want to find your utopia? Where everyone can just get along?* That was the opposite of the E.E.'s goals, but she clicked on it, anyway.

Her eyes rounded when she viewed its page. "Elia, you might want to look at this website," Vela said, surprise halting her words. "Go to elements united dot com."

"Crap on a cracker!" Elia exclaimed. "What is this? Is that *Maria* in that picture?"

There as clear as day was Maria with a group of other people all smiling at the picture. "What on earth is she doing in this group?" Vela wondered aloud.

It read like an advertisement for world peace. Something about it, though, made Vela study the page. "Does this group seem weird to you, Elia?"

Want to light a fire for your beliefs? Create a wind of change? Water your curiosity with these simple facts. The world needs to grow out of it's culture of violence and schemes. Let's all just get along!

"Don't you think it's curious that they mention all the elements in this?" Vela asked. The people in the group picture with Maria were all side hugging and smiling widely. "Do you think it's a coverup for the E.E.?"

"Maybe. It's worth filling out the contact page to find out."

"Alright. But, put a fake name in and let me know right away if they contact you. Should we ask Maria about it?"

"I don't think so. Because if they are the E.E. then there goes our cover. It wouldn't surprise me if she was a part of that crazy train. Okay," Elia said decisively, "I'll let you know what else I find out. I gotta go."

"Be careful, LeeLee. I'll talk to you tomorrow."

After they hung up, Vela continued her search around the web to see if she could find any other websites that seemed like the E.E. The first website she had found seemed like the closest she could find to an Elementals group. The more she thought about it, the more she was sure the E.E. wouldn't broadcast its hate message. It made more sense to hide their terrible group behind a positive message. Maybe that's how they found members by lying about their true purpose. Then once they had them in their grip, used them to sell their gifts to desperate Elementals across the world. It made a sick sort of sense.

Vela prayed for wisdom and for insight and safety into her dangerous search and kept looking.

Chapter Twenty-Nine

VELA TIREDLY TURNED THE page of the book her teacher was going over in class. She could barely concentrate. Despite searching for other viable options that could be the E.E., she had found nothing. Then she had faced a night of restlessness. She couldn't sleep knowing what Elia was doing. Searching for a ruthless group that would kill them if they knew they were trying to infiltrate them.

Shaking her head at Elia's sheer stubbornness, Vela caught Linc's attention. She had the seat next to him, but on his other side sat her nemesis. She couldn't get rid of the jealousy still lingering after watching Maria blatantly flirt with Linc before class started. Linc looked like he smiled politely at Maria, but otherwise ignored her.

Vela had been too tired to glare at her, however, and now that she had to keep her relationship a real secret, she didn't dare to.

Linc caught her eye when the teacher started class and he finally got a break from Maria's conversation. She smiled at him shyly, not sure how to act now that she'd told him they could be a couple. He looked at her with a question in his eyes. He could sense her distress and her annoyance at Maria, she was sure.

Vela shook her head again, silencing him. She returned her attention to the passage being read by her teacher and wished he could read it with a livelier voice. Needing all the help she could get to stay awake, Vela sighed.

A folded piece of paper pushed into her view. She glanced at Linc, who nodded at the paper, urging her to read it. Making sure Maria didn't notice the note, she read it.

> *I know something is wrong. If you're worried about that date I won yesterday, don't worry. I'll make it as painless as possible.*

Vela smiled despite herself. She wished that a date was all she had to worry about. But she wasn't sure she could talk about her and Elia's recent activities. For it to stay a secret, she'd have to stay quiet about it all.

Her decision made; she picked up a pen to write back. Keeping it from Linc was going to be difficult, but maybe she could successfully distract him.

> *I think I made it clear enough to you. I'm not too worried about a date happening. I can handle myself.*

He scratched quickly on the paper as soon as he read it.

> *Can you?*
> *Yes,* she answered just as quickly.
> *Are you worried about what would happen if we did go on a date?*
> *What do you mean? What would happen?*
> *Like a kiss?*
> *You would say that.*

Say what? That I'm going to claim one?
You wish.
I do. I wish it were right now. It's all I've been
thinking about since yesterday.
You're not thinking about a bloodthirsty group
that will kill us if they knew about us? You're
hung up on not getting a kiss?
Yes.

Vela looked up from the note with disbelief across her face. She hoped Maria hadn't noticed their exchanges, as nosy as she was, but they had also had to keep it from view from the teacher.

Meet me outside.

Raising her hand, she asked for permission to go to the restroom. She didn't care how Linc got out of the room, but he better follow soon. He would know where to find her. He only needed to follow his senses. She knew it to be a risk for them to leave so soon from one another, but he must be crazy to only think about a stupid kiss when the E.E. might find them!

She hurried through the empty hallways, searching for the quickest exit. Spotting one, she opened the door and escaped into the cool fall air. She waited under the shaded portico by the door for Linc to find her.

Just as the door opened to let Linc outside, she had the realization that Linc probably thought she left the classroom because she wanted to get the kiss he wanted.

Linc stepped outside with an interested look in his eyes.

Vela held up her hands up as a shield. He came into her personal space, reaching for her waist.

"So, where were we?" Linc asked in a husky voice.

"No!" Vela whispered angrily, pushing him back. "I did not come out here for *this*."

"What did you come out here for, then?"

"Listen, Elia has these crazy plans. I don't want to get into what they are right now, but..."

"Why not?" he asked, his voice changing deeper, darker.

"Well, it's kind of crazy what she wants to do."

"Crazy as in dangerous?"

"Yes, and I'm not sure how to discourage her."

"You just discourage her. It's pretty simple," he said flatly.

"Nothing about Elia is simple." She sighed and looked away.

"Let me guess. She's going to try to find the E.E."

She darted a look at him, then stood quietly, not admitting their crazy plan and that she was involved, too.

"If she is, then you're right, it is crazy," he said, running his hand through his hair. "These are not the kind of people you can find things on easily. And they're definitely not people you want to look for." He blew out a breath and looked out into the distance.

"I don't know how to stop her," she whispered. Her insides were a tangle of worry over their plans. But her heart lurched when she saw the principal look through the door's window at her and Linc. The door opened and her principal's bald head poked out.

"Are we skipping class or we on our way to another one?" the principal asked, his thin face pinched in annoyance. "Time to break up this little heart-to-heart and move on," he said sternly.

"Yes, sir," they both mumbled.

With the principal watching, they walked back to class, subdued and quiet. Linc didn't know Elia like she did. What could he do to stop her attempts to find this group? Nothing could stop her once she got her mind hooked on something. And with Vela's life at stake, Elia would stop at nothing. She envisioned a lot of arguments between her best friend and Linc, and it made her head hurt.

When the principal saw they had made it back to their class, he walked off with clipped steps.

"We need to stay low to the ground, blend in, not go in blazing looking for this group," Linc said in front of the door. "Elia needs to stop."

"I think it's going to be obvious no matter what we do. How can we hide this forever?" she grumbled, then a shock of alarm went through her. "Linc, we can't be seen as if we're together, remember? Was that principal an Elemental? He said we were having a heart-to-heart. Do you think he thought we were together?" In her alarm at getting caught outside the classroom, she forgot to check if his status as an Elemental or human.

"No, he's not an Elemental," Linc assured her as he reached for the door. "And don't worry, I'll just skip the rest of this class. If you go back and I don't, everyone will wonder where I am and not think about us leaving at the same time."

"What about your backpack?" she squeaked, panic crowding her throat to where she could hardly speak.

"I'll be back to get it later. Now, go back and pretend like nothing happened. Don't worry," he said, clear and confident. "No one knows. We're still safe."

She watched him leave with doubt hounding her. Maybe it would be better to do what Elia said. Not being sure of her and Linc's safety was going to make her slowly go crazy.

It *was* time to take the bull by the horns.

Chapter Thirty

VELA CONCENTRATED ON THE text she typed to Elia in her last class period. She could have waited until she saw her on the bus in a few minutes, but she needed answers. Needed to find out what Elia had discovered last night about the E.E. She also conveyed her worry that rumors would fly about her and Linc leaving class this morning practically at the same time.

"Psst!"

She finished her text and looked up.

Maria leaned toward her. "Hey!" she whispered. "Where did Linc go? He hasn't been in class since this morning."

"How am I supposed to know?" Vela asked with a frown.

"You mean, you didn't see him when you left class first period? He left right after you did," Maria said, with a knowing look in her eyes.

Vela's gut churned. She had to silence this rumor that they might've been together. "No, I went to the bathroom, and I didn't see him in the halls or anything."

"Come on Vela, it's obvious you two were together," Maria challenged with a hard look, a jealous one, by the looks of it.

She should have known Maria would look into anything to do with Linc suspiciously. She would do anything she could to make him hers. She must have noticed he and Vela's interaction in first period the other day, too. Maria was going to make it difficult for Vela and Linc to stay under the radar.

"You have a big imagination," Vela snapped. "That's not what happened. I went to the bathroom. When I came back, he was gone. That was it." Hoping her lie to be smooth enough, she waited for the teacher to pass by her seat, then looked to see Maria's reaction.

Maria sat on the edge of her seat, fuming with a hard glare. "Everyone thinks you guys were together," she announced. "You can tell me the truth, Vela."

As if Vela would ever confide in Maria. She suddenly wanted to question her about the picture of her on that website. But knew now wasn't a good time. It would raise even more questions Vela did not want to answer.

"Well, everyone's assumption is wrong," Vela said flatly. "I didn't even see him."

"Well, tell that to the principal," Maria said with a slow smile. "He'll probably question you about where Linc went, since he's skipped the rest of the day."

"And why would the principal think to question me?"

"He may have found out that you left at the same time." Maria's eyes glittered maliciously.

"By whom?" Vela asked in a tight voice.

"I may have told the teacher what I thought happened who then informed the principal."

"Why are you so up in my business?" Vela spat. Her control had snapped. She was sick of Maria's head games.

"When you made it your mission to take Linc away from me," Maria snarled. "I had made it very clear from the beginning I was interested in him. And then you had to steal him away behind my back."

"Steal him away?" Vela hissed. "He was never yours and he's not mine, either. Give the guy some room, Maria!"

"I'll do what I want and when I want to. Don't think for one second I'll listen to you. But you might want to listen to me." She leaned into Vela's space and breathed, "Stay away from Linc. He'll never want someone like you, you with your little plants and even smaller life. He's all mine. Let me handle him. He's too much for someone like you to even think of being with."

Vela sat back, speechless. Maria, satisfied she had gotten Vela's attention, leaned back in her seat and examined her nails. She may as well have scratched Vela's face to ribbons with the damage her words had caused. Maybe she was right. Linc, as the Grand Elder's son, had a bright and shining future. How could she even think to be a part of his world? Yes, they had a bond, but how far would that take them if their lives were utterly incompatible?

Not only that, but Maria could and would announce it to anyone who would listen if she knew about Vela and Linc's secret bond, especially the E.E. if it meant she couldn't have Linc for herself.

Vela's phone had gone off in her hand several times, so she knew Elia had gotten the text she had sent. Dazed, she looked at her phone, thankful the teacher gave the class some down time. She could focus on what Elia wrote.

> **Elia:** First, I might have a lead on this group you found. I found a forum that looked like it could be them and it seems like they're looking for new members.
> **Elia:** Second, what do you mean you and Linc left the class together? WHAT were you two doing together that whole time?
> **Elia:** You better give me details later, sister!

Vela: I think that you should leave this group alone. I have a bad feeling about this. And already people are talking about how Linc left class right after me. Maria's telling people about it, so now they think we were together, even the principal!
Elia: Maria is going to be a problem, Vela. She wants to sink her claws in Linc, so she'll be watching you two.
Vela: That much is obvious. We need to shut down this rumor!!
Elia: I have an idea, but you're not going to like it. And Linc really won't like it.
Vela: What?

Three little dots appeared showing Vela a text being written, but it disappeared. Then appeared again. After a minute of suspense, Elia finally sent the text.

Elia: You need to date someone else.
Vela: What? No!!
Elia: Go on a date or two, that's all I'm saying. Throw people's attention in a different direction. Then they'll forget all about anything between you and Linc.

Vela leaned back in her chair. It made a certain sick kind of sense. But could she do it? And what on Earth would Linc have to say about this plan?

Vela: I'll think about it.

Vela had a bad feeling in her stomach. Just how far would she go to throw the wolves, namely Maria, off her and Linc's scent? She was about to find out.

Chapter Thirty-One

Vela walked through her front door, tiredly shutting it behind her. She leaned her aching head against the wood, and for a brief moment, wished she had someone else's life, or at least her old one back.

Guilt chased through her for the thoughts, and she picked her head up and walked into the dining room, slumping down into a chair at the table. Thinking about Elia's suggestion again just gave her a bigger headache than she already had. She drummed her fingertips on its surface. She worried about when Linc would return her call and come over. She didn't know what he would say about the crazy idea number two, Vela was calling it, for her to date someone else, but she had a suspicion. Crazy idea number one was infiltrating the secret group. She moaned and laid her head on her arms, wanting to know when life had taken such an insane turn. It was undoubtedly when Linc came into her life.

But she wouldn't trade this for anything else. Complications were sure to come up with her dating a Festan. She just didn't expect such drastic ones as these.

A cheerful hello echoed through her home after a knock on the door. A deep voice, Kane's by the sound of it, welcomed their new guest, which Vela knew was Elia. A pealing laughter rang out, signaling Elia having fun with Vela's brother.

Elia soon walked into the dining room and dropped into the seat next to hers. Her face had a glow and Vela dreaded to hear what excited her excitable best friend.

"You ready to plan?" Elia asked, her eyes dancing.

"What has you in such a good mood?"

"Oh, nothing. Kane said something funny. He's so hilarious." Her eyes had such a dreamy look, Vela could only roll her eyes.

"You have it so bad."

"Yeah, I really do." She gazed over Vela's shoulder, and Vela knew she was in her dreamworld with her hero. Vela almost didn't want to interrupt the moment.

"Planning for what, by the way? To sell me off to the highest bidder? Or the one where we threaten our lives with the Elemental Extremists?"

Snapping out of her thoughts, Elia answered, "Vela, we're secretly looking into a private group, and you just need to go on a few harmless dates to throw off suspicions about you and Linc."

"Is that all? A *few* dates, Elia? You said a couple before. Do I need to marry someone by the time you're happy?" Vela threw up her hands.

"No, look, I have it on good authority Evan is very interested in you and would love to go on a *couple* of dates."

"No way! He wouldn't keep his hands to himself for two seconds, let alone two dates! Elia, no. Next plan. And why have I agreed to do this? Linc is going to kill me."

"And he'll really kill whoever you do date, don't forget. We need to tell him exactly why we need to do this," Elia said soberly.

Vela's senses tingled with awareness of Linc approaching. She hadn't heard the door knock, but her feelings around him were never wrong.

"Elia, shhhh! We don't want to tell Linc this just yet. Let me ease him into it," Vela whispered.

"Tell me what?" a voice asked behind their chairs.

Vela and Elia both jumped. Turning around, Vela cringed. *What did he hear?* She looked up at Linc, trying and failing not to look guilty.

"What's going on? And why do you look so guilty?" he asked with a smooth voice that shivered up Vela's spine. Wishing all she had to worry about was a date with him, not going on a dating spree with Evan, of all people, she shrugged.

"They're up to something," Kane chimed in as he joined them. "Don't trust them. When Elia gets that look on her face, you need to watch out." Elia smiled up at Kane innocently.

"Are you two going to tell me what you're talking about or am I going to have to guess?" Linc asked.

"Linc," Vela began tentatively, "we have an idea on how to throw people off our scent, but you need to keep an open mind."

"What do you mean, throw people off our scent?" he asked, his eyebrows furrowed. "No one knows we're together."

Her heart warmed at hearing him say they were together, but she focused her mind on what she had to tell him.

"People are wondering about us," she explained. "Specifically, Maria, and she has assumed, correctly, that we were together when you followed me out of class today. So, she started telling everyone that we left together, and people are asking about us now. She ambushed me in class asking if I knew where you had gone for the rest of the day," she finished, wringing her hands. She did not tell him the rest of the conversation when Maria warned Vela away from him.

"Okay, that's easily remedied. What else?" His sharp eyes turned to Elia.

"Don't look at me!" she cried, pointing at Vela. "Ask her what else!"

Vela spun to face her best friend. "What? This is your crazy idea! You should explain it to him!"

"Explain what?" Kane asked in an exacerbated tone.

"Yes, please do explain," Linc said, irritation in his tone.

"That she should date someone else," Elia confessed in a small voice.

Snapping a furious gaze to Vela, Linc asked her, "Is that what you think, too? That instead of quelling a few stupid rumors, you should *date* someone else?"

"Well," she began.

Linc interrupted with a slight tremor to his voice. "Well, what? I'm pretty sure that's a yes or no question." He was furious, just like she thought he would be. He clenched his jaw, and his eyes were like hard blue stones as he waited impatiently for her answer.

"Linc, I don't want to. God knows it's the last thing I want to do. But people will talk about us, which is exactly what we don't need. We have to throw off their suspicions." Begging him wasn't helping, judging by the look on his face, so she stopped talking and waited.

"Linc," Kane said, putting a restraining hand on Linc's shoulder, "It is a crazy idea, but it just might work. There can't be any kind of rumor that you two are together. We have to protect you and Vela. So, if she dates someone else, this'll blow over."

"If you think," Linc glared daggers at Kane and shrugged his hand off his shoulder, "that I'm going to just sit by and allow someone to *date my Intended*, you think again. She's mine and no one else's. I'll light up anyone who even thinks of touching her."

"Whoa, Linc," Elia cried. "We aren't talking about anyone touching Vela, just a couple of harmless dates. Vela can handle herself. No one will touch her if she doesn't want them to."

"I know she can handle herself," he growled. "And I would hope she doesn't want anyone else to touch her, but she is *not* under any circumstances dating anyone else to give them the chance. Period. Would you want me dating anyone else? Maria, for instance?"

All eyes turned toward her, and Vela sucked in a breath. Fury took over her, and she clenched her hands, trying to get a hot rage under control. This must be what Linc was experiencing, too. The thought of him with anyone else infuriated her.

"No, I wouldn't want him with anyone else, especially her," she finally said, willing the cloud of anger that filled her mind to dissipate.

"You see?" Linc gestured with a sweep of his hand. "She's just as disgusted with the idea as I am."

Logic wrapped its cold fingers around Vela's throat. She hated its duplicity. It would work to date other people, but they would also secretly be together. It was a concrete plan, but to act it out was entirely something else.

"You two need to consider your safety," Kane said seriously. "If you have to fool a few people along the way, then that's the route you're going to have to take. I think it would be wise for you both to date other people."

Unfortunately, Vela agreed. Everything within her screamed not to, but she nodded and looked up at Linc. "We need to be convincing. We can't risk our lives because we're jealous."

Sitting close to where Linc was standing, Vela could feel Linc's temperature rising. His heat element was going haywire. She could smell the smoke rising off him, too.

"No," he gritted out. "I won't do it. And if you do, I'm going to have a hard time forgiving you for it." Every one of his muscles flexed and his body looked like a concrete wall. He glared at her and said coolly, "If you want to prostitute yourself to justify that you're doing it for safety, that's your choice. I don't want any part of it."

"Prostitute myself?" Vela shot up from her seat and it took everything she had in her not to slap his angry face. Instead, she glared up at him.

"What you're doing is prostituting your integrity. Pretending to be with someone else. It's disgusting. We can figure out another way to deal with rumors about us. This plan is wrong, and you know it."

"Linc..." she started to say.

He slashed the air with his hand, cutting off anything she would say. With one last hard look at her, he stomped out of the room.

When the front door slammed, Vela slumped in her seat. "This sucks," she said. Her heart felt like a cold stone in her chest. Her anger gone, she felt deflated and defeated.

"It really does," Elia agreed quietly. "If it wasn't so dangerous for you two to be together, then I would say not do it. But it's so important that you fool everyone who suspects you two."

"The thought, Elia, the simple thought of Linc dating someone else, enrages me like nothing else. I know how he feels! How can we ask him to do this? To allow me to date someone when we have a lifetime bond with each other? It's by far the worst thing I can do to him." She covered her face with her hands and fought the tears threatening to make an appearance.

She didn't think she could do it. She really didn't. It would be the ultimate test of their fledgling relationship. Could she act convincingly, like she was interested in someone else? She shook her head.

"Vela, it's really the best way to handle this. You're making the right choice," Kane said gravely, patting her shoulder sympathetically.

With that last comment hanging in the tense air, he left the room and Elia said quietly, "This might not be a good time, but we need to talk about the other thing, Vels."

"You're right, it's not a good time," Vela said, her throat constricting. Tears were coming, she could feel them welling up.

"No, we do," Elia insisted. "This forum I found last night has a meeting soon. We need to talk about going."

"What, Elia?" she asked, exasperated. "You really want to go into this now?"

"Yes. It's next week. We need to come up with a plan on how to get there."

"Where is there?" Vela asked, her voice rising. "It could be anywhere in the world."

"Well, it's in Denver, so it's not too far away, thankfully."

"This is too much, Elia," Vela said tiredly, placing her head, which now had a blaring headache, in her hands. Looking up, she said, "I have to date someone else. Go to a secret meeting to spy on its dangerous members, which Maria, of all people, may be a part of. Oh yeah, and then possibly fulfill a prophecy where my child unites the world." Vela moaned. "Just give me time to sort this all out, okay?"

"Just think about it. I'm really nervous about Maria seeing us, though. We might need to think about disguises."

"*Disguises*? Are you kidding me right now?"

"Well, just in case this group is the E.E. and she's a part of them, if we're in disguises, she can't tell them who we really are. Think about it, that's all I ask."

Vela sighed heavily. "Trust me, that's all I'll be doing."

"And Vela?" Elia covered Vela's hand with hers. "Try not to worry. We need to pray that this is the direction that God is having us go. If it is, then peace will come."

Peace was good. Vela craved it, needing it to saturate her frazzled emotions.

"Okay," she whispered. "Thanks, LeeLee."

Once Elia left, Vela slumped in her chair even further. The stairs felt like they were a million miles away. Pulling herself up, she lumbered up the hateful things and went to her room.

This night needed to be over. She didn't know how much more she could take.

Chapter Thirty-Two

VELA DIDN'T THINK SHE would hear from Linc for days after he'd left her house in a rage. However, she discovered a text from him when she woke up the following morning.

In the night he had written, *My uncle has invited you and your parents to come over tomorrow after school to meet you and to talk over issues. Be prepared. We need to talk.*

Vela wanted to write back and say, "No." That the time wasn't right. But it must be important for Linc to schedule this now with his uncle. She would be agreeable and not argue, she decided. She would need to meet his uncle eventually, anyway. And she and Linc needed to talk, too. So, she responded and asked for his address.

When her phone vibrated in her hand, she thought it would be Linc again. Her stomach flipped when she read her new message. It was from Evan.

> **Evan:** *Hey pretty lady, heard you had a change of heart. Want to get coffee after school?*

Vela ground her teeth together. She was going to kill Elia. She knew Evan texting her was all her doing. She wasn't ready to do this. But she was ready to murder her best friend, slowly.

Vela: *Can't. Sorry. Have plans.* Grimacing, she then texted, *Maybe some other time?*
Evan: *Cool,* he answered quickly. *See you at school.*
Vela: *Kk,* she responded reluctantly.

Linc wasn't on board with this plan, so it was very likely he would incinerate Evan in his shoes at school if she started expressing interest in him. She would need to choose her next steps carefully, which included getting Linc on board with this fake dating idea.

Late getting ready for school, she jumped up, then rushed back to her phone to check if Linc had responded with an address. He had. After throwing on hipster jeans and a cute top, she raced down the stairs to find her parents to tell them about the afternoon plans.

She found them eating breakfast in the kitchen. Hurriedly, she asked for them to be available for a visit to Linc's house that afternoon, then rushed out the door so she could make the bus.

After furiously whispering at Elia for most of the bus ride about contacting Evan, which she had done, Vela felt moderately better. Elia moped and grumbled that the plan needed to be put in motion as soon as possible, but Vela ignored her.

Vela walked into her first period class, relieved she had beaten Evan and Linc both. Her luck was short-lived, however, when Evan sauntered into the room. He made it worse when he dropped into the seat next to her. He leaned on his arm toward her desk and smiled.

"Hi, Evan," she said, unsure how to flirt without actually wanting to. And she wasn't ready to do this when Linc would walk into the room any minute. She could sense him getting closer.

"Hi," he crooned. "So, a little birdy told me some pretty juicy stuff."

"Like what?" she asked, feigning ignorance.

"Like, you've been secretly interested in me," he answered, wearing a crooked grin. "I knew you liked me," he said, projecting confidence. If he looked any more ridiculous, she couldn't fathom it. He resembled a stupid bird puffing up its chest.

Vela froze. Linc was coming. She could feel him about to walk into the room.

"Crap!" she whispered, trying hard to come up with a good reason she would talk to Evan. He'd guess pretty quickly what was going on.

"Ha!" Evan yelled, pumping his arm, scaring Vela to death. "You wouldn't have said, 'Crap,' if I hadn't said the truth. I'm right, aren't I? I wasn't sure if it was a trick or not, but you do like me! Awesome!" His face lit up, and he draped his arm around her. "So, I'm down for this and since you are too, let's see where this goes, huh?"

Vela swallowed thickly. Linc was standing at the door watching Evan with eyes that promised pain.

"Uh, Evan," she said, throwing off his arm. She would have to fake date someone besides Evan, who had no concept of personal space. "It was kind of a joke. I don't know why Elia does these things, probably trying to keep high school interesting. But you know Elia. Always keeping us on our toes!" she rambled.

Linc's hard gaze hadn't changed, but his expression cooled when she'd removed Evan's arm. He slowly began walking to his seat.

"Look," Evan said, "You had me pretty convinced you hated me, but maybe you've been trying to get my attention another way."

Turning her head back toward Evan, she asked, "What?"

"By being coy."

The room suddenly got hot, and she looked toward the source. Linc barely restrained himself.

"It's just coffee, that's all I ask," Even asked, ever persistent. "Go on one coffee date with me."

Vela's attention suddenly went to Maria, who had just walked into the room. She looked curiously at Linc as she edged around him, fanning herself as she went. He had stopped at his desk and stood with his hands fisted at his sides. He stared at Evan, who didn't seem to notice Linc's attention.

Maria chose a seat near Linc. Sitting down demurely, she looked at Vela, her eyebrow raised.

With Maria's gaze on hers, Vela turned toward Evan and reluctantly nodded. She didn't have time to find another fake date. This one with Evan was primed and ready. And she needed Maria to see her interest in someone else besides Linc. Even though Linc would see it too, she had to do this.

"I'll go with you," she whispered, barely getting the words out.

"Yes!" Evan crowed. "I've won a date with the elusive Vela Ashcroft!"

"Don't make a big deal of this, please, Evan," she begged.

She looked over at Linc and begged him with her eyes for forgiveness.

"Hey, this is a historic moment! I've been trying to get a date with you for years! I'm hoping this will just be our first, with more to come."

Vela groaned.

"What? A guy can hope, can't he?"

Vela didn't think she could go through with this deception. She glanced at Evan and his eager, hopeful face shook her. This just felt wrong on so many levels.

In the corner of her eye, a girl jumped up next to Linc's desk, screaming.

The teacher yelled, "Fire! Everyone back!" The entire class started screaming, jumping out of their seats as pandemonium broke out.

Vela spun around to see a paper in flames on Linc's desk. Everyone asked each other how this could've happened. It was just as she feared. Linc had lost control of his gift. His face wasn't just angry, he wore an enraged expression.

Evan and Maria, the only other Elementals in the room, wore different expressions. Maria looked furious, her eyes darting back and forth between Vela and Linc and Evan just looked confused as to why Linc had lost control of his gift. Maria worried Vela. Evan didn't seem to know about her and Linc, thankfully, but Maria was aware of something.

Linc then tried to look as confused as everyone else. She figured it was the only thing he could do. If he put the flames out with his gift, it would make this situation even worse. The teacher rushed by Vela with a fire extinguisher in his hands.

"Everyone back!" the teacher yelled. Pointing the hose at the burning paper, he quickly extinguished the small fire.

"How did this happen?" he yelled. "Who started this?"

Everyone looked at Linc. "I'm sorry, Mr. Hammond." He produced a lighter from his pocket and sheepishly looked up at the teacher, turning his face into a contrite expression. "I was just flicking the lighter on and off and it must have been too close to the paper." He looked darkly in Vela's direction, but then his expression became blank.

Vela was impressed. That he would carry around a lighter when he could produce fire with a mere thought. But she figured if he had an accident, like today, having a lighter handy would answer questions about how a fire started.

"To the office, now, Mr. Stevenson," the teacher ordered. "I will not tolerate this kind of behavior in my classroom. Now, go and look for cleaning materials so you can clean up this mess." Linc looked relieved to leave the place.

It was a serious offense in the Elemental community to lose control of your gift in front of humans. If he hadn't explained this away as an accident, serious repercussions would have followed, as well as rounding up every human in the room to alter their memories of this event. He would have had to disappear from the area to help any rumors to die down. Vela blew out her breath, relieved he had successfully explained away what had happened.

Linc cast her a stony glare as he passed her seat. His eyes conveyed the truth of his feelings. This was a consequence of what she had just done. Why did she accept a date from Evan? If Linc had done that to her, she would have been just as angry. But he needed to accept responsibility for his actions, too. He cannot excuse his inability to contain their secret by blaming her. No matter how angry he got, he needed to keep his emotions under control.

But she would find a way to fix this distance between them. She had to.

Chapter Thirty-Three

THE BELL RANG, AND Vela shot out of class, her nerves frazzled beyond repair as she escaped to the bathroom. She gripped the porcelain sink and stared in the mirror and frowned at her own reflection. Her eyes looked drawn and stressed, with circles under her eyes. She looked sick and in a way; she was. Guilt plagued her chest and made her stomach feel like lead.

Putting her back to the wall, she crumpled to the floor. A tug on her heart had her bowing her head. She examined her feelings and knew conviction weighed her down. At that moment, she knew she had followed the wrong path.

"This just doesn't feel right, Lord," she whispered.

Ashamed, she hadn't prayed about whether she should be doing this course of action with Evan; she squeezed her eyes shut. She knew she had just taken it upon herself to come up with an answer about her and Linc's safety. If anyone would know about this entire situation, it was the Lord! She needed His guidance, and it was beyond time for her to give this situation to Him.

She pleaded with God. "Lord, take this burden from me and Linc. Please, Lord, protect us from those who mean us harm. Whether we're meant to be together or not, you know, Lord, you know our paths before we even take them. Forgive me for charging ahead on a plan without coming to you for guidance first. Show me what to do in the coming days, I pray. And help me right this wrong I have done against Evan. By giving him the wrong idea, I have deceived him and you, Lord, in my actions. They were wrong and I'm sorry for them. Guide me and protect me, I pray. Amen."

She basked in the peace that prayer brought her for a minute. Finally, she pulled herself up from the floor, looked into the mirror again, and took a deep, cleansing breath. It amazed her at the transformation peace gave her face. And she knew what she had to do. Rushing out the door, she clenched her backpack and prayed silently for strength to fill her as she plotted her next steps.

⤜⤜⤜⤜ ⤛⤛⤛⤛

After school, Vela had met with Evan at the coffee shop just down the street from the school, like she had promised. Now, as she typed in Linc's address using her GPS app on her phone, she felt shame as she remembered the conversation.

She spent several minutes profusely apologizing to him. Understandably, he looked confused. She tried to explain her reasoning for agreeing to go on a date with him, but silenced to secrecy about her and Linc, she ended up giving a convoluted explanation she hoped made some sort of sense. He had looked a little bewildered and a lot let down and she mentally kicked herself again for pulling this stunt on him. She had left the coffee shop and rushed away, hoping Evan had understood some of what she had said to him.

Now she was walking to join Linc and his uncle, who were meeting her parents in a few minutes, and she wanted to get there in time to be included in their conversation.

Walking fast, she prayed again for forgiveness and made it just in time to Linc's home. She probably could have tracked him like he did her not too long ago, but she didn't have the mental capacity to try something new. As she approached, Linc stood on the sidewalk in front of a modest sized home. A tall blonde middle-aged man, she assumed was his uncle was next to him. They must have waited outside for them, either that or they had just arrived, too.

Linc had his hands stuffed in his jeans pockets with his shoulders hunched as he studied the ground at his feet. Looking up, he said almost as if he read her mind, "I couldn't just sit inside waiting. I watched for you outside." Looking back down, he asked, "So, how did your *date* go?"

Wishing he had introduced her to his uncle first, she guessed she deserved that question. Judging by his look, Linc was being as nice as he could be and even that strained him.

"I canceled my date with Evan," she said, feeling guilt rise again. "I tried giving him an explanation without going into what's going on with us," she gestured between her and Linc.

When the uncle's eyebrows raised, she explained. "Basically, that it was a joke between Elia and me. That she was forcing me to spend time with him, thinking I would eventually like him as much as he liked me. Which is kind of true. Elia has said that before, but I just never believed her. But I think he understood, well as much as can be expected," she finished, knowing she was rambling but hoping Linc would stop glaring at her.

"Well, okay," the older man said, his handsome face pleasant as he clapped his hands together before offering her one of them. He gave Linc a look, and it seemed to shake Linc out of his moody thoughts.

Linc ran his hand through his hair. "This is my Uncle Richard. And this is Vela."

Richard smiled, and Vela returned his handshake with a firm one of her own. She casually studied the similarities between Linc and his uncle. Despite the man's blonde hair, the resemblance between them was obvious. Same facial structure and body build. Relieved to see his smile, she was happy he didn't drill holes into her with his eyes, like Linc did. He didn't seem to judge too harshly, but what did she know? She just met him.

"It's nice to meet you," she said. "Thank you for inviting me and my parents, who should be here any minute." Looking around, she wondered why they were running late. Richard walked up his steps and Vela was unsure if she should wait outside for her parents or go inside. She ended up following the leader of their small group up the steps. She looked behind her to make sure Linc was following. With a last long look at her, he sighed and followed his uncle up to the porch.

She wondered what that sigh was about. She hoped he forgave her. Frustration raced through her. She had done it all to protect them both. Straightening her back, she resolved to own up to her mistake, but he needed to get over his anger.

Linc wouldn't meet her eyes as they walked into a bright vestibule, and she braced herself for the upcoming meeting. He closed the door behind them, and he looked like he was ready to burst. Would she get an earful alone with him? Or wait for a private meeting with her and just rip into her in front of his uncle and her parents? She cringed, thinking of that potential scene. Her parents would not like that. Neither would she, for that matter.

Vela heard a knock on the door, saving her from either scenario at the moment.

Linc answered the door, and her mom walked in and looked curiously around, with David on her heels.

"We knew the former owners of this house," her mom began in leu of a greeting. She looked around with bright eyes. "It's always been one of my favorite houses. So quaint."

Vela looked around for the first time and agreed. It was small, but cozy. Just the right size for a bachelor and his nephew. Well, she had never actually asked if Linc's uncle was a bachelor. Did he have a wife somewhere while he traveled? She would ask later.

The vestibule opened into a small living room with a fireplace. A dark brown leather couch and its accompanying loveseat sat in an "L" shape in the room, with a glass coffee table in front of them. A brown recliner added to the ensemble. A kitchen with an open counter faced the living room, and she admired the bright yellow walls. Not really a manly color, but she guessed they didn't want to bother painting it a more somber tone.

"So," Richard said, rubbing his hands together as he walked over to Vela and her parents. "You must be the Ashcrofts."

Vela's mom was the first to shake his hand, then Vela's dad. Vela stood awkwardly, twisting her hands next to Linc, who had yet to look her way. Her stomach felt like a giant pile of knots. She was unsure how to apologize to him. She'd like to pull him aside and explain her actions in private. Or should she do it in front of her parents and his uncle? She stood uncertain until finally she had to get away for a minute.

"I'm sorry, but can I use the restroom?" Vela asked.

"Absolutely. Down that hallway, second door on the right." Richard motioned behind him.

Linc's gaze swung to hers, and she flinched at his look. It was unforgiving and hard to see. This was not a good way to start a relationship, she thought miserably. She wanted to make things better right away but had no choice to follow through on her announcement to use the restroom. Flustered, she left, following Richard's directions.

She used the restroom quickly, then stopped to splash some water on her face. She looked in the mirror and stood, unhappy with what she saw. Her eyes looked haunted. Her mom always said you could see into a person's soul by looking into their eyes. She wondered what her mom would find in Vela today. Nothing good. Looking away quickly, she wiped her hands on her pants, since she didn't see a hand towel. And she was not using the big towel hanging; it looked like it had been used. Bachelors, she thought grimly. They didn't think of little things like hand towels.

Vela left the bathroom, hearing voices further in the house. She looked curiously at the room she passed next to the bathroom. It looked like an office. Wanting to see the research Richard wrote about her clan, she was tempted to go in and look among his things but thought better of that idea. She was in enough hot water as it was.

She had to walk through a sitting area to get to where everyone waited for her. Passing by an armchair, she stopped when she saw an open book. It looked like a manuscript. *This must be Richard's writings on the clans,* she thought. She grazed her fingers over the page. Too curious to pass this opportunity by, she leaned over to see what it said.

> *It seems to me, this Gyan clan operates much like all the others. As I have thought before, even though we are divided, they hold many practices*

the same.
Such as the learning of the young. These Gyans,
too, homeschool their children, teaching them the
art of their gift, as well as basic subjects of history
and mathematics in a community center shared
with humans.
I note Gyans appear to hide their powers among
humans easier than the Festans, Boreans and
Neronians. More research will be needed to be
conducted as to why.

Leaning over the page, she caught a whiff of something familiar. It almost smelled like wisteria, a beautiful purple flowering vine that took years for her parents to coax into bloom. Once bloomed, however, the plant was toxic to ingest, causing a malady of symptoms like confusion, headaches and dizziness. *Why would this plant smell like this flower?* she wondered.

A wave of dizziness overtook her for a moment, but she blinked it away. Refocusing her eyes on the page, she shook her head and turned away from the mystery to return to her parents and Linc with his uncle.

When she rejoined the group, they were all sitting on the patio. Surprised to find such a large patio area for this small of a house, she took a seat in between her parents and Linc, settling in to hear their conversation.

"It looks to me like the E.E. has a small presence here in the Breckenridge area. Is that true for the bigger cities near here? How prolific are they in Denver?" her father was asking Richard.

"As far as I know, they seem to have a foot in the larger cities, but it's hard to tell because they do such a good job of staying under the radar."

"Yes," her father grumbled, "They seem to have long arms to just about anywhere. They put their weight behind a boundary battle just recently in Utah. That was a small town. I'm not sure how they were able to influence the Boreans to act against the Gyans there, but they did."

"How do you know the E.E. had anything to do with that?" Richard asked.

"When we rounded up the Boreans after it was over, they said some unfamiliar Boreans came into their area and incited them, giving them reasons they needed to attack the neighboring Gyans," David answered. "It sounds like just like other areas where the E.E. have done the same thing."

"So, if they can get to a town like Steinacker," Vela said, "then they could easily come here to where Linc and I are."

All the adults nodded. "Which is all the reason more to keep your relationship hidden."

If we even have a relationship. She glanced at Linc, who refused to look at her in return. She'd had enough. All conversation stopped when she stood up.

Once she faced Linc, she started right into her apology, not caring who witnessed it. "Linc, I'm sorry. I honestly never meant to hurt you. I was taking matters in my own hands, and it blew up in my face." Wringing her hands, she continued, "I'm not interested in Evan. I thought if I could start a different rumor than the one Maria was throwing around, that would fix things. I should have listened to you. But I know how important it is that we keep our bond a secret. Instead, it has just destroyed your trust in me, but I'm asking for some of it back."

He didn't meet her eyes during her apology. He was bent over, his elbows on his knees, and looked down at his hands. She bit her lip and waited. He shook his head then looked up at her, saying, "I'm sorry I've been crazy about you and Evan. This bond is making me a little overprotective. I can't stand the idea of anyone else with you but me. To have you resist our connection, then decide you do want to commit, then turn around and date someone else is almost more than I can handle."

Taking a deep breath, he continued, "But I must. I'm not a child who throws tantrums anymore. Believe me, I want to when it comes to you. I asked you to trust me and you didn't, which hurt. I told you we could find another way to handle the rumors. You trusted your instincts, which I can understand. Who am I to change who you are?"

Holding his hands out, he continued, "I need to trust your decisions, too. But Vela, you need to eventually decide about us. Start being honest with yourself and choose if I'm who you want in your life. Only me. Because without that decision, then why are we even here? Why are we even meeting?" He gestured toward the circle of her parents and his uncle.

He was right. She needed to decide what she wanted. Especially when the stakes were so high. She noticed the adults had been quiet for some time, listening to Vela and Linc's heart to heart.

Looking back at Linc, she asked, in a small voice, "Can we just take time to get to know one another? Do we have to make a lifelong decision right now? I mean, I don't even know your middle name."

"Now that's the first bit of sense I've heard all day," Richard said. "These two are starting a Kentucky Derby without learning how to run! Listen you two, a relationship is hard enough to survive, but tie in expectations like an Intended bond and that makes it ten times worse. What a bond is supposed to do is to make a couple's lives easier by pairing matched souls together. But we complicate it by fighting nature. He gestured toward Vela's parents. "Our job is to keep you two safe. Let's see how we can accomplish that."

"Now, to decide on a course of action..." Richard began to speak, but Vela's mind stuttered as Linc leaned toward her ear after she had sat back down.

"It's Anthony."

Turning her head, she became absorbed in his stormy eyes. They looked troubled, but dare she hope that his anger was cooling?

"What?"

"My middle name. It's Anthony." He stared at her for a moment, then looked away.

Flustered, she turned back to listen to Richard. Her smile was small, but her relief was huge. A weight lifted and she could concentrate on the conversation around her.

Maybe he wasn't as mad as she feared. Things could start fresh between them.

Chapter Thirty-Four

VELA BLOOMED WITH WARMTH. After their conversation during Linc's tour, she thought things would be so easy between them. But as she recalled her and her mom's conversation about falling in love, she agreed with her mom's sage advice. It would take time. They needed to get to know each other.

Tempted to reach over and grab Linc's hand, she stopped herself. She needed to make small steps after she had made such gigantic ones. She had gotten into trouble by making large decisions on her own. This was something she wanted Linc to start, not her. Holding hands didn't seem like a big decision, but to her, it was. From here on out, he needed to be included in any changes and she fully intended for him to take the lead. She had decided a while ago to give Linc a chance, to give them a chance.

So, she would wait. Even small changes were worth waiting for.

The group continued in a buzz of conversation about how to keep Vela and Linc safe from the E.E.

Fighting to pay attention, she focused on the current speaker. It was her father. "We need to have a contingency plan in place if anything concerning happens to Vela or Linc. Now it's important you come to know Vela's brothers, too. They're always available, should anything happen." After inviting Richard and Linc to their house to meet them, they continued their conversation.

David asked, "Do you mind us asking why you're Linc's guardian? Where are his parents?"

Glancing at Linc, Richard answered. "My brother and Linc's mother asked me to take Lincoln with me on my travels. It's so he can better understand our world. They're leaders among the Festans, so Linc will be when he's old enough as well. To be leaders, you need to see the world as it is for yourself, not by someone else's explanation. I'm basically a glorified tutor, here to instruct Lincoln as he studies the communities we visit. All while I make my own observations and document them."

"Who's benefited from your work?" Vela asked.

"So far, just myself. But I hope to share my work with others when the time is right. Which reminds me, I thought I caught a scent when you walked into the room." He looked at Vela, his eyes trained on her hands. "Did you touch any-thing when you came back from the bathroom?"

Vela's nerves tightened, and she felt like a little girl caught with her hand in the cookie jar. She nodded. She had touched his manuscript. Was it possible he knew?

"I've treated my manuscript with a special concoction," Richard said. "It's a spray from a special plant meant to affect humans if they were to read what I wrote," he explained. "It causes dizziness, headaches and confusion, when inhaled. It is the most effective way of keeping humans away from read-ing about us. They'll literally be too sick to read anything I've written."

Vela's eyes widened, and she looked down at her hands, noticing the wisteria scent had followed her into the room. Richard must have noticed.

"I'm sorry," Vela said, embarrassed, tucking her hands under her legs.

"It's okay." Richard chuckled. "I'll always know when someone has read my work, because I've gotten pretty good at sniffing it out."

"So, any copies you make of this book will have this spray on it?" Whitney inhaled deeply. "I smell it now, wisteria. Is it?"

"Yes. It took some research to get the right plant. Since I'm not a Gyan, I'm not trained on these things. But I managed."

"Not to be rude, but back to the topic," David said. "When will the time ever be right to share your work?" His expression grim as he continued, "The fighting among the clans is at its worst. I just don't see clans welcoming you with open arms. Not for a while."

"So far, the reception has been testy. But that's my problem and I'll bear it gladly to see my work complete."

"Since Linc's parents are Festan leaders they helped pave the way for you to negotiate with other clans?" her dad asked.

"They have. Especially Susanna, Linc's mother. Her position goes a long way in cutting corners. I'm actually pretty lucky my brother married our Grand Elder. That's why I'm here. She reached out to the Elders in this town and asked for leniency in allowing me to stay and research. I just hope it stays peaceful enough for me to remain."

"You never know when a skirmish will happen, even with a Grand Elder's blessing," David said. "It's unpredictable when tempers will flair."

"Usually, these problems happen when boundaries are being contested," Richard remarked, "and I don't see that happening in this area. Now, on to our two lovebirds. What has been done to hide their bonding?"

"I've asked my sons to keep an eye on social media for any comments about their relationship," David said. "So far, all is clear. No one seems to know."

"There's a girl named Maria," Vela said, "who has a crush on Linc and is starting to spread some rumors about Linc and I. I don't know how far she's gone, but it may get leaked onto social media soon."

"What rumors?" Richard asked.

"The other day, we left class, one right after the other, and she's saying we were together during that time," Linc answered.

"Is she right? Were you together? You were supposed to keep a low profile," David growled.

"Yes," Linc said, taking the brunt of her dad's temper and meeting his gaze straight on. "She's right. We were together. We didn't leave at the same time, but Maria has keen eyes and a rather nosy attitude. She seems to want to know everything about me."

"Ah, it's a little crush on you, then?" Richard asked.

"Unfortunately, that's what it looks like. She's made it her business to know as much about me as she can. She's quite persistent."

"You and Vela need to completely ignore one another at school," David said. "Don't even pretend to be friends. These rumors will die down, especially if there's no fuel for the fire. You must pretend you're nothing to each other."

"How will I get to know him if I can't even talk to him?" Vela asked with outrage.

"You can get to know each other outside of school," Richard said. "Out of the all-seeing eyes of this Maria, you two will get off her radar. Give it some time and you can start talking at school again. As long as we keep an eye out on social media for any comments about them, I think that should clear up this little mess."

"How about you two get some fresh air?" Whitney suggested. "This will all be water under the bridge, don't you worry. I think it's time they get to know each other, don't you boys?"

"Yes, I suppose that's true," David said as he stood up. "Why don't you two go for a walk?" He said to Linc. "You don't live too far from our house. It'll be a pleasant walk with the weather we're having today."

Vela looked shyly at Linc as they both got to their feet. She worried about how quiet he had been during the discussion.

"Do you want to?" she asked. "I mean, do you want to go on a walk with me?"

"Let's talk while we walk?" he asked, spearing her with his gaze. He looked intense. She didn't know what to make of that.

"Of course," she said with a fake smile. He must want to let her down privately that he didn't want to spend time alone with her. Now that she wanted to see him, why was this happening?

He led her toward the door and once they left the house and were going down the steps, he said, "I understand what you did," he said simply. "And I'm just going to forget about you agreeing to go on that ridiculous date with that even more ridiculous idiot."

Vela's breathing hitched. "You mean it? You're not mad at me?"

Linc's eyes softened, and Vela could breathe a little better.

He held her by the elbow as they walked down the sidewalk. "I don't want to waste any more time being angry with my Intended. I intend to make the most of every moment with you. Not everyone finds their bondmate and I want to enjoy my time with you, not spend it fighting. That doesn't mean, however," he said with a frown, "that I will pretend to like it if you want to date other people in the future."

"The future," she said thoughtfully as she walked by his side, "Who's to say, Linc, what that holds? What if you get to know me and you realize I'm a fake worthless sort of person and you find you hate my guts? We hardly know each other! It could happen!"

He stopped her, gripped her arms and said, "That will never happen."

Vela's heart rate climbed, and she put her hand over her chest to calm down her panic. It was unfolding inside of her just how much she wanted Linc to like her. She didn't want to be the reason he walked away. They were just getting to know each other, and she liked what she saw. And if they were compatible, where would that take her? Would she go away to live with the Festans? To be away from other Gyans? She really hadn't thought this through.

"Breathe, Vela," Linc's calm voice interrupted her inner monologue. "You aren't breathing, and that's kind of important to do."

She realized he was right and inhaled deeply.

"That's right. Breathe deeply and slowly," he instructed, his voice close. He had stepped into her space, which helped achieve a peace she desperately needed.

Relaxing, she looked up at him and realized he was still gripping her arms. Putting her hands on his sides, she asked tentatively, "How are we going to do this, Linc? How are we..."

"*We* are going to take this one day at a time," he said firmly. "There's no reason to plan out the future. It has a way of happening with absolutely no effort on our parts."

"No effort," she scoffed. "It'll take *some* effort."

Her disagreement made him smile. Looking her over to be sure she was alright; he released her and continued their walk. He repeated, "We'll take one day at a time and enjoy each moment. This is supposed to be an easy and painless process. We're just making life difficult for ourselves if we worry. I know you're not sure if you want me forever. But I don't have that problem. I know what I want. You're special to me. And I don't easily let go of special people in my life. So, don't expect to get rid of me easily, if that's your plan."

Her heart warmed, and she felt her panic draining away. Avoiding his eyes, she said, "I know one thing. I won't betray your trust again because I enjoy being special. It makes all this doable. Like I can see the future."

He stopped, tipping her chin up with his finger. He looked deeply into her eyes and said softly, "Remember, you don't need to force the future. Let each day take care of itself. Let's just take things slowly, 'k?" He leaned in and kissed her softly.

When she felt him drawing close, she had stopped breathing with sweet anticipation. She wrapped her arms around his neck and returned his kiss. She shivered when he ran his hands through her hair.

He pulled away a fraction of an inch. "I love your hair. Ever since I first met you, I've wanted to run my hands through it." She sighed blissfully when he played with her silky strands, and she was glad she had worn it down today.

"I'll have to remember that," she said, and interrupted him playing with her hair with another kiss. She played with the ends of his hair, too.

She abruptly giggled.

He pulled back with a confused look. "Are you laughing at my kissing?"

"No! My fingers tingle when you're nearby and when you kiss me, it's kind of distracting."

"Maybe I should start next time by kissing your fingers, each one."

"That would make it worse," she giggled some more. "Come back here." She pulled him by the back of his neck into another kiss.

But he could try. And if he was going to continue with such sweet words, she could see the future becoming very sweet indeed.

Chapter Thirty-Five

IT WASN'T A FAR walk from Linc's house and as they neared her home, she heard Jack's collar jiggling and his whining with excitement inside. He must have heard her voice and reacted. She reached the door and braced herself when she opened it. He pounced on her immediately and her back ran into Lincoln's as he supported her and Jack's weight.

"Jack! Down." She laughed. When he obeyed, she patted her leg and said his favorite word, "Outside." She followed her happy dog out the door.

Linc glanced at her while out on the porch, then held out his hand. "Shall we?" he asked. She looked down and found herself happier than she had been in a long while. She slid her hand into his.

Happy to see a lightness to Linc's deep blue eyes that wasn't there before, she could see he had made peace with everything. So, she could too. If she worried about her future now at seventeen, she'd be a sorry mess and she didn't want that for herself. She would learn to trust in the moment.

She squeezed his hand and looked up at him with a big smile. "Yes, we shall."

They all started down the steps of the porch and she led him toward a path in the reserve her father had mentioned. They passed the vegetable and herb garden. Before she could pass the gazebo, Linc stopped.

He pulled on her hand toward the flowering vines draped over the wooden beams. He picked one of the white flowers and turned toward her, placing the small flower at her ear tucking the stem behind it.

"Beauty at its finest," he said, trailing his finger down her cheek.

She absorbed the compliment but shook her head. "The flower might be beautiful, but..."

He interrupted her. "If you're about to say you aren't beautiful, I won't be responsible for my actions."

Her eyes widened, and she stilled. Blushing, she said, "I really don't think I am, Linc. But my mom said to always say thank you when complimented, so thank you."

"Your mom is a very smart woman, but you are stunning."

Changing the subject, she pulled the flower from her ear and laughed. "You picked the wrong flower to give me, though. It's a Climatis flower. It might look beautiful," eyeing the four petaled delicate beauty, "but it's actually poisonous."

"What?" he cried. Faster than she could blink, he plucked the flower from her fingers and threw it on the ground. "It's poisonous to touch, too?"

"No," she said, chuckling, "Just to eat. It'll leave your tummy hurting for days."

"Well, I didn't really think you'd eat my offering, so that's a relief." He eyed the flower where it lay in the grass.

"I didn't expect you to know." She tried to stop her giggling. "I couldn't help but tell you, though."

"Showing off your supreme knowledge of plants?" he asked as he picked up her hand again, pulling them toward the small trail she had showed him.

As they strolled together, it dawned on Vela that Linc had sparked a change in her. She didn't realize how her prejudice against Festans had hardened her and made her anger a part of who she was.

"You know I have a lot to thank you for," she said, gazing at him softly.

Stopping, he cocked his head. "About what?"

"I just realized something." She stood and gathered her thoughts for a minute. "I've hated the Festans for so long. Because of my memories of Cooper and my old home. I never understood 'till now that those memories have made me an angry person carrying all that animosity around. Now that I see it for what it is, prejudice and misplaced anger, I don't like what I see in myself."

She shook her head and started walking. "Until you came along. I should be angry at our way of life that's created all this bitterness our races have toward each other. I've been angry all this time at the wrong people."

He walked with her and looked at her with understanding. "It takes a lot in a person to admit things like what you've just described." He squeezed her hand. "It's perfectly natural to be angry at the events in your life, Vela. Don't blame yourself for normal feelings."

"But it kept me from you," she said in a pained whisper.

He squeezed her hand in response, but stayed silent.

Once they reached the path, Linc turned to look around. "How about we walk this way?" He pointed to the right, where a fork offered a choice. But there was barely any trail at all going that way.

"Are you sure?" she asked, eyeing the well-worn trail to the left. "That's not really a trail."

"It'll be an adventure," he pressed. "Come on, let's see if we find something."

"Adventure? Haven't we had enough of those?"

"You can never have too much adventure."

Lost in the blue depth of his gaze, she agreed. "Okay, but we aren't going too far. I don't want to get lost out here."

"You got it, come on."

She ignored her worries as she and Jack followed Linc, enjoying the beauty around her. Trees spiked into the sky with a majestic grace that humbled her. These sentinels had been on Earth much longer than she had. She loved them. They not only provided shade and beauty, but the oxygen that helped make Earth livable.

It was a science that delighted her.

She wished it were mid-September when the leaves changed colors brilliantly, but it was coming soon. When the forest displayed hues of yellows, oranges, and reds that painted the vistas with breathtaking scenes, she loved it. The greens in August still boasted a beauty she admired, though. Every leaf, branch, and trunk had a stately elegance she would love in any variation of color. The greens calmed her, and she allowed its tranquility to soothe the last of the stress she had endured today.

Brushing her hands on each trunk she passed, she gave them some of her energy, gifting them with a healthier life. Jack barked happily every time she touched a tree.

"Are you using your gift?" Linc asked as he pushed some branches out of their way.

She nodded. "Why?"

"I was wondering why you were touching each tree we passed. I sensed that's what you were doing."

"It makes me happy to give some of my energy to them. Makes me feel like I'm a part of a bigger picture. Jack loves it, too."

"I could tell. And I kind of know what you mean. There aren't too many opportunities to burn something down.

But occasionally I get to give some of my energy to an animal who needs it."

"Do you heal them?"

"Not really. But, since I can bend their minds to do what I want, I enhance their senses, making them sharper. I can make a predator even more vicious, more lethal. Making their sense of smell more precise enhances their ability to hunt. Or, for herbivores, to forage."

"Wow," she said, impressed. "Can you make an animal, like a squirrel, jump higher or farther, too?"

"No, I can't make their physical traits better, only their mental ones. It's like taking a drug that sharpens your senses. Their will to please me increases too. Animals have always loved me; they're drawn to my gift. I can pretty much tame any animal."

"Even a lion?" she asked with a laugh.

"No." He chuckled. "Well, I don't know, actually. I've never tried. I'm sure I can influence them, but to have them cuddle up to me might be a stretch. I've only ever tried on small animals."

"So, like a wolf or big dog."

"A dog, yes, but I've not tried on a wolf. Haven't had the pleasure of meeting one, yet. Maybe we'll meet one today," he said with a wink.

Vela's blood went cold at the thought of encountering a hungry wolf. "Let's hope not."

They continued walking for a while, talking about everything and nothing. It was perfect. But she eventually grew tired of skirting brush and pushing through branches. She eyed an opening ahead with a fallen tree they could rest on.

"What do you think about sitting for a while?" she asked. "I'm sick of fighting these branches."

"Sure. That spot ahead looks comfortable."

"That's what I was thinking, too."

They reached the fallen tree, and she sat comfortably against a branch that jutted out to the side. The sun warmed her skin, which was good because their walk had been well shaded. It was getting cold in the evening, and she could feel the temperature steadily dropping as the day went on. The temperature in September sometimes dropped in the fifties, which wasn't too bad, but she hadn't brought a jacket. She let Jack roam the area, exploring as he went.

"We should head back soon," she said. "I don't want to get caught out here in the dark."

"Sure. But let's just sit for a few minutes. I thought we were supposed to use this time to get to know each other."

Tucking her leg under her, Vela adjusted until she was comfortable. "I thought we've been doing that. So, what do you want to know? My favorite color?" she joked.

His eyes twinkled, and he sat next to her. "That's a conversation for another day. Let's talk more philosophically."

Examining her growing feelings for Linc, she bit her lip. She needed to ask him something that had been on her mind but was suddenly unsure how to ask. Bracing herself, she said, "Okay. I need to ask you a serious question."

"Haven't you been asking me a bunch of those?" he asked with a crooked grin.

"Yes." She blushed. "But this one's important to me."

He straightened, his blue eyes serious on hers. "Ask away."

With no other way to cushion this question, she just blurted out what she needed to know. "Do you believe in God?"

Linc's eyebrows shot up.

"Is that a hard question for you?"

"No," he said slowly, "just wondered where this is coming from."

"I just thought we should have this conversation. Being as we're each other's Intendeds." She twisted the end of her shirt nervously.

"True." His eyes examined hers.

"It's kind of important that we're on the same page with this," she said quickly.

"True."

"Is that the only thing you're going to say?"

"No. As a matter of fact, I do believe in God."

Vela inhaled. She didn't realize she had been holding her breath, waiting for his answer.

"I take it you do, too?"

"Yes! Definitely."

"For a minute there, I thought this conversation was going a completely different direction."

She cocked her head in a silent question.

"Well, you were being so antagonistic for a minute." The corner of his lips turned up and his eyes twinkled. "I never know what's going to come out of your mouth."

"You're teasing me, aren't you?"

"Yes. I am. Is it that obvious?"

"Whew! That is a load off my mind," she said, falling back onto the tree. After a silent minute, she mused, "What's hard to believe is that years ago, the world had a collective belief in a higher power. It at least explained, in their minds, the calamities we brought about when we fought over territory lines."

"That God was punishing their errant ways?" Linc asked with a reflective look on his face.

Vela nodded. "And I guess it would be hard for humans to believe in us as Guardians if most of the world doesn't even believe in a higher power now. That God would give us the responsibility to care for the Earth. That would be inconceivable because most humans don't believe He exists. I wish they didn't have such a lack of faith. God's perfect balance in nature is beautiful.

"I mean, think of nature," she continued. "Can't they see the sun's rays expertly feeding the grass underneath them and the trees above them? How does that happen organically without Someone telling it to do so? How could they not rejoice when God sends buckets of water from the sky to blanket the earth? Only to sink miles underground to feed into aquifers that's ultimately fed into sinks and showers."

"It might be a mystery to some how it all happens, but I understand what you're saying," Linc said in a thoughtful tone. "God, The Creator, designed all of Earth for mankind to enjoy," he said softly, almost reverently. "But ultimately, He did it for those who enjoyed His gifts to give Him all the glory. God showcased His gifts to the world, with Earth providing a beautiful place for humans and Elementals to love and worship Him.

"Sadly," Linc said with a frown, "there are Elementals, even, who abuse their gifts and ignore God's presence. Fights over boundary lines between the clans are often by those who always want more and can't be happy with what they have."

"Some people," Vela nodded. "choose to believe that every miracle of nature and life is a cosmic accident, like humans evolving from monkeys. But I guess coming up with those kinds of conclusions is what happens when they don't believe in God."

Vela wondered what Darwin would have thought if he had been given proof of Elementals' existence. She voiced her question, then asked, "Would Darwin have believed in a higher power, then?"

"Who knows?" Linc said, his mouth in a tight line. "He probably would have thought your ancestor was a tree." He looked out into the distance and his brow furrowed.

"What is it?" She sat up.

"I sense something large coming our way, but I don't know if it's a person or a large animal." His gaze searched the distance, but Vela couldn't hear or see anything.

"With your heat signature ability? Is your range for sensing only animals?"

"I can sense anyone or anything with warm blood within a mile."

Jumping up, he held his hand out to Vela to help her up. "Let's not take a chance that a pack of wolves has caught our scent. Let's go."

"I think you're right." Looking at Jack, though, he didn't seem too concerned. He still sniffed the bushes. "But I'm sure it's a nearby hiker or two. Do you sense more than one?"

"Yes," he said grimly. Still holding her hand, he urged her with him down the trail.

She called Jack to her as they left the area.

Vela wondered who would be out in this part of the woods, casually hiking. She had never been in this area before herself and she had lived here for years. Trying to hurry, she grew frustrated fighting the plants and realized she could move the plants easily.

"Linc, stop."

Standing with her feet braced, she raised her hands and ordered the plant life ahead of them to move. Like a mole that dug a tunnel through the dirt, she uprooted bushes, laying them gently to the sides of her new path. Ferns, plants, and even saplings were gently dug up with her mind's power and laid to rest where they fell. Her path went as far as her vision allowed. Sad she couldn't transplant these plants and saplings, and feeling drained from the exertion, she turned to Linc, who looked at her with awe.

"Let's go. We should be able to walk much easier now," Vela said.

"It looks like it," he said, shaking his head. With a determined look, he then ordered, "Let's jog. They're coming straight for us."

Nodding, Vela started jogging down her trail. Linc stayed right behind her and soon she wished she had spent more time running. Her lungs burned, and she wished for better endurance. She pushed herself, through, and kept going. Her heart lurched when Linc yelled and pushed her ahead. Looking back at him, she stumbled when she saw his expression. It looked like he was tormented. How could he know whoever or whatever was near was dangerous?

"Vela, go, go, go! Whatever it is, they're closing in!"

Her heart in her throat, she pushed her speed into a full sprint. Sweat streamed down her face, blinding her for a moment. She swiped her face, clearing her vision. How far in were they? She didn't see the opening to the trail yet. Pumping her arms, she thanked God she had cleared a path for them. She forced her legs to go faster.

With no warning, a sudden wind swirled around her, picking up leaves and twigs in its path. It soon became a cyclone, picking up speed, and she had to stop and shield her face from the rocks and sticks that were being slung through the whirling air. Thankfully, Jack was right next to her, and she kneeled, bringing him close to her. She couldn't see anything through the debris flying around. The screaming wind nearly picked her up, and she held onto Jack to prevent being lifted into the air.

This stormy weather was unnatural. This was the work of a Borean Elemental.

Chapter Thirty-Six

WILD WINDS ATTACKED VELA, and she tried looking around to see the Elemental causing this storm, but she couldn't see a thing. Leaves and brush blew all around her and she put her hand up to shield her eyes. Where was Linc?

"Linc!" she screamed his name over and over until she was hoarse. How dare these people attack them. She didn't know if he answered her call because, with the sound of the storm and Jack barking, she couldn't hear anything. Her hands trembled with fury as she ducked over Jack, and she willed herself to find a defense against this storm. She took control of the nearby plants and pulled them around and up over her and Jack's head.

Roots, bushes, and tree branches all answered her call. Leaves brushed her face as branches wrapped themselves around her and Jack, making a cocoon. She needed to protect herself from any more damage. She could feel cuts on her face and arms, but she pushed past the pain and concentrated on her shelter. Settling herself on the ground, she waited for the wind to die down. There was no way of knowing what was going on outside, whether Linc was in a similar cyclone.

Finally, it became quieter outside of her little dome. Unsure of what other Elementals she dealt with, she waited. Hearing voices, she strained her ears to hear what they were saying. The branches and trees around her muted most of the sound. Jack, however, started growling dangerously.

"Looks like our little Gyan has gone all earthy on us boys," she heard a voice sneer. There was no trouble hearing that. She couldn't pick up the rest of the conversation. The speakers who answered must be too far away. "Well, little lady, don't keep us waiting. Come out of your little hole, why don't you?" the voice beckoned. "Sounds like you have a little guard dog with you. Why don't you shut it up for us?"

"Who are you? Why are you attacking me?" she called out. She fisted her hands, keeping a tight control over the plants. Unless they had hatchets, they weren't breaking into her cocoon. She would get some answers before she came out.

"We're just interested in your love life, that's all. How about you come out and talk to us?"

Were these Elemental Extremists? If so, she was in terrible danger. Nothing good could come from this conversation. Afraid to come out, she stayed silent.

"Steve, get this thing down," the voice ordered. Soon after, she felt the top of her sanctuary shudder. Then someone cut the top completely off with a quick slice of air.

Hands reached in and hooked under her arms before she or Jack could react, hauling her out easily of her sanctuary. They dumped her on the ground, and she sat stunned by the impact it had caused.

Jack barked wildly, still stuck in her dome. Looking up, she saw five figures standing around, looking down at her. A molten rage filled her when she narrowed her eyes at no one else but Maria. So, she was a part of the Extremists. She and Elia were right.

Maria looked at her smugly. She wore dark pants and a camouflage shirt, and she stood, feet braced apart like she expected Vela to fight.

She was right.

Scouring the dirt under her for the strongest roots, Vela sensed and dismissed several weaker options before finding what she wanted. A beautiful, thick one pricked her awareness, and she mentally got ahold of it. Slowly, she moved it through the dirt so as not to alert Maria to what she did.

Vela snarled, "What do you want?"

"What? No hysterics? I'm almost disappointed," Maria said in a deceptively soft voice.

The other four snickered.

She now had the root just where she wanted it. Holding onto it for the right moment, her attention flew to the cocoon when it shook with Jack's attempts to free himself. She didn't want them to hurt Jack when he couldn't move to protect himself. There was no sign of Linc, either.

The four men with Maria ranged in age from twenties to forties. And they all featured hard muscles through their clothing. They also looked at her with sneers and hard looks in their eyes. It looked like they hated her already.

"Why should I be hysterical?" Vela asked, "I'm not the least bit surprised that you're a part of a psychotic group, Maria."

The leader, she assumed, with thinning brown hair and a long face, said, "You know who we are then? Good. That makes this easier, then." The man had a crooked nose that looked like it had been broken more than once. She would remember his ugly face, she vowed. His arms crossed over his chest, he stood before her with confidence. The man looked tall and skinny, but there was strength in him. He was an Elemental, that much she knew, but had no way of deciphering which. He stood just far enough away.

"Where is my friend?" she asked, flicking her eyes at Maria.

"Your *friend*? Is that what you're calling him these days?" Crooked Nose said, turning to look at Maria, who rolled her eyes and looked away. "We heard he was more than that to you."

She studied her captors before answering. Maria finally looked back at her, raising her eyebrow.

"How did you find out?" Vela directed her question to Maria.

"That you and *my* Linc have a bond?" Maria spat, her eyes flashing in anger. "The usual way. He told me." She then smiled, slow and catlike.

Alarm spiked her blood, wondering why Linc would tell Maria of all people they had a bond.

"We're a lot closer than you might think, Vela." Maria stood tall with her hand on her hip, feasting on the pain Vela knew showed in her eyes.

Vela didn't believe it. Linc wouldn't start a relationship with Maria. He barely tolerated her.

She turned her attention to the men. They wore determined expressions. There was no mercy to be found in this group. She asked again, "Who are you?"

"Let's just say we're *not* friends," the man answered.

"Yeah, I've got that figured out. Where is Linc? What have you done with him?"

"He is no longer your concern, little girl. We just want to know one thing. Is he your Intended?"

This conversation was over. No way would she answer that question.

At that, she struck fast. Her root burst from the ground in a shower of dirt, tackling Maria, but Vela wasn't finished.

She whipped the end of the root at the heads of the other men. One after another, she knocked them all to the ground. Before she got up, she stopped a moment and in one motion secured them all with smaller roots around their ankles. *That would do for now.*

Lurching to her feet, she opened the cocoon with her powers, freeing Jack. Grabbing him by the collar, she ran wildly away from her attackers, giving Jack the command to follow. He whimpered. He wanted revenge. She gave another order, and he kept up with her.

Vela dashed through the trees; glad she could depend on them as her weapons. With her powers operating in medium strength, with all the energy she had spent already, she made a tangle of bushes behind her as she ran. But with Maria in their group, she'd be able to untangle her mess easily. She prayed she could outrun this group.

Immensely thankful she had trained her dog well, she ran as fast as she could, Jack keeping up with her easily. She ran in the direction she thought her home was. She was ridiculously turned around in these woods. She spied the trail she had made earlier crowing in relief. Searching her pockets for her phone, she grabbed it and as she ran, called her dad.

Breathing was getting difficult, but she sucked in air and willed herself to go faster down the trail. She listened for any attempts to follow her as she waited for her father to answer. "Pick up Dad, please!" Her heart soared when she finally heard his voice answer. "Dad!! I'm being chased. I think it's the E.E.! Please help!"

"Where are you?" he demanded.

"I'm in the woods behind the house. We didn't go down the main trail, we went to the right. I'm trying to get home. Please find me! Jack's with me."

"Vela, don't stop! We will find you," he promised in a pained voice. "Keep Jack close and whatever happens, keep me on the phone, okay?"

"Okay," she wheezed. Her lungs were starving for air, but she didn't dare slow down. She knew those guys would catch up and who knew what would happen to her and Jack?

Vela heard footsteps catching up to her just before someone heavy slammed her to the ground. Her phone flew out of her hand. A yelp sounded and distantly she realized they got to Jack, too. They had completely knocked out her breath, and she lay stunned. A moment was all she was given before a man yanked her up. Her attacker held both her arms clamped next to her body and shoved his face into hers.

"Think you could get away, did ya'? You thought wrong, little girl. Your little Gyan tricks won't get you away that easily. And your little dog? He's under our control now." Her captor was the leader, but she could see another man with him, who had his arm out toward a lump on the ground.

Jack twitched as he tried telling his legs to stand up, but the man, a short beefy guy with shocking red hair, controlled him using the same powers Linc had.

"The roots kept the rest of you down, didn't it? Where are the others?" she mocked. Bucking in his arms, she fought to break his hold. "Let me go! And my dog, too!"

"And get our legs bitten off? Not a chance. Maybe you should understand who you're dealing with first. This is what I do to people who don't listen very well." Putting his hand in front of her face, he focused and the sweat on her face slowly turned to ice. She shivered, but he wasn't done. Soon, the ice began digging into her skin. She screamed when the ice broke the skin on her face. Blood trickled down around her eyes and cheeks as he continued. Pain radiated from the small wounds and she whimpered. What else was he capable of if he would do this?

"Please," she begged. "Stop. I won't run. I promise."

"Now you're making promises. Any more problems from you or your rangy mutt and there'll be plenty more of that for ya'."

Holding her against his side, he started walking back down the trail, dragging her along when she didn't keep up with him.

She looked over at Maria, who had caught up to them. Vela could see Maria had made a trail to help them catch up to her. She also had an uncertain look on her face. Vela expected her to gloat over what the man had done. Instead, she looked uncomfortable.

With the blood running down her face, Vela must look like a nightmare. The ice chips soon melted, joining the lines of blood on her face, but still she shivered.

She wished she hadn't dropped her phone when she fell but hoped her dad would reach them soon. He could track her last location with the tracking app on her phone. Hearing voices, she looked for her dad and brothers only to see the group of men she had felled running toward them.

"'Bout time you made it here. We need to hurry; she called for help," the leader growled. He pushed Vela toward a muscled bald man and her spirits sunk. She could never get away from him. He was monstrous. His arm was bigger than her leg.

She prayed silently for a rescue, but the group of captors was walking quickly and there was no sign of her father or brothers. A kernel of hope grew as she thought maybe they were hiding, trying to find a good time for a rescue.

"Please don't kill my dog. I'm begging you," she pleaded.

"We'll see," he grunted noncommittally.

It was difficult to not watch for a sign of her family. She didn't know where these guys were taking her. She knew of nothing in this direction, so she did not know where they could be going.

Vela knew she was in trouble. The E.E. were unspeakably violent and ended the lives of their victims. So why was she being taken? They could kill her out here as well as anywhere else. With that disturbing thought in mind, a fight took root deep inside and rocked her insides. She wouldn't go down easily. Wrenching violently in her captor's steel-like grip, she fought to loosen his hold, hoping to catch him by surprise.

It worked.

He loosened his hold just a fraction, but it was enough to tear herself away. Bursting into action, she sprinted in the opposite direction, screaming her father's name.

She had gone a handful of steps when steel arms wrapped around her waist and she flew to the ground again. Her attacker held her face down and she winced as branches dug into her cheek. She squeezed her mouth shut to avoid eating dirt. She fought to break the hold on her, but it was useless. She wasn't going anywhere.

"You couldn't come nicely, could ya'? You just made things a lot worse for yourself," a voice growled in her ear.

She heard the blow before she registered the pain of it. Moaning, she moved her head, making sure she still could. He had hit her hard and stars danced in front of her eyes.

"Still here? Well, let's fix that."

Another blow struck her head and blackness took over.

Chapter Thirty-Seven

WHEN VELA WOKE UP, she saw nothing but gray. It hurt to move her eyes. It hurt to turn her head. Her head just hurt. It hurt so badly it throbbed; she didn't dare move. She laid on a table; it seemed. She could feel its hard surface with her fingers. Her first thought was Jack. Did they let him live? Her heart wrenched at the thought of them hurting her precious sidekick.

She couldn't move her eyes, but she could focus them. She trained them on the gray to better see what she was looking at. Lines ran through at regular intervals. She realized they were slats. She must be in a cabin or house of some kind.

Squeezing her eyes shut, she assessed her pain. She almost screamed at her head's slightest movement, and the cuts on her face hurt in small stinging places. She cringed at the thought of the scars her face would now grace but shrugged off that worry. Vanity had no place here. She wished, again, that she could heal herself.

Other than that, she seemed fine. Her arms, legs, everything else was alright, sore, but good. She gingerly felt around her head until she found the two places it hurt the most. Her hand came away sticky with blood. Head wounds bled the heaviest, so she hoped her wounds had clotted. She didn't want to bleed out. Frustrated, she couldn't move, she closed her eyes and breathed deeply, trying to stay calm.

What she wouldn't give for a pain reliever. Where was she? With nothing else to do, she rested. No one else was in the room with her, that she could hear anyway. Closing her eyes, she figured sleep was her only option.

Sleep wouldn't come, though. Especially when she was afraid of who might march into the room at any second. She couldn't wait till her family found her. These people would see one fight they would never forget. Smiling grimly, she enjoyed her imagination going with that thought. Twitching her fingers, she thought through her current situation, weighing the good with the bad.

Vela didn't know where she was being held. That was bad. But she wasn't dead; why they hadn't killed her, she didn't know, but it was good to be alive. She was injured, which was also bad. She wasn't sure the extent of her injuries, but her eyesight was clear, and she wasn't dizzy, which was a good sign that she didn't have a concussion. She ticked that off on her fingers as one more good thing. This group was extremely dangerous, which was bad. There wasn't much good she could find in that, no matter which way she spun it.

Her head hurt from her thoughts pinging around. All this thinking was not good. Ah! That was another bad thing. She really needed to stop.

A creak sounded nearby. Was that inside the room or out?

Panic started creeping up her throat. Not being able to move was beyond frustrating. There was no way she could defend herself. Was this her end? Would she die lying here? She started hyperventilating.

Tears filled her eyes, and she stiffened when she heard a door open. Furiously blinking her tears away, she tried to see who it could be. Someone walked into the room with quiet steps, and she heard them putting something down. It hurt too much to turn her head, but it sounded like a bunch of little things sliding around. They must be on a tray.

"Now, now. Calm your breathing down," a large woman crooned as her round face came into view. She wore her hair swept up in a twist and she wore a patterned dress. "I can see your pulse jumping out of your neck from here. You're going to pass out if you don't calm down. I'm here to help you." She sounded kind. It was a giant step up from the leader of the band of guys who had abducted her. She'd take it.

"Where am I? Who are you? What do you guys want with me?" She moaned. Even moving her jaw was painful.

"I know it hurts. You have quite the wounds here. You must have had a terrible fall to have wounds like these. Tsk, tsk. Look at all these cuts on your poor face. Well, no matter. Soon, you'll be all better. Just hold still and let me work." The woman ran her hands over Vela's head and body, being careful not to jostle her.

It was like someone had taken their fist and bashed Vela's head in. Wait, that *is* what happened. Why was this lady saying she had fallen? She may have a head injury, but she was positive someone had hit her, not once but twice.

"Fallen?" she asked, barely moving her lips.

"Yes, that's what the Searchers said when they brought you in, that you had taken a nasty fall. Thank goodness they were looking for you, dear."

Before Vela could argue, the woman placed both her hands on Vela's two head wounds. Vela groaned when a healing warmth emanated from the woman's hands. Vela became lost in a world of hazy bliss as the woman healed her.

She closed her eyes and finally relaxed. The woman continued for several minutes. Once she finished with Vela's head, she moved her hands to the cuts on her face. Small points of warmth followed as she healed each wound. She then moved down to reach the rest of her body. Wherever she touched, aches and pain disappeared, and Vela was immensely grateful for this woman's gift. She was a Gyan Elemental. Only Gyans could heal wounds like this.

Now free from pain, Vela's mind could wander. This group was a mix of Elementals, that much she knew. She was being healed by a Gyan but a Borean, Festan and Neronian had attacked her. Why were the two experiences with this group so different from one another? And why did this woman think she received her injuries from a fall?

Now that she could, Vela sat up. The woman had just finished her healing on the small cuts on her legs. She looked up at Vela with kind brown eyes.

Wanting answers, Vela said, "Look, thank you for healing me. You're very gifted to heal wounds like I had. But they weren't from falling. I don't know who you think these Searchers are, but they are *lying*. First, they kidnapped me and then they attacked me when I tried to run away. All the blood on my face? It's from a Neronian turning my sweat into *ice*. He then cut my face by digging the ice chips into my skin. Now, who are you people? And where is my dog?"

The woman's face drained of color, and she opened and closed her mouth like a fish. "That can't be," she protested. "Searchers found your body after you had fallen down a ravine. Why would they attack you? We want to *help* you, not hurt you. And what dog?"

Vela rubbed her head, trying to ease a blooming headache, despite her healing. Everything she knew began twisting around in her mind, and she fought to make sense of it. This woman was either deluded or she had been lied to. She hoped Jack had gotten away and not been killed. Maybe they were holding him somewhere.

Vela shook her head. All Vela knew about this group was evil, but this woman was certainly not that. For what reason had those Searchers lied about what really happened?

"Who are these Searchers? What are they looking for?" Vela asked.

"Not what, but who," the woman answered. She eyed Vela with interest. "We're waiting to find the couple who will give us the prophesied child. The Searchers are looking for them. They're quite diligent."

"That's not the word I would use," Vela mumbled under her breath. Louder, she said, "They're crazy. They *hurt* me."

"Honey, they would never harm a potential mother to the prophesied child. You must have knocked your head pretty hard. Your memory isn't right."

Swinging her legs over the table, Vela gritted out, completely done with this conversation. "I just want to go home. I'm leaving."

The woman jumped in front of the door, holding her hands out. "No! You can't go! You really can't. Sorry."

"I will throw you to the ground if I have to, lady. I am leaving."

"Look," the woman said, "You must stay. There's no choice here. We would never hurt you, but we will contain you if left with no other choice."

"You would keep me here against my will?"

Her captor looked at her grimly. "Yes. We would. It's imperative to find the right couple and there are some tests we perform that will confirm if you are the couple or not."

"Wait, you have Linc, my friend, too?" Her heart jumped. And instantly she felt guilty she hadn't asked about him first.

"Lincoln is here. But we must keep you apart to accurately complete the tests. Sorry, but you can't see him."

Vela could sense that Linc was close, now that she thought about it, but didn't know much beyond that. She stood still, thinking through their conversation. This was madness. She'd been abducted, then healed by someone who did not know what her group was capable of. There was something strange happening here. She intended to get to the bottom of it.

"Please. Just calm down and wait here," the woman requested. "There's someone you should talk to who can explain things better. Just hold tight." She turned her ample form around, picked up the tray she had brought in, which Vela could now see had rags and soaps on it. She held out the tray to Vela and said, "I'll bring in some water and you can clean up a little." She walked out of the room and Vela could hear the lock click into place behind her.

Her shoulders slumped, and she hung her head. This was ridiculous. She should have knocked the woman out from behind when she had the chance. Well, she thought, desperate times call for desperate measures. She walked over, yanking on the window, grunting with the effort. It didn't budge. How was she getting out of here?

Frustrated, Vela sunk to the floor.

The woman opened the door, bringing in a bucket of water. She laid it on the floor next to the door, never coming in completely, and promised someone would bring a meal soon. Vela had no chance of getting the upper hand then, either. Resigned, she got herself cleaned off as best she could. She didn't have a mirror, so she wasn't sure if she had gotten all the dried blood off her face.

Time moved slowly, and Vela thought they had forgotten about her. She had given up sitting on the table and had gotten as comfortable as she could on the floor, leaning against the wall. Being alone with her thoughts hadn't made anything clearer. Questions ran around in her mind.

Where was Jack? Did they leave him behind and did her family find him? Was she sure she had seen Maria look uncomfortable with the force the Neronian had used on her with the ice? Would Maria help her out of here? And what tests did they run on couples like her and Linc? Was Linc okay? The lady who healed her said he was fine, which calmed her some.

More questions abounded. Would they really let her go if she failed the tests? What did it mean if someone passed their tests? *When* was she going to get to talk to someone? She ran her hands through her hair, tempted to pull it all out.

Vela knew she needed to calm her mind. Prayer was what she needed.

Closing her eyes, she breathed in deeply, allowing the air to soothe her frayed nerves. Emptying her mind of all her questions, she relaxed her tense muscles and opened her mind to time with God.

It was her only chance of a reprieve right now.

Chapter Thirty-Eight

CLOSING HER EYES, VELA breathed in deeply, allowing the air to calm her frayed nerves. Emptying her mind of all her questions, she relaxed her tense muscles and opened her mind to time with God.

"God," she whispered, "Still my nerves, help me, God, trust you have me in your hands and won't let go."

Bending her head, she squeezed her eyes as her troubled heart still beat painfully.

"Help me, God, please."

Stillness permeated the room, and a thick silence blanketed her, wrapping her in a cocoon of warmth and blessed peace.

In that moment, she basked in His presence, because she knew He was there, always would be, always had been.

Then she heard a loud whisper in her mind, "Let go, my child. Forgive."

Her eyes flew open, and she sucked in a surprised breath. She looked around to see what voice had just said that. But knew she wouldn't find anyone there.

God had just spoken to her.

"Forgive?" she whispered, trembling. "Forgive who? The E.E. for capturing me? Who?"

In her mind's eye, an image blazed, imprinting her once again of its devastating image. A fire racing up surrounded the walls of a single door. Familiar whimpers and cries of her precious friend sounded in her mind, like she was there all over again.

"It's time, child. To heal," the resonating whisper said in her mind again.

Vela bowed her head, tears leaking from her eyes. Her terrible, familiar pain clenched her chest, making it hard to breathe.

Sobbing, she whispered desperately, "I can't. I can't let go. He'll die in my memories, if I do. Cooper needs to live on." Her memories raced through her mind, faster than she could catch them and stuff them back down. She imagined her familiar wall, as terrible as it was tall, she now knew, between her mind and the images. Blocking them from coming out. Blocking her from healing.

"It's time." God spoke again, this time in a firmer voice.

Nodding, tears ran down her face and she finally relaxed and watched as old crusty memories cracked through the barrier she had erected and exploded into an avalanche of memory.

Vela slept in her bed in the dead of the night. The noise of her brother Drew bursting through her door woke her. He ran into her room, screaming at her to get up. Pulling her out of bed, he pushed her down the stairs where smoke had already begun billowing through the first floor's rooms. She stumbled with her sleepy legs but forced herself to keep moving.

The smoke was too thick to see where the worst of the fire raged. But she trusted her brother to lead her out safely. He didn't take her to the front door, but to an open window instead. Her father was already outside waiting for them. He stood; arms open as her brother pushed her through.

Vela immediately saw her mother when she landed outside. She was in her mother's arms in seconds, bursting into tears as the frightening reality unfolded around them. She looked around for Kane but didn't see him.

"Where's Kane?" she yelled.

Vela's father looked around with horror stamped on his face. He started pushing himself back into the house when Vela's heart stopped. A noise pierced her ears like he called just for her. Her dog. Cooper's terrified howls flooded her eyes with new tears. He was deep inside the house.

"Dad!"

His shoulders pushed out, and he looked at her.

"Cooper's inside too! Please!" It was all she could beg before her throat closed in fear.

He glanced over his shoulder and then back at her.

"Kane's my priority, Vela, sorry."

Vela's heart slammed with grief. She watched her dad disappear into the house. She looked over at her mom. Vela's eyes must have conveyed her intent because her mom's face crumpled. Steel streamed into Vela's veins.

"Vela, no."

"I can't just let him die!" Vela turned toward the house.

Drew jumped in front of her. He grabbed her arms, pinning them to her sides.

"Vela, I can't let you do this."

She tried shaking off his hold, but it was too tight.

"If I have to, I will force you to move," she said through gritted teeth.

"I can't let you go into a burning house, Vela. He's just a dog!" He shook her.

Her eyes bugged out. "He's my best friend!" she screamed at both her mom and Drew. Her mom's hands were over her mouth, and she refused to speak up for what Vela wanted. For someone to save Cooper.

Distressed, Vela did the only thing she knew to do. One long root tore from the ground at her command and wrapped Drew tightly. He let go of her to grab at the vice that held him. She held control of it as Drew tried to wrestle it from her mind and ran.

Jumping up to scoot into the open window, she threw her legs over and ignored the frantic screams of her mom and her angry brother. She jumped down inside and nearly twisted her ankle on the landing.

Vela knew this was dangerous. Madness, really, to go into a burning house, but she couldn't ignore Cooper's cries for help. Her eyes frantically searched for her father and Kane. She tucked herself into a wall as she saw her father carrying Kane fireman style over to the window.

Thankful he had found her brother, she focused on her mission. Following the sounds of Cooper's yelps, she made her way to the other side of the house. Smoke filled her lungs, and she choked. In the dining room, she had to hunch over as coughing spasmed through her dry airway. Straightening, tears streamed down her face, and she put her arm over her eyes, continuing her almost blind walk.

Cooper sounded closer the deeper in the house she went, but she hadn't reached him yet. She grew aware the further she got, the hotter the air felt. At that point, it was impossible to see anything more than a foot in front of her, so she relied on her ears to find him.

Taking short, shallow breaths, she prayed she could reach her best friend in time. She had made it to the kitchen and through the smoke saw flames racing up the living room wall to the left of her. Keeping well away from the fire, she turned toward the direction of the mudroom. It sounded like he was stuck in there. The door was closed. An image of her dog burning alive in blazing flames flashed through her mind. No! She had to reach him! Squeezing her eyes shut, she shook her head at the *image and focused on the door.*

Knowing a little of fire safety, she checked the door handle before she grabbed it. Tapping it, she yelped when it burned the tips of her fingers.

"Vela!" someone called from behind her.

She whipped her head around, searching. Taking a breath, she called out, "I'm here! By the mudroom!" Normally she would feel relief at getting help, but all she felt was terror for her dog. She turned back toward the door. Smoke now leaked under and around the cracks. His cries turned to howling, and she panicked.

Desperate, she looked around for a towel. Spotting one, she grabbed it and brought it back to the door. She paused, not knowing what waited for her on the other side. The oxygen in the air could hit the fire and create a back draft, a terrifying explosion of new flames. Cooper spurred her on, however, she had no choice. She cracked open the door with her arms up to shield her eyes.

Fire exploded toward her, blasting her to her back. Stunned, she couldn't move, but knew she must. Searing pain on the underside of her arms where she had guarded her face alerted her, but she needed to move. The flames hungrily sought fresh places to burn and licked up the walls beside her and hurried toward her on the floor. Whimpering, she scooted backward to avoid being food for the flames.

Jumping up, she cradled her arms as best she could and stared hopelessly toward the mudroom. Heat seared the front side of her body, and she turned her face away from the heat. She choked on the smoke and her sobs.

She couldn't reach him, save walking through the flames. For the first time in her life, she wished she was a Fire Elemental. Frantically, she screamed Cooper's name, begging him to jump over the fire somehow. Waving away the smoke, she saw his out-

line avoiding the flames on his side of the door. His increasing cries tore at her heart.

"Cooper!" she screamed. Toeing her way through patches of unburned floor, she had to do something.

It seemed hopeless. But she would do anything, even if it meant she would injure herself. In between coughs, she screamed, "Cooper! Jump! Come, boy!"

She taught him this trick as a puppy, and he always obeyed her. He had to now.

Tears clogged her vision, and for a moment, she thought she saw him crouching for a jump. Her heart in her throat, desperation filled her as she pushed her arms through the flames to catch him. Blinding pain tore through her arms, her scream piercing the air and she fell, darkness meeting her. In that moment, she wasn't sure if it was death that had caught her, or her arms filled with Cooper.

Vela woke days later. "Cooper?" she croaked to her family, who sat around anxiously watching her.

Silence filled the room. It felt heavy, a monster in the room.

It was fairly easy to read their expressions. Her father and Drew were angry at her for putting herself in danger. Her mother and Kane just looked at her with sorrow in their gazes.

"He's gone?" she asked in a dead voice.

"Thank God you aren't," Drew said, stuffing his hands in his jean's pockets. He turned his frustrated gaze to her arms.

She followed his eyes, and her heart wrenched. Both her arms were wrapped in gauze from her elbows to her hands. When she moved slightly, she flinched in pain. She sucked in a breath as agony tore through the arm with the movement.

"Honey, don't," her mom said, coming to her side, patting the bed next to her, not knowing where to put her hands.

Vela swallowed, trying to get moisture in her dry throat, then asked, "No one could save him?" She searched all their faces for *answers.*

"Honey, there was nothing they could do. Your father and brother found you passed out on the floor and barely got you out in time," her mom whispered. "And the whole room was on fire. If they were Fire Elementals, they could have walked through the fire to reach him, but we aren't. So..."

"So, he's dead," Vela said in a flat voice, her heart tearing into a million pieces, almost matching the number of memories she had with her best friend.

Her mom gave a short nod. Everyone else looked away.

"He was murdered," Vela spat. "By the Festans. I will never forget this. And these," she nodded toward her wrapped arms, "will always remind me of what they did."

Vela had never known such pain at Cooper's death. It hurt worse than the burns that had melted her arms. She grieved; heartbroken, Cooper was not there to love.

She had been thirteen years old. It felt like a lifetime ago, but it was only four years. Movement to the left had Vela's head whipping in that direction. Something had moved over there, she was sure of it. Studying the area, she looked around to see what had moved.

There! She blinked her eyes free from the tears that blurred her vision. A butterfly was sitting on the table's edge. It fluttered its wings and paused before it took flight. Vela watched it and wonder filled her chest as her face streamed with fresh trails from her terrible memories. She knew Linc had sent her this message. That he was here, and they would be alright.

It seemed impossible in this moment to think she would escape, but she had somehow survived a fire, even though Cooper didn't. She missed him desperately and knew she always would.

She knew, then in that moment, that forgiving the Festans who burned down her home and inadvertently killed her dog would not erase her wonderful memories of Cooper. Forgiving the Festans was what she needed to do. Linc might be sending her a message with the butterfly, but it was God sending her this message of forgiveness by using Linc, a Festan.

Linc had blown into her life so thoroughly she knew her life would never be the same again. And part of this experience was letting go of her past. It had handicapped her in her relationship with Linc and taken too much of her life in its angry claws.

Deep shame built through her as memories of all the times she had spent her anger out on Linc ran through her mind. Raising her fists to her eyes, she groaned. *I hurt Linc, over and over, but he's been an innocent in this all along*, she thought miserably. The Festans' act had hurt her, but she had done the same thing, hurt Linc in the act of revenge.

Lifting her head, she straightened. She was ready to let go. Ready to lay to rest the memory of her precious Cooper. Ready to finally forgive.

New tears flowed down her cheeks, and she turned her face up and opened her heart up, baring her soul completely. "God, I forgive them. I forgive what happened with Cooper. I forgive them for burning down my home. I give all that pain and all the anger to you. I lay it at your feet. That's what you did at the cross, died so I could have a life free of anger and prejudice."

She bent her head as she sobbed, tears dripping onto the floor, remembering. All that anger was such a loss. What did it ever do for her? Nothing. She shook her head at the thought. "Forgive me for all those years of wasted time hating others. Help me to see what you want me to see. Help me to let this completely go and never pick it up again. I give this to you to throw as far as the east is to the west, like you said in your Word."

The old weight that she had long carried lifted off her. It was a move, so sudden, so permanent, Vela sat in amazement and continued to weep, but this time, with tears of joy and beauty. She felt light, not weighed down with her grudges and misplaced anger.

She moved her head to look at the butterfly again and she felt her collar was wet with tears. She worshipped her God and Savior right then, giving Him the proof of His light leaking out of her, while accepting His gift of forgiveness.

Her own memories had imprisoned her, holding onto anger and hatred. All the while, God promised her healing, if she had just asked for it. Hiccupping, she wanted to savor this moment of freedom... of peace. So, she bowed her head and sat in the stillness of the love that washed over her, the transformative power of healing she had just received.

Because she had been damaged. Not just the scars on her arms, but in her heart, in her mind. By not letting it go, she had only hurt herself. And it had distanced herself from her Creator, who had wanted to heal her of this long ago.

All those times she'd had flashbacks, she thought were reminders of her pain, but now she knew it was God reminding her to let go and forgive.

Taking a deep breath and wiping her drenched cheeks, she wiped her hands on her pant legs and got up on her knees, reaching her finger out to see if the beautiful message, the butterfly, would let her hold it. She wanted to feel as close to God as possible in that moment by connecting with what He had Linc send her.

She burst into laughter. She thought then that if Linc sent this, he could probably sense that she was close to him, too.

This little insect told her she would escape, and soon. Linc would find a way to her, and they would get out of here. She hugged herself and wished she could be near her Intended right now.

How did he get a butterfly in here, anyway? She looked all around and couldn't figure it out. It didn't come through the window; they locked it shut. Under the door, maybe? She looked up and realized he had probably used the air vent. Sneaky. How she was going to get this thing out of here was another question. As much as she loved its message, she wanted it to live its life.

She strained her ears for any noise outside her door, telling her someone would be coming in. Whether it would be one of the insane Extremists or the sane ones, she had no idea.

Vela cradled the beautiful blue and white butterfly in her hands and centered her thoughts. She stopped obsessing about the door and prayed instead. Prayer was her best and only weapon available to her right now, so she closed her eyes, calmed her overflowing heart, and whispered her plea. She hadn't trusted God before with her fears, but she would right now.

"Please, Lord. I don't know what is going to happen. I don't know who these people really are, but You do. I know to trust in You in everything, even at the worst of times. And this is one of those times. Lord, protect Linc and me. I'm afraid for our lives. Help us out of here and to live through this. I pray for protection and safety. Confuse our captors and divert them from their plans, whatever they may be. I trust in Your plans, not theirs. Thank you, Lord, for loving me and helping me find love in this. I pray all this in Your precious name. Amen."

Vela knew in her heart of hearts Linc had fully found a place there. She loved him, and that thought thrilled her. When she next saw him, she would share her news with him.

She thought too of King David in the Bible. He had been through countless terrifying moments running for his life from Saul, the king who wanted him dead. Saul had chased David for years, afraid David would take his throne, which God had blessed David with. She would trust God like David did. God spared David's life over and over and had given him the throne by the end.

A calm washed through her, and she bowed her head, feeling thankful. By putting her trust in God and placing this all in His hands, she was leaving it up to Him what happened. She was thankful for the fear that had left her. She was as ready as she could be to face the future, whatever it may be.

The door finally opened, and Vela cupped the butterfly in her right hand and put it behind her leg. She didn't think anyone else would understand Linc's message. She hoped Linc's message would escape when she did.

Chapter Thirty-Nine

A DARK-HAIRED MAN WALKED into the room, and she knew he had to be one of the leaders. He stood tall and confident in his perfectly pressed polo shirt and khakis. He had a bland face, not anything too handsome or ugly. No defining features besides his thin lips, she noted, if she ever needed to identify him later.

He did intimidate Vela with his stare, though. His lips formed a smile, but it never reached his eyes. He didn't ooze warmth like the healer had. He just stood and studied her.

Vela was the first to break the silence. "Do I pass your examination? And are you going to say I fell down a ravine, too, or can we be honest with one another?" She surprised herself with her brave words, but she wouldn't take them back.

He smirked. "You're braver than most."

"Why? Have the other Elementals you killed cowered and begged? You will not get that from me, I promise you. I want to know what you people did to my dog, too." An anger surged through her, and she wished she was outside so he could get a taste of her powers. It was possible for her to create an earthquake indoors, but it was extremely difficult to do without touching the earth. She didn't have that kind of power yet.

A speculative gleam came into his eyes, and he said, "They say the prophesied child will have warriors for parents. You have a fighting spirit, so yes, you have passed one of my tests. And your dog is alive, the last I heard. He got away from my men," he said as an afterthought.

Relief crashed through her, but then asked bluntly, "Are you going to kill me and Linc?"

His eyes widened with surprise at her knowledge of what they did to suspected couples who could possibly parent the Chosen Child.

"I know what you do to couples like us," she announced.

He quickly masked his face into a neutral expression before he glared at Vela and put his hands behind his back as if he truly contemplated their deaths.

Silence reigned, and Vela's shoulders stiffened with adrenalin. She'd have to put this butterfly somewhere so she could have use of her hands.

"I haven't decided what to do with you and Linc yet."

"What are you people? Monsters? Why are you doing this to people like Linc and I?" Her heart rate spiked. She turned slightly to hide her hand and placed the butterfly on the table, praying it wouldn't fly away. She at least needed her hands free.

"Did you ever stop to think," he said in a chilling, even tone, "if someone came along and united our clans, that that would be nothing short of terrible for our way of life? You know our world to be a division of clans, with changing borders, yes, but that's been the way of things since the beginning of our time. Our world, as you and I know it, would cease to exist if this child comes about. Who would rule us? The child?" he sneered.

He continued, "Who would be under him or her, for that matter? There are too many unknowns for this to ever happen. For a child to bring that kind of change would be disastrous. Our entire community of Elementals could collapse under this kind of regime. Would it be a democracy or a dictatorship? Would he or she want to be king or queen? Who knows what our system, our entire way of life, would be? Never has anyone united us before. And never should," he spat. "I'm part of this society that's merely trying to protect our way of life."

"You're just trying to protect your income of secreting in Elementals to other clans!" Vela shouted, finished listening to his monologue. "Don't give me your ridiculous reasons and expect me to believe this has nothing to do with the money you would lose if our clans united." Her hands clenched the table, and she struggled to contain her rage. She didn't know what element he had, and she didn't want to fight until she knew.

Before she could blink, he advanced on her and grabbed her arm. He put his face in front of hers and growled, "People like me have been *protecting* our way of life for hundreds of years! I will not, we will not, just stand by and allow our way of life to be threatened by some snotty-nosed brat. We have freedom now. What will we have if someone is over us all? Think about that."

She leaned in even closer, unafraid. "Your supposed freedoms cause problems every day. Disputes over boundaries have been the root of hundreds of Elemental-made disasters. Why not put a stop to all this fighting? If someone can stop it, why not?"

He squeezed her arm painfully. "This is just the kind of thinking that will get you killed, girl. You better hope you fail the other tests."

"What other..." Before she could finish, he was out the door, and she was left alone again.

Not long after the man left, three men came in and marched Vela to another room. They led her down a hall, passing several doors. It looked like this place was an actual home. She wondered how big the house was. None of them spoke to her despite her asking questions, and once they deposited her in a lone chair in the middle of a barren room, stood at various spots along the walls. They each wore dark clothes; she wondered if they were uniforms or had just dressed alike. It was creepy too, to be watched and not spoken to, so she ignored them and studied her surroundings.

The room was small and dark. Windows sat high in the walls, offering little light in the room. She couldn't see out of them, so she didn't know if she was on a second floor or not. Her chair was the only thing here. She briefly considered picking it up and throwing it across the room, only to see if she could get a reaction from her guards. They each stood staring unseeingly into the walls and they reminded her of the British castle soldiers that stood ramrod straight with no expression whatsoever. The more she thought about it, the better and better the idea of throwing her chair sounded.

Before she could come to any decision, however, the door opened. A line of robed people walked through. They filed in and stood facing her chair in one long line. She counted thirteen in all. Their crimson robes had deep hoods hiding their faces. Even though Vela couldn't see their eyes, she could feel the intensity of their stares. She felt she was being judged, and she wondered what her face told them. Vela straightened her back and raised her chin, meeting their gazes with a fierce one of her own. She wouldn't grovel and beg. They would find that out quickly enough.

They were looking for the prophesied child's mother in her; she knew that much. But she didn't know what they knew. What signs to look for. She would just be herself, she decided. If her destiny was to be a part of this, she would take that mantle and wear it proudly. But first she was going to wait silently until they revealed something, *anything*. She could sense they were Elementals, but nothing further than that. Maria popped into her head, and she studied in her mind's eye the look on Maria's face when Vela had been cut with ice. She wondered if she could sway her to help her out of here. If she was even here.

After several minutes, one of the figures stepped forward. He or she was in the middle of the line and now this person stood flanked by six others on each side. After another moment of silence, he spoke.

"Vela Ashcroft, you are here to submit to questioning and a test of your powers."

"I was given no choice but to submit," she snapped.

"You may be the mother of the prophesied child; we have retained you to determine that possibility," he said, ignoring her attitude.

"And if I'm not? What then?"

"Then you will be sent home."

"Like all the others before me? They never made it home. Is that to be my fate as well?"

Murmurs erupted from the line of robed people before her. Whether at her audacity or at the truth of her words, she didn't know.

"You will submit to our questioning, Miss Ashcroft. No harm will befall you, despite the outcome."

Vela snorted. Now that she did *not* believe. She would answer their questions, but at the first opportunity, she was escaping. She wanted to get this over with. "What's your first question?" she asked.

"What is your element?"

"Earth."

"You will demonstrate your gift, please."

Rolling her eyes, she waited as a guard brought over a pot of dirt. When it reached her, she reached her hand out and searched the pot to see if they had planted a seed to grow. She found one buried deep, and she fed it some of her energy. Effortlessly, she grew it until she could see the fruits of her labor peeking over the top of the dirt. A green shoot unfurled itself into a stem and leaves. With just a bit more effort, she watched as a white daisy bloomed. Looking up, she folded her hands in her lap and waited.

"Now that we have proof of your element, we will begin our questions," the leader said.

She didn't expect him to be impressed, but she had showed her gift rather quickly, so she brushed off his disinterest and waited for the rest of the questions.

"We have in our records you were born on August 23rd. Is that correct?"

Shock rocked through Vela. Why do they want to know that about her? "Why?" she asked uneasily.

After a long moment, he answered, "When the day and night are of equal length, a warrior star who will bear the child will rise."

That must be part of the prophecy. It's had such an impact on her life, she'd like to hear the whole thing.

"Was that the whole prophecy?" she asked.

"No."

"I'd like to hear it."

He exhaled, as if her answer annoyed him. After a moment of consideration, he relayed by memory, "When the day and night are of equal length, a warrior star who will bear the child will rise. Under the Winter Solstice, the Hunter will emerge. He will capture the Goat under the Northern sky and they will produce the one who will unify. Though their elements are diverse, through them the child will command them all."

"Now is that your birthdate?" he asked again in a hard voice that brooked no patience with her.

She had to think for a minute. She needed to hear the prophecy again to make complete sense of it. What did he mean that the Hunter would have to capture the Goat? Was she the Goat or the Hunter? She bit down on the inside of her cheek, drawing blood, focusing on that pain instead of her absolute powerlessness.

"Miss Ashcroft?"

She had no idea if her birthday fell on a date that would have both day and night of equal length. But she knew they could trace this information with or without her help, so she answered, "September."

"What day?"

"The twenty-third."

A shock wave moved through the robed Elementals, followed by harsh whispering and gasps. What was the significance of her answer?

"What is it?" she asked impatiently.

Her inquisitor had turned to speak to another behind him when she had answered. He faced her again and said, "Your birthday falls on the Autumn Equinox."

"Is that when the day and night are the same length?"

After studying her for a moment, he nodded.

She sat back in her seat and thought carefully. If she were to continue to pass these tests, she would never be seen again. They would kill her; she was sure of it. She had inadvertently passed this one. As curious as she was to know if she could be the prophesied child's mother, it wasn't worth her life. She would have to be sure to fail the rest of the tests.

Vela looked around the room and thought that anytime now would be a great time for Linc to stage a rescue. She wondered where he was. He was close. She could feel him, but she didn't know where he was being held.

The speaker demanded her attention again. "Were you born in the United States?"

It was such a general question, she answered honestly, "Yes."

"Miss Ashcroft, we're going to have a stone brought to you. Please tell us if you have any reaction to it."

She decided right then that if she felt anything, she would have to pretend that she didn't, even if she was on fire.

One of the twelve figures came to stand in front of her. "This stone," a woman produced from her robes, "will tell us if you are indeed bonded to a Festan Elemental. It may hurt."

Vela shivered with fear. She was getting her wish. That stone would burn her because of her connection to Linc, a Festan.

The robed woman set a small gray stone on Vela's forehead. Instantly, a terrible heat raced through her head and down into her body. She clenched her hands and prayed God would help her fake a non-reaction.

She felt like she was burning alive but gave no indication of it. She stayed absolutely still but screamed inside her mind. Her eyes were closed, so she didn't have to hide their reaction, but she desperately tried to contain tears of pain. What she couldn't hide, however, was her body's reaction to the heat. Sweat beaded on her forehead. After what seemed like excruciating minutes, but most likely just seconds passed, the woman mercifully lifted the stone off of her head.

"Did you feel any reaction?" the woman asked, eyeing her.

Making sure she could talk without a tremble in her voice, she opened her eyes, pretended to think by cocking her head to the side, and said, "No."

"Interesting. No feelings at all?"

"No," Vela answered, deeply relieved she could act as well as she had.

Vela prayed desperately that they wouldn't test her again with that stone. She wouldn't be able to hide that kind of pain again.

The woman walked back to rejoin the others, and Vela could have cried with relief. She thanked God for answering her prayer and focused on her inquisitor.

"I am not convinced," he announced. "Why are you sweating if you didn't feel any heat?"

"I'm nervous," Vela said, injecting force into her words. "All of you are watching me and it's made me a nervous wreck. I sweat when I'm nervous. Don't you?"

Ignoring her question, he asked, "Even so, you didn't have any feeling come over you when the stone was placed on you?"

"No," she lied. She needed to be believable. She couldn't go through that again.

"Very well, Miss Ashcroft," he said after studying her. "Our next question has already been answered by one of our own, so you are no longer needed here."

"Wait! What question was it? When did you ask me anything?" she asked with panic rising in her. How did she know if she had failed it or not?

"That will be all," he intoned, dismissing her. "Let's bring in Mr. Stevenson."

"Will I get to see him? What question did you ask me?" she asked, as the guards by the door came to escort her out of the room. "You can't keep me here! I demand to be released!"

Her guards seized her arms, forcing her to get up out of the chair and walk out of the room. She struggled against their hold while searching her senses as they led her out to see if she could determine where Linc was. But all she could find was that he was close.

The building she was being held in seemed small, all the rooms were tiny. She didn't see much of the place as they led her quickly down the hallway to the room, she had woken up in. She wondered where they held their meetings to fit their members. How many members did they have, anyway? Questions raged in her head, and she clamped down on her frustration with no clear answers.

She suddenly remembered that Elia had discovered that this group was having a meeting tonight. Was this a satellite location of the E.E. or was the meeting being held here? Hope soared through her that Elia would have told her family and they could possibly be on their way right now.

As she settled back in the room, she attempted to not look too gleeful at the thought. Plus, Linc was here, and he had some kind of plan, too. Both thoughts cheered her, and she got as comfortable as she could on the floor to wait out her uncertain future.

Chapter Forty

ONCE THE MEN GUARDING her had roughly deposited her back in her room, she searched the small space for her little friend but couldn't find the little thing. It must have gotten out when she had left the room earlier.

Relieved it had escaped, she paced the room and hoped for a similar fate. She had wanted to fail all the tests, but the only one she had control of was the stone and its effect on her. And she wasn't positive they had believed her act. As far as the first test, she didn't have any control over her birthday. She couldn't have anticipated that her birthday would fall on the Autumn Equinox. And then she couldn't remember answering the last test or any other question. So, she didn't know if she had passed or failed that one.

But wait, the man who had come into her room, who she had argued with, told her she had passed his test. He had said she had a fighting spirit, a warrior. He must have relayed what he had determined to the robed figures. Hanging her head, she didn't know what more she could do to protect her life.

One thing was certain. She could try to escape when she got new visitors. She had to try something to free herself. She couldn't stand waiting around like this. Jumping in place, in an attempt to do something with her frayed nerves, she had to do something. If only she had access to the earth, she could use her powers to get out of here. But there wasn't even a houseplant in this austere room. The only thing in the room was the table she had woken up on.

If she had a way to sharpen the legs into points, she would break the table legs off to make a weapon. Wait, even without the legs having sharpened points, a table leg was better than nothing to protect herself. She was thankful the table was made of wood. If it had been plastic, implementing her plan would have been impossible.

As quietly as she could, she turned the table over. She didn't want to alert anyone outside her door to what she was doing. With the table upside down, she braced her legs on either side of one corner. She put one foot down on the belly of the table, got a good grip on the leg and yanked, using all her strength. She heard a crack, and she jumped in place, happy that she had partially broken a leg. Hoping the crack wasn't too loud, she gave the leg another yank to break it completely free.

Holding the table leg in her hand, she looked at it with fierce pride. It broke in a jagged point, which was good because it looked sharp enough to pierce if she needed that. She frowned. Could she stab someone? Shaking her head, she hoped it wouldn't come to that.

But finally, she had something she could use. She wasn't helpless now.

Bracing it on her shoulder like a baseball bat, she faced the door, ready for her next visitor. Standing in a defensive stance, she got ready to stand there forever if she had to. Different scenarios ran through her mind about how she would incapacitate someone. She changed her position. It would be better if she put her back to the wall next to the door. That way, they wouldn't see her as soon as they opened the door.

She needed every element of surprise she could get.

The only kink in her plan was if it was Linc or her family who came through. Because she planned on knocking heads first and asking questions later. After all, she didn't know what gifts the Elementals had, and she couldn't afford to be attacked by them. She only knew Gyan battle tactics. From what she had seen when she had been abducted, she was far outclassed in fighting other elements.

She could only hope she would sense Linc or recognize any of her family before she brought her weapon down on their heads. She was desperate enough to make a terrible mistake like that.

Heavy footsteps sounded outside her door, and adrenaline raced through her arms and body. She was ready for battle.

The door opened, and she got a quick glimpse of an unfamiliar head before she brought down the table leg, striking them on the back of the head. They dropped immediately and a tray of food clattered to the floor. Was there only one? She looked in the doorway and didn't see anyone else.

The hallway was clear.

Breathing a sigh of relief, she threw down her weapon and looked at who brought her food. It was the woman who had healed her earlier. Vela cringed and hoped she would be alright. She bent down to grab hold of the woman and pulling her under the woman's armpits; she used all her strength to drag her plump body into the room. Then she promptly cleaned up the food scattered in the doorway. She hoped desperately she hadn't killed her.

Sliding her fingers down the woman's neck, she searched for a pulse and was relieved to find a strong heartbeat. Vela held her breath, searching the woman for keys that might open locked doors. She searched through all the pockets she could find but came away empty-handed. *Oh well, I could at least take some food.* She snatched up the roll that had come with the tray and stuffed it in her pocket. She would need food after her escape, if she got that far, she thought grimly. Still, it helped to be prepared.

She reached for her weapon, stood, and strode out into the hall. Her adrenaline gave her an energy that surprised her. She had never felt so alive. Her resolve was firm. She would escape this, she *would* survive.

The table leg rested on her shoulder, and she gripped it firmly as she took careful steps into the hallway and closed the room the healer woman now rested in. The interrogation room was a few doors down and she walked past it, hearing no noise. They must be finished with their interview with Linc. She wondered what they had discovered. This prophecy ruined her life. She wished people would just forget it.

All senses alert, she strained to listen for footsteps. She heard nothing. Where was everyone? She kept going until she reached the end of the hallway. That's when she realized she was upstairs. There was a stairwell around the corner, and she paused. This wasn't good. The stairs might open into a room where she wouldn't be able to hide. Fear washed through her. She stopped to wipe her clammy hands on her pants. She needed a good grip.

Taking a deep breath, she started down the stairs, listening intently. This was going too easily.

The stairs took a turn, and she raised her makeshift bat and continued. That's when she heard a voice. Peering down the stairs, she looked to see what kind of room the stairs opened into. She couldn't see much because of the turn in the stairwell. The voice continued, and she heard a murmuring from what sounded like a group. They must be having a meeting.

Two, maybe three people she could handle, but not a group. Her spirits sunk, but she bolstered herself.

Maybe she could sneak past them somehow. The only thing she could do was continue. She was not going back to that room to wait for whatever sick fate they had for her. She reached the bottom step and could see the rooms now.

There was a hallway stretched in front of her with the hope of a front door, a kitchen on the right and a living room on the left. She put her back to the wall next to the living room, hiding her presence. She took a quick look into the large room. Sweat beaded on her forehead as fear gripped her. The room held a group of people who, from what she could hear, were listening to a speaker. And she could hear that the speaker was talking about *her*. She paused.

Did they think she was the mother they had been waiting for? She couldn't help being curious about what they had discovered.

"It looks like this girl is the closest match we've found," the speaker said. "Everything matches up to the prophecy, with the stone being the exception. But you found, Lincoln, that she is impervious to your fire?"

Shock rocked through Vela's body. She was sure she hadn't seen Linc in the room. Just the backs of the heads of those listening. No one was being guarded, that she had seen. Was Linc sitting and listening *with* the E.E. members? She bit down hard on her fist so she wouldn't cry out. She shook her head, denying what this could mean. Tears leaked, and she rapidly blinked to clear her vision. In her surprise, she had missed the first part of his answer, so she held her breath to better listen to every word.

"... when I hugged her to me, my fires did not hurt her. She *is* my Intended, make no mistake."

Why would he be a part of this discussion? When she had glanced into the room, she had seen a group listening to every word the speaker was saying. He was *part of the group.*

Vela's heart ripped apart. Was this why he wasn't captured with her? He had re-joined the group that had *hurt* her. This knowledge felt like he had been the one to knock her out.

Had he been a part of this sick group all along? Was he one of the ones who thought they were helping the prophecy along, or one of the ones who wanted to eliminate it? She realized the speaker had asked another question she didn't hear.

"Sir," Linc answered, "Vela trusts me implicitly. She would go with me anywhere."

"She really would." Vela heard Maria's voice add on.

Vela didn't want to hear anymore. She wiped the tears she had shed, listening to his poisonous words. He wasn't worth any of them. The things that were making sense warred with the ones that didn't. Did he know she was his Intended from the beginning? Did he attend the school to find her, only just to drag her to his demented friends? If she was the prophesied mother, then *he'd* be the father. Did his membership to this group protect his life, but not hers? Was he replacing her with *Maria*? Conversations with him ran through her mind. She shook her head.

She'd have to analyze those later. She was getting out of here and she would do anything to accomplish that.

Vela would have to cross the entrance to the room everyone was in, but she thought she could do it quickly enough, hopefully without raising suspicion. She looked in the other direction, checking to see if she was missing someone in the kitchen. Finding the way clear, she didn't want to waste any more time, so she dashed across the living room entrance into the hallway.

Racing down the hall, she was rewarded with the front door. Just when she thought she had made a clean break, she heard a cry of discovery behind her. She dropped the table leg and her fingers fumbled to unlock the deadbolt. Throwing open the door, she was out and racing down the front steps in seconds.

She glanced over her shoulder just in time. A spear of ice flew toward her, and she dove onto the ground to avoid being impaled. Scrambling up, she flew toward the tree line.

A wealth of pines surrounded the house; it looked completely isolated. Dashing toward them, she could only hope and pray she would lose her followers in the trees.

She fought through her heartbreak. She felt like her chest had been crushed, crippled with the knowledge she had been terribly used. How could Linc have completely fooled her? She had been right all along to hate Festans. She should *never* have trusted Linc. She ran, allowing anger to fuel her pace.

The wind pressure changed, and she felt rather than saw a funnel chasing her down. She would not make this easy. She zigzagged, narrowly missing being caught up in the windstorm as it blew past her. Swerving to avoid its massive wind tearing through the yard, she ran around it and used it to hide her from view from who chased her.

At her first chance, she'd make a hole in the ground and bury herself, effectively hiding. She broke through the tree line and looked behind her. Several Elementals were hot on her trail, and more followed.

She needed to distract them.

Getting creative, she waved her arm and uprooted small pines as she passed, felling them. Cries of pain sounded behind her as her efforts worked. A grim determination filled her, and she ignored her guilt at hurting anyone.

They brought this fight on. She would finish what they started.

Vela continued her punishing pace, ignoring her name being yelled. She jumped over brush and fallen logs and looked for a good place to implement her plan to hide. She screamed when a tree came down in front of her. Skidding to a stop, she looked for a way around it when a sweet sound filled her ears, a barking. Jack!

Spinning around, she had time to brace herself before Jack's hundred-pound body jumped on her torso.

"Jack! You're safe! Thank God!" she managed to say between slobbery licks on her face.

Drew reached her next. He wrapped his arms around her and Jack. She cried in relief. If they were here, her family was too, maybe more.

"Vela, we've got to get you out of here," he said, pushing Jack away from her. "We've staked this place out. There are about twenty of them and five of us, well, seven, with you and Linc. Where is Linc? Is he still in there? He can take you and keep you safe."

She fought down her crushing disappointment in her Intended.

"Vela? Where's Linc?"

Her expression told him more than words could say. She fought through her dark feelings of betrayal and growled, "He's one of them, Drew. He's been an E.E. all along."

His face reflected his complete shock. He bared his teeth and clenched his hands. Sounds of an Elemental fight reached them. She looked toward the house and could see flames and wind battering the tops of trees. "I'll deal with him," he growled, his expression darkening. "Come on, let's go."

"No! I want to help you! I will not let you guys fight while I run away! This is just as much my fight as yours. Now, let's go."

He warred with his decision, clenching and unclenching his fists and jumping on his toes. "Vela, they're targeting you. I don't want to deliver you right into their hands."

"They can't get away with kidnapping me that easily. And you guys need my help." Grabbing his hand, she called Jack to her, pulling him toward the fight, and Drew finally succumbed to her decision.

Together, they raced toward the fight of their lives.

Chapter Forty-One

WHEN VELA RAN INTO the clearing, her eyes widened. The elements had come alive. She saw bursts of fire, currents of air whipping around, and ice knives flying through the air. Those were just some weapons being used. Thirty or so Elementals were fighting in a desperate bid to outlast each other.

Jack, sensing the fighting atmosphere, growled. She spotted some of her family, but stopped in her tracks at what she saw next. She recognized some E.E. members who were now fighting each other. It seemed some had figured out the true nature of this group and were helping her family.

She saw they had made it back just in time. Behind her mother's back, Vela blocked a fireball with a wall of dirt she threw up, saving her life. Whitney glanced back and her face reflected immense relief.

"Vela! Come stand next to me. Are you okay?" She grabbed Vela's hand, squeezing hard. She looked her up and down, but her distraction cost her. She flew to the ground by a powerful gust of wind, landing on her side.

Vela focused her attention on the female Borean who had dared attack her mother. She opened a hole underneath her. The Borean dropped, but before her head disappeared, Vela tightened the hold until the woman struggled for breath. She gasped for air. Before she could try any desperate attacks, Vela squeezed the dirt hole until the woman passed out.

Vela's stomach dropped and rage followed when she saw Elia next to her facing two Elementals. She mentally grabbed onto two roots, ripping them free. In a shower of dirt, she slung them both like a whip. The attacking Elementals cried out when the roots tore into their backs. They fell, writhing in pain. Jack pounced and bracing his front paws on one, holding him down, he bit into the other, subduing them both.

Vela stumbled when Elia crashed into her. Her small arms wrapping Vela in a tight hug. "I knew we'd find you here," she said breathlessly. She looked wild. Her hair was free, tangled all around her and her eyes held a light Vela had never seen before. Elia looked like a warrior. "Are you okay?" Elia asked.

"I'm fine. Pay attention, don't ask me stupid questions right now!"

Elia doused a fire wall, advancing on them with an explosion of dirt. "Stupid? Do you know how worried I've been about you?"

"Elia! If you die, I will freak out, so please, just fight!"

A voice had her twisting her gut, and she looked behind her.

"So, the Bobsy twins came to play," Maria drawled.

"Maria! You *are* a part of the E.E.!" Elia gasped.

Vela's eyes narrowed on her nemesis and slid her feet apart, preparing herself for a fight.

"My dad told me since I was a little girl, the Chosen Child will ruin our world!" Maria shouted at Vela. "I can't let you be responsible for bringing him or her about," she continued, her beautiful eyes deceptively hard.

"So, you've known nothing but lies like that. No wonder you turned out the way you did," Vela countered, suddenly feeling sad for Maria to grow up in that kind of angry world.

"And the worst of it is, you took the one person I wanted," Maria continued, like she hadn't heard what Vela had just said. "But is his betrayal enough for you to let him go, I wonder?"

Maria's reminder of Linc's involvement with this group made Vela's blood race in fury. Elia gasped in shock at the news. Vela barely saw the fighting around her or even when Elia turned and fought hand to hand with another Elemental, protecting Vela.

"Don't remind me," Vela gritted out.

"Oh, I will," Maria shouted, her eyes flashing. "How do you think I know Linc so well? If it wasn't for your stupid bond, he would have chosen me. Maybe," she yelled, a maniacal look coming into her eyes, "if you're dead, he'll forget you even existed."

Vela's eyes widened and her heart froze. Maria wanted her dead?

Maria then looked at Jack at Vela's side. Her eyes narrowed in concentration and before Vela could think of a defense, Maria swept her hands apart. Her action opened the ground underneath Jack, and, with a yelp, he fell, disappearing into it.

Vela cried out and mimicked Maria, opening her arms to hold open the hole Jack was in. Vela heard Maria screaming in frustration. Furious at Maria, who tried burying her dog alive, Vela tried to think of what to do.

With her attention focused on her dog, Vela didn't see Maria changing tactics. In a spray of dirt, Maria tore a long root out of the ground and whipped it around Vela's neck, wrapping it tightly.

Vela's hands flew to the painful hold it had, choking. Panic coursed through her, and she tried desperately taking control of it, but Maria's mental grip was like iron. Spots soon formed in Vela's eyes. Her fingers dug into the root, praying for a savior. She looked around for help, but it was as if she and Maria existed in a vacuum. Fighting raged around them, everyone focused on their own opponent.

She dropped to her knees, losing all hope, her mouth opening and closing, begging for air. Looking up at Maria, tears swam in her vision as she looked at her would-be murderer.

Maria's eyes, once hard with anger, now flickered with uncertainty. Maria's arm stretched toward her, and it shook. Her hand clenched and unclenched like her hand itself choked Vela.

God, give her mercy, please save me!

Vela's eyes begged Maria to let her go. Maria looked away, like she couldn't watch the life being drained out of Vela.

Vela continued to try sucking in air, but it was useless. She tried one last time, mentally grabbing onto the root, but her lack of oxygen drained her of the energy she'd need. Why wasn't her extra power from being bonded with Linc helping her? Her lack of oxygen robbed her of it.

Vela tried one last thing. She slumped to the ground next to Jack's hole, bracing herself on all fours. Immediately, her connection to the ground revived her powers a little, and she turned her head toward Jack.

She commanded the dirt under him to rise, pushing him up out of the hole. She continued to give the last of her energy, bringing her dog and her last chance of survival to the surface like an elevator. Finally, black closed in on Vela's vision and she fell to the side.

Distant barking sounded and suddenly the root loosened, giving Vela life-saving breaths. She rolled to her side, dragging in breath after breath into her starved lungs. Wheezing, she looked up with blurry vision and found Jack on top of a screaming Maria.

Forcing herself up as she breathed in the sweet air, she got to her feet and walked slowly over to her. Jack bit down on Maria's shoulder, a growl in his throat warning her against moving.

Maria looked up at Vela, terror in her eyes, and screamed, "Get him off me!"

"Why would I do that, Maria?" Vela asked, each word painful coming from her abused throat. "So, you can try to kill me again?"

Maria squeezed her eyes shut and, with gritted teeth, said, "I just wanted you out of the picture. My father says you will be the death of our world if you exist."

"Our world will be fine, Maria," Vela rasped, trying to project over the noise of the fighting around them. "Even if I am the prophesied mother, our world was always meant to live together, not apart. We would have God's blessing if we united. Can't you see that?"

Maria cried out in pain when she tried to move. Jack growled again and tightened his bite. Vela looked around and realized her family needed her to fight, not trade words with her psychotic rival.

Just then, in the corner of her eye, she saw Jack let go of Maria and jump toward her blind spot. She crouched and ducked her head, not knowing if someone threw a weapon toward her or what the threat was.

Picking her head up to vicious snarling, Jack stood in front of her with his front paws bracing his body in an attack position. He protected her from three Elementals. Forced to have her back to Maria, she faced her new threat.

Two guys and a woman looked at Jack and paused their attack. They looked at each other and seemed to come to an unspoken agreement as they focused their attention on her dog.

They knew a threat when they saw one.

One minute Jack was snarling and the next he was in the air, pouncing on one Elemental biting into his chest before bouncing off the first and flying toward the second, the woman. He ripped into her arm as soon as he had his paws on her, then in another circus-like flying leap, landed on the third. Like a steel trap, his mouth cut into his victims like butter. Jack performed beautifully. His movements looked choreographed and rehearsed, they were so perfect.

Vela watched, amazed. She had never seen him like this. He had them all on the ground writhing in pain in seconds. He stood over them, daring them to get back up. He hadn't even given them a chance to defend themselves.

He behaved like he was on steroids. Didn't Linc say Festans could heighten animals' senses? But what Festan would give Jack a boost like that? She looked around the battlefield. Was it one of the E.E. who had turned on the other members who did it?

No one seemed to pay any attention to her and Jack, so she chalked up his prowess to his natural fighting abilities.

Vela scanned the yard to see if she could help anyone. That's when she noticed the group of thirty had diminished drastically. She didn't see that many fallen bodies. Most of the Elementals had fled the fight. It seemed a lot more even now with the reduced numbers. She wondered if they now fought the actual monsters of the group. Which reminded her. Where was Linc?

Her dad stood near the tree line and dodged an ice knife, then lunged forward to punch the Neronian in the nose. Blood squirted, and he fell.

To Vela's right, Kane fought near Elia. He grappled with an Elemental before he picked him up and threw him into the dirt. He put his foot on the man's stomach, then secured him with a cage of roots.

To her left, Drew held off two men by peppering their faces with dirt clods, impairing their vision. He then bent a nearby sapling and swung it into their bodies, sending them flying. They didn't get up.

Satisfied her family was managing, she looked around for Maria, but she had fled. Then she scanned the fighting for the one person she did want to confront. She didn't see Linc anywhere. *Did that coward run too?*

She didn't have time to figure it out. Because deep in the fray, the searcher who had kidnapped her had his sight set on her. He sported a black eye since she last saw him. She wondered who he had irritated. Other than Linc, this was one person she wanted to fight. Payback for what he did filled her mind. He moved with ease around flying ice knives, wind gusts, and smoke from fire bursts. He came right for her. She crept backwards, closer to the forest line. She needed as many weapons as she could find.

"Jack, follow me," she commanded.

"Little girl, look at you play like you know what you're doing," he sneered as he prowled closer his ugly face contorting. "And you got your mutt back. We should have killed him earlier. That can be remedied soon enough."

Rage raced through her, and she struggled to form a coherent sentence. "I know what I'm doing," she shot back. "And you'll regret messing with my dog and my family."

"Is that who these people are?" he glanced at her mother, looking her up and down. "They look *very* capable."

Vela screamed and flung a nearby branch at him to shut him up. She wanted to whip the man's mouth off. He dodged her attack, and a feral light came into his eyes.

"You're going to regret that." He raised his hands and Vela watched as ice crept over them, morphing them into jagged, icy blades. "Now, let's dance," he purred.

Vela jumped backwards when he lashed both arms at her, coming perilously close to slicing a hole through her stomach. She tried opening a hole under him, but he jumped over it easily. Jack lunged toward him just as he landed and bit into his ankle. He somehow shook him off. He was off balance though and tried reaching Jack with his ice knives for hands, but Jack jumped out of reach.

"Is that all you guys got?" he snickered.

Inching further toward the tree line, she lured him closer. "You want to dance? Let's go," she snarled. She created another hole, which he jumped over again. She made hole after hole to keep him busy hopping. Her plan was working. She was bringing him into the forest. Jack snuck behind the Neronian and snipped at his heels, trying to get a bite, but his jumps evaded Jack's teeth.

The Neronian cursed as he continued to avoid her holes and Jack's bite. He didn't seem to notice when she had drawn him into the trees. With a powerful thrust, Vela wrapped the man in enough branches from a nearby maple to cover him from head to foot.

She left his foot out for Jack to snack on, which he did as he lunged toward his treat. The man howled at Jack's attack. He tried hacking at the branches with his ice weapons, but Vela wasn't done. She squeezed his leafy prison. His screams were cut off with his breath. She turned her back on his struggles and walked back toward the clearing to see who else needed help.

Calling Jack to her, she took a breather while she looked around. She reached out to the nearby trees, siphoning energy from them to re-energize her. Some leaves wilted and fell off, others just went limp. She didn't drain them dry, just enough until she felt replenished.

Vela froze at the sound of howling wolves. Those sounded too close. "He wouldn't," she whispered. "Please, God, no." Before another thought could follow, the back of her neck prickled. She slowly turned around.

The fringe of the forest revealed a line of wolves peering through the trees, their eyes fierce and teeth bared. She couldn't count them all. Linc strode through them, and her heart nearly punched through her chest. He held his arms down, signaling the wolves to stay.

Linc had just brought wolves to a dogfight.

When all the Elementals noticed the wolves, the fighting abruptly stopped, fire poofed into smoke, wind funnels vanished, and ice and water dropped to the ground. The Elementals they fought grinned when they saw Linc, and it only confirmed to Vela that he was a part of them.

Jack's eyes were trained on his dog cousins and snarled ominously. She grabbed hold of his collar. She did not need him to get mauled by a pack of wolves.

Vela's body burned with the need for revenge. She saw a haze of red. "Linc!" she screamed. "How dare you!"

His eyes widened in surprise and then confusion. Letting go of Jack, branches answered her call, and she threw one after another at him, trying to knock him out. He burned to ash everything she attacked him with.

"Vela! What are you doing?" he screamed.

"What am *I* doing? *You* are the traitor! How *dare* you try to hurt my family! I will kill you first!"

"What?" Kane yelled. "What do you mean, he's a traitor? Vela?"

Drew joined them.

"No!" Linc yelled.

"He's an E.E., Kane," Drew said. "I'm going to kill him. Don't trust anything he has to say. He's been a part of them all along."

Vela heard Elia and her mom gasp.

"No! It's not like that. You've got to let me explain!" Linc yelled.

Movement made Vela look behind Linc to the tree line. Maria raced through trees and ran toward Linc until she stopped breathless next to him, holding her bleeding shoulder.

"It's okay, Linc, you can be your true self now," she said, smiling up at him. "You don't have to hide. I'm here with you."

He frowned down at her and looked back at Vela, frustrated. Vela tried tamping down the white hot anger rising fast through her. She already knew Linc was a traitor.

"Not now, Maria," he said, dismissing her.

Maria glared first at Linc, then Vela.

Kane shook himself from his shocked expression. "Is this true Linc? Are you a part of these people?"

The man who had spoken to her alone in the room and who'd been fighting with her father strode over to stand in front of Linc. "It's time you showed your true loyalty, Lincoln. To us." His tall form oozed superiority as he leaned on his heels and put his hands in his pockets. The man easily projected confidence. Linc would follow him. Maria left Linc to stand next to this man.

Was this Maria's father? Vela wondered.

"Yes," Linc said grimly, "It *is* time." With a wave of his hands, the wolves drew closer. But they didn't approach Vela's family. They growled at and guarded E.E. members, herding them into a circle in the clearing in front of the house. Linc dropped his hands for the wolves to stand guard on the now shocked members. He looked straight at Vela with a strained face as he held control of the wolves as he tried to communicate something with his eyes.

He flicked his glance away and, addressing the E.E. leader, said, "I've never actually been a part of your group. I was planted here to find information on all of you. That I found my Intended wasn't expected, but it gave me further insight into your group's motives and actions. Now, I suggest you stand down. We're leaving with Vela. You will *not* hurt her."

"I see," the man responded. "In that case..." He fixed a glare at Vela and that was the only warning she got before a root shot at her.

Before she could blink, Maria screamed and flung her arm her out, changing the trajectory of the root. The only sound she could hear was a sickening squelch. Vela looked in horror at what had just happened. The root had missed her but speared her mother in the chest. In what looked like slow motion, Vela watched as her mother's body fell to the ground and lay there, still. Vela's hoarse scream penetrated the air as she crawled on the ground toward her unmoving mother.

Chapter Forty-Two

SHOUTING AND FIGHTING ERUPTED all around her. Vela barely noticed as she reached her mother and gently moved her until she laid her onto her back. Jack crouched on the ground next to her mom, whining softly. With shaking fingers, Vela felt for a breath. It was there, but barely. Her mother's eyes fluttered open, and Vela cradled her face.

Why would Maria try to kill her just to save her later? Did she mean to kill her mother now?

"Vela," Whitney whispered.

"Mom don't talk. Save your breath," Vela said, her own voice shaking. She couldn't tear her eyes away from the root protruding from her mother's chest.

"Vela, come here. There's something... tell you... before too late," she wheezed. Blood moved in a line down her cheek, and she gurgled, choking.

"Mom, please hold on," Vela sobbed, not knowing how to help heal this terrible wound. She could heal some things, but she knew if she removed the root, her mother would bleed out before Vela could stop the bleeding. "I don't know what to do," Vela whispered, barely able to talk with the horror trapped in her lungs.

"Nothing... can do... please... come," Whitney's eyes, filled with tears, beseeched Vela.

Vela moved closer, leaning over her, tears splashing on her mother's white, strained face.

Whitney squeezed her eyes shut, then opened them, tears dripping onto the ground. She looked intently at Vela and, with both hands, clutched Vela's arms with a sudden strength.

"I... love... you," she wheezed. Vela nodded her head, trying to keep her sobs soft to better hear her.

"I love you too, Mom."

"But you aren't... mine. Not... truly."

Whitney coughed and Vela squeezed her eyes shut when blood splattered on her face. She opened them again, not wanting to miss a single second with her mother.

"Mom, no!" Confusion spread through her. What did could her mother mean?

"We... adopted... you... Vela... my precious... girl."

With wide eyes, Vela looked at her mother with a new horror. Her world fell away at those words. She leaned back, shock combining with her terror at losing her mother. Or was she?

"What?" Vela's voice sounded far away to her own ears. "Mom?"

The little light that was in her mother's eyes slowly faded. Vela shook off her confusion and cradled her mother's head in her lap. She started begging. "No! Mom, don't leave me, please. I can't lose you, please, Mom. I don't care, you're mine, you'll always be mine."

Vela stroked her mother's hair away from her face, whispering her plea over and over. Hands squeezed her shoulders, and she looked up, barely seeing who was behind her for the tears flooding her vision.

The fighting had stopped; the wind stopped howling. Water and ice didn't streak the air and roots lay by the feet of the other Elementals. Vela blinked her tears away to see that Drew, Kane and her father all kneeled around her mother's still body.

"We need to get the root out," her father said urgently, his hands taking over. "All of our healing abilities will be needed. Drew?"

With a pale face, Drew nodded and scooted closer.

"I'm going to pull it out and then, together, we'll feed her our energy," her dad instructed. "Everyone's hands need to be touching her. Vela and I will close the wound in the back and Drew, you and Kane, close the front. Now!" He had rolled her mom over with careful hands to reach the root behind her. He yanked the protruding root out in one quick motion. Vela locked the squelching sound it made away, deep in her mind, for another time. For now, she had work to do.

Vela's hands clapped over the open wound, and with all her strength, poured all her healing energy into her mother. The bleeding needed to stop. With another sob, she watched her mother's face for any sign of a change. It was ashen and showed no improvement.

Not yet anyway.

She prayed like she had never prayed before, begging for a miracle. A heat blistered through her as she pushed her gift into her dying mother. She had never given this much energy before, but she would give more, all of herself, if it meant her mother could live.

Vela knew that the root had caused internal injuries, puncturing organs, most likely her lung. This was where Vela was least gifted, but she strained to see what it had pierced. Reaching out with her senses, she searched the grievous wound. Her shoulders slumped. It was a mess. Muscles, tendons, the root obliterated everything in its path. She didn't have the gift to search deeper, to see if the lung had been punctured.

So, she focused her healing on what she had been told to do. To close the wound. Drew and her father could seek and heal the deeper wounds. She hoped.

Vela ignored who watched their desperate attempt to save her mother's life. She squirmed at the twinge in her chest. It was difficult, at best, to trust Linc to fight for them and not against them. His control over the wolves was impressive. She could hear the animals' snarls and knew they waited for more victims.

She concentrated on her healing. Her muscles burned with pain. Her powers were dwindling. But with her dad's help, the blood slowed and seeped out now instead of pouring out. The wound was closing.

"Please God," she begged, "Help us!" Her vision was darkening as black spots floated in and out.

Suddenly, a warmth covered her shoulder, and she looked over at its source. Linc's hand rested on her, and he gripped her, feeding her his energy. Their energy as Intendeds shot through her. Directing all her attention and now renewed power, she poured healing into her mother's grievous wound. Finally, the wound slowly closed. She searched her father's face, for his reaction alone would tell her whether they were successful. Linc's hand fell away, and she missed his warmth. She shook her head at the confusion rocking her; she didn't think what to think about her Intended. He had denied being involved with this group that might have killed her mother.

Giving her attention back to her father, who looked absolutely determined as he ran his hands over her mother's back, holding his hands over certain areas.

"Dad?" Vela asked, "Is she alright?"

"Hold on, Vela," he bit out. "Drew, how's your side? What are you seeing?"

"We need help," he answered. Drew barked commands at Kane as he leaned over their mother, pouring all his energy into her. He gritted his teeth and Kane yelled out as they attempted to heal the enormous damage in her mother's chest.

Using all her powers today, even with Linc's help, Vela wasn't sure how much more she could give, but she would give her last breath to save her mom. "Dad, want me to help?" she asked in a shaky voice.

"I can."

Her heart stopped.

Linc crouched next to them. "If you can heal the internal injuries, I can seal the wound," he said gravely. "I can cauterize it."

Drew and Kane's faces showed Vela they were exhausted. "As much as I hate this idea, it would work," Drew mumbled. "Kane and I will finish here if he can close it." He looked up at Linc, who watched soberly. "But, if you so much as breath wrong in my mother's direction, I *will* kill you."

Linc nodded and waited.

This was his chance to redeem himself. "I will bury you alive if you hurt my mother, Linc," Vela vowed.

He speared her with his gaze. "I would never hurt her, Vela, never. You're going to have to trust me." Scanning all their faces, he said, "You all are."

Drew looked like he was going to fall over. He focused intently on his mother's wound and closed his eyes, as if he could see every vein and artery inside of her. He probably could.

Vela watched as the blood flowing out of the wound slowed down until only a small stream slipped out.

Drew fell over with his arms limp by his sides. Kane wasn't too far behind. Both had dark circles tracing under their eyes. "Your turn," Drew heavily breathed, glaring at Linc, warning him with his eyes to remember his promise.

Linc furrowed his brow and held his hands over Whitney's slowly rising chest. Her breathing was better, but not where it should be.

Vela looked on with worried eyes and prayed even harder. A whimper escaped her throat.

"Please! I need absolute quiet," Linc demanded. He focused on his hands.

Vela didn't know much about Festans' gifts, but she had to assume that to knit flesh together with their fire would be extremely tricky. She watched with hope in her heart and tears in her eyes as Linc's gift tried to save her mother's life. She vowed in that moment that she would forgive Linc for anything if he was successful.

Blood ceased to trickle out and Vela's breath hitched. She didn't dare make a noise. She grabbed her dad's hand and squeezed hard. He must feel so helpless at that moment. She knew she did.

The edges of her mother's wound soon melted together, closing in a miraculous blend of muscle and tissue. Vela had seen a lot of injuries healed by her parents whenever her brothers got hurt. And this looked nothing like those healings. A Gyan's healing would look like a seam or a line on the skin. Linc's heat had melted her skin shut. It wasn't pretty, but it was a life-giving miracle. And it couldn't look more beautiful to Vela.

Tugging on her father's hand, she asked breathlessly, "Dad, did it work? Linc?"

Vela's dad let go and kneeled by his wife, running his hands carefully over her wound, inspecting Linc's work.

Linc sat back on his heels, then slumped over, leaning his hands in the dirt, his breaths heavy. He had spent even more energy than she had in the fight with the E.E. members, controlling the wolves and now her mother's healing.

Vela dug her hands into the dirt and fed her core with the life force that only nature could provide. She soaked up as much as she could for a quick burst of healing ability.

Laying her hands on Linc's back, she fed him a remedy that would replenish his depleted stores of energy. His breathing slowed and didn't sound as labored when she picked up her hands. Still leaning over, he looked over at her with his hair falling in his eyes. His gaze held a gratefulness reserved only for her. Her mouth turned up in response.

It wasn't a big smile, but it was the kind that spoke volumes about how she felt. She was grateful but didn't trust him completely. Not until he answered her many questions about his involvement with the E.E. and why he had hidden it from her. Was he really turning his back on this group? Or was he drawing away suspicion from himself by looking like he sided with Vela's family? And when they were on their walk, did he know the E.E. would capture her? Was he aware she had been hurt?

On the other hand, she didn't think he would bother healing her mother if he had truly sided with the E.E. He would have wanted her out of the way, preferably dead.

Pulling her thoughts away from Linc, she shuffled over to her mom, whose breathing looked much better. Her dad, Drew and Kane were leaning over her, examining her.

"Dad? What are you doing?"

"Checking every inch of her. I want to be sure there's nothing, not even a scratch, or anything that could harm her.

Once we're done, we need to take her home where she can rest. She'll need a lot of restorative sleep to see her completely well."

Nodding, Vela then turned to Linc, who stood off to the side, his attention trained on the woods.

"Where did they go? The wolves?" she asked. She hadn't seen them leave, as focused as she was on her mother's healing.

"I sent them away. But they've had a taste of flesh now and want to return to get a few more bites." Shrugging, he said, "It's instinct for them. It's not exactly natural what I did to them."

"Can you keep them away?"

"With what you just did, yeah, I can. I'm keeping them back."

Huffing, she said, "I just wish they'd come back and eat every one of these E.E. people when we leave."

Looking back at her, he said, "You don't know what you're asking. Some of these people hold absolutely no animosity for the Chosen One's parents. They want to protect you, not harm you."

"Is that why you joined them? To help find the Chosen One's parents?" she baldly asked him. Her eyes speared his demanding answers.

He studied her for a moment. "My parents..."

"Yes, I heard what you said to that leader about your parents, but why did you do it? You have free will, Linc. You could have, at any time, acted on your own. Was it all an act with us?"

Linc reached for her and placed his hands on her shoulders. Leaning to look her in the eye, he said in a deep voice, "Believe me, it was as real to me as it was to you. You are still my everything. I just had a role to play with these people. Please believe me."

Shaking her head, she looked down to avoid his piercing gaze. She couldn't think straight. His vicinity, his touch, his scent. It all swam in her senses. "I don't know what to think," she whispered.

"I found that many of these people genuinely want to find the Chosen Child. They want change," Linc said as he rubbed her arms.

His touch soothed, and he shared the energy she just gave him to her, so she didn't move away. "Why did so many of them leave the fight?" she asked. "They didn't want to fight me?"

Nodding, he said, "They've been lied to by the leaders of this organization. They thought they were searching for people they could revere and protect. This must have been a terrible surprise for most of them."

Linc's gaze shot up to look over her shoulder. "It looks like your father and brothers finished going over your mom's injuries. They need to take her home. It's time to go." He hooked her chin with his finger and brought her gaze back to him. He looked at her with a question in his gaze.

Eyeing him, she said, "You have *a lot* to explain."

He nodded grimly. "I wouldn't expect anything less from you. By the way, did you get my little message while you were being held?"

"What? The butterfly?" she asked.

"What other message did you get? Was there more than one?" His eyebrows raised in surprise.

"No, yours was the only one. And I got it, loud and clear. Thanks for that. I needed it."

"I know," he whispered.

"Now, let's go home," she said.

Vela, Jack and Linc followed her brothers and father as they carried her mom away. Elia must have left to get the car, because Vela saw her driving it toward them.

She really had the best of people surrounding her. She couldn't be happier about the answer to prayer she and her family had received. And for God forgiving her. They were all moments she would not soon forget. Right now, she didn't want to think about the house she was leaving, or the E.E. members she and her family had left half buried in dirt.

They could dig themselves out of the mess they had made, as far as she was concerned.

She was going home, and she appreciated that statement more than she had ever before.

Chapter Forty-Three

Vela's chair was as comfy as comfy could be, but she chafed as she sat in it. Her leg jiggled as her busy mind spun all kinds of scenarios that could be the true account of her birth.

Whitney rested in her bed under Vela's careful care, but it had been two days and Vela was no closer to answers about her true parentage than before. Her dad said he wanted her mom to be awake for all of Vela's questions to be answered. It would take time for her to wake up, however.

How much longer would it take?

Vela wanted to give her mother all the time in the world to recover. Her injury should have been fatal, but by God's own miracle, she had survived. The bombshell she had dropped on Vela, however, destroyed Vela's patience and it wore thinner as the days went by.

Vela studied Whitney's form on the bed. Thankfully, Drew's training as an EMT helped him give her fluids intravenously. They didn't want to lose her to dehydration just when they had gotten her back. As she watched her mom sleeping, Vela relaxed into the flowered armchair, thankful her mom was alive and breathing, but she had so much to share with her as well. She wanted to tell her how God had healed her anger and forgiven her. It was such a momentous moment; her mom will be ecstatic to hear about it.

Jack's head lay on her lap, and he looked up at her with soft, soulful brown eyes. She played with his ears and smoothed her hand down over his head.

He had been brilliant in the fight. So had Linc, even though it was still hard to believe he had been an E.E. member.

Linc sat downstairs with her father, talking about their safety. She wasn't sure what their plan could be; the E.E. knew where she lived. How were they going to protect themselves? She was pretty sure, too, her father questioned Linc on his loyalties. She had yet to have that conversation with him, but she planned to when her dad was done with him.

So many questions and not enough answers.

Linc had been holed up, he said, sharing his insights into the E.E. organization with the Gyan Elders for the past two days. This was his first day here, in her home. He had talked to her a little on the phone about his conversations with the Elders.

The fight with the Extremists had revealed their true motives, and certainly reduced their numbers. Without Linc in their meetings, it was hard to know what their numbers actually were, but that was just one cell. There were hundreds of cells all around the world. And the E.E. had valuable resources in computer technology that they used to find potential mothers and fathers of the Chosen Child.

Linc could recognize the E.E.'s faces he had met, so he identified them to help the Elders. Her father, David, was in contact with the Elders, too, about the kidnapping and the following fight. They were going to contact other Elders of other Borean, Neronian and Festan clans and spread the knowledge so they could take action against more kidnappings. This was one of the few times the Elders worked together for the safety of the clans.

Linc had told the E.E. about his and Vela's bond, only because it would ingratiate him further into the leader's trust, he said. He thought it would protect Vela from any harm. He had been wrong.

Vela still wasn't sure about how Maria had found out about the bond. Was it directly from Linc, like she said? He vehemently denied that accusation.

It was awfully convenient for him to defend her family with wolves when his double nature was revealed. He would have to do something drastic to be convincing to her family to believe he wasn't in the E.E. And all it would take for him to ingratiate himself back into that organization is a little information only he would know and some groveling. It didn't take a rocket scientist to figure that out.

He said that Maria must have connected the romantic dots between Vela and himself or found out about the bond from her father, who was that cell's leader.

As much as she wanted to trust Linc wholeheartedly, a little nugget of doubt stayed with her.

She remembered what she had overheard at the E.E. meeting. It had burned into her brain. *Vela would follow me anywhere.* He was right, she would have. He had sounded so confident, so sure. She wondered if he really believed in their cause. But which one? The gentle one where the members just wanted to find the Chosen Child for the chance of a peaceful world? Or the bloodthirsty ones who wanted anyone connected to the Prophecy of Connection dead?

It sickened her, if it was the latter. She just wasn't sure what to think. What to believe.

The question most on her mind, however, was her parentage. Her biological mother and father, that is. As much as she loved her parents, they would always hold that distinction, she vowed. But she needed to know how she came to be in this life. Where did she come from? She had another whole family, and she itched to know who they were. She had always thought she looked like Whitney, but now she knew it was just a coincidence.

Vela eyed her sleeping mother and asked God for patience. Her mother needed this restorative sleep. She shouldn't want to rush her healing. She tapped her fingers on the arm of her chair. Whitney had cautioned Vela on praying for patience. That God would teach it to her through experiencing difficult situations. She snorted. She didn't know how much more difficult things could get. But before she could wish for things to get easier, she stopped herself. Things could get always get worse. Her mother could have died.

That was a sobering thought.

She got up, deciding she would join the conversation with her father and Linc. That seemed more productive than sitting here.

With her hand on the door handle, she thought she heard a slight noise behind her. She cocked her head and listened. There it was again. Turning around, she approached her mother's bed. Her mother's hand twitched.

"Mom?"

Whitney's eyelids fluttered. That was all the proof Vela needed. She raced to the door and yelled for her father to come upstairs. She ran back to the side of the bed and mother's hand, willing it to move again. Right now, she didn't think about her questions. She just wanted to see her mom's big, beautiful eyes, awake and alive.

Her dad burst into the room, breathless and anxious. His gaze ran over his wife's body, searching for a new sign that she was well. When he didn't see anything, his questioning eyes turned to Vela.

"She moved her hand, Dad. And her eyelids twitched. She might be waking up," she said with excitement.

Vela could hear Drew and Kane bounding up the stairs and lunged into the room. Her bond told her Linc was approaching, too. But he seemed to hang back and lingered outside the door. Probably to give them privacy, she thought. She went to the door and peeked her head around the door frame.

"Come here," she requested. When he held back, she reached for his hand and pulled him in. "You belong in here, too. Without you, she wouldn't be waking up at all."

"It should only be family right now, Vela," Linc protested, but allowing her to lead him inside the room.

"Well, you practically are, so stop that."

Vela froze. It was the closest she had come to committing to him and their bond permanently. As much as she didn't fully trust him, she could not deny they shared a bond for a lifetime. And she *wanted* to trust him.

She could see he had noticed the same thing, and he stood still, watching her. His eyes burned with an intensity that didn't surprise her.

"We'll talk more about this later," he said after a moment.

She held his gaze with her own and slowly nodded. She made her way to the side of the bed and asked her brothers if anything had developed. Drew indicated with a jerk of his chin for her to pay attention to what their dad was doing.

David started talking quietly to Whitney, asking her to open her eyes. He told her who was in the room waiting for her to wake up and rubbed her hands gently, reverently. Vela knew he was probably also using his gift, giving her mother an extra boost of healing energy. They all held their breaths and waited. Her father's voice was soothing, and it resonated through Vela at the same time. She hoped her mother felt the same.

It had taken all of them standing here to help heal her mother. God's gifts of healing and fire had saved her.

The room went silent when David bowed his head over his wife's hand. He prayed, his lips moving silently. Vela closed her eyes and silently joined him. Linc's hand found hers and he joined them in prayer.

One of her brothers shouted. Vela's eyes flew open, and a great relief washed through her when she saw her mother's sleepy blue eyes blinking open.

"Hi," her mom whispered. She scanned the room and her gaze welcomed everyone who was there. "How did I survive?" Her voice was weak, but Vela could clearly hear her astonishment.

David told her how he, Vela, and her brothers fed her their healing energy, that they gave her all they had. He shot a grateful look at Linc and continued. "Linc closed the wound completely."

"I shouldn't be here," she said softly and turned her tortured eyes to Vela. "I thought I was dying. That's the only reason…"

Vela rushed to her dad's side, reaching around him to grab her mother's hand. She said, "Mom, it's okay, I understand. I have questions, believe me, a million of them, but what's important now is for you to get well. To heal. Don't worry about me," she urged, her eyes wet with tears.

"That's my job, baby, to worry."

"Well, put it on hold until you're strong enough to handle that kind of stress, because it's too big a job to worry about me," Vela joked.

Linc snorted and said, "It's true." Vela gave him a look before she returned her attention back to her mother.

"Vela, I want to explain... everything... but..."

"Shhh, Mom, not now. For now, you need to rest and get well."

"Whitney," David said, "We can talk about things later. You just went through a lot and Vela's right. You need your rest." He looked over at Vela and her brothers and jerked his chin toward the door, asking them to leave the room.

Drew and Kane nodded, said goodbye to their mother, and left. Vela touched her mom's hand again, told her she loved her, took Linc by the arm and walked out.

Vela closed the door, leaned against it, and sighed.

"That was good of you."

"What was?" she asked Linc tiredly.

"To not attack her with questions about your parentage. I'd imagine it's hard to wait to know what happened. To know the truth."

"Yeah, well, I can wait. The important thing is that she's alright. My questions are secondary. It is hard, I'll admit, though." She hung her head.

"Vela," Linc said, then stopped. A moment later, reached for her hand. "We need to talk."

"Yes. Yes, we do."

"Come on. We can talk downstairs."

Vela allowed him to lead her. Was he going to finally explain in full his involvement with the Extremists? And why he kept it hidden from her? Or did he want to talk about her parentage? The list was endless.

He led her out the back door to the porch, and they settled into two rocking chairs. He scanned the yard uneasily and Vela did too, knowing someone could easily find them in plain sight of the yard.

"Did you mean it I'm a part of your family, now?"

Swallowing, she looked anywhere but at his intense look now trained on her. She had said it in a rush, but did she really mean it? With her suspicions wildly attacking her mind, she had doubts. Still, he inspired a trust in her and she couldn't deny she was cautiously trusting him. But was it enough?

"Yes," she finally said. "I wish you would have told us about your part to play with the Extremists, but I am choosing to trust you. With me, with my family."

"Good." He took a deep breath and said, "Because I need you more than ever to trust me right now."

He studied her look when she stayed silent. She nodded, encouraging him to continue.

"I need to take you away." His deep voice was firm. He turned his attention back to the yard and continued to study every inch.

"Away. Away where?" Confusion settled over her.

"Out of this town, far away from here," he answered, giving her the full attention of his dark blue eyes.

"Linc, the Elders went back and cleaned out that cell. We should be fine." Suddenly, she remembered his words at the E.E. meeting again. They flashed clear: *Vela trusts me implicitly. She would go with me anywhere.* A cold suspicion claimed her.

"They will regroup, trust me. Some of their members ran away from the fight, but they'll have contacted other cells and given them our information and descriptions. We need to be far away from here, and soon. Vela, we need to leave tonight. We're both in danger here."

It was time for some very needed explanations. "How did you get involved with them, Linc?"

He sighed heavily and leaned his arms on his knees. "My parents. They're deeply involved in the Festans investigation into that organization. They thought I would be a perfect person to infiltrate them because I would look young and impressionable." He hung his head and studied his hands.

"When were you going to tell me?" she asked, hurt lacing her tone. "That you were a part of these people? Were you always going to keep it a secret from me?"

"No," he said firmly. "I would have told you, but my parents didn't want to threaten my secret involvement. They were afraid you would tell your parents who're Elders, and they might have leaked it."

"Why did you turn against them? Are your parents mad you revealed your double position?"

He turned his head toward her, his hair swinging. "I think it's rather obvious why I turned against them. They were going to kill you, Vela," he said, his eyes heavy with meaning. "And my parents are not happy with me." He returned his gaze to the backyard.

Vela couldn't help her suspicion still. He was being vague and a part of her wanted to trust him, but she couldn't help it. He had fooled her once and she wouldn't be a good warden to her heart if she wasn't careful.

Despite her misgivings, however, there was something she needed to do right now. She had learned what holding onto something could do to her spirit and she didn't want to hold on to any kind of hurt or anger anymore. It was time.

He had been a part of her healing with that little butterfly, so it was only right to ask him a question that would completely absolve her of her guilt.

"Linc, I need to ask something of you."

"Sure." He leaned down to look into her eyes.

Vela almost couldn't meet his gaze. But she had to. Looking deep in his warm, blue orbs, she said, "I'm sorry. For all the times I lashed out at you, hurt you for something you had no part in. I'm sorry for my prejudices against your clan. I've asked God to forgive me for my actions, but I need to ask you for forgiveness, too." He might not be completely honest with her, but she couldn't live with herself without her being completely honest with him. She searched his eyes and only found more warmth and kindness, more than she should have received.

"Vela. I understood from the first time I talked with you that my clan had harmed you deeply, almost irreparably. I only wanted to show you I'm not those people. My kind, your kind, have done a lot to harm to each other over the years. But you and I, our generation, can start fresh."

Vela shivered when Linc brushed a hand across her arm.

"Of course, I forgive you. Let's start over, Vela Ashcroft. For us. For our people."

She nodded eagerly. "I want that. More than anything." She took a deep breath. She had to ask him, find out about her suspicions. "But why, Linc, wouldn't you tell me about the E.E?"

"Vela, I couldn't tell you." He sounded resigned. "I couldn't risk your safety. It was better you not knowing what I did. I knew they would test us. The less you knew, the better. The more believable it would be that I was a part of them. I suspected we would pass their tests." He gave her a significant look that reverberated through her.

She nodded, accepting his explanation. "I did pass those tests, didn't I? So, you took them too?"

When he nodded, she asked, "Does that mean we're the prophesied parents, Linc?"

His face went pensive, and he studied the yard for a long moment. "It's not for certain. But it's very likely we're the ones they're looking for. Vela, the fact that we passed those tests is a very bad thing. It's a death sentence. We need to hide. And I have a place we can go where we should be safe. Or, it can be a death trap," he finished under his breath.

"What do you mean, 'A death trap?' Linc?" She held her breath, suddenly aware his answer would change her life and her future.

Chapter Forty-Four

LINC'S VOICE HELD A somber note, and Vela listened carefully. "There's a place I know where Elemental couples, like us, live. They've created a secret community where they hide from the E.E. If they ever discovered it, they would slaughter the whole place. It's either the safest place for us, or the worst."

"Really?" she asked with astonishment. "How did you find out about it?"

"Because my parents helped create this community and help keep it secret."

She looked at him in wonder. "You're a part of the fight against this group, and then you develop an Intended bond, with me, a Gyan? How coincidental is that?"

His mercurial eyes held fondness when he responded, "I know, believe me, it was as much of a surprise to me as it was for you."

She blushed when she remembered her reaction. "I ran away."

"And kept running, too. You put me through a merry chase," he said, smiling.

"Now, you want us on the run together. What about my family? Finishing high school?" Her words twisted inside her, and she tried to foresee what a trip like this would be like and all its consequences.

"They have children and teens there too, where they homeschool them. You won't get an official diploma, because that would alert the E.E. immediately to run paperwork like that, but you'd get an education," he assured her.

"Linc, are you saying we would have to stay there forever? Will we ever not be hunted?"

"No. We will, from now on, always have to watch our backs. But there are other communities like theirs. We can travel to those, if that's what you want."

Vela's heart thumped painfully in her chest at her next thought. "What if we were to ignore the bond?"

His look burned into hers. "What? And go our separate ways?"

Not trusting herself to speak, she swam in the raging blue waters his eyes depicted. Then she nodded. "Maybe my brother was right. That we're safer apart than together."

He looked away, swallowed and asked, "Is that what you really want? To end... us?"

"No," she said immediately, and that felt right. Deeply, she knew Linc would always be a part of her and she a part of him. She could never harm him. And that's what would happen if she ignored their bond. She would scar him forever. She couldn't do that to him. "But if ever there was a reason to part, this would be it," Vela said softly, her throat closing painfully.

"Vela," he said in a gruff voice and leaning toward her, "you will *never* be safe. Now that they know about you, whether you choose me or not, the very fact that you exist threatens their beliefs. I want to keep you safe, with what I know and with my gifts. That means you need to be with me. And I say that selfishly too. I don't ever want to be apart from you. Vela, I've come to...love you. It's not just the bond that makes me feel this way, not with me."

Before she could respond, he reached for her hands, caressing them with his warm touch. "You may not feel the same, right now, or as deeply as I do. But, for you, I'll wait. I will try with everything in me to completely win you. I love your fight, your spirit of forgiveness, your capacity to love. And I want that to include me. Don't fight your feelings. Do this for me," he asked earnestly, "Explore those feelings I *know* you feel."

Vela's emotions swirled so wildly inside of her, she had to gasp and fill her lungs with a breath she didn't realize she was holding. She had gotten somewhat used to the intoxication of feelings the bond inspired in her, but this was different. This was terrifying. Her eyes blurred at the declaration he had made, and she impatiently wiped them free of the tears that had leaked through.

"Linc," she began uncertainly, "how can you know all this so fast? You've barely met me. What have I done?"

"What haven't you done, Vela? Everything you've said and done has only cemented that I need to be near you. I knew with absolute certainty the day of our duel that I would do whatever it took to make you mine," he said, his eyes shining and a wide smile making him look more handsome than she had ever seen him. "Anyone who would challenge me like you always do is someone I want to spend a long time getting to know as well. And the more I discover, the more I need to know."

He *was* certain, she realized. These weren't just words to him. His actions, too, had spoken loud and clear about how he felt about her. It was unbelievable, and she needed to let it sink in.

"I do care for you," she said, allowing honesty to fuel her words. "I know I don't want to ignore our bond. I want to be near you, too. I fought our bond, at first, but you've come to mean more to me than anyone. I meant it when I asked for your forgiveness. I treated you terribly and for no reason. I don't want to let you go. But I need to trust you, Linc. I need to believe wholeheartedly that your involvement with the E.E. is finished. What I overheard was…"

"A *lie*," he said vehemently. "I would have said anything to make them believe what *I* wanted them to believe."

"When they captured me, they hurt me, Linc. Did you know they would?" Hurt leaked from her eyes, and she studied his reaction carefully.

He shook his head fiercely and said, his gaze burning, "I didn't know, and when I found out, I didn't take it very well. When they went after you with that cyclone, I fought to get free to help you. But there were too many holding me, leading me away. I tried calling out to you, but the cyclone swallowed any noise. You must not have heard me. When I got to the house, I made sure Greta was the one who tended your wounds. She's the best healer I know."

Vela grimaced. "I may have knocked her out with a table leg." She avoided looking at Linc's expression.

His chuckle was her answer that he wasn't mad. "I figured you would do what you had to do to get out of that room. Then, they kept us in separate rooms. I made it known I was not happy about that, but I had a role to fill, too. Maria was glued to me, and I knew she would report anything back I did to her father."

Vela wanted to talk about Maria but thought of the black eye the leader of the abductors sported when she fought with him in the clearing.

"The black eye that guy had?"

"He should have had worse," Linc spat. "They pulled me off him before I could do more."

"Thanks, I got my revenge, though. Linc, Maria is obsessed with you. And with me, but she saved me in the end. I wonder why. She tried to kill me; you know. I barely got away. If it wasn't for Jack…"

"I honestly had no control over what Maria did. She was always a wild card. She made it obvious from the beginning she was interested in me, but I never encouraged her. I think she has her own demons to work through, though. She's been fed all that garbage her whole life. It can't be healthy for her to live in that family.

"Vela," he said, squeezing her fingers. "Come away with me and be safe. I can't have anything happen to you again. When they took you, I wanted to kill every one of those Elementals that dared put a hand on you. They promised me you wouldn't be hurt, but that didn't mean anything," he said, his mouth twisting in a grimace. "I should have known they would lie. I made sure the wolves took care of each one of them that had gotten rough, as you say. I made sure they regretted it."

"Did the wolves kill them, Linc?" She didn't want their deaths on his conscience. She worried, too, about those she had incapacitated.

"No, but it will take a few healers to put them back together again," he growled. "Vela, it was war. That they started. One we made sure not to lose. They would have taken our lives without question. We were only defending ourselves."

"I know," she agreed, sliding her fingers through his and interlocking them. "That doesn't mean we can't feel. I would feel every death I had a part in, and I know you would, too. I don't want you to suffer that. And did you, by chance, give Jack an energy boost back at the fight? Before you showed up with the wolves?"

He smiled, "Yes, I did. I waited out in the woods for the right time to reveal the wolves I had collected and saw those three Elementals come for you. I wanted to even the odds."

"Well, you did. He was magnificent!"

He looked at their hands and pulled them up to his lips. He softly kissed her every finger, and she could feel the heat of his breath, that ran hotter than most. But it was the fire of their bond that rushed through her, making her catch her breath.

"I love that about you," he said softly.

"What?"

"You fought fiercer than my wolves. And the fact you care about what happened to the people who hurt you says a lot about you. You're gentle to the core, but don't mess with those you love. I love that."

"Linc, you really want to go to this place? Tonight?" She couldn't help worrying about all the consequences if they *didn't* leave.

"It would be better to leave tonight." Looking at her gravely, he said after a pause, "And telling no one where we're going. It's stayed secret for a reason. Vela, we can't even tell your parents it's location."

Vela let those words settle in her like a rock sinking to the bottom of the ocean. That's where she felt she currently was, but worse. It felt more like she was in the middle of a raging storm where she was desperately fighting the towering waves of an angry sea. What he said made sense. Too much, in fact. She bit her bottom lip as she considered going. He had told the E.E. she would go with him anywhere. Was she handing herself over on a silver platter if she went? He was slowly convincing her it was a necessary plan. His next words only confirmed it.

"Your dad agrees with me," he said quietly.

He let that statement still the waters she was fighting. She slowly felt her resistance slipping away. If her father agreed, she needed to consider his opinion.

It was true. The E.E. knew where she lived. It was only a matter of time before they came back. She might have hours, minutes, before they reappeared. Her family was in danger with her being here.

"When do we leave?" she asked. She needed a little time. There was one conversation she was going to have before she left this house. And she intended to have it. "And I'm taking Jack. That is non-negotiable."

Chapter Forty-Five

AGREEING TO LEAVE WITH Linc was one thing, but Vela soon discovered that doing it was another thing entirely. She couldn't bring herself to choose what to take with her, and then there was the fact that she loved her home. She wanted to leave on her own terms, not the E.E's.

Her father had closeted himself up with her mom since Linc left, so she hadn't been able to talk to him yet about Linc's plan. She had gone up to her room to pack and currently she was staring into the abyss that was her closet, having no idea where to start.

"Vela Marie Ashcroft! Were you planning on even telling your best friend that you were leaving?"

Vela spun around and looked at Elia guiltily. Her hands were on her hips, her small stance quivering with anger.

"How'd you know?"

"I didn't, until I saw the suitcases on your bed!" Elia shouted. She carried a hurt look that twisted Vela's insides.

Vela looked over at the three empty suitcases lying open, waiting for her to fill them. She sighed. "Linc just told me over an hour ago. Honestly, I didn't know Elia. He says it's safer for us both if we leave and go hide."

"Leave, where?"

"I can't tell you. I don't know where. It's a secret place that no one can know about. I'm sorry, Elia."

Suddenly it was too much. All of it. The kidnapping, the fight, her mother nearly dying, and now Linc's plan to escape into the night.

Vela crumpled to the floor.

She tried covering the sobs tearing from her throat with her hands, but there was no escaping her cries. She was leaving her family, but also Elia and everything she knew. It was the unknown that crushed her. Why was this what she broke over? Anger replaced her grief, and she pounded her fists into the carpet where she had dropped.

It wasn't fair. None of this was what she had asked for.

She didn't realize she had said the last part out loud when Elia responded to it. Her arms wrapped around Vela's scrunched up legs and back. "When do we ever ask for what the future gives us?" she said into Vela's hair. "God has a plan, though, Vela. It may not make any sense at the time or for a long time, but we need to trust that He knows how it will come together, for His good and yours. He is molding you to be a magnificent woman, and that is never a simple process. Granted, what you've been through has been nothing short of terrifying, but look at you! You survived it, more than survived! You kicked butt and took names, too."

Elia smoothed the hair back from Vela's face and leaned over to look into her eyes. "I was never prouder than seeing you belt out of that E.E. house like the hounds of hell were after you. When you ripped out those trees blocking anyone from coming after you—Vela, that was brilliant! You were and are pure brilliance, like a daughter of the sun. There's a strength to you I never saw before, well, before, Linc."

Vela gave a watery laugh. "I guess he has brought out something in me."

Elia laughed, too. "Pure awesomeness, is what I've seen!"

"Elia, how will I ever see you again? This place Linc wants to take me to has couples like Linc and I there, all hiding from the Extremists. For their safety and mine, I can't tell anyone where it is. But I can't imagine you not being in my life." Her tears had slowed during Elia's speech, but they trickled out again at the huge loss she was already feeling.

"I can always come with you." It didn't sound half-hearted. She was serious.

"No! You have a life to live! You can finish school, go to college if you want. Maybe one day, date Kane," she said with a soft smile.

"Kane, right," Elia said with a big sigh. "Put that carrot in front of me. That's a low blow, Vels."

"It's the truth. And you know it."

"Yeah, I've been in love with him since you guys moved in. Maybe it's just a crush, though," Elia said, shrugging.

"It's definitely a crush! But that's how a full-blown love story starts and one I don't see going anywhere. And Elia, I think he feels the same and is just waiting for you to grow up."

"I *am* grown!"

"Elia, you're a Senior in high school. You just turned 17. I think he's being a mature adult and waiting till you're at least 18. He'd get arrested if he looked at you the wrong way right now."

"Yeah, you're right." Elia moaned. "Wait! Why don't I leave with you for a year and come home in all my 18-year-old-glory and blow him over with all that I have to offer? It could work!"

"Elia, your parents would never let you leave, and you know it." Vela straightened her legs into a more comfortable position and leaned her head on Elia's shoulder. "I'm going to miss you, LeeLee."

"Please let me go with you, Vels," Elia said, a sob catching in her throat. "What would I do without you? We're the M&M's, remember? One doesn't exist without the other."

Vela giggled at Elia's reminder of their old nickname. Her mom had called them that years ago, and it had stuck. She reached for Elia's hand and clenched it. "You will always be the 'M' to my 'M,' LeeLee. There will never be another friend like you." Vela's throat constricted again.

"Why does this feel like goodbye already?" Elia asked in a broken voice.

Vela needed to give her best friend purpose in staying. "Elia, I need you here. There's no one better at trailing leads on the Net. You can help my parents and the Elders get a track on where the Extremists are and who they are looking for. You can help protect those of us hiding. We need you behind the computer; will you do that? For me?"

Elia looked up with watery tracks trailing down her face. She nodded and hung her head. "Yes," she whispered. "I can. I will," she said in a stronger voice.

"And when it's safe to do so, I'll contact you. We might be miles apart, but our hearts will forever be together, I promise you that. This is not goodbye, it's just an 'Until it's safer,'" Vela said in a strong voice, which she was desperately wanting to believe. "And I'm only a phone call away."

"So, this is how I find you," her dad said dryly, leaning against the doorframe. "Sharing tears with Elia. Why am I not surprised?"

Vela studied her dad's face and saw easily the pain his eyes reflected. "Hey Dad."

"I see you talked to Linc." He noticed her suitcases, his brow furrowing.

"Yes. I know Mom isn't strong enough, but I need to talk to you both before I leave. Can you help make that happen?"

He frowned but nodded. "Yes, I can give her some more of my energy. Enough for that conversation."

"What are you guys talking about?" Elia whispered, picking up on the tone of the conversation. She knew something was up.

"I'll tell you later," Vela promised.

"Give me at least twenty minutes," he requested.

"Linc's picking me up in a couple of hours. I can give you more time if you need it."

"Okay, how about an hour? That gives her more time to rest."

When he left, Vela could feel Elia staring at her. She took a deep breath and blurted, "When my mom thought she was dying, she told me something."

"What? Don't leave me hanging here, Vels."

"She said I wasn't her child. That my parents adopted me. I guess she didn't want to die before telling me the truth."

"But you saved her," Elia said weakly.

"Yeah, and now, before I go, I need to know the truth behind my birth."

Elia sat silently. She was quiet for so long; Vela nudged her shoulder. "Wow, this is the first time I've left you speechless."

"How did your birth parents choose your parents to leave you with? I have so many questions."

"Me too," Vela said flatly. "Believe me." She got up. She had an hour to pack her entire life away. She had to get started. Walking over to the closet, she started ripping her favorite outfits off their hangers and throwing them into the nearest suitcase. She started making trips back and forth between the closet and the bed where she was packing her life away.

"Vela, your parents could be anyone. I wonder who they are," Elia said in a soft voice. She suddenly straightened and, with wide eyes, looked at Vela like she had never seen her before. "Wait a minute. What if they're two different Elementals, like you and Linc?"

Vela's stomach dropped. Her world tilted, and she dropped the clothes she had been stuffing away. She leaned on the bed, and shock spun her gaze around. She looked at her door. "Elia, I can't wait another second. I need to know."

She ran in three long steps to the door, yanking it open. In just another few steps, she was at her parents' door. Taking a deep breath, she knocked. She could hear talking inside, so instead of waiting for an invitation, she gripped the handle and opened the door.

Her mom sat propped up on several pillows and Vela stuffed down the guilt that washed through her. Her mother had no business being up. Vela knew that, but she had no choice. She had to know the truth. A desperate urge filled her until she thought she would burst from the pain of it.

"Who. Am. I?" she bit out. She fisted her hands at her sides to stop their trembling. She would tear through the walls if she didn't get some answers.

Whitney's eyes filled with anguish and tears. She looked over at David, imploring him silently with a question Vela could only guess at. But she was tired of guessing.

"Mom, I *need* to know. Please tell me. I think I'm going crazy." Her voice broke, and she grabbed the sides of her head. The unknown raged through her, giving her a full-blown headache.

"Vela, we'll tell you what we know," her dad said from across the room. "But we'll apologize now because it's not much."

"I don't care. Anything is better than what I know now, which is nothing."

"You were a tiny baby when we got you," her mom started in a shaky voice. "The Elders brought you to us, in a soft blue blanket. When I saw the blanket, I thought you were a baby boy, but the first time I saw your beautiful blue eyes, I knew you were a little girl.

"We had been wanting another baby; we were trying for a girl, remember David?" Whitney asked in a tremulous voice.

When he nodded, she continued.

"You had been put on the doorstep of the community center in a little basket. It was early in the morning when an Elder found you. You were crying. I don't know how long you'd been left there, but you ate voraciously when they gave you the bottle of milk that was in your basket." She took a deep breath. "I sometimes wonder if you'd been out there all night, poor thing." She had a faraway look in her eyes as if she were back in that moment years ago.

"And?" Vela urged.

"The only other thing in the basket, besides the blue blanket and the bottle, was a brief note. We didn't understand it at first. Well, we understood the first part, just not the second."

Whitney held her hand out to David. He walked to her holding a small piece of paper. He held it out to her. She shook her head and tilted her head toward Vela.

He looked at it for a second before holding it out for Vela to take.

Without hesitation, Vela lunged for the note. When she had it in her hands, she realized it was a 4x6 index card with only a few lines on it.

Her birthday is September 23rd.
She is a child of the prophecy.
Keep her safe.

Vela studied the writing, wishing it said more. For a wild moment, she had wondered if she had been given a birthday by Whitney and David, which would have canceled the chance of passing the birthday test the E.E. had given her.

"We gave you your name. We already had one picked out. We didn't get to birth you, but we kept you and loved you completely. There has not been one day we haven't loved raising you."

Vela could see Whitney was tired. Her eyes drooped and her hands lay limply on the bed. But she had to have one more explanation.

"How do we know which prophecy this note was talking about?"

"We don't know," David answered for Whitney. "Over the years, we researched different prophecies. We knew about the Connection Prophecy and all signs seem to point toward that one. It seems the E.E. thinks so, too."

"Because of Linc?" Vela asked. "And my bond with him?"

"And your birthday, too," Whitney supplied.

"Could it be possible I'm the child the prophecy predicts? Or a parent? I need to hear it again," she said heavily, feeling a weight of responsibility settle on her shoulders.

"I don't think you're the child," her mom said. "Unless your parents were two different Elementals. Then it's a possibility, I guess. But there's no way of knowing that."

"Do you know the prophecy? I'd like to hear it, if you do."

David recited, "When the day and night are of equal length, a warrior star who will bear the child will rise. Under the Winter Solstice, the Hunter will emerge. He will capture the Goat under the Northern sky and they will produce the one who will unify. Though their elements are diverse, through them the child will command them all."

"When the day and night are of equal length, that's the Autumn Equinox, isn't it? And it seems like that would be the mother because it says the star will bear the child," Vela surmised. "So, the Hunter is the father, and he will capture the Goat. Is that the mother?"

"What we've figured out," David answered, "is that during the Winter Solstice, the Hunter, who is the father of the Chosen Child, will find or capture the mother, who is the Goat. And Linc being part of the E.E., it can be said he captured you. Anyway, it's said the Hunter and the Goat will have a child. The parents are different elements, which the child will inherit and use to rule the Elementals."

"Why do they call the mother a goat?" Vela asked.

"That confused us," David said, rubbing his face. "We thought, at first, it would be your astrological sign, but you're a Libra, which is a lion, not a goat. But, looking into it, we saw you can see the Capricorn constellation during the month of September in the Northern sky. The Capricorn is represented by a goat, a Sea Goat, actually."

"The prophecy does mention the Northern sky," Vela remembered.

"That's where the parents meet," David said.

"The Northern sky could be anywhere," Vela said.

"We think it means the Northern hemisphere," her mom said.

Vela held her head. This was a lot to take in. She rubbed ineffectually at her headache. She wished she could get rid of this pain. One thing was certain. She was a part of the Connection Prophecy. And she needed to find out if her parents were different elementals. If they were, she could be the Chosen Child. If not, it was a good chance she could be the mother of this child.

Whitney patted the spot next to her on the bed. "Come here, baby girl."

Vela dragged her feet over to where her mother lay. She was exhausted. And she still had a trip to take tonight, which she hadn't even packed for yet. She slumped onto the bed and nestled her head into her mother's soft chest. Her mother's heartbeat soothed her. She was so thankful to hear it thumping regularly. What would she have done without her? She was going to find out as soon as she left. But leaving, knowing her mother was alive and well, was a heck of a lot different than leaving when her mother didn't live in this world any longer.

Her mom smoothed Vela's hair, running her hand down the length of it. Vela relaxed. Her headache eased. Vela's eyes popped open, and she lifted her head. "Mom! You can't heal me!" she scolded. "You're not in any kind of shape to give me any of your energy!"

"Shhh," her mom said soothingly. "I will do whatever I can while I still have you." Love shined in her eyes and Vela blinked away sudden tears.

Vela suddenly wanted to share her path of healing. "Mom, I want you to know that I've forgiven my past, the Festans, for everything."

Whitney sucked in a breath. "Really, baby? That's wonderful. How did it happen?"

"They locked me in this room, and I had nothing in there but my thoughts. God encouraged me to remember," she whispered.

"Baby. I know that must have been very hard." She softly ran her hand over Vela's hair again.

"It was. But you know what was the best feeling?"

"What?"

"Letting go. Giving it all to Jesus, who had wanted it all along. He knew the burden I carried all those years."

"He knows the burden and the cost. He wanted you to be free of that life."

"Of hatred and animosity. I didn't understand what a burden it was until it melted away. When I asked Jesus for forgiveness, I felt lighter. It was like pure goodness and love flooded my body. It was amazing. Still is. So, thank you, Mom."

"For what, baby?"

"For praying for me all these years. I know you and Dad have. I couldn't have gotten to that moment without you and Dad getting me there through your prayers."

"Oh, honey," Whitney soothed, holding Vela to her chest. "That's what I'm on this Earth for. To be there for you and pray for you. I will always, you know."

"I know." Vela paused before she said, "So, you know about Linc and I leaving?"

"David told me. And, as much as it pains me to say it, I agree. You are safer away than here. Every moment you remain is a risk. They know where you live, sweetheart."

"I don't want to leave you," Vela whispered. "Any of you." Her heart broke inside her chest. It had suffered so many abuses lately. It was a wonder it still beat at all.

Whitney moved a lock of Vela's hair behind her ear and said, "I don't want to lose you either, but I'd rather know you are alive and well somewhere else than to grieve your death."

Vela cried softly into her mother's shoulder. That's what she had just thought about her mother. It seems they shared the same thoughts, just not the same blood. She breathed in her mother's familiar scent, lavender and vanilla.

"Vela," her father said gently, "you need to get packed. Linc will be here soon." He rested his hand on her shoulder and rubbed it in small circles.

Vela grabbed his hand and pulled him down so she could hug both her parents. She cried, knowing she needed to treasure this moment. There was no telling when she would get to do this again.

She didn't know her future. But she knew her past, and she knew her heart. It was full to the brim with all the memories she had experienced with the two people who had raised and loved her since she was a baby. They had provided a family she would forever treasure and love. And she needed to protect them by leaving them. The longer she stayed here, the more they were in danger. She would not tolerate that. Not if she had anything to say about it. She had to leave to keep them safe.

Whispering her goodbyes, she also made promises. She would let them know how she was doing and what was going on. She would stay safe and be the daughter they had raised her to be. She would never forget them or betray her faith. It was what had gotten her this far, and she thanked them for instilling every good thing in her and teaching her to have faith in God.

And then, after she had packed, she said her final goodbyes. She didn't want a big scene at the car before she left. So, she had dragged her three suitcases to the door and tearfully hugged her brothers and Elia. She would be strong. She was an Ashcroft, through and through, no matter what her blood showed. She would prove it to them and, most importantly, to herself.

Epilogue

"Are you sure you know where you're going?" Vela asked for the millionth time. Jack yipped in the back seat as if he agreed with her. Thankful he had finally stopped whining, she guessed he finally lost his fear of riding in the car after two whole days of traveling.

They drove Linc's new car. His parents had wired funds for them to buy something quickly. So, they had found the closest car lot they could find and bought a fairly new sedan. Nondescript and bland, the car blended in well with its gray color and style. She pressed her fingers into her lap, trying and failing to avoid knotting the end of her shirt. It was a wrinkled mess from all the times she had already done it.

"Vela, yes, I know where I'm taking you," Linc said in a tired voice. "How many times do I need to assure you that we are not lost?"

"I'm not saying you're lost, just being sure you know where you're going," Vela said stubbornly.

"Isn't that the same thing? If I didn't know where I was going, we'd be lost. Really," he sighed.

"Look, I'm leaving everything I know behind me. You're taking me somewhere I didn't know even existed before now. Is it so wrong for me to need some assurances from the one person I am trusting with my whole life?" *Besides the fact you could be taking me straight to the E.E.* She tried to squash her suspicion, but it had taken deep root.

"No," Linc said softly. "It's not so wrong. So, yes, I know where we're going. Don't worry." He glanced at her with a small smile and Vela reluctantly returned it.

"I'm sure you're going to love this place. It's beautiful there," he said. He had told her that yesterday, and Vela drank in any information he could give her about her new home.

"How many people did you say lived there?"

"The last time I was there, there were about fifty. But it might have grown some since then. It also may have split into another community. There are other places like this one," he reminded her, "and they sometimes move around visiting each other."

"I hope I can make some friends there," Vela said wistfully. "It won't be the same, though."

"No. It won't. Elia certainly is one of a kind." He squeezed her fingers gently. "We'll visit them."

"My family?" Vela asked with surprise.

When he nodded, she whispered, "You promise?" She studied his face for traces of sincerity. She didn't know why she bothered. He always meant what he said. But this seemed like a big thing to promise her.

"When it's safe."

Nodding, Vela knew there was an indeterminant amount of time involved in that statement. She moved her gaze to the scenery passing by. It all looked the same. The same stretch of trees, the same long road. They were going west, and she wondered how different it would be from where she'd lived before. It was all going to be different, every experience, every person she met. She tried to still the nervousness that stirred her stomach. They didn't feel like butterflies, more like birds wildly flying around inside her.

Thinking of butterflies, she smiled. Linc had brought over the most gorgeous blue and green Monarch butterfly when he picked her up on the day they'd left her parent's home. He said it was a promise that he would keep her safe. Then he whispered in her ear, "That includes your heart. I'll protect it with my last breath."

He really said the cheesiest things sometimes. But she loved it. She'd smiled, leaned back and asked, "Do you have to be so serious all the time?"

And he'd quickly responded, "When it comes to trusting me with your heart, yes. I take that very seriously. You can trust me."

And she would try to. At this point, she had no other choice. She would abandon that niggle of fear he was lying to her about rejoining the E.E. She had made the leap and now flew the coop with him. She looked at his hand in her lap. She didn't have much in her life; she had Linc, Jack and three suitcases with everything she owned in the world in them. But she had God on her side, too, and that meant more to her than any one thing she had. And she had her memories. Of people who loved her and were praying for her every day. She couldn't ask for much more. So, she didn't.

"I'm ready," she finally said.

Linc's teeth shone in the wide smile he gave her. "I've been waiting for you to say that. Let's do this."

Vela nodded, agreeing to a future she never could have imagined for herself. But, for the first time, trusted to meet all her expectations and more. Much more.

Free Book!

Receive a free novella, Operation Kane, from the Terra, Torch, and Tempest world if you join my newsletter!

Elia will do anything to get her best friend's older brother to notice she's a woman now, even become a spy.

Dive into this world of Elementals, unrequited love, and the power of hope. Enjoy the best friend's older brother, forbidden love, fake dating, and friends-to-lovers tropes in this powerful story of faith and young love.

Go to: www.sofiasimpson.com to find this charming novella. Connect with me there if you'd like to have me on your podcast.

And if you enjoyed this book, please leave a review on Amazon, Bookbub or Goodreads, or if you're especially generous, all three! It means more to us authors than you know.

Fill your rooms with
the delicious scents of
my book candles!

Vela, Honey Butter Rolls
Linc, Roasted Marshmallows
Rayne, Evergreen and Ash

Go to:

https://linktr.ee/sofiasimpsonauthor

Also by Sofia
Available on Amazon
DREAM WEAVER
SOFIA SIMPSON

Acknowledgments

I could not have written this novel without One Person, guiding me, loving me, encouraging me: Jesus Christ. I would, at times, stop, bow my head and pray for the next word, for the next scene. He never failed me. I have failed Him many times over, but He never quit on me.

I also could not have written this book without certain pom-pom-waving cheerleaders pushing me through:

My husband, Matt. How do I explain what half of my heart is screaming at me to write down here? You are my biggest fan, even though you haven't fully read my books. I know fantasy isn't your thing. You listen whenever I need you to and stop what you're doing to read what I push in front of you. You support my dream. Thank you.

Jenny, my sister from another mister, so close to my heart, you were born there, I'm sure. I love that I could call you, text you the words, "Pray for me," and I knew you would stop everything and do just that. For going across country with me so I could attend a writer's conference-what friend would do that? You would. Thank you and I love you.

Nicky, Nicky, Nicky, where do I start with you? How about at the beginning? I knew when I had your name picked out in middle school, you would be a part of my heart forever. You challenge me to change my ideas, fight with me about which son is my favorite, and when I beg enough, give me a hug when I need one....or two. I love you. I must be thankful or I wouldn't have dedicated this book to you.

Darcy, you are one of the calming souls I had ever met, and also the most sincere. Those endearments drew me to you immediately when I first met you. Thank you for introducing me to Marco Polo and for the many, many, many video messages you listened to and sent me. You've been an incredible encourager, champion and most importantly, friend. This book would not have been finished without you, my friend. Thank you from the bottom of my heart.

Nicky's Amazing Group of Friends. Talk about cheerleaders. You have been on my podcast, Sofia Talks, or beg to be on it. You come over and help me make a TikTok, that went viral, thank you very much and are basically the best group of teenagers I have ever met. I've written this book with you guys in mind, I hope you know that. Brooklyn, you are the best, I love you!

To all my Beta Readers...you know who you are. Without you, this book would be a skeleton. You added muscle, skin, eyes, nose and mouth. You made this book real.

To my Mom-in Law, thank you for all of your encouragement. You listen patiently, advise wisely and have always told me to never give up. Thank you from the bottom of my heart. None of my dreams would have become a reality without your and Papa's prayers.

Mashew and Milana-you two supply the fodder for much of my material. Your antics and fun interactions are hard to capture but hilarious to witness. Milana, thank you for loving my son so much and I could not have gotten through this book without your non-fat "carrots" to sugar me into finishing and our many movie nights to dull my brain. Mashew, you believe in me, unquestionably. When I say I have a plot hole, you say, "Fix it." When I get stuck, you tell me, "Get unstuck." Simple advice, but true. Thank you, both of you.

www.ingramcontent.com/pod-product-compliance
Lightning Source LLC
Chambersburg PA
CBHW021403310726
48971CB00005B/1181